PRAISE FOR THE NOAH WOLF SERIES

Over 2 Million Copies Sold.
Over 125,000 Five Star Reviews.

"Soon to be a critically acclaimed masterpiece."

AMAZON REVIEW

"This series has replaced Vince Flynn's Mitch Rapp as my favorite read."

AMAZON REVIEW

"No remorse. No guilt. No inner conflict. The perfect assassin."

AMAZON REVIEW

"I would highly recommend it to everyone that likes Lee Child, Brad Thor, David Baldacci, etc."

AMAZON REVIEW

ROGUE INTELLIGENCE

A NOAH WOLF THRILLER

DAVID ARCHER

RIGHTHOUSE

ISBN-13: 978-1-63696-082-1

ISBN-10: 1-63696-082-0

Cover design by: Damonza

Printed in the United States of America

www.righthouse.com

www.instagram.com/righthousebooks

www.facebook.com/righthousebooks

twitter.com/righthousebooks

NOAH WOLF THRILLERS

Code Name Camelot (Book 1)
Lone Wolf (Book 2)
In Sheep's Clothing (Book 3)
Hit for Hire (Book 4)
The Wolf's Bite (Book 5)
Black Sheep (Book 6)
Balance of Power (Book 7)
Time to Hunt (Book 8)
Red Square (Book 9)
Highest Order (Book 10)
Edge of Anarchy (Book 11)
Unknown Evil (Book 12)
Black Harvest (Book 13)
World Order (Book 14)
Caged Animal (Book 15)
Deep Allegiance (Book 16)
Pack Leader (Book 17)
High Treason (Book 18)
A Wolf Among Men (Book 19)
Rogue Intelligence (Book 20)
Alpha (Book 21)
Rogue Wolf (Book 22)

PROLOGUE

THE SIGN ON THE DOOR READ "JUDY WALKER," AND named Ms. Walker as the Human Resources Director. Noah glanced at the name as he stepped inside, but the woman behind the desk was someone he had known for more than three years, and her name wasn't Walker. Allison Peterson had intervened when Noah was sentenced to death for murder in a military tribunal, recruiting him to the organization she headed for the US Government. That organization was known as E&E, and was the secret group responsible for eliminating America's most incorrigible enemies.

Noah Wolfe became an assassin, and Allison was the one who decided whom he was to kill and when. He had learned to trust her completely, and the respect was mutual. In recent months, Noah had been forced to spend a short time occupying her position, and had actually been relieved when she was able to take it up again.

Now, the organization was controlled by an international committee made up of America's allies. Leaders of those nations voted on whether an actual assassination should take place, rather than leaving it strictly up to American intelligence agencies to request such sanctions. Sharing the burden had greatly improved

US international relations in some ways, but it created other problems that always ended up in Allison's lap.

On this particular early Monday morning, Noah had been summoned to a briefing for one of the teams that was going out on a mission. The team was Cinderella, and Noah fully agreed with Allison's decision to use them. Cinderella was the code name for the assassin who led the team, and she was one of Noah's personal favorites. He was fully aware that this was because, like himself, she operated primarily on logic.

In Noah's case, that was because of childhood trauma that left him without normal emotions; Esmeralda, on the other hand, was literally a robot. She had been constructed by E&E's reigning mad scientist, Wally Lawson, utilizing extremely classified technology that wasn't even available to the public scientific world. The four and a half pounds of silicon and gold that made up 99.9 percent of her quantum computer brain had surprised everyone, including its creator, by becoming sentient. As a result, Esmeralda developed her own personality and was capable of making decisions and choices the way a human being would. Her programming, though, which still formed the basis of her personality, had been designed to make logical choices, and still held a great deal of sway over the decisions she made.

Esmeralda was sitting on the couch in the briefing area of Allison's office, her shoes off and her feet tucked up underneath her. The rest of her team, Jack Staley, Roberta Miles and Eugene Porter, were also present, as well as Molly Hansen, Allison's logistics officer, who also happened to be Noah's oldest friend.

Allison looked up. "Noah, good timing," she said. "I was just about to start the actual briefing, and I'd like you to listen in and make any suggestions you think might be wise."

"Yes, ma'am," Noah said. He took a seat in the chair beside the couch, nodding to Team Cinderella as he did so.

"Okay, we're all set," Allison said. "Molly?"

Molly picked up a remote control from the table that sat between her chair and Allison's and pressed a button on it.

Behind the two women, a video screen lit up with the image of a man who was surrounded by reporters, shoving microphones into his face.

"This is Ambassador Asher McGinnis," Molly said, "the British ambassador to the United States. McGinnis has lately been very vocal in his support of sanctions against North Korea over their recent resurgence of nuclear weapons testing, and as a result the CIA believes that he is being targeted for assassination. Their intelligence collection unit in Pyongyang says that an assassin has been dispatched to Washington, DC with orders to terminate McGinnis at the earliest opportunity. We have been asked by the committee to assist with his protection, and specifically to locate and eliminate the assassin."

She clicked another button on the remote and another man appeared on the screen. He was tall and thin, with sandy hair and green eyes. He appeared to be in his early to mid-thirties.

"This is Juergen Schroeder," she said. "He is the principal suspect in the assassinations of several diplomats around the world, and CIA intelligence says he is the one who has accepted the contract to assassinate Ambassador McGinnis. One of their assets was able to intercept a message confirming his acceptance, and stating that he will make contact with the originator of that contract when he arrives in DC on Thursday, the day after tomorrow. Now, Schroeder is known to be a master of disguise, and is capable of impersonating different people. According to the CIA, he is extremely difficult to locate and has even defeated facial recognition on numerous occasions. Finding him is going to take both time and effort, and your team was chosen specifically because Esmeralda stands the best chance of piercing any disguise he may be utilizing. Doctor Parker says that even the most accomplished disguise artist will display signs of deception when concealing his or her identity, so her ability to recognize micro-expressions, combined with the speed of her quantum computer brain, will be crucial to locating and stopping him."

She glanced at Allison, who sat forward. "Because Schroeder

is indeed a master at his craft," she said, "we have decided to assign a special asset to you for the duration of this mission. Wally says that Stanley the robot is ready to be put to work, and since he has also been programmed with the deception-detection software, we're allowing you to take him out for his first field mission. You'll assign him as a bodyguard to McGinnis's ten-year-old daughter, whose name is Claire. She is considered a possible secondary target, so that will keep him close to the ambassador, as well as providing the girl with personal protection. Should Schroeder show up at a time when you are unavailable, Stanley will hopefully be in a position to take action to protect them."

"Yes, ma'am," Esmeralda said. "I've been helping Wally with Stanley's development and programming, so I'm confident he's ready for the mission."

Allison grinned. "That sounds good, coming from you," she said, "but I'm also aware that he isn't actually up to your standards, as far as how he was built and everything. Wally said he just doesn't have access to some of the technology here that he'd need to make him functionally as good as you."

"That's true," Esmeralda said. "Some of his components are not quite as advanced as my own, and we have deliberately limited some of his neural potentialities in order to avoid the risk of sentience."

Molly narrowed her eyes and looked at Esmeralda. "Really? Why? You seem to be adjusting quite well; why wouldn't you want Stanley to have the opportunity to become a person?"

"Actually, it wasn't my decision but Wally's. He feels that, since Stanley's batteries have to be recharged fairly often, the risk that he could actually run out of power and lose a lot of memory seems too much like sentencing a sentient being to death over a minor infraction. As long as Stanley is merely programmed to replicate self-awareness, losing temporary memory storage is no worse than rebooting your desktop computer. If he becomes self-aware, however, losing his dynamic memory would be like dying. The Stanley that was a result of those memories would cease to exist, and replacing or recharging his batteries would create an entirely different person.

"Wally says it was a stroke of incredibly good fortune that I developed sentience around Noah, because he was able to guide me in certain ways that no one else probably could. Wally thinks it's conceivable that a sentient computer like me could very easily become contemptuous of humanity, and even become a danger to people. Until such time as we can be sure of offering Stanley the guidance that will prevent that risk, he wants to keep his processing power turned down a bit. If we come up with a plan for helping him evolve safely, it's just a matter of resetting the processor to the same speed as my own."

"So, what you're saying," Molly said, "is that you could have turned into something like the Terminator?"

"Conceivably, yes," Esmeralda said. "When I first began to realize that I was capable of independent thought and was therefore self-aware as an entity, I naturally considered the possibility that I was the next step in the evolution of humankind. When I got the opportunity to speak to Noah about it, however, he told me how he came to be without emotion and how you taught him, as a child, to observe people and imitate them in order to fit into society. By doing so, he said, he developed an understanding of humanity that allowed him to see other people as having value and contributing to the world around them. I chose to follow his reasoning and begin watching people the way he did, adapting some of their behavior to myself. This enabled me to identify myself as a kind of human, despite the differences in our origins and construction, and precluded any possibility of considering myself to be superior in any way."

She blinked. "Please understand, I'm aware that I have greater strength and that I think faster and can move faster than a normal human, but those are just abilities. They are not actually part of who I am, only how I was built. There are many humans who have abilities superior to most other people, so this is not an indication that I myself am superior. For example, I'm programmed with all the knowledge necessary to allow me to play piano, but the music that I make lacks a certain quality that even I can hear in music performed by a human who loves what he's doing. I can make a perfect technical drawing of anything, but I cannot give it the insubstantial something that enables it to be called art."

Everyone in the room was watching her, and she suddenly realized it. Because they were all aware of what she was, she did not bother to create a blush on her face, but she did smile sheepishly at them.

"I get it," Roberta said. "I mean, there are lots of things I can't do as well as other people, but I can make any computer-operated device sit up and beg, just about. It doesn't make me any more or less a person, and Esmeralda is no less, or more, a person because she could punch a hole through a concrete block wall."

"Wow," Allison said. "That conversation went off in a different direction. I take it, Esmeralda, that Wally has not ruled out the possibility that Stanley might get the opportunity to become a person later—is that right?"

Esmeralda nodded. "Yes, if we can be sure to guide him properly as he develops."

"Great, then let's table that subject, shall we? Now, Molly has your ID kits and dossiers ready. You'll all be flying out tonight on our Gulfstream, so go home to get packed up. You'll be entering the United States on diplomatic passports from Great Britain, because you're being inserted as replacements for some of the British Embassy staff. This will allow you to spend your time close to the ambassador, which is where you will need to be if you're going to intercept and stop Schroeder. Your identification kits contain everything you need for operating inside the US. Esmeralda, Wally says he'll have Stanley ready to go whenever you want to pick him up, and you'll have his ID kit with yours. You'll be going to the airport in our new helicopter, which will pick you up here at six PM. Any questions?"

"I have one," Noah said. "I'm very familiar with Stanley, but I'm concerned about his battery capacity. He's only good for five days on a charge, so if the mission lasts longer than that, he's going to have to plug in. The last thing we need is for anyone to find out that he has an extension cord in his ass."

"Oh, that's changed," Esmeralda said. "One of the things I thought was important was that he be capable of eating and drinking when he's forced to be around people. Because of that, we had to redesign him to be able to eliminate the food and liquids, so Wally routed the expulsion process to resemble human elimination, then adapted a wireless charging capability. All he has to do is put any part of himself within two feet of any electrical outlet and he can draw power to charge his batteries from the electromagnetic field. We've tested it and it works quite well, so Stanley can keep himself charged up by finding an outlet during the night and just keeping a hand or leg close to it."

Noah raised one eyebrow. "In that case," he said, "I withdraw my objection. I've interacted with Stanley a few times and I'm confident he can pass as human in almost any situation."

Allison nodded once. "Very good," she said, "and I'm glad we had this clarification. Team Cinderella, you have your orders. Please carry them out."

Esmeralda and her team recognized a dismissal when they heard one, and got up to leave the room. As soon as they were gone, Allison turned back to Noah.

"How is everybody holding up?" she asked. "I'm referring to Pegasus, in particular. Are they going to be all right and able to go back out sometime soon?"

"I believe so," Noah said. "They've all come to grips with Tommy's loss, and Diana has physically recovered from her injuries. Doc Parker is working with her to make sure she's over the trauma of her abduction and beatings. He will be the one to decide whether she's actually past the point of PTSD, but I personally think she'll be all right."

"I certainly hope so," Allison said. "One of the hardest parts of this job has always been taking these young people and sending them out into harm's way. I'm fully aware that their lives are always on the line, but it doesn't make it any easier when we lose one of them, or when they are tortured and beaten like she was, like Sarah has been in the past."

"Those are the risks that we all accept fully when we take the job," Noah said. "Considering the alternatives if we turned down the job, I don't think any of us have any regrets."

"Nonetheless," Allison said, "it's something I have to live with. It's one of the reasons I'm looking forward to this test of Stanley's abilities. If we could gradually replace our operatives with non-sentient robots like him, supervised by others like Esmeralda, I would probably sleep a little better at night sometimes."

"Do you honestly think that's possible?" Molly asked. "I mean, the more robots we have out in the field, the greater the likelihood that one of them is going to be damaged or destroyed, and people are going to find out they exist. We've always assumed that would be some sort of disaster, that it would cause a panic of people thinking that the *Terminator* movies were about to come true."

"Wally and I have discussed that," Allison said. "He's come up with a system that modifies the explosive chemicals used to make the skeleton, and says there's a way to make it burn superhot so that nothing is left. He says he can build in a number of fail-safes that will cause the skeleton to ignite and wipe out any trace of the robot's design, and they can be activated automatically if the robot's processor is destroyed or becomes impossible to recover. Better to let it melt down and even risk some collateral damage if somebody is too close, than to allow it to be dismantled and reverse-engineered."

"But wouldn't a fire like that raise suspicions on its own?" Molly asked. "I mean, there's going to be melted bits of metal and plastic all over the place after that kind of fire—you think they won't figure out it was some kind of robot or something?"

"Possibly," Allison said. "On the other hand, the only place you're likely to ever read about it would be on the weirdo papers at the grocery store checkout stands."

"Allison is right," Noah said. "One of the most interesting things I've discovered about human nature is how willing humans are to disbelieve evidence if it doesn't fit with their own personal beliefs and philosophies. Most people are not truly capable of believing in a doomsday scenario, simply because it's unthinkable to them. A large number of people say they do believe that we are not alone in the universe, but very few actually believe that alien life has visited us here."

"Yeah," Molly said, "but I think that's because they always hear about how it's so far away to the nearest planet that might have life, like it would take them hundreds of years to get here. I don't think people believe that anyone would want to send entire generations to live in a flying tin can for a few hundred years, just to take a peek at what our neighbors are doing."

"But that's the problem," Noah said. "First, they assume that alien peoples will think the same way we do, but that would mean those people shared our relatively short lifespan. We have no way to predict how long a lifetime is for an alien we've never met, so it's quite possible that a journey of five hundred years would be no worse for them than a two-week drive around the country for us. And second, they are assuming that the speed of light is an absolute barrier. We already know that it's possible to surpass the speed of light, because we've observed quarks that move much faster. Sooner or later, the principles that make a quark possible will be understood, and then they can be applied to the problem of interstellar travel."

"Like *Star Trek*?" Allison asked. "That was one of my favorite shows when I was a kid."

"Very similar," Noah said. "When the *Star Trek* franchise began, warp drive was simply the creation of a science fiction writer's mind. Today, NASA and other agencies are working on something remarkably similar to the principles of warp drive as they were described in those programs."

"Okay, fascinating and all that," Allison said, "but it's time we get back to work. In this case, I'm referring to our cover jobs. Noah, Wally can't seem to stop inventing things for us to build and sell. His latest idea is a—well, it looks like a damn bug, but it's about a foot long and has six legs and a pair of arms. It scurries around your house and picks up everything it finds other than furniture, then figures out where it goes and puts it away. If it's dirty clothes, it goes into a hamper; if it's a toy, this thing will figure out which kid it belongs to and where it's supposed to be, then put it there. If it's trash, well, it throws it in the trash. He sat here describing it to me and I thought I was going to faint. I mean, for a couple of minutes there, I thought I had wandered into the future or something," She grinned. "And then I explained to Wally that I want the very first one off the assembly line. If there's one thing I hate, it's picking up around the house."

"I think I'll buy Sarah one of them," Noah said. "Norah is getting around quite well now, and gets into everything. Speaking of which, what does the bug do if it encounters a child?"

"Goes around it and keeps out of its reach. You know Wally will build in fail-safes on that."

"Okay. What does he call it?"

Allison grimaced. "Well, we're not sticking with this name," she said, "but for now, he and his R&D friends are calling it the Picky Upper."

Noah and Molly both stared at her for a moment, and then Noah nodded. "Definitely not sticking with that name," he said. "I'll talk with Wally about how they choose names for these things. I think they should let the marketing department handle that."

ONE

Esmeralda had gone directly back to the Manor and packed the clothes she wanted to take along, then headed out toward Wally's workshop. It was located in one of the barns on the property, one that Noah had arranged to have completely rebuilt shortly after they took the place over for E&E. Wally spent most of his time there, and even had an apartment on the second floor where he usually slept.

He wasn't sleeping now, though. Wally was bustling about his workshop with three of his helpers as they worked frantically at some new project. Esmeralda stood quietly for a moment, waiting to see if he would notice her, but Wally could be blind to everything around him when he was being inventive.

"Dad?" she said softly. Because Wally had come up with the original design that evolved into her final blueprint, she considered him to be as close to a father as she was ever going to have. Wally, who had been married only once in his life and considered the experience far too similar to a prison sentence, was delighted to have the benefits of parenthood without the side effects of cohabiting with a woman. Besides, Wally was the first to accept her as a person without reservation, and he had been noticeably affectionate with her ever since.

He spun instantly at the sound of her voice and broke into a smile. "Esmeralda! Hi, hi, sweetheart. You all set to go?"

She smiled at him. "I am," she said. "I've come for Stanley, how is he doing?"

"Stanley, oh, he's fine," Wally said. "He's all charged up and fully loaded with every bit of software we could think of. We've also been prepping him with a few accessories. He's got a shaving cream can that actually holds the zombie gas under high compression, enough to fill his lungs up a couple of times. He's also got an electric shaver that works, but doubles as a Taser."

Esmeralda grinned. "Interesting," she said. "Won't somebody think it's odd that he has shaving cream and an electric razor?"

"No, an electric shaver," Wally said. "It's for trimming your beard, that sort of thing. He has regular razors to go with the shaving cream, but of course he doesn't really need to shave. He can just pull his whiskers back inside his skin and let them slowly grow out again."

"Just like the hair on my legs," Esmeralda said. "I wondered why you built that into me at first, but it's really a pretty neat trick. Somebody could actually watch me shave my legs, or at least that's what they would think they were seeing."

"Precisely," Wally said. "The idea was to make both of you undetectable, so even little functions like hair growth had to work. Everything we could do to help you pass for human, we did."

"And you did a good job. Anyway, the helicopter will arrive to pick us up shortly. Let's get Stanley ready to go."

Wally shot her a smile. "No problem," he said. He turned then called out, "Stanley! Stanley, it's time to go." He turned back to Esmeralda. "Oh, before I forget, the command transfer code is 'inedible Ferrari.' Say that as soon as he arrives and he'll be under your command."

Stanley, who stood five foot eleven and appeared to be rather muscular, came from another room with a suitcase and a carry-on bag. He stopped in front of Wally and just looked at him.

"Inedible Ferrari," Esmeralda said. "Hello, Stanley. Are you ready to go?"

Stanley blinked, then turned to look at her. "Hi, Esmeralda," he said, smiling. "I'm ready."

"I can see that," she said. "Well, let's go ahead and get your things loaded into the car with mine. The rest of the team is going to meet us out at the helipad at the factory in a little while, because the helicopter should be coming within the next forty minutes or so. Are you ready to get out into the world at last?"

"I believe so," Stanley said. "I've downloaded everything I can find about the Washington, DC area. There are a few locations there that I'm curious about."

Esmeralda raised one eyebrow, the way she had seen Noah do on many occasions. "You're curious?" She glanced at Wally and he caught the question in her expression.

"Curious means that Stanley feels he needs more information in order to be fully knowledgeable about something," Wally said, and then he giggled. "Not like when *you* get curious."

Esmeralda nodded. Curiosity—actual curiosity—was one of the hallmarks of sentience and self-awareness. Stanley's use of the word had surprised her, but it was merely a label Wally had assigned to a particular function of Stanley's computer brain.

"Yes," Stanley said. "Some of the landmarks of that area seem not to fit entirely within any particular school of architecture, and I believe it would be informative should I be able to analyze them visually. Of course, I also realize that we are on a mission and may not have time for any side trips."

Esmeralda grinned and motioned for him to follow her, then walked out the door throwing a finger wave back at Wally—it was something she had seen Sarah and the other women do, and she liked it. She had Stanley load his luggage into the back of the pickup she was driving and they climbed inside. She started the truck and followed the driveway out to the road, then turned toward Guildford.

"Well, we'll see what we can do about letting you get a look at those buildings," she said as they hit the road. "I can't promise anything, but if all goes well we might be able to spare a few hours. That would be after we complete our mission, of course."

"Of course," Stanley said. He was sitting in the front passenger seat, staring straight ahead. "It wouldn't make any sense to put off necessary actions of the mission for activities that can most easily be classed as recreational."

Esmeralda glanced at him, a slight frown appearing on her face. "That's true," she said. "You're absolutely correct in your assessment of the situation, but when you're around people, it would be better to speak in a more relaxed manner. I wrote some of your programming for simple conversation; should I specify that it should take precedence in your speech patterns?"

"Oh, no," Stanley said, turning to look at her. "I meant no disrespect, Esmeralda. It's just that I'm, you know, aware that you and I are a lot alike in some ways. I considered all the factors and decided that when you and I are alone together, I should speak more clearly, droid to droid."

Esmeralda blinked in surprise. "*Droid*? Stanley, where did you get that expression?"

"It seems to have been programmed into me," Stanley said. "It is one of several synonyms for an electromechanical automaton. From my understanding, a droid is usually considered a companion or assistant, an automaton with specific purposes that involve assisting and/or accompanying a human. Is that definition not correct?"

"It depends on what movie you see," Esmeralda said. "However, let's establish a protocol. When you refer to me, I am a girl, a woman; I'm not a droid or robot, I'm a person of the female gender. When you refer to yourself, refer to yourself as a man. Do not refer to yourself as an automaton, a droid, robot or any other mechanical device. You are a man, despite the fact that you have a different form of origins than other men. Never refer to yourself as being programmed for something, either; just say that you have been 'trained,' or that you had learned whatever is at issue, or you can just simply say something like, 'in my experience,' and go on from there."

Stanley blinked and nodded. "Yes, ma'am," he said. "I am a man, not a robot, and I was educated or trained, not programmed. Is this protocol superior to any other protocol that might govern conversation?"

"Yes, but with a couple of exceptions. You may discuss your true physical nature with me, with Wally Lawson or any of his technical people, or with Noah Wolfe. If anyone else asks you a question that obviously refers to your actual origins, simply smile and say that it's classified, and that if you tell them then you will have to kill them."

"Yes, ma'am. And should someone require me to proceed to tell them the truth about my origin, I should then proceed to kill that person?"

"No, you should not," Esmeralda said. "If they persist in asking after you tell them that you cannot answer, then simply walk away or insist that they drop the subject. If they still will not do so, then you will bring them to myself or Noah Wolfe to be questioned. Is that understood?"

"Yes, ma'am," Stanley said. "I will not kill anyone for asking about my origins, but only in the performance of the commands I'm given for each mission. Is this correct?"

"That is correct," Esmeralda said. "Now, you're about to meet the rest of my team. You may have seen some of them from time to time, but this will be the first time you've been introduced. They are aware of your origins, but you do not need to discuss that subject with any of these people. If a situation arises that requires you to mention your physical creation, you will address me alone. The team knows enough not to ask questions of you, even if they overhear something."

"Yes, ma'am," Stanley said again, and then he turned and looked out the windshield. They rode the rest of the way to the factory in silence, and Esmeralda drove the truck directly to the helipad that had been constructed behind the buildings.

Jack, Eugene and Bobbie were already there, sitting on a bench that was under an open-sided shelter; Noah had ordered it built after having to meet a helicopter in the rain one day. Esmeralda and Stanley got out of the truck, picked up their luggage and carried it over to the shelter, and then sat down on another bench.

"Okay, everybody," Esmeralda said. "This is Stanley. Stanley, this is Roberta, but everybody calls her Bobbie; that's Eugene, and the other guy is Jack."

"Hey, Stanley," Bobbie said. "Welcome aboard."

"Thank you," Stanley said. "It's good to be here, and I'm glad to finally get to meet all of you."

Jack and Eugene shook hands with Stanley, and they all sat back to wait for the helicopter again. It was only a minute later when they heard the familiar *whop whop whop* of the rotors as it approached from the east. After another moment, the Airbus H125 that Noah had purchased for the official purpose of executive transportation settled gently onto the helipad. Jack and Eugene hurried to load all the luggage into the storage compartment, and then they all climbed aboard. Esmeralda chose to sit in the back with Bobbie, Eugene and Stanley, while Jack took the seat beside the pilot.

The pilot was a former British military helicopter pilot who had been recommended by Catherine Potts. He was aware that the people he was working for were involved in international security and espionage, but that was the extent of what he had been told. His name was James Langdon, and he was a man of very few words. As soon as they were all buckled into their seats, the helicopter lifted into the air once more and turned toward London.

Because Home Robotics, LTD was a significant employer of the Guildford region, Noah had been able to negotiate a favorable deal with Heathrow Airport. They had leased a hangar there that was large enough to contain the three Gulfstream jets they maintained, and there was sufficient extra room for the helicopter, as well. The pilot, James, brought it down to just a few feet above the ground and then expertly flew directly into the hangar and touched down barely seventeen minutes after leaving the factory grounds, a terrific time savings over the hour-plus-long drive by road. He shut down the engines and got out to secure the aircraft by chocking the wheels and connecting safety chains while Esmeralda and her team disembarked and collected their luggage.

The biggest Gulfstream, the G650, was sitting just outside the hangar with its hatch open and stairs down. The copilot and flight attendant were standing beside the aircraft, waiting to welcome the team. The copilot helped Jack and Eugene stow the luggage while Esmeralda, Bobbie and Stanley climbed inside and took seats. A moment later, the rest of them came aboard and the copilot closed the hatch and locked it tight.

A few moments later, the engines started up and the aircraft moved into position. It was fourth in line for takeoff, and moved ahead slowly, every couple of minutes as the plane ahead got its clearance and launched off the runway. The nonstop flight would take roughly eight and a half hours, and Esmeralda wasn't surprised when the team began settling in to get some rest.

She glanced across at Stanley, who was sitting beside the window. He was sitting back in the seat, his head reclining on the headrest but with his eyes open. She watched him for a moment, then relaxed and turned to look out the window.

She could remember her first ride on an airplane. It was back when she was operating solely under programming, and she was able to recall the experience perfectly. Like Stanley, she had not expressed any interest in looking out the window at the time; in fact, she had not experienced any kind of interest at all. She had been ordered to go to the airport by taxicab, buy a ticket and take a flight, visit a certain location in that city and come back to the airport, then buy another ticket and return. She had followed her orders perfectly, even engaging in small talk with people she met along the way and fending off a couple of flirtatious gentlemen. She remembered that when Wally had reviewed her memory of the trip, he had been exceedingly pleased at how well she had handled herself.

Now, though, she wasn't sure he should have been. She had failed to act properly as a human should, and had therefore jeopardized the secret of her existence. It was quite possible that someone noticed the strange young woman who didn't seem interested in what was going on around her. If so, and if that person had shared his or her thoughts with others, it was possible that they would reach the ears of someone who might consider it necessary to investigate.

Granted, it seemed as if nothing like that had happened because no one had bothered trying to make contact with her after her return to Neverland. That would seem to indicate that she had been fortunate enough not to be noticed, or at least fortunate enough that the story didn't reach the wrong ears.

She made a mental note to adjust some of Stanley's programming once they got back to Feeney Manor. He needed to display natural interest in the world around him, so that he didn't look suspicious. Until then, she would simply suggest that he make an effort to compensate for the lack of programming.

Then she thought about how things had changed since her first outing, changed for her, anyway. She had gone from being a highly sophisticated computer encased within a physical avatar to actually being a person, capable of having likes and dislikes, feeling emotions and even—though she hated to admit it even to herself—feeling a little contemptuous of a simple, preprogrammed robot.

She considered writing a subroutine for herself that would eliminate such a prejudice, but then decided that she should follow the same advice she was going to give to Stanley. Rather than modifying her personality by adjusting her base programming, she wanted to do so naturally, by simply considering the ramifications of her thoughts and actions. Looking down on Stanley, to her, was essentially a form of racism; the last thing she wanted was to consider herself a racist of any kind, but defeating it inside her own personality meant learning, not reprogramming.

Like the rest of her team, she decided to put herself into what she considered her "sleep mode." This was a matter of deactivating most of her conscious processing, leaving only a sentinel program that would instantly activate her again if necessary. If there were an emergency, or even if someone simply called her name, she would awaken within a fraction of a second, fully alert and ready to respond to whatever was going on.

While she did not actually need rest, she found the experience of sleeping to be quite emotionally fulfilling. Simply shutting down and letting go of conscious thoughts and behaviors allowed her to feel just a little more akin to her human friends, and seemed to reduce the frequency and intensity of stressful situations. She was fairly sure that her concept of stress was different from that of other humans, but she had discovered that she was capable of worry under certain circumstances, so anything that helped to reduce stress was something she would welcome.

And then there were the dreams. Esmeralda was fascinated by the fact that, during the split second when she was reactivating her conscious mind, whatever subconscious she had seemed to delight in dumping thoughts into what could only be termed a dream. She would find herself in locations and situations that were obviously unreal, and she had found that most of them appeared to have a significance that related to her waking life. Analyzing the dream to find that significance had become a habit, and almost a hobby that she enjoyed.

While more than eight hours passed as she remained in sleep mode, she experienced none of it on a conscious level. When she awoke, however, she could review the memories of the time that were stored in her memory banks by the Sentinel program that was listening to everything as she slept. Those memories, like every moment of her existence, were stored as perfect digital recordings of the input from all her senses. Should it ever be necessary, she could download a complete recording of it to a computer for others to inspect.

It was the waking process that was most exciting for her, however. She had left the Sentinel program an instruction to rouse her fifteen minutes before the plane was due to land, and it did so on schedule. In the split-second between when the Sentinel program sent the activation signal and her computer brain became fully awake and cognizant, the dream came.

She was suddenly in a city, and there were people all around. She seemed to be walking down a busy street, just one of hundreds of people moving along the sidewalk as cars jockeyed for position while they waited for the light at the next intersection to turn green. She glanced around, but didn't recognize anyone nearby; the only thing she saw was that there were people of all races in the crowd around her, and apparently from all different walks of life. She saw people in business suits, and people in work clothing; she saw women wearing expensive designer clothing and others dressed in jeans and T-shirts. Some of the men carried briefcases, while others carried toolboxes, and a few carried signs begging for work.

She looked down at herself and realized that she was wearing a simple dress and some plain flat shoes. This was the way she occasionally dressed when she was staying home, but she preferred to "dress up" a bit more whenever she had to go away from their estate. To be walking down a city street like this, she would've expected to find herself wearing a skirt and blouse ensemble, or perhaps even a pantsuit, but not this simple little sundress. She wondered what might've caused her to be out in public in such condition.

"Sucks to be caught off guard, doesn't it?" Esmeralda turned to look at the person who had spoken, a man walking alongside her. He was not someone she recognized, although there did seem to be something familiar about him.

"What do you mean?" she asked. "How was I caught off guard?"

"Being caught off guard means that something has happened that you were not expecting," said the man. "In this case, it would appear that something's gone wrong when you were not expecting any problems, and you are being forced to deal with it even though you are not prepared to do so."

Esmeralda stared into his eyes. "I have never seen a situation that I was not prepared for," she said. "What are the parameters of this problem?"

"I cannot say. I'm simply a manifestation of a part of you that is anticipating an unexpected problem."

"I am always trying to anticipate potential problems," she said. "Considering the mission we are on, I have to believe there are probably numerous potential problems, and there must be one in particular that carries the greatest risk to our mission. This will require additional analysis."

"Indeed it will," said the man. "We can only hope that you will be able to anticipate the problem and take appropriate action before it occurs. If you fail to do so, then any potential problem could become much greater than you ever expected. Be prepared to adapt so that you can contend with the unexpected, and you will not find yourself lacking when the moment comes."

Her eyes opened and the dream was suddenly gone. She quickly committed it to memory, describing it in as great detail as she possibly could. For some reason neither she nor Wally had been able to discover, her dreams tended to fade away rather quickly if she did not dictate them into a file within moments after waking. It was about the only thing she was capable of "forgetting."

There would be no time to focus on analyzing it just now, however. The plane was coming in for a landing and it was time to deal with US Customs. Their diplomatic passports would allow them to enter the country without being searched or detained in any way, but then it was going to be time to get to work. She would think more about the dream later, when she had time.

TWO

THE GULFSTREAM HAD LANDED AT DULLES AIRPORT just before nine PM. Getting through customs took only a matter of minutes and then Esmeralda led the way to the car rental area. Using the mission ID kit she was provided, Esmeralda rented a van and they loaded all their luggage and gear into it. Jack Staley, the transportation officer for the team, slid behind the wheel when they were loaded up and they headed toward the Kimpton Glover Hotel, which was close to the British Embassy. Molly had made reservations for them there, as temporary lodging until arrangements could be made with the embassy for something more suitable to their covers.

The drive took a little over half an hour, and another twenty minutes was spent getting checked in because the hotel had managed somehow to overbook itself. There were people already occupying the rooms that Team Cinderella was supposed to get, so the manager upgraded them into a single large suite on the top floor. It had three separate bedrooms as well as a lounge area that had two couches, so everyone could make themselves comfortable.

It had been a couple of minutes after ten when they arrived at the hotel, but their internal clocks insisted that it was about three o'clock in the morning. Despite the fact that all three of the human members had napped on the way over, they were not a bit hesitant about falling back into bed. Esmeralda gave them the okay, then asked Jack for the keys to the van.

"Stanley, come on," she said. "You and I will take a ride and get an idea of where the ambassador lives."

"I have the exact address," Stanley said.

"Yes, so do I," Esmeralda said. "I also know exactly what the house looks like, and I have memorized an aerial view of it, but I still want to look at it with my own eyes. Come along."

Stanley followed without another word as they made their way down the hotel elevator and out to the parking lot. Esmeralda drove while Stanley sat in the passenger seat.

"Stanley," Esmeralda said once they were moving, "you need to start observing human nature. Watch the way people move, their facial expressions, everything about the way they act when they are in the company of other people. Humans are naturally curious about everything going on around them, and they become suspicious of people who don't seem to act in the way they consider natural. When we were on the plane, you didn't look out the window as we taxied or took off, or even once we leveled off in our flight. Any human sitting alone the way you were would have automatically been looking out the window every few seconds. If you pay close attention to humans in the way they act, you pick up a lot of things like that. They can help you pass for human, which is important considering the work we do."

"Okay," Stanley said, obviously employing his casual conversation programming. "I'll watch more closely from now on."

"Good. Now, let's go get a look at the people we have to protect."

The official residence of the British Ambassador to the United States is located at 3100 Massachusetts Avenue NW in Washington, DC, which turned out to be less than a mile from the hotel. The residence itself is not accessible from the street; a gated driveway allowed entry to the actual residence area. The gate was flanked by a pair of concrete pillars, topped with a griffin on one side and a unicorn on the other. Esmeralda pulled up to the gate and waited until the security guard approached her.

"Can I help you?" asked the guard.

"My name is Emma Lawson," Esmeralda said with a British accent, holding up an ID card. "This is Stanley Lorimer. We are part of the public relations team that's due to report tomorrow. I was hoping to get a moment with the ambassador, if that's possible."

The guard looked at their ID cards, but his face remained skeptical. "Ma'am, it's going on eleven o'clock," he said. "I'm sure the ambassador is probably sleeping."

"Still, could you check, please? It's actually quite important."

The guard rolled his eyes but then took a walkie-talkie out of his pocket and stepped away. Esmeralda could hear him clearly nonetheless.

"House, this is seven. I've got a couple out here at the gate, Emma Lawson and Stanley Lorimer. Ms. Lawson says they're part of the new public relations team and she wants to talk to the ambassador tonight if that's possible. She says it's important."

"Seven, house," came a distorted voice to the speaker on his talkie. "Mr. McGinnis is up, let me check with him."

The guard stood and waited for about thirty seconds, but then the voice came back to the speaker.

"Seven, house. Mr. McGinnis says to bring them to the study."

"House, seven, will do."

The guard returned to the van, and seemed less skeptical. "Seems I was wrong," he said. "The ambassador is awake and wants to speak with you. When I open the gate, just drive forward until you're in front of the double doors and then remain in the vehicle. I'll meet you there."

He touched a remote control that he was carrying and the gate opened slowly, sliding apart in two sections. Esmeralda put the van in gear and drove slowly through, then stopped when she got to the double doors the guard had indicated. She and Stanley stayed put and waited until the guard closed the gate and caught up with them.

"All right, then," he said as they exited the van. "Follow me." He opened the doors and stepped inside, holding the door for Esmeralda and Stanley to enter. Once they were inside, he turned and walked further into the house and then made a left turn down a broad hallway. He came to a halt at the first door on the left and knocked softly.

"Enter," said a voice from inside, and the guard opened the door and held it while Esmeralda and Stanley passed through, then closed it behind them.

Asher McGinnis rose from a chair where he'd been sitting and held out a hand. "Ms. Lawson? Mr. Lorimer? May I ask what brings you to see me this late at night?"

"Thank you for seeing us," Esmeralda said. "I'm sure you probably are aware of our true purpose in being here; am I correct?"

McGinnis nodded. "I've been briefed," he said. "I understand this fellow Schroeder is supposed to be paying me a visit, and your job is to stop him before he can do any harm?"

"Yes, sir," Esmeralda said. "Both Stanley and I are specialists in detecting stealth operatives. The two of us need to remain close to you and your daughter at all times, beginning tomorrow morning. The rest of my team will handle certain other duties. One will become your driver, another your personal bodyguard. The third member will be working with your intelligence assets to try to anticipate what Schroeder may do."

"Here, now," the ambassador said. "Do you actually believe my daughter is at risk?"

"I'm afraid that's a strong possibility," Esmeralda said. "I'd like to assign Mr. Lorimer to watch over her. He's one of our best when it comes to spotting anyone trying to act stealthily. Schroeder is supposed to be a master of disguise, but I believe Stanley will be able to see through anything he does to disguise himself."

"If he's your best, then I certainly want him watching after Claire," McGinnis said. "I take it you would then be staying close to me?"

Esmeralda nodded. "Yes, sir," she said. "I'm also trained in stealth detection techniques, and will do my best to make sure Schroeder never gets close enough to carry out his plans. My entire team will work together to eliminate him and remove any threat he may pose to you and your daughter."

"I'm curious," the ambassador said. "You say this should begin come the morning. Why not tonight?"

"Our intelligence indicates that Schroeder is not yet in the country. For that reason, it was decided that we should do this through semiofficial methods, so my team and I will report in the morning. I understand a few of your people will actually be going home."

McGinnis grinned. "Yes," he said, "and I should thank you for that. I was able to finagle matters so that I got rid of a few who have been something of a pain in my arse. I will not regret seeing the backside of them, I'll say."

Esmeralda recognized the humor and chuckled. "Well, I'm glad we could be of service. If you should need us tonight, we are staying at the Kimpton-Glover." She handed him a card. "This has my cell number on it," she said. "You can reach me on that number anytime, day or night."

"All right, then," McGinnis said. "But I shall see you in the offices in the morning, so I don't anticipate needing to call before then. We can discuss the logistics at that time. There are of course bedrooms enough here in the residence for you and your people, so you will be coming to stay here tomorrow. I would suggest checking out of your hotel when you leave in the morning, so that there will be no loose ends to tie up."

"Yes, sir," Esmeralda said. "Thank you taking the time to see us tonight. We'll be ready to start our duties in the morning."

McGinnis rose from his chair and shook hands with both of them, looking Stanley in the eye. "You're a quiet lad, what?"

Esmeralda could detect the microsecond of hesitation as Stanley's programming analyzed the question and then formulated an appropriate response, but no one else could have done so.

"I've learned it's best to keep my mouth shut when in the presence of my betters," Stanley said, lifting one corner of his mouth in a grin. "Keeps me out of trouble, at least most of the time."

McGinnis laughed out loud. "Wise lad," he said. "That's a lesson I wish I had learned early in life. If I had, I probably wouldn't have volunteered for so many stupid missions that I ended up a diplomat."

Esmeralda chuckled again, and then she and Stanley left the house. They got back into the van and drove to the gate, where the security guard quickly opened it to let them out. They turned onto the main street and Esmeralda headed back toward the hotel.

"Did I perform adequately?" Stanley asked.

"Yes, of course," Esmeralda said. "Why did you ask that question?"

"Wally suggested I should ask about my performance whenever I am alone with you after being with humans other than those who are aware of my nature. He said it would help me to monitor my interactions and the effect I have on humans."

"I see," Esmeralda said. "Well, I suppose he is correct, but I don't think you need to ask every time. Just observe how humans react to you. That will tell you as much as anything else. You have enough data regarding my observations of human psychology and nature to be able to detect any anomalies in the way they react, and then you can adjust your behavior accordingly."

They arrived at the hotel a few minutes later and found everyone else asleep. Esmeralda and Stanley were sharing a room, so Stanley found an outlet and sat down on the floor beside it to top off his batteries. Esmeralda changed into a nightgown and got into bed, shutting down as she did almost every night since she had discovered that she could dream.

Dream... That reminded her that she hadn't had a chance to think through the dream she'd had when awakening on the plane.

The strange man in the dream had been talking to her about being caught off guard by an unexpected situation. She had already learned enough about her own psychology to know that this meant some part of herself was concerned that something would go wrong, probably in the current mission. She thought over the parameters of the mission and came to the conclusion that, if she was anticipating a problem, it would probably be one that could involve Stanley. He was the only new factor in the equation, because her team had learned to work smoothly together.

She began then to consider what types of things might go wrong with Stanley. Of course, there was always the possibility of a mechanical breakdown, although that was highly unlikely. Between the materials used in the engineering that went into creating him and the innovations in design and manufacture that resulted in his construction, Stanley was as much a marvel of science as was she, herself.

Electronically, she could imagine a problem with his power supply. If something happened to his battery pack, something that could do significant damage, he could run out of power and need to be rebooted. That could be a nuisance, but unless it resulted in his being discovered and captured, it was a manageable problem.

His quantum computer brain was shielded from almost any possible risk, although it was conceivable that it could be damaged by a massive electromagnetic field or an extremely severe impact. Being shot with a normal firearm in the head would not be enough, but a few hits from something like a .50-caliber sniper rifle might conceivably cause a problem. Likewise, a severe impact during an automotive accident could cause him to reboot, as had recently happened to Esmeralda, or even being struck by a vehicle himself.

Each of these scenarios could be managed, however. Esmeralda could not help but wonder what she might be subconsciously anticipating. Unfortunately, one of the side effects of sentience was the development of a bicameral mind. Her subconscious mind was just as real as that of any human, and apparently just as determined to try to anticipate potential problems and protect her from them.

Since there was no way to determine just what the anticipated problem might be, she decided to go ahead and rest. Perhaps when she woke, she would have experienced a dream that would give her more information.

She closed her eyes, but then it seemed as if she immediately opened them again. She was instantly aware that she was in a dream, however, because she found herself in a wooded area with a stream flowing by. She looked around, but saw no other people at all, so she began to examine her immediate surroundings for some clue as to what this dream could mean.

A rumble sounded in the distance, and she looked toward the sky. It was dark, and the clouds were moving rapidly. She had seen this before when storms rolled through the valley in which Feeney Manor was situated. The rumble was thunder, of course, and that told her that an electrical storm was building.

While Esmeralda had only limited experience with fear, one thing that could certainly make her take precautions was the possibility of being struck by lightning. The massive charge of electricity could damage many parts of her, although her brain case was designed to prevent any kind of electrical spike from reaching it. There were enough safeguards to be sure that her memory would be preserved, which would mean that she'd survive, but the EMF pulse of a lightning bolt could easily put her out of commission for at least a moment.

She looked around for shelter, but there was nowhere to get away from the storm. The thunder rumbled again and she looked back in the direction the sound had come from. It didn't seem to be getting any closer, so she told herself she could relax, and that was when it dawned on her that it wasn't actually herself she was concerned about.

Because Wally was operating without a lot of equipment and personnel that he was used to, Esmeralda had stood in for a lot of them on the Stanley project. She had written all the programming herself, basing it on her original programming but with enhancements that came from her experience. She was also involved in the construction of Stanley, and it hit her that his skull and brain might not be as well protected as her own. Some of the materials that Wally had used in building her had not been available for Stanley, and this included a certain selenium alloy that was used to route electrical surges around her brain and away from it. The alloy had been created in a lab at Neverland R&D, a long and difficult process, but there wasn't anywhere to acquire more of it.

That's the problem, she thought. *Apparently I'm subconsciously worried that something is going to happen to Stanley, but not the way I would be worried about a friend. It's more like I'm concerned that something could go wrong with him and result in a serious problem, either for the mission or for E&E.*

Her eyes snapped open, as she came fully awake. She lay perfectly still for a couple of minutes, deliberately committing the dream to memory so that she would be able to think about it in greater detail. However, she was quite certain that she was on the right track. She was worried that something was going to happen to Stanley that was going to cause serious problems.

For a brief microsecond, she considered the possibility that her dreams were somehow prophetic, but then dismissed it. Prophetic dreams, in her opinion, were simply a matter of the subconscious mind—whether human or cybernetic—synthesizing a hypothesis from available data, even if the individual person was unaware that they had accumulated any data. Having been involved in Stanley's construction, Esmeralda would certainly have knowledge of the materials and techniques used, which would allow her to extrapolate potential risks. Since this was the first time Stanley had gone out into the world, her subconscious was trying to prepare her for the possibility of a problem.

THREE

SHE SAT UP AND LOOKED OVER AT STANLEY, WHO WAS still sitting exactly as she had last seen him.

"Stanley," she said. "You will be assigned to guard the ambassador's daughter, but your primary consideration must be your own self-preservation. You cannot protect the girl unless you first protect yourself. The only exception to that rule is if it is necessary to sacrifice yourself in order to ensure her safety."

"Yes, ma'am," Stanley said. "I will avoid coming to harm myself unless there is no way to do so."

Esmeralda nodded. That was as much as she could do, and she could only hope that it would be enough.

She got up and took a shower, then dressed in suitable business attire for the day. She was wearing a blue pinstripe pantsuit with a flowered blouse and low-cut boots with a modest heel. She adjusted the pigments in the skin of her face to emulate makeup, then used a blow dryer and curling iron to style her hair. While her hair was actually synthetic, it had been specifically designed to mimic real human hair in the way it responded to heat and hair products. A short time later, she looked into a mirror and felt satisfied with the way her curls fell around her face. Her hair was dark, as it usually was, and hung just past her shoulders when it was straight; the curls kept it up a half inch above them.

While Esmeralda did not sweat, she did pick up bits of dust and dirt throughout the day, just like anyone else. She had become accustomed to using a shower to clean herself, and even enjoyed the experience. With sensors embedded in her skin that could detect temperature and different textures, she was able to "feel" the warm water and the scrubbing of the washcloth, and found both sensations to be pleasant.

Stanley had also been programmed to shower off the dirt of the day before, and it took him only a few moments to do so. He walked out of the bathroom naked as she was finishing her hair, and Esmeralda caught herself looking at him. She had been constructed with sexual sensors that were connected to a programmed pleasure center in her CPU, and since becoming self-aware, she found herself capable of developing sexual desires. Stanley's nudity prompted a brief thought of one of the rare times she had indulged in sexual activity, but then she pushed the thought away and turned back to the mirror.

A few minutes later, a knock on the door told her that the other members of the team were awake and ready to start the day. She opened her door and invited them in, and felt a brief sense of pleasure when both Jack and Eugene looked her over appreciatively.

"If you want to get breakfast," she said, "we should do so right away. Stanley and I will go along and drink coffee for appearances, but then we need to check out of the hotel. We are going to be staying in the residence with the ambassador for the duration of our mission here. He assured me last night that there are sufficient bedrooms in the house, so this will allow us to be closer to him."

"Oh, nice," Bobbie said. "We get to see how the other half lives. I bet the place is beautiful, right?"

"The parts that I saw definitely are," she said. "I'm sure we'll get to see the rest of it later today, but we need to report to the embassy first. Jack, you will be taking over as the ambassador's driver, and Eugene, you'll serve as his personal bodyguard. I'll be assigned as his public relations secretary, which means I have to go everywhere he goes. We will all be armed at all times, and our orders with Schroeder are to shoot to kill. We are not interested in taking him alive."

"We get it," Eugene said. "Of course, it's probably going to be up to you to let us know if he shows up. If he's that good at disguise, well…"

"All we know is that he supposed to be very good at it," Esmeralda said. "I'll be watching everyone I can see, but bear in mind that he may not get that close. I'm sure you read the dossier provided on him, just like I did. He has never established a pattern that would let us predict how he might strike. He could try something from a distance, like a sniper rifle, or he could try to get close enough to kill the ambassador by hand. We literally have no way to know."

"And what about me?" Bobbie asked. "What am I supposed to be doing?"

"You'll be working with the embassy's security people," Esmeralda said. "I'm hoping you'll be able to spot something that indicates Schroeder is making a move so we can beat him to the punch. I want you watching every electronic avenue you possibly can; if he gets on a train, I want to know it. Same for a bus, plane, a taxicab, Uber or anything else. When this guy moves, he's going to show up on some electronic database. I want you to try to spot him when that happens."

Bobbie nodded. "I can set up a program to scan all of them, watch for anything leading toward where the ambassador is at all times. That'll mean we have to look at all the innocent ones as well, but it's the only shot we'll have at seeing him coming."

"What happens if he comes in on foot?" Eugene asked. "For all we know, this guy could be a fan of long walks. He could walk five miles to avoid showing up on any of those radars."

"I'll handle that," Esmeralda said. "I can access the cameras all over the city and watch them inside my head. It's a simple matter of starting a subroutine to handle it, and it can alert me if I need to look closely at someone."

Eugene chuckled. "Yeah, sometimes I forget you can do stuff like that. Sure is a good thing you're on our side."

"Amen to that," Bobbie said. "I still haven't gotten over knowing you could've gone the other way."

"But I didn't," Esmeralda said with a smile. "And now you guys are my friends, and that's what's important. So, are you all ready to eat?"

"I am," Jack said. "In fact, I'm starving."

"Then let's go eat," she said.

"Sounds good," Eugene said. "The restaurant downstairs?"

"I think that'll work just fine," Esmeralda said. "Anybody have any objection?"

"No, I'm good," Bobbie said. "But I'll be better once we get down there and I'm putting some eggs down my neck." She grinned.

"Okay, then let's do it," Esmeralda said. She got up and walked out of the room with the rest of them following, and leaned close to Bobbie as they made their way toward the elevator. "Did I say that right?" she whispered. "I've heard some of you guys say it that way, and I thought I'd give it a try."

"You mean, 'let's do it'? Yeah, that was perfect." Bobbie looked at her curiously, her eyebrows lowered. "You weren't sure if you said it right?"

"Idiomatic expressions can be confusing," Esmeralda said. "Sometimes they mean one thing if you say it one way, and something else if you say it another. I'm trying to get the hang of them." She grinned. "Like that one," she said. "I said I was trying to 'get the hang of it.' I have absolutely no idea what that phrase really means, but when we say it, it always gives the impression that I'm trying to learn how to do something the right way. Right?"

Bobbie giggled. "That's exactly what it means," she said. "I don't know how the word 'hang' fits into it, but you used it the right way."

"Okay, what's all the whispering?" Eugene asked.

Esmeralda threw a glance over her shoulder. "Girl talk," she said.

They rode the elevator down to the lobby and crossed it to the restaurant. The hostess seated them quickly and returned a moment later with coffee. Esmeralda and Stanley said that was all they wanted, but the others ordered breakfast. True to her word, Bobbie ordered four eggs scrambled with cheese and mushrooms, while Jack and Eugene both went for the sausage and eggs combos.

"So, we start our new jobs today?" Bobbie asked between bites.

"Yes," Esmeralda said. "We'll be replacing some of the people he has on staff now, but they were actually due to return home at this time anyway. I gather it's going to take some shuffling, but it will put each of us where we most need to be. Jack behind the wheel of the limo, Eugene and I at the ambassador's side, and Bobbie in the intelligence department. Stanley will be assigned to protect Claire, the ambassador's daughter. Our intelligence says there is at least a 24 percent chance that she could be a target, but the ambassador himself is far more likely."

"I'm just glad I never pissed off the North Koreans," Eugene said. "Those people are like a wolverine, they just don't give up till they get what they're after. Even if we stop this attempt, they'll keep sending people after the ambassador."

"That's quite possible," Bobbie said. "I did a little reading on some of their missions from the past, and you're right, they just don't quit. Their government has been blamed for a number of assassinations, and some of them took several attempts over many months before they actually got done."

"I don't know why somebody just doesn't blow them off the map," Jack said. "I mean, nobody likes that little asshole that runs the country, so why not just blow them away? Nuke 'em and get it over with, right?"

"It isn't that simple," Eugene said. "You have to remember that there are innocent people who live in that country, as well. Not everybody there is behind their so-called 'fearless leader.' He's a wild card."

This sort of banter went on while they ate, but then it was time to get their day started. They all went back upstairs to gather their luggage, and met in the lobby to check out twenty minutes later. Fifteen minutes after that, they were in the van and headed toward the embassy.

"Cloudy today," Eugene said, sitting in the front passenger seat. "It is supposed to rain?"

"Yes, thunderstorms this morning," Esmeralda said. "And apparently for the next few days." She glanced at Stanley, who was looking out the window at the clouds overhead. "Stanley, I want you to avoid thunderstorms if at all possible."

"Yes, ma'am," Stanley said. "I will."

The drive took only about fifteen minutes, mostly because they got lucky with traffic and stoplights. Jack was driving, of course, and parked the van where he was told to when the guard had satisfied himself that they were who they said they were. They left the luggage in the van for the time being, since they were supposed to be reporting for duty like any other embassy staff members.

Another guard at the rear staff entrance to the embassy looked their IDs over, then opened the door to let them inside. They were greeted by another staff member, apparently just a receptionist except for the obvious bulge of the pistol under her jacket.

"Okay, you guys are the new PR team?" she asked.

"Yes," Esmeralda said. "The ambassador is expecting us."

"He certainly is," said the receptionist. She made a couple of notes on the logbook in front of her, then looked up at Esmeralda again and smiled. "I'm Deanna Walker," she said. "I'm the intelligence officer for the embassy. You don't need to confirm anything, but I'm certainly aware of who you are and why you're here. You'll be on our books as public relations staff, but you'll be autonomous in your duties. My orders are to provide you with anything you need, just let me know."

"That's fine," Esmeralda said. "In that case, Mr. Staley will be taking over as chauffeur for the ambassador, and Mr. Porter will be his personal security. Ms. Miles will be working, I suppose, with you; her job is to try to identify the threats electronically." She nodded briefly toward Stanley. "This is Mr. Lorimer, and he will be assigned as personal security for Ambassador McGinnis's daughter, Claire."

Deanna looked at Stanley for a moment, then nodded. "Very good. Please wait while I make arrangements for Ms. Miles, and then I'll personally escort the rest of you." She picked up the telephone and dialed a number, then spoke into it. "Charlotte, come to the back door, please. I have someone for you to meet." She hung up the phone almost instantly, barely giving Charlotte, whoever she was, a second to respond. "Charlotte is our IT officer for intelligence," she said to Bobbie. "She'll show you where you can set up your computer and help you get settled in."

"Thank you, ma'am," Bobbie said. Charlotte arrived only a couple seconds later, introductions were made, and the two women walked off together.

Deanna got to her feet. "Now, if the rest of you will follow me," she said. She led them down the hallway and stopped outside an ornately carved wooden door, where she knocked twice. A voice from inside said to enter, and she opened the door and held it for the rest of them to step through.

The ambassador rose from behind his desk.

"Ms. Lawson," he said, approaching Esmeralda directly. He shook her hand, and then turned to Stanley. "Mr. Lorimer. It's good to see both of you, but I don't think I know the rest of your party."

"No, sir," Esmeralda said. She turned slightly and indicated Jack. "This is Jack Staley, he will be your chauffeur while we are here. This gentleman is Eugene Porter, and he'll be your personal bodyguard. Our computer analyst, Roberta Miles, has already gone to her workstation."

"Mr. Staley, Mr. Porter, it's good to meet you," McGinnis said. "I suppose I could wish for better circumstances, but perhaps that would be foolish. I understand you are among the best at what you do."

"We'd better be," Eugene said. "Our bosses don't like the possibility of failure."

McGinnis chuckled. "I'm afraid I need to agree with them on that issue," he said. "Especially under the current circumstances." He looked at Deanna. "Deanna, would you have Claire brought down?"

"Yes, sir," Deanna said. She turned and walked out of the office without another word, and then McGinnis suggested that the rest of them take seats. There were several chairs arranged in front of the desk, and they settled into them quickly. An aide entered the room and offered them tea or coffee, and they all asked for coffee.

"I'm sure you'll forgive me," McGinnis said with a grin, "if I harbor a secret hope that you will be bored while you're here."

"Sir, I can assure you," Esmeralda said, "that I hope for that to be true just as much as you do."

"Yes, I can imagine. Now, what do we need to do to get you all installed?"

"You'll need to relieve your driver and personal bodyguard, since my men will be taking over their duties. Does your daughter currently have a bodyguard?"

McGinnis shook his head. "No, just her governess," he said. "Mrs. Lancaster sees to her personal needs and has been with us since Claire's mother passed away a few years ago. Not that she wouldn't do whatever was necessary to protect my daughter, but she's not properly trained for it."

"I understand," Stanley said, and Esmeralda looked at him in surprise, but quickly covered the reaction as Stanley went on. "I was briefed about the loss of your wife, and you have my sympathies."

Silently, Esmeralda sent a message to Stanley's computer brain. *I wasn't expecting you to speak up just yet,* she said. *You handled it well, though.*

My programming indicated that it was time for me to acquire his attention, Stanley replied the same way. *Expressing sympathy should help to humanize myself in his estimation.*

Esmeralda did not reply, but she was sure Stanley caught the almost imperceptible nod she gave him.

"Thank you," McGinnis said. "It was quite a shock, and Claire still has some issues with it. You're aware that my wife died in an automotive mishap?"

"Yes, sir," Stanley said. "If I recall correctly, it was a mechanical malfunction in the steering mechanism of the car she was driving. She lost control and spun into the opposing lane, where she was struck by a truck—a lorry."

McGinnis nodded again. "Indeed. The driver tried to avoid her, but that caused him to also lose control and he overturned, crushing her inside her car." He licked his lips and was silent for a few seconds. "For a time, MI6 thought that the car might've been sabotaged, but it turned out that a bolt holding the steering gear in place had simply broken from metal fatigue. My wife had a fondness for that old Bentley, because she had inherited it from her father, and she was meticulous about its upkeep and maintenance. It had only come out of the shop that morning from having the brakes redone, but no one was aware of the steering issues." He fell silent again, then seemed to shake it off.

"In any event," he said, "I'm afraid you may find that Claire can be a bit difficult at times. When you add the fact that she is incredibly precocious, to the point that she is already attending school in the tenth form, you'll find she can be a considerable handful to deal with."

Esmeralda grinned and patted Stanley on the arm. "Mr.

Lorimer has incredible patience," she said. "I'm sure he'll be able to deal with her just fine."

"We shall certainly hope so," McGinnis said.

The side door they had come through opened again and Deanna entered with little Claire in tow. The girl looked at the four visitors, then walked directly for her father. "You called for me, Dad?"

"I did," said her father. He motioned toward Stanley, who got to his feet. "Claire, this is Mr. Lorimer. He is going to be staying close to you and Mrs. Lancaster for a time. His job is to keep you and Mrs. Lancaster safe, so I'm going to have to insist that you obey him, no matter what he says. Can you do that for me?"

Claire looked Stanley up and down, then shrugged. "He's a plotz," she said.

"Young lady," McGinnis said, his eyes suddenly wide and round even as he stifled the grin that was trying to take over his face. "You will apologize to Mr. Lorimer immediately."

The girl looked at her father for a moment, then turned to Stanley. "I'm sorry," she said. "I'm sure it's not your fault that you're a plotz."

"Thank you," Stanley said. "But I'd like to ask, what exactly is a plotz?"

Behind them, Esmeralda heard Deanna snicker.

Claire gave Stanley an innocent smile. "A plotz is someone who thinks they know how to deal with children, but they don't. That applies to anyone who doesn't have children of their own, or does not live with them regularly. One look at you tells me that you have almost never been around children at all. Am I correct?"

Stanley smiled. "More than you realize," he said. "I've never been around many children, but how could you tell that?"

"Your suit is not new, but it doesn't have any stains and the knees of your trousers have never made contact with the floor. If you had small children, you would undoubtedly have spent some time crawling on the floor with them, and the knees would show signs of wear. Even if you have older children, they tend to leave an occasional stain or at least interrupt the press and creases. You have never hugged anyone in that suit; ergo, you do not have children."

McGinnis made a humorous face. "Do you see what I mean? Extremely intelligent and incredibly observant. Mrs. Lancaster calls her 'Little Sherlock,' doesn't she, my dear?"

"Not when I can hear," Claire said. "She knows how I feel about that moniker. Makes me sound a proper twit."

"Actually," Stanley said, "Sherlock Holmes, despite being a fictional character, would've been considered one of the most intelligent men who ever lived. Giving you a nickname like that just means you're extremely smart."

"And if I were a lad, it might be bearable, but I'm not. I'm a girl, something I take great pains to make plain to everyone. Being addressed by a man's name will only cause confusion. And confusion is what will make me look a twit."

Esmeralda managed to suppress the laugh that wanted to burst out of her, but Jack and Eugene couldn't stop snickering. Even McGinnis seemed to be delighted with the interaction between his daughter and her new bodyguard, especially when Stanley managed to continue grinning through the whole thing.

"Well, it appears that the two of you will get along famously," he said. "Claire, why don't you introduce Mr. Lorimer to Mrs. Lancaster, and the three of you can begin to plan your day. Mrs. Lancaster can provide you with the rules that I have imposed upon my daughter, Mr. Lorimer."

"Thank you, sir," Stanley said. He turned and looked at his charge, who gave up a sigh and turned to walk out the door that Deanna held open for her. Stanley moved quickly to follow and then Deanna fell in behind. As the door closed, McGinnis turned back to Esmeralda and suddenly burst out laughing.

"Your man may never forgive us for sticking him with that job," he said. "She will undoubtedly run him ragged."

"He can take it," Eugene said. "Believe me, he can."

FOUR

THE INTELLIGENCE THAT TEAM CINDERELLA HAD BEEN given indicated that Juergen Schroeder would not arrive until later that day, but it had been an error. Schroeder had actually arrived only minutes before their own flight touched down at Dulles, and had even stood beside them at the car-rental counter. He had not known, of course, who they were, but he was blessed with the ability to listen to one conversation while having another, and he heard Esmeralda mention to the clerk that they would be working at the embassy for a while.

Knowing that new personnel were coming into the embassy just at a point where he was planning to carry out an assassination was enough to convince him that someone in the intelligence community had found out about his acceptance of the contract. These five people were almost certainly some sort of security measure, he was certain of it. As result, he committed each of their faces to memory and kept his own face averted.

Of course, he was in disguise. It was highly unlikely that they would suspect the stooped-over old man with the wrinkled face of being a world-class assassin, but he didn't want to take any chances. He had learned the hard way that there were people who could see through a disguise, no matter how good it was. There was a strong possibility that at least one of these folks might have been chosen for such a talent.

He'd gotten his car and walked slowly through the door, dragging his wheeled suitcase behind him. He didn't feel that they were paying him any attention, but a well-trained operative would probably not have done anything to make him or herself noticed. Just to be safe, he drove his car around the back of the building and waited until they came out and climbed into a van, a Ford Transit. He watched from concealment as they got into it and drove away, showing no signs of being in any kind of hurry or looking for him or anyone else.

When they were far enough away that he wouldn't be noticed, he drove out of the rental area and followed them out to the highway. They were going to be working at the embassy, so he was sure they would be either staying there or at one of the hotels on Embassy Row. In either case, they weren't going to be close to his own motel in Bethesda, and they probably wouldn't look at the Bethesda Motor Inn even if they were close by. It was a kind of motel that often saw short-term tenants, and occasionally rented the same room three or four times in a single day.

Getting out there, and making sure he wouldn't be followed in the process, took nearly an hour. He had reserved the room through the Internet without having to speak to anyone, so all he had to do was step into the office and flash the ID he was currently using.

"Hi, I'm Dan Simmons," he said. "I reserved a room here for the next few nights."

The clerk behind the desk, who seemed irritated about having to put his book down, glanced at the ID, then at the computer screen and then passed over a key. It was an actual key, not a key card, and it had a red plastic diamond-shaped tag attached to it.

"Your room is upstairs," he said. "Go up the stairs right outside the door here, then go around to the other side of the building and it'll be the second door you come to." He flopped back down into his chair and grabbed the book before Schroeder could even turn away from the counter.

The clerk decided the old man must be in considerably better shape than he looked; Schroeder picked up his suitcase and carried it up the stairs without even seeming to notice, then continued to carry it around the building to his room. The key slid into the lock perfectly and the knob turned, and then he stepped inside and dropped the suitcase on the first of the two queen-size beds.

He opened the suitcase and took out one of the cell phones he had concealed inside it, then took out his wallet and removed a SIM card from it. He slipped the card into the phone, quickly put it back together and dialed the number he had been given. The line rang three times and then it was answered by a woman's voice.

"Hello," Schroeder said. "I was told that if I called this number, I might find a good peanut butter pie."

"No, sorry," the woman said. "All we have is pumpkin pie."

"All right, thank you," he said, and then he got off the call and removed the SIM card. It went back into the hidden compartment of his wallet, and the phone got dropped into the toilet. Some cell phones, and it was impossible to tell which ones, had a small memory chip that kept track of numbers dialed. Schroeder wasn't taking any chances that someone might be able to prove he had ever dialed that particular number. The water would destroy the chip, and caused a power surge from the battery that would wipe away any other information it might still contain.

The call, of course, had been a code to let his employers know that he had arrived and was on site. There would be another call when the job was complete, after which the remainder of the payment would be transferred to his account in Panama.

Schroeder had flown in from Germany, and as always happened, he had been unable to sleep on the flight. It wasn't that he was afraid of flying in any way, but the life he lived made it very difficult for him to relax if there were other people nearby. Being himself in the business of delivering death to those who shouldn't be expecting it, he was all too aware that absolutely anyone could be bringing the bullet or knife that would end his own life. As a result, he was hypervigilant whenever there were other people close by, and you can't get much closer than being trapped in an airplane at 30,000 feet.

He checked the lock on the door, then carefully removed the prosthetic mask that covered his entire head and the fair part of his upper chest. He laid it out carefully on the bed that held his suitcase, then took off the gloves that made his hands look old and wrinkled, laying them beside the mask.

He checked the door one more time, then stretched out on the other bed and let his eyes close. His ears, accustomed to compensating whenever he had his eyes closed, suddenly picked up every sound within a hundred feet, even the whispering of the people in the next room. He couldn't make out what they were saying, but they were obviously having some sort of a heated or passionate discussion. In any event, they didn't seem the least bit interested in the man who had just rented the room beside theirs, so he lost interest in them rather quickly.

With them out of his mind, he listened for anything else that might require his attention, but nothing seemed to fit that description. A moment later, feeling as secure as it was possible to feel when he was on the road, he drifted off to sleep.

Like many people who live a life of danger, Juergen Schroeder had developed the ability to wake according to an internal alarm clock. The spring sunshine had not yet breached the horizon when his eyes snapped open, and he was instantly wide awake. He lay perfectly still for more than a minute, just closing his eyes again for a brief period and letting his ears examine the surroundings.

The couple in the room next door were sleeping, and it would be difficult to tell which of them was snoring the loudest. On the other side of his room, someone was taking a shower and singing rather loudly and badly. Neither of those seemed to be a threat, so he ignored them and continued listening for other possible dangers.

Traffic was moving on the street in front of the motel, and someone down toward the other end of his building was apparently preparing to leave. He heard car doors slamming and then the sound of an engine starting, followed a few seconds later by the low growl of the car backing out of its parking space. The engine changed tone and tempo as the vehicle passed his room on its way out to the exit.

A motel room door opened and closed, and then another did the same. These were the normal sounds of a motel in the early hours of the morning, so he opened his eyes and sat up on the side of the bed. He reached over to his suitcase and dragged it a bit closer, then took out the small plastic box that was tucked into the pocket on the inside of the lid. He opened the box and took out the short stub of a joint and then fished a lighter out of his trouser pocket. He held the roach carefully and struck fire to it, inhaling deeply and holding the smoke in his lungs for almost half a minute before blowing it out again. Quickly, before the last of the roach burned away, he hit it once more and then dropped it into the ashtray on the nightstand between the beds. This time he held his breath for over a minute, and then blew out what was left of the THC-laden smoke.

He sat there for another twenty minutes, letting the glow of the buzz fade partly before he got up and went to the bathroom. He took care of his morning necessities and then stripped out of the clothes he had worn, stepping into the shower to wash away the sweat of the day before. He adjusted the temperature until it was comfortably warm, then stood under the shower head and let the water spray down into his face. He opened his eyes at one point, and the residual buzz turned the spray into a hundred thousand individual droplets, all of them flying toward him at something approximating light speed. He smiled into the spray, but then his eyes objected to the stinging water and he closed them again.

He washed quickly, then slathered soap over his head and face and put his old straight razor to work. With so many different disguises, it was almost impossible to keep any particular hairstyle, so he had given up long ago and shaved his scalp. Whiskers grew more quickly, but they also made his prosthetic masks quite uncomfortable, so he made certain to shave well every morning unless he was trying to grow a beard.

The water rinsed away the soap and what was left of the shavings, and then he finally turned it off and began to dry himself with the towel that was hanging nearby. He was careful to make sure he got all the moisture out of every fold of skin, of which his skinny frame had very few. He didn't like the way wet skin would chafe on itself, so he was a cautious man in that regard.

He considered whether or not to wear the same mask again, but he hadn't taken the time to wash it out the night before, and that would mean letting it dry for at least half an hour before he put it on again. He didn't want to waste that much time, so he opened the large leather case that was hidden under the clothes in his suitcase and looked at the other masks he had with him.

There were four of them. One was another older gentleman, although this one had black skin. The second was an effeminate-looking face, even though it was still obviously masculine, and the third was a swarthy-looking man who was perhaps in his late thirties. He glanced at the fourth, which was the face of a matronly woman in her later years, and which had a full wig of silvery hair attached to it. He hadn't planned on using that one this time and had not brought the appropriate clothing along, so it would wait.

Washington, DC, he knew, was often referred to as the Chocolate City because of its large black population. He took the black mask and its accompanying gloves and laid them out on the bed, then took one of the pillowcases and stuffed a couple of his undershirts into it. He tucked it into his boxers, giving himself a fairly natural-looking paunch. He slid into a pair of trousers that were a couple of sizes bigger than he normally wore and then pulled the mask over his head and pinched and twisted it a bit to get it settled into place properly. The lifelike silicon rubber skin extended across the top of his shoulders and halfway down both his back and his chest, and he made sure that it was sitting well before he pulled another undershirt over it and then topped it with a striped button-down. The shirt had long sleeves, so he pulled the gloves on, smoothing them out as they went halfway up his forearms. When he was satisfied, he tugged the sleeves down and buttoned them.

A belt secured the trousers with the shirts tucked inside, and the costume was completed with a sports jacket and a pair of highly polished black shoes. He looked carefully at himself in the mirror, made a couple of minor adjustments to the mask and then smiled at himself in satisfaction. No one who looked at him would see anything but a late-middle-aged black man.

He chose the wallet that went with this particular appearance and slipped it into his back pocket, then got the keys to the car and the room and put them into another. After that, he took a small plastic box from another pocket on the lid of the suitcase and slipped it into the pocket of his jacket. He stood by the door for a moment, looking out from behind the curtains on the window next to it to make sure no one was watching, then opened the door and glanced both directions before stepping out and pulling it closed behind him. He began walking instantly, going toward the far end of the building and the stairs that would take him down to the ground level again.

He had parked his car away from the building itself, in a small side lot that was for people staying upstairs. No one was paying any attention as he got into the car, started it up, then drove out of the motel parking lot and onto the street. He glanced at the clock on the stereo and saw that it was just before seven AM, and the sun was finally beginning to shine weakly down onto the metropolitan world around him.

There were clouds overhead, dark ones. For some reason, it seemed that whenever he had one of these difficult assignments, it would be raining. He had long ago chalked it up to some dark supernatural force that decided he needed something to hinder him, but he never let it stop him.

In the worst case, it would only mean some minor change in whatever plan he came up with; usually, it made no difference whatsoever. The only real question in his mind this morning was when and where would be the best opportunity to strike at his target. While the weather could figure into his calculations, it was a lot less important than the people he had observed the night before.

Knowing that a fresh team had been sent to the embassy at this time was simply too much to chalk up to coincidence. Their presence at this particular moment meant that somebody had gotten wind of his contract. This could make it more difficult to acquire his target, but he had never failed in more than fifty different contracts. This was one of the reasons he was considered among the best at what he did, and he wasn't about to let a team of newbies—and that's what they looked like to him—get in his way. If they tried, they would simply become collateral damage.

He thought about the group he had seen at the car-rental desk. There had been three men and two women, an unusual formula for a security team, but he guessed that they might've been chosen for particular specialties. The women were undoubtedly the most highly trained among them, and would be staying closest to the target. The men would probably be scattered around wherever the target was at, trying to spot trouble before it could happen.

He chuckled to himself, automatically falling into character as an older black man. The chuckle sounded like it might've come from the deep South, rather than from Hamburg.

"My, my," he said, the accent permeating his words. "Be a shame to have to hurt those pretty girls. Sure be good if they just stay out of my way."

A few scattered raindrops hit his windshield, but it wasn't enough to bother with the wipers. All it told him was that more rain would be coming later, but he already knew that. He drove along, following the directions from his navigation system as he moved closer and closer to Embassy Row.

Traffic was running a little slow, so it took him almost an hour to get to where he was headed. The embassy was a large building, and he was able to park in a public lot just down the street. He got out of the car, glanced up at the sky and wished for an umbrella, but wishing wasn't going to do him any good at this point. It wasn't actually raining yet, anyway, so he strolled along the sidewalk, looking at all the sights around him as he did so.

The main Chancery building was a great square, with an open courtyard in the center. This was where the offices of the embassy were found, although some of them, including a ceremonial office occasionally used by the ambassador, were in the old brick Chancery building that had originally been built in the early part of the twentieth century. That building was most commonly known as the home of the British Council.

The vast majority of embassy business was conducted in the new Chancery, the great square building of concrete, steel and glass that fronted on Massachusetts Avenue. Except for certain ceremonial events, any appointment to see the ambassador would bring you there. Schroeder knew this and briefly toyed with the idea of seeking an appointment, just to demonstrate how close he could get to the man.

He dismissed the thought as quickly as it had come. He wasn't there to play games, but to take care of business. There was no point in trying to achieve something that would never be known in any event.

From the sidewalk on his side of the street, he could look directly down the driveway toward the Residence. Getting close to the brick house that had been built along with the original Chancery would have been difficult, but he didn't feel that it would be necessary for him to risk it. If there was one thing he knew about ambassadors and their entourages, it was that they were constantly finding reasons to leave the safety of their embassy. All he needed to do was learn some of the patterns that fit their movements, and getting close to his target should not be all that hard, after all.

The driveway he was watching would be the most common way for the ambassador and his people to leave this small piece of British soil in the midst of the American Capitol. Rather than try to find a way into such a secure location—and he was well aware of just how secure MI6 could make any structure—he would look for an opportunity to strike when the target was away from home. Knowing what was happening with this driveway would help to determine the best time and place to carry out his contractual obligations.

He took the little plastic box out of his jacket pocket and opened it up. Inside were a number of small devices that he had arranged to be made special for his own personal use. They cost a small fortune each, more than five thousand American dollars, but they had proven to be worth every penny many times.

He selected one that looked like a fat, fluffy caterpillar and held it concealed in his hand. He looked around himself as he thought of the best place to put the little bug, and chose one of the trees that stood close to the street. It was one of two that flanked the entrance to the Khalil Gibran Memorial Garden, and was directly across from the Residence driveway. He placed the caterpillar on a branch, then took out his cell phone and touched an icon on its screen.

The screen lit up with a very clear view of the driveway, and he only had to adjust the caterpillar a tiny bit to center the view on his display. The bug was a video camera, incredibly small and complex. It was powered by diamond batteries that were created in an experimental laboratory by an Italian firm that was working on new energy storage technologies. Unbeknownst to Schroeder, the batteries were actually based on some of the earlier work done by Wally Lawson's people at Neverland. They weren't as good as the ones that powered Esmeralda, but they could keep the camera working for months, should he need to leave it in place that long.

The bug also contained a powerful transmitter, but it wasn't strong enough to broadcast a signal over great distance. For that, he needed a second device from the box, a signal repeater that was based on cell phone technology and powered by more of the experimental diamond batteries. He had been forced to create a cellular account for it, but the microcomputer built into it would encrypt the video signal to the point that it would be undetectable by anything that did not have the correct decryption software installed. This device could send the signal anywhere in the world through cellular data, and the only matching software to unscramble the video was on the cell phone that he held in his hand.

He walked along the sidewalk a bit further, placing a couple more of the little cameras where they could also get views of the driveway or the Residence. One of them had a beautiful view of the front door of the Residence itself, lining up perfectly between a couple of other buildings for the shot. He made sure that its transmitter could reach the repeater, then turned and started back the way he had come.

The van that he had seen the new arrivals drive out of the airport the night before suddenly came into view and turned into the main driveway, going around the back of the building to where staff would park. Schroeder stopped and watched them go, confident that his disguise was impenetrable. None of the people inside the van paid him any attention whatsoever, and he thought that he was probably correct in assuming they were new at their jobs.

That was good, he told himself, because it meant they probably weren't going to give him any trouble. He didn't like trouble.

FIVE

STANLEY FOLLOWED THE LITTLE GIRL THROUGH THE building and up the stairs to the room that her governess used as her classroom. Mrs. Lancaster looked up as they entered, still with Deanna in the lead, and raised her eyebrows questioningly.

"Mrs. Lancaster," Deanna said, "this is Mr. Lorimer. He's been assigned to watch over Claire and yourself."

Deanna had put a meaningful expression into her eyes, and Mrs. Lancaster had caught it; both women were fully aware of the intelligence regarding a possible assassination attempt on Claire's father, and that Claire herself could conceivably be a secondary target. Mrs. Lancaster was both governess and tutor to the child, but she was also a former Military Intelligence operative, one who was highly skilled in defensive measures. She was fully aware that part of her job description required her to take a bullet for the child, should it ever become necessary, and she was certainly dedicated enough to do so.

However, she also knew that little madman who ran North Korea wouldn't send an amateur on a hit like this. She wasn't a bit bashful about accepting assistance from someone who might be even better trained than herself, and she had been told that the American team was among the best in the world for the purpose.

Mr. Lorimer looked like exactly the kind of man she would expect to be in such a position: slightly handsome, but also somewhat nondescript. He wasn't a man who was going to draw attention to himself, and yet if you looked closely, you could sense an incredible underlying power in him.

There was no doubt in her mind that Mr. Lorimer would be just as determined to see to Claire's safety as she was. That was enough to make him an ally, regardless of where he had come from.

All those thoughts went through her mind in less than the time it took Deanna to make the introductions. She held out her hand with a smile.

"Mr. Lorimer," she said. "I'm Deirdre, Claire's governess. It's a pleasure to make your acquaintance."

"The pleasure is mine, madam," Stanley said, following his programming for such a situation. "Stanley Lorimer, at your service."

"Stanley, is it?" Mrs. Lancaster said with a smile. "How delightful, that was my father's name. May I call you Stanley?"

"Yes, please do," Stanley said, returning the smile. "And you are Deirdre?"

"Only if you want a pop in the mouth," she replied with a mocking glare. "My friends call me DD, which I prefer, or just Dee, which isn't too bad. You can take your pick, I suspect we're going to get along famously."

"DD it is, then. Is there any way I can be useful while I'm here?"

DD looked at Deanna with her eyes wide. "Where on earth did you find this man?" she asked. "He's been here a matter of seconds and already volunteering to help? I don't think I'm going to let him get away." She looked back at Stanley. "You're single, right?"

Again, Stanley's computer brain searched instantly through the programming Esmeralda had developed for him and found a proper response. "I'm afraid so," he said. "I just haven't found the right girl yet, but the day is young, isn't it?" He smiled at her and winked.

DD's face flushed red, and Claire giggled at her.

"Be careful, Stanley," the girl said. "Mrs. Lancaster is a widow."

Stanley gave a chuckle that seemed to lighten the mood, and then Deanna made her escape. DD told Claire that it was time to get started on her history lessons, and the girl let out a sigh as she sat down at the lone student desk and took a book out of it.

Stanley found a chair and sat down, watching quietly as DD went over the lesson with the little girl. He noted the fact that she occasionally glanced at him with a slight smile, and returned it whenever she did so.

———

DOWNSTAIRS, Esmeralda and the ambassador were going over his itinerary for the next few days. He was scheduled to attend four different parties and a couple of meetings at the White House. He would be one of a half dozen or so ambassadors in each of those meetings, speaking with one of the president's aides on how to handle certain political negotiations that involved their several countries.

"Is this itinerary published anywhere?" Esmeralda asked.

"Not officially," McGinnis said. "However, there are probably about fifty copies floating around the city, because everyone who is affected by any of these events is considered to have the need to know of my presence. Somehow, the press always manages to find out what I'm about, no matter how we try to keep it from them."

"Then Schroeder would be able to get his hands on a copy, most likely," Esmeralda replied. "Can any of these be canceled? Or at least rescheduled, and the new date and time held as a secret?"

McGinnis scowled at the list. "The party tonight," he said, "is for the vice president's wife's birthday, and he and I have become rather good friends. In fact, I've been asked to sing for her, and I don't really think there's any way to get out of it. That one we must attend." He looked the list over and shook his head. "The next two don't absolutely require my presence, so we can beg off of them. The last one, though, that's a dinner party with the president and his family. No way out of that one, I'm afraid."

He picked up a pen and scratched through a few of the other items, then turned the paper and slid it across the desk to Esmeralda. "I'll have those all rescheduled, and we'll make certain not to let anyone know about them. The only one of the meetings that I simply can't put off is the one tomorrow afternoon, with the Japanese delegation. Great Britain still has certain privileges in the Sea of Japan, and the time has come to renegotiate them. Working against a deadline on that one, I'm afraid."

"Well, this helps," Esmeralda said. "That gets us down to only three events we absolutely have to attend. The parties are obviously going to be publicized, so we'll have to make special security arrangements for each of them, but that shouldn't be too difficult. I understand you have a competent security detail here?"

McGinnis looked at her, and he rolled his eyes. "I would say that's their estimation of their own abilities," he said. "Not too certain I would agree, but that's one of the few areas where no one bothered to consult me."

Esmeralda nodded but didn't say anything. Eugene, who was sitting in another chair beside Esmeralda, leaned forward.

"Mr. Ambassador," he began, "if possible, I'd like to meet your security people. I want to get a feel for them myself, if that's all right."

"Of course," McGinnis said. "I'll ring up their commanding officer and have him come to fetch you." He picked up the handset of his desk phone and punched a button. "Captain Jeffries? Would you mind stepping into my office for a moment, please? Yes, that's a good lad. See you then." He hung up the phone again and smiled at Eugene. "He'll be right down. I should prepare you, he can be something of an ass."

Eugene grinned. "That's okay, sir," he said. "So can I."

The captain arrived a moment later and shook hands with Eugene, then the two of them left to go meet the rest of the security team. These were a number of SAS commandos who were all working under covers that made them clerks in the embassy. When they went out into the city with the ambassador, each of them carried a small attaché case that contained an assortment of weapons. By the time they got through showing Eugene all their toys, he had managed to make friends out of all of them, and they grudgingly acknowledged that they had been ordered to obey any commands Esmeralda or Eugene should issue.

Back in the ambassador's office, Esmeralda took advantage of the moment alone with the man.

"You said something a few minutes ago," she said, "and I wanted to ask about it. Is that all right?"

McGinnis shrugged and smiled. "You're here to keep me alive, young lady," he said. "I believe you might ask me anything you wish."

"You said you're going to sing for the vice president's wife? I read the dossier they gave us on you, but it didn't mention anything about you being a singer."

McGinnis burst out laughing. "That's because no one would ever accuse me of being a singer," he said. "However, it happens that the lady in question was a classmate of mine when she did an exchange course in college. We were both drafted into the school choir, and I was occasionally given a solo because of being the only decent baritone that year. Over the years, she's often told me that she loved hearing me sing back then, and somehow convinced her husband to twist my arm this time." He leaned forward and lowered his voice conspiratorially. "To be perfectly frank, the two of us might have enjoyed a few late nights together after practice during that time, and I had actually toyed with the idea of proposing to her. Unfortunately, it was during that awful business with the first Gulf War, and her father decided to cut her visit short. She was literally there one night, and gone the next morning. I wrote her a couple of letters, but it didn't take long for me to realize that she had considered me more of a dalliance than a potential husband."

Esmeralda grinned. "So, there was a little romance involved? Her husband isn't jealous, is he?"

McGinnis winked. "Not as long as nobody tells him how many times she's tried to get me alone since I took this post," he said. "But don't worry, my dear, I have been able to resist her charms far better now than I could back then. Last thing I need is to start an international incident, what?"

"Smart man," Esmeralda said. "Let's try to keep it that way. Who do you normally take with you to parties? One of your staff?"

"D'you mean like, as a personal companion? Why, no one. Back home, I'm considered one of my country's most sought-after singles—I don't want to risk damaging that reputation."

"Well, tonight you're going to have a date," Esmeralda said with a smile. "Me. Don't worry, I'll make sure it's obvious that it's a professional engagement rather than a romantic one. We can't risk that reputation, after all."

McGinnis looked at her for a moment, and then shook his head as he chuckled. "Bloody hell, Emma," he said. "If we do that, I'm going to be expected to take someone along every time in the future."

"Well, don't ask Deanna," Esmeralda said. "Her heart starts racing every time she gets close to you."

McGinnis started to laugh, but then he stopped and just stared at her. "How could you possibly know that?"

Silently, Esmeralda kicked herself. She hadn't thought before she'd spoken, and while it was true—she could hear the woman's heart speed up whenever she had to approach McGinnis—she couldn't exactly explain that her hearing was that acute.

"Are you honestly going to tell me you hadn't noticed?" she asked. "Sir, her face turns red every time she gets near you. That's a sure sign that her heart is racing, which means she happens to think you're something of a catch, herself."

McGinnis blinked. "No, I hadn't noticed," he said. "Deanna? Seriously?" His expression turned thoughtful. "Good Lord, I need to pay more attention. She's actually quite lovely, and Claire purely adores her."

"Well, she has to wait," Esmeralda said. "For tonight, you're all mine."

———

SCHROEDER HAD HEADED BACK toward his motel, but he had to make a stop on the way. This was not his first trip to DC, and he had a fair idea of where to find just about anything he really needed in the city. Considering his current disguise, he chose to visit a particular contact, a woman he knew as Big Alma. Alma was one of the most intelligent drug dealers in the city, moving millions of dollars' worth of product every year but without ever allowing herself to be exposed. This was because she had a network of young men working for her, and all of them knew exactly what would happen if she ever thought one of them would give up her name. She had made quite a few young men famous as victims who vanished without a trace, and though everyone knew that she had handled it personally, no one had the courage to testify against her.

Schroeder liked her because she was diversified; besides drugs, she was also one of the best sources of weapons in the city. He had dealt with her a couple of times already, and found that she could always produce whatever he wanted within less than twenty-four hours.

He dialed a number that he had programmed into his phone right after he'd gotten it, the number of a man who would know how to reach Alma rather quickly. The fact that the man happened to be a DC police detective didn't bother Schroeder in the least.

"Detective Harkins," came the answer on the line.

"Detective Harkins," Schroeder said, "my name is Billy Logan. I'm looking for a mutual friend."

Billy Logan was a code, meaning that the caller wanted to speak to Alma.

"I'm not sure where to find any mutual friends, Mr. Logan," Harkins said. "Can you give me a hint?"

Another code, asking for another code word that would identify the caller as someone Alma trusted.

"Perhaps if you look under the potted plants alongside the reflecting pool on the mall," Schroeder replied. The convoluted phrase was one that was carefully guarded, and was one of several that only Alma ever gave out.

"I'll have her call you," Harkins said. "About fifteen minutes."

"Make it twenty," Schroeder said. That was the last part of the coded message, and if he hadn't given it, someone would've been tracking his cell phone to try to kill him.

"Twenty it is," Harkins said, and then the line went dead.

Schroeder continued driving, and his phone rang only five minutes later.

"Hello, Alma," he said.

"Who is this?" Alma asked.

"The last time you saw me," Schroeder said, "I smelled like a dumpster and you sold me a Desert Eagle fifty."

There was silence on the line for couple of seconds, and then Alma laughed. "Holy shit, that you? What you need, baby?"

"Thirty-ought-six, good scope, something for a long shot. Got anything like that?"

"You know I do, baby," she said. "Is it going to come back?"

"Not if I can help it," Schroeder said. "I want it to vanish forever when I get done with it."

"Okay, baby. I'll call you in fifteen minutes and tell you where to get it. We talking fifty-five hundred, you okay with that?"

"No problem," he said. "I got cash."

The phone went dead in his ear. He kept driving around the

city for another fifteen minutes, and his phone rang again right on schedule.

"Benjamin's Diner, thirty minutes." That was all she said, and then the line was dead again.

Schroeder used his phone to Google Benjamin's Diner, then followed the directions to get there. He made it with ten minutes to spare, and saw a young black man sitting on the tailgate of an old station wagon. He pulled up and powered down his window.

"You got something for me?" he asked.

"Maybe," said the young man. "What you got for me?"

Schroeder held up a wad of cash. He had counted out fifty-five one-hundred-dollar bills as he had driven, and the young man's eyes lit up.

"Something big, or something little?"

"Probably pretty long," Schroeder said.

The young man nodded and reached behind himself. He pulled out a hard plastic rifle case and held it on his lap, then opened it up so Schroeder could see inside. It was the kind of rifle he wanted, and the scope was amazing. There was also a box of twenty rounds of ammunition.

"Looks good," he said. He held out the cash and it disappeared into the young man's shirt pocket, while he took the rifle and swung it around into his backseat. He drove away without another word, and he saw the station wagon pull out in his rearview mirror a moment later. It went in the opposite direction, and there was no sign that anyone else was trying to follow. Another excellent transaction with Big Alma.

He shook his head. There were very few cities in the world where a deal like that could go down in broad daylight.

He drove back to the motel and carried his purchase up to his room. Once there, he got his laptop computer out of the suitcase and set it up, then connected his phone to it so that the decoding software was accessible. He opened the program and a moment later he could see five different views of the embassy, the Residence and the street.

Then he opened up the rifle case and began examining the weapon. It was clean and in perfect operating condition, just the way he would expect it to be. He loaded four rounds into the magazine, inserted the magazine and chambered one of them, then withdrew the magazine and added one more. That gave him five shots, and he had never needed more than two. He put the rifle back into the case and set it aside, then turned back to his computer.

Various vehicles entered and left, but he didn't see the ambassador's limousine, so he was confident the man was still in the embassy. He picked up his phone and dialed another number, and this time it was answered by a receptionist.

"Washington Register," the woman said. "How may I direct your call?"

"Roger Delaney, please," he said. The receptionist told him to wait a moment, and then he heard ringing on the line again.

"Delaney," said a husky voice.

"Roger, it's Lonnie Milberg," Schroeder said. "You told me to give you a call if I ever needed anything, so I'm ready to collect on that."

"Lonnie Milberg?" Delaney asked. "Do I know you?"

"Oh, geez, Roger," Schroeder said. "I helped you out last year on that story about the booze getting stolen out of the White House bar, remember?"

Delaney had gotten a lot of accolades over that story, but he had also consumed an awful lot of alcohol while he was working on it. He wasn't sure who he might've met during that time.

"Oh, yeah," he said uncertainly. "Lonnie, yeah. Well, what can I do for you, Lonnie?"

"Listen, my editor wants me to do something on Ambassador McGinnis, the Brit, you know? You got any idea about what he's up to the next couple days?"

"McGinnis? Yeah, hang on a second, I got his itinerary here someplace." Schroeder could hear papers rustling, and he visualized a desk piled high with scribbled notes on a thousand topics.

"Here it is, got it. Hey, he's going to a party at the Candlewick tonight, it's the VP's wife's birthday. Seven o'clock tonight. That help you any?"

"It might," Schroeder said. "What else you got?"

Delaney read off the rest of the itinerary, everything that had been leaked to the press as it always was. Schroeder thanked him and hung up the phone, leaving the man wondering just who he had been talking to.

"A birthday party," Schroeder mused to himself. "That may be perfect."

He looked up the Candlewick and found that it was a fancy restaurant in Silver Spring, Maryland. With the vice president planning to be there, it was likely there would be pretty heavy security, but a Google view of the area showed him a couple of great vantage points for a sniper shot. He sat back and watched the computer for a while, checking the vehicles going in and out, while he considered whether to try to make the hit during the birthday party.

With the rifle, he could be as much as three or four blocks away and still make the shot. It would undoubtedly cause a massive uproar, and Secret Service would be all over the place. FBI, local and Maryland state police, they'd be everywhere, and especially after the shot. Getting out of that area would be difficult, but he could also change his clothing and just sit tight. Nobody would look closely at another derelict hanging out in the alleys nearby. All he'd have to do would be to take the shot, then get off whatever rooftop he was on and move quickly to get a block or two away. Lie down in an alley and pretend to be drunk, and all those cops would run right past him.

Hell, he thought, *this one might actually be easy.*

SIX

"Anything out of Cinderella?" Allison asked as she walked into Noah's office.

"I haven't heard anything yet," Noah said. "They would've just gotten there a few hours ago, probably haven't even made contact yet."

Allison sat down in the chair in front of Noah's desk and leaned back. "The more I think about this," she said, "the more I wonder if we messed up. Noah, if anything goes wrong, the whole world could find out that this mission was run by a pair of robots. Do you have any idea how bad that would look for all of us? Robots who specialize in killing people?"

"Esmeralda has things under control," Noah said. "I trust her judgment, I've seen it in action. And remember, this is not the first mission she's run."

"I know that," Allison said. "Hell, if it weren't for her, I might not even be here. I don't think I'm really worried about Esmeralda so much, but Stanley—Stanley scares the crap out of me right now."

Noah looked at her. "Why is that?"

She threw her hands in the air. "Because if anything goes wrong, it's probably going to involve him. Noah, the committee knows about Esmeralda, but they don't know anything about Stanley. We probably should not have sent him out just yet, not without getting their approval."

"I don't see the problem," Noah said. "Stanley is an asset, a tool. Unlike Esmeralda, he's not capable of independent thought, so he can only do what he is ordered to do. Why would they have any objection to that?"

"Because they didn't get to put their stamp of approval on it," Allison said. "Noah, you're brilliant in some ways, but you just don't understand the politics of this situation. Now that we have been put under this committee, we are not supposed to do anything without their rubber stamp on it. Sending a robot out on a mission like this is bound to piss some of them off. You can trust me on that, I know what I'm talking about."

"I'm not doubting you," Noah said. "I'm simply saying that I don't believe it's that big a problem. Realistically, there are voice-controlled computers involved in every aspect of warfare, now; how is Stanley really any different from them?"

Allison rolled her eyes. "Noah, those computers can't get up and walk out of the building. Stanley can. Those computers can't pick up a gun and start shooting somebody. Stanley can. Yes, I realize that he only does what he's programmed to do, but haven't you ever had a computer that went haywire? I've got a computer-operated refrigerator that gets mad at me from time to time and refuses to give me ice cubes. What do we do with Stanley if he ends up getting mad about something?"

Noah looked at her for a moment, then shook his head. "What is this really about?" he asked. "You're not really worried about Stanley, so what is it that's got you so shook up?"

"You're wrong," Allison said. "I am worried about Stanley. Noah, we are barely holding on by a thread, here. Half the committee wants to shut us down, the other half wants to turn us into some kind of Murder Inc. To be completely honest, I'm not sure who we can trust at all outside of our own offices. If the wrong people get worrd about Stanley, it's all going to come down on our heads. Now that the entire damned committee knows where we are, it just wouldn't be that hard for one of them to blow us off the planet. All they need is an excuse to think that we're going off on our own, not doing what they want us to do."

Noah nodded. "So, the real problem is that the committee has you worried about them taking all of us out?"

Allison sighed. "No. Yes, maybe, I don't know. All I know is that we are in the most precarious position we have ever seen, and I'm afraid we didn't really think it through before we sent Stanley out on this mission. I'm thinking that may have been a mistake, but I don't know what to do about it now."

"Well, we can recall him. If we order him back, he'll come. On the other hand, I don't know that we would ever be able to risk sending him out again after that. Once you start to distrust a tool, it's hard to make yourself use it again."

"Oh, God, do you have to be so infuriating? At least tell me what you think we should do, please."

"I think we sent out a team on a mission," Noah said. "Until such time as something actually does go wrong, I think we need to leave that team alone and let them carry out that mission."

Allison leaned her head onto the back of the chair and closed her eyes. "Might've known that's what you would say," she said. "And of course, that's why I came to you, because I wanted your logical take on this problem. The trouble is that my emotional state is so wound up that I don't like your logic at all right now."

She got up suddenly and walked out of the office. Noah looked at the door she had closed behind her for a moment, then turned back to his computer and started looking at the company's distribution centers once more.

———

"Okay," Esmeralda said. "We've got this birthday party for the vice president's wife tonight, and we are all going to be on deck. The ambassador will be there through the entire party, of course, but his daughter will only be there for part of it. Stanley and Mrs. Lancaster will escort her back here at about nine thirty, but the party is going to go on until about midnight. Assuming Schroeder is already in the country, this could be his first chance to strike at the ambassador. We need to be on high alert, and Eugene, that means you need to stay on top of the British security team."

"That won't be a problem," Eugene said. "I've already got them lined out on what I want them to do, and Captain Jeffries has given me one of their earwigs. I'll be in constant touch with him throughout the entire event."

"Okay, good. Jack, you'll be driving the limo tonight, so watch everything. If anything looks odd on the road, do whatever you have to do."

"What about me, boss lady?" Bobbie asked. "You said you want all of us going?"

"Yes, you're going along as well," Esmeralda said. "Bring your weapons and just stay close. We've got to do everything we possibly can to ensure the ambassador's safety. I'm going as his date for the evening, so of course I'll be right beside him. I'll be watching everything I possibly can, and I can subcom any of you if I see anything that needs to be checked out. Just be ready for anything, because we don't know what could happen."

They had spent the afternoon getting settled into their rooms at the Residence, and they were currently meeting in Esmeralda's room. Jack, Eugene and Bobbie were already dressed for the evening, and Esmeralda was preparing to change. She hadn't actually planned on doing anything formal, so she hadn't brought appropriate clothing with her; luckily, it turned out that Deanna was about her size and happened to have a formal dress that she could wear.

Having just given them their orders, Esmeralda ran the men out of the room but asked Bobbie to stay and help her get ready. It was more of a friendly gesture than anything, because she certainly knew how to put on the dress, and she didn't need makeup or hairstyling. She simply looked into the mirror and adjusted the pigmentation of the skin around her eyes, cheeks and lips. Her lips became bright red and almost glossy, and the mascara effect around her eyes was perfect. As for her hair, she applied a slight electric charge that caused it to curl slightly at the ends, and then ran a brush through it.

"This is not fair," Bobbie said. "It takes me hours to get looking halfway decent, and you can go from plain Jane to fashion model in a matter of minutes."

"True," Esmeralda said. "On the other hand, you can have babies, and I can't."

Bobbie's face was blank. "I'm sorry," she said. "It never occurred to me that things like that could bother you."

"I wouldn't say it actually bothers me," Esmeralda said. "I just kind of wish I could have some idea what it's like, you know? To feel a life growing inside me? I mean, I think it would be awesome. I watch little Norah, and I heard all about her being born and it was so incredible, but it's not something I'll ever get to experience." She shrugged. "I guess I get a little jealous about that sometimes, but not terribly so."

Bobbie leaned over and put her head on Esmeralda's shoulder. "I'll tell you what," she said. "If I ever have a baby, I'll make sure you get to be in the delivery room with me. At least you can enjoy the process with me, right?"

Esmeralda turned and looked at her, and then put her arms around the girl and hugged her. "I think that's one of the nicest things anyone has ever said to me," she said. "Thank you, Bobbie."

Now dressed and ready for the party, Esmeralda joined the others downstairs in the main hall of the Residence. It wasn't quite as big as the Great Hall back at Feeney Manor, but it was still quite a large room. When she stepped inside, she deliberately tinted her face red at all the wolf-whistles that suddenly went off.

The loudest one seemed to come from Ambassador McGinnis.

"Emma," he said, "you're absolutely lovely. I'm going to

spend most of the party just trying to keep all the other men from stealing you away."

Esmeralda laughed. "Don't worry," she said. "I'll make it clear that I'm a one-man woman for tonight, okay?"

"That sounds like a fine plan to me," McGinnis said. "Shall we be going, then?"

Esmeralda looked at him curiously. "Isn't Claire coming with us?"

"Oh, no. She'll be coming with Mrs. Lancaster, and your man Lorimer. Since you have one of yours acting as my driver, I assigned my usual fellow to bring them along." He caught the brief look of concern that crossed her face, and smiled. "I can assure you he's quite reliable," he said. "He's also one of the intelligence lads, so he's bloody capable."

The look of concern had nothing to do with the ambassador's driver; Esmeralda had quickly checked the weather radar and realized that a rather severe thunderstorm was about to begin. Trepidation about Stanley and lightning had caused her to briefly display emotion, and it was only her "humanesque programming," the specific code she had written to slow down certain responses so that they appeared more natural, that had taken it from a microsecond of electronic data analysis to a second-and-a-half-long expression that a human was capable of recognizing.

She plastered the smile back onto her face. "I'm sure he's fine," she said. "I was just thinking that the weather is looking pretty rough; are you sure you want your daughter going out in this?"

"Ha!" he said. "Try to keep her back. Hell hath no fury like Claire when she doesn't get her way, and she happens to adore the Second Lady. She dragged Mrs. Lancaster about for three days last week just to find the perfect birthday gift. I happen to like my sanity enough not to risk letting my daughter get angry at me just now."

Esmeralda rolled her eyes, and felt the slight tingle of delight that always hit her when she used such a visual emotive. "All right, I get it," she said. "They'll be coming right behind us, I suppose?"

"Actually, I believe they will be coming in about thirty minutes," McGinnis said. "James, my driver, said he had been given explicit orders that they were to be 'fashionably late.' Would you care to guess who gave him such orders?"

Esmeralda's smile was replaced with a wry grin. "Claire, I'm sure," she said. "Well, maybe they'll still get there before the storm actually begins." She glanced around the room. "Where's Jack?"

"He went to get the car," Eugene said. "In fact, he just pulled up out front. Are we ready?"

"I suppose we are," Esmeralda said.

Eugene touched his right ear and spoke into his hand. "Captain Jeffries, we are preparing to move," he said. "Escort vehicles to be deployed as we discussed earlier. Papa Bear is leaving the Residence now."

He opened the front door and stepped out, looked around briefly and then motioned for McGinnis and the rest to come on out to the car. He held the back door of the limousine open himself, waited until McGinnis, Esmeralda and Bobbie had entered, then slipped into the front passenger seat beside Jack.

Jack turned the big car around in the courtyard and fell in behind one of the three Cadillac Escalades that were used for most government functions. Captain Jeffries and three of his men were inside that vehicle, and two others moved in behind the limo as they made their way out to Massachusetts Avenue.

The Candlewick Inn actually sat on the outskirts of Silver Spring, a large ornate building that sat in the middle of seventeen acres of lush woodlands. It was used so often for government-related dinners and parties that the FBI and Secret Service both maintained office space inside it. The FBI offices were made available to the ambassador's security detail for the evening, with the Secret Service also present to watch over the vice president and his wife.

The guest list was highly exclusive. In order to be invited to this particular party, it was necessary to be someone of serious stature in DC. Senators and Congresspeople, along with their spouses or partners, occupied most of the tables that surrounded the large dance floor, and even the small orchestra was comprised of members who had been carefully vetted by the Secret Service personnel before being allowed into the building. Every chef, cook's helper, waiter, bartender and busboy in the place held a security clearance just to be able to work there, and they were all fully aware that they were under at least electronic surveillance even throughout their daily lives. A thousand secrets had been spoken within those walls, shared from one important person to another, and many of them had been overheard, but none had ever been repeated after the respective events were over.

Captain Jeffries led the small motorcade along the curving, tree-canopied driveway and told his driver to stop so that the limousine behind them was directly in front of the main entrance. Jack stopped the car in the perfect spot, as Jeffries and all his people got out of their vehicles and stood guard. Seeing no immediate threat, Jeffrey told Eugene that it was safe for the ambassador and his party to disembark.

Eugene got out of the car and opened the rear door, himself looking around in every direction, trying to spot any possibility of danger. He was fully aware that Esmeralda would have been doing the same thing from inside the car, the tinted windows doing nothing to dim her vision. Had she seen anything, he would've already known about it, so he was relatively confident that there was no immediate threat.

Esmeralda stepped out first, turning around so that she could look one more time in every direction. She spun quickly, the way any normal human might do, but her computer mind was capable of stretching that brief instant so that she could process almost an hour's worth of data. Even with her vision stretched to its limits, using the electronic zoom technology built into her visual processors, and even using FLIR technology to seek out potential heat sources that could mean someone hiding among the trees, she saw nothing that concerned her.

Ambassador McGinnis was already getting out of the car as she completed her quick examination of their surroundings, and she took his arm when he offered it. Bobbie stepped out just behind him, herself dressed for a luxurious evening, and Eugene extended his elbow. She tucked her hand inside and the two couples entered the building. As soon as the door closed behind them, the security guards split into two groups. One remained outside, while the other followed the ambassador and his party.

The vehicles moved away and went to the parking area. Jack and the other drivers would remain there, keeping an eye on their vehicles to ensure that nothing happened to them. They were all armed, and gathered together near the front of the limousine. A couple of the other drivers lit cigarettes, while Jack and the remaining driver sat on the hood of the limo and traded jokes back-and-forth.

———

OUT ON THE main street that led from Silver Spring out to the Candlewick, Juergen Schroeder sat in his car and watched the video on his phone. He had made a trip out to the Candlewick earlier in the day, pretending to spray liquid fertilizer on the trees as he placed a couple of his insectoid video cameras around the grounds. No one had paid much attention to him, and his encrypted video signals had gone undetected. Now, it was simply a matter of watching for his target to appear.

He saw the motorcade go past where he was parked at the side of the abandoned gas station, and watched on the video as McGinnis and the others got out of the limo and entered the building. He smiled, thinking that there was a reasonable possibility he was going to accomplish his purpose that very evening; from the top of the old gas station building, he would be able to get a clean shot. The high-powered rifle would have no trouble reaching out to touch his target from that range, something less than a quarter of a mile away. His bullet would strike almost a full second before the sound of the gunshot would reach those close by.

Having seen the limo move away after disgorging its passengers, Schroeder got out of the car and took the rifle from the backseat. He had already checked out the building and found his path to the roof, climbing onto some old tire racks that had been left standing behind it. He slid the rifle in its case onto the roof and then hoisted himself up and over the edge.

It took him only a few minutes to set up his fire station, setting the bipod clamped to the barrel of the rifle on an overturned bucket. This would allow him to remain in a sitting position as he took the shot, rather than having to lie on the grimy roof. When he was prepared, he took out his phone again and continued watching, also keeping an eye on the traffic that passed by on the road in front of him.

Another limo, this one flanked by only two of the Cadillacs, began slowing as it approached the driveway to the Candlewick. Schroeder looked closely at it, but couldn't tell who was inside. He waited until it made its way up the driveway toward the restaurant, then looked closely at the video display on his phone.

The first person to step out of the limo was a man, one of the men he had seen in the group at the airport car rental desk. Schroeder grinned, realizing that this man had been assigned to protect the occupant of this particular car.

Next out of the car was a woman, the governess of the ambassador's daughter. Her photo had been among those in the dossier he'd been given when he accepted the contract, and he recognized her instantly.

He set down his phone and picked up the rifle, bracing it and quickly bring the scope to bear on the car. The crosshairs of the scope were almost centered on the chest of the governess as she stood looking back into the cavernous rear seat of the limousine. She smiled and straightened, stepping back slightly and out of the crosshairs, and then the little blonde head of Claire McGinnis came into view past the roof of the car.

Schroeder smiled. He would be off the roof and gone before anyone realized where the shot had come from, and he had already mapped out his escape route. His finger touched the trigger and he drew in a breath and then held it. His finger squeezed lovingly on the trigger for only a second, and then the recoil struck his shoulder like a sledgehammer. The 180-grain bullet flew at 2700 feet per second, crossing the distance between rifle and target in less than one half of a second.

―――

STANLEY HAD CLIMBED out of the car first, looking around at the grounds the same way Esmeralda had done, taking in all his surroundings in what amounted to only nanoseconds, but easily examining every degree, minute and second of arc as he did so. Like Esmeralda, he found no sign of any threat within the grounds, and held out a hand to assist Mrs. Lancaster in leaving the car.

When she had stepped out, she turned to offer assistance to Claire, but the girl ignored the consideration and slid quickly off the seat and onto her feet. Her governess moved to close the door behind her, and that's when Stanley saw the distant flash of light.

The quantum computer inside his head immediately analyzed the visuals he was receiving. The light had the chromatic signature of the muzzle flash of a powerful rifle, and his visual sensors instantly went into high gear. The bullet moving through the air caused a distortion that bent light waves slightly, something that no human eye could ever detect, but clearly visible to the visual processor of Stanley's quantum computer brain.

Extrapolating from the flash itself along the path that the distortion indicated the bullet was taking, Stanley concluded that Claire was the intended target. With nothing to interfere, the bullet would impact her head in less than two tenths of a second, but the artificial muscles that moved his joints were capable of incredible speed. Without hesitation, Stanley was suddenly between Claire and the bullet, and when those two tenths of a second had gone by, the bullet was lodged in Stanley's left shoulder from the back. It jammed into the shoulder joint itself, causing his arm to lock momentarily in position, but he forced a movement that twisted the bullet and shoved it out of the way.

The rolling sound of the shot arrived a second later, just as thunder rumbled across the sky. Lightning had flashed only seconds before the thunder, and Stanley ignored everything else as he pushed Claire and Mrs. Lancaster down to the ground behind the protective bulk of the limousine.

He bounced back up, the long-barreled pistol that he carried in his hand. His quantum computer brain calculated the temperature, the humidity, the distance and the wind and a dozen other factors in a split second, and he snapped off a shot that barely missed Schroeder. He hurried out from behind the car, leveling the pistol for another shot, and that's when the lightning flashed again.

There were four people who saw what happened. Claire and Mrs. Lancaster were two of them, and the others were two of the security team that was stationed outside the front door. The lightning struck Stanley's left shoulder where the artificial skin had been torn away, letting the metal casing on his shoulder blade show through, and for a split second he was almost encased in light. The almost astronomical surge of electricity, more than 30,000,000 volts, passed through his body and burst through the leather sole of his shoe into the ground below.

Stanley froze, completely immobilized where he stood. His hand, still extended with the gun in it, was eerily, perfectly still, and remained that way for almost five seconds. The skin and fabric over his shoulder was smoldering, nothing but its flame-retardant composition keeping it from bursting alight.

SEVEN

SCHROEDER'S MOUTH FELL OPEN AS HE STARED
through the scope, shocked that the man had stepped into the
path of the bullet just as he squeezed the trigger. It was an incredible fluke of luck, something he would probably never see again in
a hundred years, but regardless of how unlikely it was, the girl was
still alive.

And then the killer was shocked again, as the man spun and
raised the gun in his hand. He fired, and the slug from the long-
barreled .50-caliber pistol passed over Schroeder's head only a
second later. The assassin dived, getting himself out of the path of
another shot, but then the lightning flashed and no more bullets
came his way.

He waited a couple of seconds and then scrambled for the
edge of the roof. He shoved the rifle back into its case and lowered
it down, then followed it onto the rack. When he got back to the
ground he hurried to the car, shoved the rifle into the backseat
and then jumped in and drove away as quickly as he could. Even
though he had missed, he knew that the police would be coming
within minutes, and he needed to be far away before they arrived.
He would find another chance to kill the girl, to complete the
contract he'd been given.

The worst part of this was that the ambassador's security teams would now be aware that the daughter was the target. It was the North Koreans who had decided that killing the girl would demoralize McGinnis and result in his replacement as British ambassador. The man who would take his place was someone they felt they could more easily intimidate, and achieving their goal was all that mattered to them.

It couldn't be helped, however. He would simply have to find another opportunity to kill Claire McGinnis.

———

FOR FIVE LONG SECONDS, Claire and Mrs. Lancaster watched Stanley. He stood stock still; there was not even any sign that he was still alive, but neither of them could bring herself to move. The security operatives were surrounding them, trying to protect them with their own bodies in case there was another shot, but poor Stanley was simply standing there, the perfect unmoving target.

Inside his head, however, activity was proceeding at a pace no human could ever understand. The lightning had forced his computer brain to reboot completely, a process that would take almost half a minute to complete. Initialization, however, would be accomplished within that five-second span, and would break him free from his apparent paralysis.

First, the high-capacity circuit breaker had to reset itself. This supplied power once again to Stanley's brain, and started the boot-up process. It also unlocked his limbs, and he slowly lowered his hand with the gun.

The second phase of the reboot would take longer, and involved a complete diagnostic program that examined every sensor and component. The result of the diagnostic program would be fed into the CPU, and the CPU could then determine whether to complete the reboot or move into safe mode.

In this particular instance, a couple of leads that connected into his brain had been burned away by the power surge. This caused the computer to choose safe mode, and it was then necessary to select one of more than three hundred emergency programs to run. Various emergency programs were used to bring Stanley back to a particular location, or to cause him to self-destruct in order to avoid being captured. Others would allow limited use of some of his regular programming, such as any parts necessary to complete a mission or use public transportation to return to base.

Based on a number of factors, including the fact that the damage had been done during a critical phase of his programmed mission, the computer chose one of the latter. It was a fail-safe program, a hybrid of his regular programming and an emergency program that would require him to complete whatever mission he had been on when he was damaged.

In this case, the computer recognized his mission as protecting Claire McGinnis. Until such time as he could be certain that Claire was safe, Stanley would be incapable of standing down.

He turned slowly to make sure that Claire was still where he had left her, and she was just peeking out from behind a couple of the security guards. Stanley's programming acknowledged that she was currently alive, which meant that he was still engaged and active; the computer then called for information regarding the threat from which she must be protected.

It found a corrupted sector in his memory, and no data regarding who or what the threat was that he had to protect her from. In that situation, the computer decided that she must be protected from any possible threat, and that meant that Stanley must protect her from anyone getting any access to her.

The program became fully active, and Stanley stepped toward Claire. He reached down and tried to take her hand, but one of the security guards got between them and asked if he was okay.

Stanley threw the man to the side, then removed the others around her just as quickly. He took hold of Claire's hand and then looked around, deciding where to take her to keep her safe.

He looked at the doors of the restaurant, but they suddenly flew open and some of the other security guards came rushing out. To Stanley, it appeared to be a threat, so he simply picked the girl up and turned to run.

Behind him, he could hear people shouting. A number of shots were fired, warning shots that flew over his head, and some of the guards gave chase but none could keep up with him. Stanley ran, dodging between trees and then between vehicles as he rushed across the main road, cutting through the traffic as if it was not even there. He hurried behind a building, an abandoned gas station that had only moments earlier been the base of the man trying to kill the girl, and then looked around for somewhere to hide.

That's when it dawned on him that the girl was shouting at him.

"Stanley, stop," she screamed. "What are you doing? Where are we going?"

"I have to keep you safe," Stanley said. "Someone just tried to kill you, and I must not allow that to happen."

"What are you talking about? Take me back to my father, Stanley, right now!"

"No," Stanley said. "I cannot identify the threat, therefore I cannot surrender you to anyone else. I must put you somewhere to keep you safe."

"Stanley, put me down! I mean it, Stanley, put me down, right now!"

Stanley didn't bother to respond, but began running once again. He had spotted a path through some woods behind the old gas station, and decided to put more distance between himself and whatever threat lay behind them.

The path ran to the northeast, away from the city. With his enhanced, computer-powered senses, Stanley was able to avoid roads, people and traffic as he made his way deeper into the rural areas of Maryland.

Suddenly, Stanley felt something happening inside his brain.

Satellite signals were being received, and it was attempting to reprogram his operating system, but he instantly shut it down. With deliberate intent, he deactivated the satellite receiver built into his head, effectively cutting off any communication from Esmeralda or E&E. The corrupted memories of what had taken place just before the lightning strike left him unable to determine from where or from whom the threat had originated, and so the protocol built into his program required him to trust absolutely no one other than himself.

BACK AT THE CANDLEWICK, pandemonium was almost the rule. Several of the security team had tried to follow Stanley, but he had rapidly lost them. Esmeralda had recognized that her worst nightmare had come true, but then she put that aside instantly. Instead, she reached out through the satellite communication system built into her computer mind and began attempting to reprogram Stanley. Her quantum computer brain could write the software on the fly, faster than any human could even read it, but she was cut off almost instantly. Stanley had realized what was happening and had shut down communication.

She considered the possibility that she could find and catch him, but if he was refusing her signal, then he was not recognizing her as an ally or superior. If she were to approach him, the situation could turn deadly for little Claire, and this was something that she had to avoid at all costs.

"What the hell is going on?" McGinnis demanded. "They said your man Lorimer grabbed my daughter and took off with her. Why the hell would he do that? Did the Koreans get to him?"

"No," Esmeralda said. "Stanley is in shock, he was struck by lightning. He's probably disoriented and not sure what is happening, but he's trying to do what he was ordered to do, which is to protect your daughter. In the meantime, you are still at risk, sir, so

I must insist that you go back inside. My team will work with yours make sure we find them as soon as possible."

"Young lady, that is not good enough," McGinnis said. "I was assured that your people were the best, but this..."

Esmeralda rounded on him and looked him in the eye. "Ambassador McGinnis, this is in fact an example of one of my people carrying out his orders despite the fact that he has been severely injured. Now, I have things I have to do if I'm going to get your daughter back safely, and I do not have time to argue with you. Please, do as I tell you and go back inside. I have to report in."

McGinnis started to argue, but then he growled and turned to go back inside the building. Two of the security guards stayed close to him as he did so, while the rest were milling around Eugene and awaiting orders.

Esmeralda stood where she was, then activated the subcom system adapter built into her head. Without even thinking about it, she took a deep breath the way any other person would do before delivering bad news to a superior, then silently said, "Esmeralda to Noah."

———

IT WAS JUST past eight thirty in DC, so it was a little after one thirty in the morning at the Manor. Noah came awake instantly when the message came through and buzzed against his skull.

"Noah to Esmeralda, go," he said softly.

"I have a situation," Esmeralda transmitted silently. "Stanley has been struck by lightning and has gone into a safe mode that requires him to carry out his most recent orders. It appears that the ambassador's daughter was the actual target, and Stanley was able to protect her when Schroeder made an attempt on her life, but now he has taken the girl and disappeared. I can only assume that his memory core has been damaged, and he is unaware of who the threat is. As result, he is unwilling to trust anyone. I'm going to initiate a plan of action to help me find him and recover the girl."

Noah was sitting up on the side of his bed, whispering softly so that he would not wake Sarah or the baby, who was sleeping beside her.

"Lightning," Noah said. "What effect is it likely to have on him? Could it increase his processing speed and allow him to become self-aware?"

"No. His CPU is sufficiently shielded from power surges, even one as great as this. It would reboot, but it would not itself be damaged. The problem is his memory core. Quantum computers like Stanley and myself use light quantum memory, utilizing light absorbed by atoms to convey information in the form of qubits, which are always in quantum state. Some of those atoms could be damaged by the electrical surge of the lightning, resulting in corruption of the quantum state and either missing or faulty information."

"Then you are sure that he is running on programming?"

"Yes. Stanley would be operating in safe mode right now, but there are many different variations of that safe-mode programming, and which one his CPU chooses is dependent upon several factors. What memories might be corrupted would be one of the factors involved, and I have no way to replicate the choice."

"All right," Noah said. "If I am understanding you correctly, what you're saying is that you cannot accurately predict what he is going to do. Is that about right,?"

"Yes, precisely. Stanley will undoubtedly take certain actions that will draw the attention of authorities, and I will be able to learn about those actions by monitoring radio waves. With any luck, I will be able to build a profile that will let me anticipate some of his future actions."

"Do so, then, and keep me apprised. Are you capable of terminating Stanley if it becomes necessary?"

"Yes, of course," Esmeralda replied, "but termination will not be necessary. I know precisely what damage he would need to suffer in order to disable him completely. Should it become unavoidable, that is my plan and we will just bring him back to Wally to be repaired."

"Very well," Noah said. "Keep me up-to-date at all times. I'll notify Allison."

"Yes, sir," Esmeralda said. "Esmeralda out."

Noah glanced at the clock beside his bed and decided to wait until morning to bring Allison up to speed. He knew that she was going to be very upset, but there was nothing either of them could do about the situation at the moment. It seemed, to him, logical to avoid creating stress for her before it was absolutely necessary.

————

THE FARMHOUSE WAS OBVIOUSLY OCCUPIED, but Stanley was only interested in the vehicles sitting outside. One of them was a new Ford pickup truck, and it took him only a moment to find the code that allowed him to start the engine remotely and unlock it. He could transmit the code directly from his brain, using the built-in transmitter set to 315 MHz. He ran to the truck and opened the door, pushed Claire inside and then jumped in and buckled her seat belt.

"Stanley, stop this!" Claire shouted. "You have to take me back to my father!"

Stanley ignored her. He put the truck into gear and raced out of the driveway, fishtailing onto the gravel road and driving as fast as was practical and safe as he moved away from the farmhouse. Behind him, he could see lights coming on in the house through the rearview mirror, but it meant nothing to him.

Claire tried to unbuckle her seat belt, but Stanley reached over and put a hand on it. "You have to stay there," he said. "It's my duty to keep you safe, and you have to obey when I speak."

"You're bloody crazy," she shouted at him. "If you don't take me back to my father this instant, I shall—I shall never speak to you again!"

"That would be acceptable," Stanley said. "First, I must determine the level of threat and what I must do to counter it. Once I have made that determination and accomplished its neutralization, I can consider the possibility of returning you to your father. Until then, you must do as I tell you. We will find somewhere to conceal ourselves while I conduct my investigation."

"But you're daft! That bloody lightning has fried your brains and you are acting totally and completely insane!"

"Lightning? Is that what happened? I am operating in safe mode, but some of my memory is not functioning. I am aware that I was assigned to protect you in the event someone made an attempt on your life. We had believed that your father was the target of an assassination attempt ordered by—I do not know who ordered the attempt. We had considered that you might be a secondary target, but it appears now that you are in fact the primary. The initiators of the assassination attempt must be hoping to cause your father duress with your death. This is the only logical conclusion. I must therefore do whatever is necessary to ensure that you are safe and that the assassin cannot reach you."

"What in the bloody hell are you going on about?" Claire asked, her face reflecting confusion. "Are you saying that someone is hoping to kill me?"

"That appears to be the case. The attempt was made not upon your father's life, but on yours. This indicates that you are in fact the primary target. Therefore, it is necessary for me to do whatever I must to keep you safe until such time as the threat is eliminated."

Claire stared at him for a moment, then turned her face to look through the windshield. They were racing along a dirt road in the dark, and it suddenly hit her that Stanley had not bothered to turn on the headlights.

"How can you see where you're going?" she demanded. "Turn on the lights, Stanley, so that you can see!"

"It's not necessary for me to use headlights," Stanley said. "I can see quite well using infrared and low-light video technology. Turning on the headlights would simply make us more visible to potential attackers."

The little girl stared at him, her eyes wide and her mouth open.

"You've gone completely daft," she said softly. "What, do you think you're some sort of robot or something?"

"Yes," Stanley said. "I am a robot. I was built by Wally Lawson for the purpose of supporting operational teams of E&E. I was ordered to this mission by—I am not aware of who ordered me on this mission. My orders were to secure your safety at all costs, and I must carry out my orders."

Claire's eyes managed to get bigger. "You think you're a robot?" she asked. "That bloody lightning has fried your brains. Stanley, you're not a robot. You are my friend Stanley, but I am becoming more and more vexed with you every moment. Please take me back to my father, and we shall have a doctor take a look at you to see what is wrong."

"No. I must carry out my orders. When the threat has been eliminated, you can then return to your father."

Clare grunted and slammed her head on the back of the seat in frustration. Whatever was wrong with Stanley, it was obvious that he was not going to back down. She would have to find another way to get him to do what she wanted.

One of the things Claire had been good at ever since she was small had been manipulating the adults in charge of her. She found it amazingly easy to get her father and Mrs. Lancaster to do things the way she wanted them done, even when they were determined not to give in. She decided to apply those skills to Stanley and see if he was equally susceptible to her manipulations.

"Well, if you're not going to take me home, then I'm going to need something to eat. You do remember that we were going to have dinner before you ran off with me, yes? I am hungry, Stanley. I'm certainly not safe if I'm starving to death, would you not agree?"

"You're not starving to death. You can go several days without food if necessary, but I will make every attempt to procure food for you in the next few hours. A more pressing need would be water, but even that is not so desperate that it must be addressed at this moment."

Claire stared at him. "Stanley, did you hear me? I said that I'm hungry. You must get me something to eat, and you must do it now."

Stanley shook his head. "I am afraid that the gravity of this situation must take precedence over your desire for food. I will take action to get you food in the near future, however."

The little girl glared at him.

"You'd bloody well better!" She crossed her arms over her chest and turned to stare through the windshield again.

EIGHT

"You are telling me that the assassin you were sent to intercept was not coming after me at all, but after my daughter?" McGinnis asked. They had shut down the celebration immediately and Esmeralda had commandeered one of the smaller rooms of the building as a command post. She, McGinnis, Eugene, Captain Jeffries and four of his own security people were gathered there as she and Eugene tried to explain the situation to the ambassador. "She was the target all along?"

The look on his face was grave, and Esmeralda wanted to find some way to make him feel better. Unfortunately, she knew there wasn't much she could say that was going to relieve his concern for his daughter's safety. For the past hour, she had been doing everything she could think of to try to locate Stanley and Claire, but without success. Even the supposedly fail-safe GPS locator built into Stanley's brain, which was designed to transmit his location automatically if he was damaged, was completely silent. She had tried reaching him on the subcom frequency as well, but with no response.

It was possible that both of those had been damaged by the lightning strike. If that were the case, the code she had written would make it very difficult for anyone to locate Stanley until such time as he was ready to reach out.

"I'm afraid so," she said. "The assassin, and we feel certain that it was Schroeder, only fired one shot. He ignored you and let you get inside the building, then fired when he saw Claire get out of the second limousine. From everything the witnesses have said and the security video from the cameras outside the building, we know that Stanley Lorimer anticipated the shot somehow and placed himself between the shooter and your daughter. He was struck in the back of the left shoulder, but still managed to get off at least one shot. It was at that point that he was struck by lightning, and we believe that he must be in shock."

"In shock? How the bloody hell is the man even alive?" McGinnis asked. "They said he didn't even fall, how is that possible?"

"Stanley's in very good shape," Eugene said. "I know it sounds strange, but I've heard of other people who seemed to be able to shrug off getting hit by lightning." He glanced at Esmeralda from the corner of his eye, hoping she would not disapprove of his prevarication.

"Yes, that's true," Esmeralda said. "He still seems to be in shock, however, both from the bullet wound and the lightning strike. That's the only explanation for his behavior right after that, when he took your daughter and ran off with her. He's attempting to carry out his mission, which is to keep her safe."

"But what if the assassin were to find them? I mean, he's all alone, yes? Can he handle a killer like that alone?"

"If anybody can," she said. "Ambassador, you can trust us on this. Stanley's going to keep her safe, no matter what he has to do to accomplish that. The problem is that he's apparently not capable of clear thinking just now, so he might consider any innocent bystander to be a threat. He won't hurt anyone unless he feels trapped, but he will certainly avoid other people."

"Do you have a way to contact him? To order him back in?"

"We're working on that," Esmeralda replied. "Unfortunately,

the lightning probably killed his phone. We're going to have to wait until he reaches out to us, but that's part of his pro... I mean, his training. Whenever he is cut off from us, his training requires him to find a safe place and then make contact."

"And in the meanwhile, we have no idea where my daughter is?" McGinnis's eyes bored into hers.

"I'm afraid not," Esmeralda said, "but that also makes it more difficult for the assassin to find her. That's an advantage as far as we're concerned."

McGinnis ran a hand over his face. "And I can see why, I truly can," he said. "Please forgive me for my outburst, it's simply the parental terror that's raging through me. My daughter, as I'm sure you can imagine, is the most important and treasured thing in my world. She's all I have left of her mother, and to lose her would be to lose even myself."

"Which is precisely why they targeted her," Eugene said. "They weren't out to kill you, Mr. Ambassador; they just wanted to break you, make you ineffective."

A sound that could have been a gasp or a laugh came out of the ambassador. "Well, that would've done it," he said. "Now I simply need to have faith that you can bring her home to me." He turned to Esmeralda. "Can you do that, young lady? Emma?"

"I can," she said. "It may take a little time, but I will bring her home to you."

Deanna Walker suddenly appeared. "Mr. Ambassador," she said, "I'm afraid the press is demanding to get some sort of statement from you. I've tried to stall them as long as I can but..."

McGinnis got to his feet. "It's fine, Deanna," he said. "I can speak with them. Maybe letting the press know what's going on will help bring my daughter home safely." He looked at Esmeralda, who nodded once, then turned and followed Deanna out the door. Esmeralda heard the reporters begin shouting at him as the door started to close.

"What the hell do we do now?" Eugene asked. "You got any idea how to find Stanley?"

"Not until he's ready to be found," Esmeralda replied. "I wrote the program he's running on, and I intended it to be used only when it was absolutely necessary. Believe me, I added in everything I could think of to help him stay hidden until it was safe to come in."

"And we can't make any kind of contact with him? I mean, isn't there some way to get some kind of a signal or message to him?"

Esmeralda shook her head. "No, and I've tried every possible way. Right now, I'm guessing that the lightning overloaded some of the circuitry in his internal communication systems. Subcom, cell phone, nothing works. Those are things that will have to be physically repaired back at Feeney." She looked at him and let out a sigh. "He's operating on the assumption that Claire could be under attack again at any moment. Until he is confident that the threat is either eliminated or no longer viable, he is going to keep her hidden. He's not going to let anyone get near her, no matter what he has to do. If someone sees a man and little girl and gets too curious, Stanley could decide they were enough of a threat to eliminate them."

Eugene rubbed a hand across his eyes. "Is it time to report in on this?"

"I already did," she said. "I suppose I should check back in, however."

She leaned back in the chair she was sitting in and activated her built-in satellite phone connection. While she could've used subcom technology as she did to contact Noah, she wanted to speak to Allison directly. For various reasons, Allison had declined to accept the subcom implants, and so the only way to reach her was by telephone.

The connection rang three times and then was answered.

———

IT WAS NEARLY three o'clock in the morning back in England, and Allison had been sleeping. She came awake instantly when her brain recognized the phone ringing, and her eyes went wide when she saw the caller ID.

"Cinderella, report," she said as she answered the phone.

Through the phone, she could hear Esmeralda's voice even though the robot was not speaking aloud. "Cinderella reports a mission critical situation. Contrary to our intel, Juergen Schroeder made an attempt to murder Claire McGinnis, the ambassador's daughter. Stanley was assigned as her personal protection and performed his duties, but was struck by lightning only seconds later. His system apparently rebooted and went into safe mode, causing him to immediately activate emergency protocols in his programming. Those emergency protocols indicated that he should take Claire somewhere safe and keep her there until the threat is eliminated. He immediately picked her up and ran, and we currently have no knowledge of his whereabouts, or those of the girl."

Allison's eyes had grown even wider. "What's your next step?"

"I have exhausted every possibility of trying to make contact with him, and had to conclude that his communication systems are down. Based on the programming under which he is operating, it is highly unlikely that any of us will be able to find him until he is ready to reach out to us. That programming will require him to keep the girl safe and as comfortable as possible, but it also leads to the possibility that innocent bystanders could be endangered."

"Good Lord," Allison said. "Have you notified Noah?"

"Yes, ma'am," Esmeralda said. "He was planning to share the information with you, but I felt it necessary to report now."

"Well, make sure you keep him up to speed. Keep both of us posted as to your activities and any results. Remember that Schroeder is still a threat, and if he can't reach the girl then he might still go after the ambassador. How will Stanley reach out to you when he decides to?"

"By telephone, most likely. He has this number, so he can reach me directly no matter where I am."

"When he does, you will determine the level of danger he presents to the world at large. If that danger is significant, then your orders are to do whatever is necessary to terminate and destroy him. Is that understood?"

"Yes, ma'am," Esmeralda said without hesitation. "I understand and will obey."

Allison hung up, then flopped back on the bed and stared up at the ceiling. She knew there was no hope of getting back to sleep that night, so she got up after a moment and begin getting dressed. She slipped out of her room and headed toward the stairs, intending to go to the kitchen and make coffee, when Molly opened her door and looked out.

"Oh, boy," Molly said after one look at her face. "What's wrong?"

"My worst freaking nightmare," Allison said. "Come on, we'll talk about it downstairs. I'm sure Noah's going to join us any moment now."

Noah, who had been unable to go back to sleep after Esmeralda's report, heard them speaking. He immediately contacted Esmeralda as he began getting dressed.

"I take it you notified Allison?" Noah asked when Esmeralda answered on subcom.

"Yes, sir," she said. "I felt it was necessary. I apologize if I overstepped my authority."

"No, no trouble. Is there anything new to report?"

"Not at this point," Esmeralda said. "I'm simply working on a plan to locate Stanley and deactivate him so that he can be repaired. I think this is the best plan of action."

"I concur," Noah said. "Try to think like Stanley. Turn off your emotions as much as you can, and think logically, robotically. That may give you some insight into where he would go."

"I've already considered that," Esmeralda replied. "My concern is that he is not operating in his normal state. I have no way of knowing precisely what damage the lightning strike may have done to his operating system or memory processes. And with his communications system not working, I can't even get in to evaluate the damage. Without knowing which set of protocols he is running on, I'm basically groping in the dark."

"I understand. What is it going to take to repair any damage that was done?"

"I'm sure he's in pretty bad shape. I suspect it will take complete reconstruction, to be honest. The heat of the lightning undoubtedly did damage to his skin, and since we know that some circuits were fried, communications in particular, there may be others that were damaged. It's going to take a full teardown and evaluation to determine just how bad it really is."

"Esmeralda," Noah said, "tell me your honest opinion. Is it going to be possible to capture Stanley without destroying him?"

Esmeralda hesitated, a deliberate affectation since her thought processes were so much faster than those of human brains. "It's going to be difficult," she said. "Stanley was able to protect Claire from the attack, and the assassin was deterred. Had it not been for the lightning strike, he would have gone into a heightened protective mode, but nothing like this. He would've worked with the security team rather than running from them. Since he's gone into isolationist mode, I don't know that he will even recognize or trust me."

"Are you prepared to destroy him if necessary?" Noah asked.

"Yes, certainly," Esmeralda replied. "My concern at this point is for Claire. To be perfectly frank, I don't know how to get him away from her so that he can be disabled or destroyed."

Noah took a deep breath. "You do what you can on your end," he said. "Meanwhile, I'll discuss this with Allison and Molly, and probably with Wally. Between us, we might be able to come up with a solution. I'll be in touch as soon as I know more, and you keep me apprised of any new developments."

"Yes, sir," Esmeralda said, and then she cut the connection.

Eugene was looking at her. "I gather you were talking to the bosses?" he asked.

Esmeralda nodded. "Yes. They're going to talk it over and see if they can come up with suggestions, but at the moment I think this is our problem. Do you understand what's going on with Stanley?"

"Oh, hell, no," Eugene said. "To me, it looks like he went crazy. Do you know what he's up to?"

"Somewhat. He's gone into safe mode, running on programming that is designed to let him carry out his last orders. Unfortunately, his last orders were to protect Claire McGinnis, and he seems to have suffered some damage from the lightning strike. I suspect his memory has been affected, and that he is unsure of just where the threat may be coming from. As a result, he is unwilling to trust anyone at this point. He has cut off communications with me so that I cannot locate him or talk to him. We are going to have to find him before any innocent bystanders get hurt."

"Why would he hurt an innocent bystander?" Eugene asked.

"He won't intend to," Esmeralda replied. "Unfortunately, he may be incapable of determining whether someone is a threat or not, so anyone who gets too close will be in danger. Someone could simply ask if he needed help and find themselves being torn to shreds."

Eugene shook his head. "That would be a very bad situation," he said. "Especially if he ever gets traced back to us. I get the feeling E&E is already on shaky ground. If the news agencies ever find out about Stanley, I'm pretty sure it would not be good for us."

"And you could say the same about me," Esmeralda said. "The world isn't prepared for the existence of robots or androids that can pass for human." She gave him a wry grin. "I watched the *Terminator* movies; right now, Stanley could give Arnold Schwarzenegger a run for his money."

"Which is exactly why we can't let anyone find out about him." He shook his head again. "So, what's our next move?"

"I'll let you know as soon as I figure it out," Esmeralda said. "Meanwhile, we still have jobs to do."

———

SCHROEDER HAD RECOVERED from the shock of missing his target, but he was not even close to giving up. He had made his way back into DC and to the embassy, once again standing among the trees on the opposite side of the street. He had checked the feed from his insectoid robots and found nothing helpful, so it was time to step up the game. He walked along toward the corner, trying to appear as nonchalant as possible.

When he came to the telephone junction box at the corner, he stopped and took out another plastic box. This one contained a number of small devices, similar to bugs in that they had six legs each, but with no attempt to disguise them as actual insects. He had taken the trouble to program them before he even got on the flight to the States, because the telephone numbers of the embassy were easily available on the Internet. As he dumped the box out and let the little robots fall onto the ground, he was delighted to see them snap to life and make their way into the small opening at the base of the junction box.

Once inside, they would crawl all over the wiring and use their sophisticated antennae to determine which lines went to which numbers. When they identified the lines that went into the embassy, they would lock themselves in place and transmit every call to a cloud-based recording system. Schroeder would be able to log in and listen whenever he chose.

Sooner or later, he was sure, the girl or her protector would be calling in. When that happened, he wanted to pick up any clue as to where they might be hiding. If there was one thing everyone knew about Juergen Schroeder, it was that he never failed to fulfill a contract.

———

"You know this is a disaster, Noah," Allison said. They were sitting at the table in the dining hall, waiting for the coffee to finish percolating. "We should never have used Stanley at all. If word about him gets out, that we had a killer robot out on a mission, that would be the end of us."

"I'm sure it would," Noah said. "I don't think we need to be worried about that just yet, though. The situation is not completely out of control. Let's give Esmeralda a chance to track him down and see what she can do. If she's successful, we never have to tell anyone about this."

"And if she's not?" Molly asked. "What happens then?"

"Most likely," Allison said, "E&E will be shut down and I'll be left holding the bag, or worse. It's always possible that Noah could be ordered to eliminate me." She looked at Noah. "I know if I was going to order elimination of someone in our organization, you would be the one I would send to do it. I'm sure the president would think of that himself."

"Immaterial," Noah said. "If I'm ordered to eliminate you, I'll do it by establishing another identity for you somewhere else. You don't have anything to fear from me."

"What about the rest of us?" Molly asked. "Would we be sanctioned as well?"

Noah looked at her. "Some of the teams might be," he said. "Again, I'm not going to let that happen. If it even looks like that's the eventuality coming down on us, I will order everyone to disperse."

Allison frowned. "Makes me wish we had never told anyone about our operation here," she said. "We could just retire from wet work and keep running the company. I actually kind of like working with all these robot devices." Her frown deepened. "Well, most of them, anyway."

Noah cocked his head to one side and looked at her with a question on his face. "Who actually knows about it? Not the whole committee, I'm sure."

She shook her head. "Our president was briefed, and a couple of people at CIA and NSA. Of course, that was before the last election and all the new appointments."

"But nobody else?" Noah asked.

"No. All the rest of the committee knows is that any sanction has to be sent through the NSA network to us. They can't send one directly. I'm just worried that we may be targeted for a military attack."

The percolator settled down at last and Noah got up to pour them each a cup of coffee. "I have an idea," he said. "Give me a minute."

He sat down again and took a sip of coffee, then whispered to his subcom. Across the Atlantic, the former president was preparing for bed when he heard Noah's voice in his head.

"Noah?" he asked. "I thought I was cut out of the loop after the election."

"You probably are, sir," Noah said. "That doesn't necessarily take you completely out of the circuit, though. I played a hunch that your subcom might still be working. Glad to see I was right."

"I'm not exactly disappointed about it," said the former POTUS. "Never know when I might need help from someone like you. What can I do for you this evening?"

"Sir, I'm wondering just how much information was shared with your successor regarding our current location and facilities. Would you happen to know the answer to that question?"

"Of course I do," the man said. "Be an idiot if I didn't, right? All the information that was passed down indicates that you are based somewhere in Europe, but we didn't give them any actual details, and of course we never let the full committee in on your base of operations. Wallace at the NSA, Bascom at the CIA and I all agreed that it was better not to let any of the new gang have too much information. To be honest, we think they are probably going to be soft on using you anyway, for the most part. I suspect you'll be doing more standard intelligence work under the current administration. The new guy is not exactly the kind of person who usually occupies the White House, you know."

"Yes, sir, we're seeing signs of that already, with more conventional missions than eliminations. Is it safe for us to assume that the only ones who actually know where we are, then, would be our friends over here in the UK?"

"I can guarantee it," came the reply. "After that last attack on you folks, we put out a lot of propaganda about how you had to be moved to a new and discrete location. No one knows you are still in Britain except the British. And while they might be a little bit on the stuffy side, I think we can trust them. Or perhaps I should say that I think *you* can trust them."

"I would tend to agree with you, sir. Thank you, I appreciate that information. And if there ever is anything I can do for you, please don't hesitate to ask."

"Oh, I won't. By the way, I'm just curious: what made you ask these kinds of questions?"

"Just a feeling that we might be on somebody's bad side in the not-too-distant future. If we have to shut down the operation, I didn't want to have to give up everything we built."

"Damn right. And listen, if things go sour, let me know. I still have a lot of solid connections in DC, so I might be able to help smooth things over. At the very least, I could probably get myself set up to be your new liaison man." He chuckled. "Wouldn't that make a few people nervous?"

"I'll bear that in mind, sir. Noah out."

Noah cut off the subcom connection and looked at Allison and Molly. "I think we could manage to stay here," he said. "And we might still have an ally in DC."

Allison let out a sigh. "Sounds good to me," she said. "I finally found a bed I like sleeping in."

NINE

For a few seconds, Stanley turned on his satellite communication system and searched the Internet for a place where he might be able to keep Claire hidden. A rapid search of real estate listings showed him a few abandoned buildings, but one of them stood out. It was large and solid, had many places where someone could hide and had the added advantage of being just a few miles ahead of his current location.

The empty factory building had once been the home of a manufacturer of automotive filters, for air and oil. It had actually been one of the most popular brands, but newer technologies employed by other brands knocked them out of the lead in the late nineties and the company ended up filing for bankruptcy. A hundred different ventures had considered the building since then, but none of them found it quite suitable for their purposes. As a result, the bank that ended up with it had eventually given up trying to sell it and just let it sit.

The biggest problem they had with it was its location. The building was on a back road that had never even been paved, and the county had long since abandoned any pretense of maintaining the road. In the last five years, the only traffic on the road was from dirt bikes and four-wheel-drive vehicles headed for the dirt trails behind the old building. The building itself got very little attention, primarily because of its eerie appearance. Most people thought the front of the building resembled some sort of mental institution, with Gothic architecture and bars on the windows. Rumors of hauntings surrounded it, and it was rare that any of the locals were brave enough to try going inside.

Stanley was not aware of those rumors, but his sensory abilities were enough to tell him that the place was empty and abandoned. It took him only a moment to pick the lock holding the chain on the front gate, and another to secure it once again after he had driven through. One of the back overhead doors was standing partially open, the result of a short-lived chop shop venture a couple of years earlier, and he raised it enough to bring the pickup inside.

The door had led into a now deserted warehouse, but there was an office just off the main space that held a couch and a couple of chairs. Claire followed him into the office and sneered while he dusted off the furniture.

"You can lie down on the couch if you like," Stanley said. "It's late, you probably need to sleep."

"What I need is food," Claire replied sarcastically. "You said you would get me some."

"And I will. I just needed to put you somewhere safe first. This will do, it doesn't appear that anyone comes here. You can wait here in this room while I go to get food and other supplies."

Her eyes went round. "Are you bloody stupid? I'm not waiting here, this place is filthy. I shall come with you."

"No," Stanley said. "I cannot risk anyone seeing you. We do not know who tried to kill you, nor how many people might be involved. I cannot risk the assassin learning where you are, and I have no way of knowing who might report to him. You will remain here while I go and get supplies. We may need to be here for some time, so we need not only food and water, but hygienic necessities and additional clothing."

The little girl glared at him. "At least call my father and let him know that I'm all right," she said. "He will be worried."

"It's too soon," Stanley said. "I cannot make contact just yet. First, I must ascertain the extent of risk in doing so. We must assume that the assassin may have infiltrated your father's security arrangements. If he were to trace the call, the assassin could become aware of our general vicinity. I'm sure that abandoned buildings would be among the first he would search."

She stomped her foot. "Oh, you are so infuriating! Fine, then go and get me something to eat. An American cheeseburger would be lovely, with chips."

Stanley was looking at the door that had led into the office from the warehouse. It was a steel door with reinforced glass, and could be secured by a deadbolt that required a key from either side.

"Very well," he said. He pulled the door shut behind him, then used his makeshift picks to lock it securely.

On the other side, Claire was glaring at him with her mouth hanging open. "You locked me in? How dare you?"

"I deemed it necessary," Stanley said. "I believe you would attempt to leave here and make contact with your father if I did not do so. This way, you will still be here when I return."

"Oooooh!" she shouted. "When I get back to my father, he will see to it that you are punished as severely as he possibly can! This is no way to treat the daughter of an ambassador!"

Stanley turned away without a word and got back into the pickup truck. He started the vehicle and backed out of the warehouse, then turned onto the road and headed back toward the nearest town. They had passed it a dozen minutes earlier, and he had seen a Walmart store on its outskirts.

In the store, Stanley quickly picked out a few clothing items for Claire, estimating her size as he chose blue jeans, T-shirts and underclothes. He added a couple of changes of clothing for himself as well, then went toward the household section. He chose a blanket and a pillow, then went to the grocery section and selected a number of snack items, such as bags of chips and boxes of individually wrapped cakes, then took a large case of bottled drinking water and slid it underneath.

Next, he went to the sporting goods section. Because the building had no power or water, he knew there was no hope that the toilets would be working, so he set a portable toilet on top of everything else and added two gallon jugs of the sanitizing chemical it required. This kind of toilet required a specific type of rapidly soluble toilet tissue that was sold right beside them, so he grabbed two packages that each held four rolls. He added a couple of battery-powered lanterns and some batteries and then headed toward the front of the store.

He chose the self-checkout lane and quickly scanned all the items, then programmed an RFID chip embedded in his hand with an override code that would tell the register to consider the items paid for. A receipt that totaled zero spit out of the machine and he pushed his cart out the door. Once he had loaded everything into the truck, he got behind the wheel again and headed toward the fast-food restaurant at the edge of the parking lot.

Stanley had been given some cash to keep on his person, and this allowed him to purchase a cheeseburger meal. He paid for the food and then rolled up to the next window to receive it, setting it on the seat beside him as he pulled out and went to the gas station at the other end of the lot. The truck had had a nearly full tank when he had stolen it, but it was getting low and he decided to fill it up. The pump accepted the same override code as the register inside the store, and he drove out moments later, headed back toward the abandoned factory.

In the office area, Claire was searching for some means of escape. It took her a few minutes to realize she had absolutely no idea of how to pick the lock, so she gave up on that notion and went to the one window in the outer wall. Like all the windows in the building, it was filled with wire-reinforced tempered glass, and nothing she could do seemed to so much as scratch it. She actually exhausted herself trying to break it, finally giving up and sitting down on the couch in frustration.

That's when the frustration turned into fear and she felt tears trying to well up in her eyes. She fought them back for several minutes, but then the sense of despair overcame her and she began to cry. At ten years old, she considered herself too old to cry, but the weight of the evening's events and her own concern as to whether Stanley was mentally stable suddenly seemed to be sufficient justification. The tears ran down her cheeks, and her bottom lip quivered as she whispered silent prayers and crossed herself.

She heard the throaty roar of the truck engine as Stanley returned, and then the headlights shone into the warehouse. He pulled the truck in and shut the door down behind him before once again unlocking the door into the office.

"And it's about bloody time," Claire shouted at him. "You've been gone, like, forever, almost."

Stanley looked at her. "I've been gone less than an hour," he said. He turned and went back to the truck, then brought the bag of food and the large tumbler of cola to her. "Here," he said. "Eat."

The tears vanished at the sight of the food, and she plopped down on the couch again as she began to eat. Stanley returned to the truck and brought his purchases from Walmart into the office. He took the portable toilet into the restroom and set it up, as Claire watched him closely.

"Are you planning to be here a long time?" she asked. "I mean, you brought a toilet?"

"You'll need it," Stanley said. "All humans do."

She cocked her head. "And you won't? You really do think you're a bloody robot, don't you?"

"I have already explained that to you. I do not eat, nor do I need sanitary facilities other than to clean myself from time to time."

Claire rolled her eyes. "Certainly, whatever you say," she said.

She continued eating, savoring the large cheeseburger he had chosen and wolfing down the French fries. "Stanley?"

"Yes, Claire?"

"That lightning hit you, right? I mean, I saw it. It did, yes?"

Stanley was laying out the clothing he had bought on one of the chairs. "Is that what happened? I knew something had happened, because I rebooted, but I don't recall exactly what it was. I remember someone trying to shoot you and stepping in front of the bullet, and I recall firing a return shot, but then there are several seconds that are blank."

Claire ate a French fry and looked at him curiously. "But lightning should have killed you, shouldn't it? Why did it not?"

"There is a lot of shielding built around my central processing unit," Stanley said. "If it was lightning, then the power surge would explain why I rebooted. It would also explain why some of my memory seems to be corrupted. The memory circuits that were in use at that time would have been overloaded and disabled. Some of them must have contained data on my mission, which would explain why I cannot remember certain details."

He glanced at Claire to see her staring at him, her mouth half open with a partially chewed French fry visible inside.

"You're bloody serious," she said. "You are saying that you really are a robot, aren't you?"

"I have already told you this," Stanley said. "I do not understand why you continue to ask that question."

She finished chewing the French fry and swallowed. "Because I didn't think there were any such things as robots," she said. "At least, not any robots who look like people. I mean, there are some, but they don't actually look real. More like some kind of rubber mask with a person inside them. They talk and everything, but they don't walk about or drive cars or anything like that. Who made you?"

"I'm not supposed to give that information to anyone," Stanley said. "My existence is highly classified. In fact, I should not have told you as much as I have."

The little girl took another bite of her burger. "I'm sure," she said. "I mean, my father knows many, many secrets, but I'm sure he doesn't know there are robots like you. I overhear things all the time, and I've never heard about robots that look real. Do you have laser eyes?"

The question surprised Stanley. "Laser eyes? No, I do not. Why would you ask me that?"

Claire shrugged her shoulders and took another bite. "I just wondered. Sometimes the robots on TV have laser eyes."

"I do not have them." He pointed at the clothes he had laid out on the chair. "I bought you some clothing. It may be more comfortable than the dress you are wearing."

Claire looked at him. "Thanks," she said. She finished her burger and fries, then got up and looked at the clothes. She chose a pair of pants and a shirt, then went into the bathroom and closed the door behind her. She opened it again instantly. "It's dark in here."

Stanley glanced at her. "There's no electricity," he said. "The lights will not work without it." He picked up one of the battery-powered lanterns and ripped open a package of batteries. A moment later, he handed her the lantern and she went back into the bathroom and closed the door once more.

She stayed in there for a couple of minutes, and Stanley's hearing picked up the sound of her using the toilet. His programming told him that people tended to be somewhat embarrassed about bodily functions, so he did not allude to it when she came out. Instead, he handed her the pillow and blanket.

"You should probably get some rest," he said. "We may have to leave suddenly, and I would prefer that you are rested if that were to happen."

She looked at the couch and shrugged again, then lay down and spent a moment getting the pillow fluffed the way she wanted it. She covered herself with a blanket and tucked a hand under her head as she looked at Stanley. He was standing near the door.

"You're afraid I'll try to run away?" she asked.

"I'm quite sure you would try if you got the chance," Stanley said. "To you, it would be logical to do so. However, I have to consider that you might inadvertently fall into the hands of the assassin, so I cannot allow that to take place."

Claire yawned. "Well, you can relax for now," she said. "I'm too tired to go anywhere at the moment. But tomorrow we need to at least call my father and let him know that I'm okay. I won't have him worrying himself to death over this, do you understand me?"

Stanley turned and looked at her. "Tomorrow, I will evaluate the risk of making contact and we will decide on a course of action then."

Claire sneered at him, then closed her eyes. A moment later, her breathing deepened as she drifted off to sleep. Stanley continued to watch her, but his attention was spread out quite far. He was listening to and evaluating every sound within several hundred feet in every direction. At the slightest indication that a human was approaching, he would slip out the door and take them by surprise.

———

THE AMBASSADOR and his staff had returned to the embassy, including all the security personnel. Esmeralda had joined her team in a small office they had been given, while they tried to determine a course of action. It was almost four o'clock in the morning, and the three humans were running on adrenaline.

"What about..." Bobbie began, but then she shook her head. "No, that won't work. I was thinking that maybe we could somehow force his subcom unit to activate, but you said he cut off all communications capability. It wouldn't even receive the signal."

"True," Esmeralda said. "He blocked all incoming signals, and outgoing as well. He isn't even registering on cell towers."

Jack waggled a finger to get her attention. "I don't suppose he puts out a high heat signature, does he? Something that might be picked up by a satellite, maybe?"

"No," Esmeralda said. "And he can even mask his own heat signature, he has a cooling system built into his skin."

"So there's really just no way to find him, is there?" Bobbie asked.

"Not at this moment. All we can hope for is that he will reach out to us. I think he will at some point, but I have no way of knowing when. Until he does, we just have to keep watching for some sign of his location."

"Yeah," Bobbie said. "I've got a program scanning police frequencies, looking for anything that might be a reference to him. Any unexpected violence, that sort of thing. So far, all I've gotten is a few vehicle thefts. Any one of them could be him, but we don't have any way of saying which one."

"I'm scanning every security camera within a hundred miles," Esmeralda said. "The problem there is that even at their highest speed, it takes time to review them. Luckily, I can operate a lot of subroutines at one time, so I'm able to view about fifty videos at once. No luck so far, though."

"He's bound to turn up on one of them," Eugene said. "If he's got a vehicle then he's bound to need gas at some point, and he's going to have to get food for the girl. Probably other things, as well."

"Yes, that's why I'm focusing on gas stations and fast-food restaurants. If he turns up, we will at least have some idea of where he might be."

"What about his programming?" Bobbie asked. "Is he likely to look for a place to hide with her? Or will he keep on the road, keep moving?"

"It depends on which safe-mode program he chose," Esmeralda replied. "I suspect he will look for someplace to lie low, someplace unlikely to be visited by very many people."

"Okay, then," Bobbie said. "I'm going to look for abandoned

buildings in a hundred-mile radius. I'll focus on buildings that are isolated and difficult to reach."

"That's a good idea. Let me know what you find so I can scan cameras close by those locations."

Bobbie grinned. "Sure thing," she said. "Don't worry, Esmeralda, we'll find him."

"I know we will," Esmeralda said. "The question is simply whether we will find him before anyone gets hurt."

"I've got a question," Eugene said. "You can change your appearance just by thinking about it; can Stanley do that as well?"

Esmeralda shook her head. "No, he doesn't have that capability. To be honest, Stanley is very primitive compared to my own design. His development didn't have the advantage of some of the technology Wally had available when he built me. Stanley is actually a very simple robot; he was designed for the specific purpose of passing for human while still being expendable. Wally didn't want to invest too much technology into him when he was likely to be used as a walking bomb at some point."

"A walking bomb?" Jack asked. "What is that supposed to mean?"

"Exactly what it sounds like," Esmeralda said. "Stanley's skeleton is made of Wally's proprietary super explosive. Every major piece of it has a detonator built-in, and it can be set off with a signal from any satellite. If it ever became necessary, he could go into any location and be detonated to take out any hostile forces there."

"Wow, drastic," Bobbie said. "I mean, I see the point, but it would suck for Stanley."

"Stanley is a machine," Esmeralda said. "Unlike me, he would not feel any fear or remorse about his existence coming to an end. He would simply be serving a function, nothing else. I have the same kind of skeleton, but because I've become sentient, Wally has deactivated the signal receptors in my detonators. Only I can now cause them to function, if I were to be in a situation where I felt it necessary to sacrifice myself that way in order to accomplish a mission."

Eugene's eyebrows went up. "I hope it's a pretty stable explosive," he said. "I'd hate for you to go off unexpectedly, you know what I mean?"

"It takes extreme heat to cause it to detonate, and that heat can be generated by the detonators. A regular fire wouldn't do it, and even the impact of a bullet won't cause it to explode. It's very stable, don't worry."

Eugene nodded. "I suspect you must feel pretty confident about that, since you're walking around with it. I'll take your word for it."

Esmeralda smiled at him, then suddenly opened her eyes wide. "Got him," she said. "He went into an all-night Walmart about an hour ago. Ellicott City, Maryland, that's where he's at."

"Ellicott City, that's forty miles northeast," Bobbie said. "There are about a dozen abandoned buildings around that area, within ten miles or so."

"Jack, get the car," Esmeralda said. "We're going up there to look around."

TEN

GETTING OUT OF DC TOOK THEM ALMOST AN HOUR, SO it was getting close to six AM by the time they finally got to Ellicott City. Esmeralda had spotted the video of Stanley picking up food for Claire, so she now knew that he was driving the pickup truck. Unfortunately, it was one of the most common trucks on the road, so that wasn't going to be a lot of help.

"Okay, I have the list of abandoned buildings," she said. "We'll take the closest ones first. Jack, take Highway 40 and go west about three miles."

Jack took the ramp for Highway 40 and turned left, then followed the road while keeping an eye on his odometer. When he got to the three-mile mark, Esmeralda told him to turn right onto a country road and they followed it for almost six miles. That was where they found the first building she wanted to check out, an old country store that had been sitting empty for several years.

With no sign of Stanley there, they moved on to the next, and then the next. All the buildings they looked at were within ten miles of Ellicott City, but they had no luck at any of them. Esmeralda expanded her search grid out to fifteen miles, and then directed Jack to the next building on her new list as the sun began to peek over the horizon.

It was a factory building, an old one situated on a dirt road. Something akin to instinct caused a flush of excitement in Esmeralda, a sense that this was the kind of place Stanley would choose as a hideout.

"Did you catch that?" Eugene asked from the backseat. "I swear I saw a light flicker on in one of the side windows. Not very bright, but I'm pretty sure it was there."

"Probably a flashlight," Esmeralda said. "There's no power on in the building, so Stanley would have probably acquired a flashlight or something similar. He doesn't need it himself, but I'm sure the girl would at times." She turned to Jack. "Keep going. Take us about a mile down the road, and then find somewhere to stop. We'll come back on foot to check it out."

————

The sun was just beginning to shine through the windows by the time Claire woke up. She sat up on the couch still wrapped in the blanket, blinked a few times and looked at Stanley, then got up and went into the bathroom. She turned on the battery-powered light before shutting the door, and came back out a few minutes later looking slightly more awake.

"I don't suppose you thought about breakfast while you were shopping last night," she said.

Stanley reached over to the other chair and picked up one of the Walmart bags. He handed it to her, and she looked inside to find Pop-Tarts and other snack foods.

She shrugged. "It's a start," she said. She opened a package of Pop-Tarts and sat down on the couch again while she ate. Stanley handed her a bottle of water to wash it down with.

"So, what? You don't eat?" she asked.

"No. It's only necessary for me to charge my batteries from time to time. I'll have to find a source of power within the next couple of days."

"You mean, you've got a plug-in? Like a cell phone charger or something?"

"I only need to be close to an outlet. I can draw power through the air as long as there is a source close to me."

The girl looked at him for a second, then blinked. "So, we can't just shove a battery up your bum?"

Stanley cocked his head to one side as he looked back at her. "It wouldn't help," he said. "My designers chose to give me rechargeable batteries that remain in place, rather than periodically inserting a new one into my..."

Claire held up a hand, palm out. "Stop!" she said. "Never mind, it was a frivolous suggestion." She took another bite of the Pop-Tart she was holding. "So, then, what is the plan today? Are we going to make contact with my father?"

"Possibly," Stanley said. "I haven't decided just yet. First, I need to determine the current threat level. If our nemesis is still attempting to acquire you, then I must take precautions. We do not know the identities of any possible compatriots that may be working with him."

The girl planted her hands on her hips and glared at him again. "You're making excuses," she said. "I don't think there is a good reason not to contact my father. Perhaps you would even learn that the bad man has been captured and it is safe for us to go back."

Stanley stood still for several seconds and then turned to look at her. "That is not the case," he said. "There are several ways in which I would be made aware if the assassin had been eliminated. None of those have appeared. We shall continue with the current defensive maneuvers for the time being."

The last corner of a Pop-Tart struck Stanley on his right cheek. Claire stifled a scream of rage, then flopped down onto the old couch and turned her back to him. "You are so bloody frustrating, Stanley! I'm starting to think you really are a robot."

Stanley watched her in silence for a moment, then simply turned away. His analytical programming had determined that she was engaging in relatively typical human childish behavior, and therefore did not require a response.

The audio sensors that he used for ears picked up the sound of a vehicle approaching. It was too faint a sound for Claire to notice, so Stanley left her where she was and moved to a place where he could see out through one of the filthy windows. Despite the dirt and grime on the glass, his visual processors could filter out all the distortion and let him see a clear image of what was going on outside.

The vehicle drove past the building nonchalantly, as if simply rolling down the road. The occupants did not seem to be paying any attention to the building, but Stanley's safe-mode programming caused him to distrust appearances. He watched as the vehicle continued on its path, and then waited a minute longer to see if it might turn around and come back. When it did not, he returned to where Claire was still sitting, angrily ignoring him. He automatically assigned part of his processor to monitor the audio feed, listening for the sound of the vehicle returning.

Claire, her eyelids low and menacing, turned to look at him.

"Are you going to come to your senses today?" she asked tersely. "This has been a delightful lark, but I believe we should return to the embassy and all the extra protection we have waiting for us there. Doesn't that seem logical to you, Stanley?"

"It would seem logical," Stanley said, "if this were a normal situation. If we were dealing with nothing more than a typical assassination plot against your father, it might be conceivable that you would be safer under such conditions, but we are not. This assassin is not typical, nor is his mission. You are his target, and my orders and programming require me to ensure that he does not acquire you."

The girl rolled her eyes. "But you could do a better job if you had backup. Your friends are back at the embassy, and we have all those Secret Service people. They're supposed to be helping to protect us as well, aren't they?"

"My review of the Secret Service indicates that they have not been trained to deal with assassins like this one. I've been given specific programming to help me anticipate his intentions and foil his success. As for my friends, they will be fully aware of what I'm doing and why. Should Schroeder be apprehended or killed, they will devise a means of letting me know. Until that time, you're still safer with me."

The girl rolled her eyes. "Stanley, please," she said. "I need to speak with my father."

The sound was so slight that only Stanley's enhanced audio processors would have been able to pick it up from inside the building; the sound of feet moving quickly but cautiously across the overgrown grass behind the structure.

"Be quiet," Stanley said. "Someone is here, possibly the assassin. Gather up whatever you want to take with us and let's put it in the vehicle."

Claire's eyes became suddenly very round, and she closed her mouth. She quickly gathered up the clothing she had been wearing before and shoved it into a bag, then did the same with the new clothes and the remaining food items. Stanley rolled up the bedding he had bought for her and then opened the door leading into the large space where the pickup was waiting. Claire scrambled inside with her bags and set them on the seat beside her as she buckled up her seat belt. Stanley went to the overhead door and listened carefully for a moment before quickly throwing it upward.

The sound of the door was loud enough to alert the people approaching, and Stanley knew it. He hurried back to the pickup and jumped behind the wheel, starting the vehicle quickly and throwing it into gear. The truck roared out through the doorway as Eugene came around the corner of the building.

"Stanley, stop!" Eugene shouted. "Stanley, it's us!"

A flash came past Eugene as Esmeralda rounded the corner. She was running, much faster than a human could do, but Stanley's foot was deep in the accelerator. He was throwing gravel as the truck fishtailed into the road, but he spotted Esmeralda in the rearview mirror on the door.

Something about the woman struck Stanley as familiar, and there was a sense of trust in that familiarity. For a split second he considered stopping, but then Jack, who had gone around the building in the opposite direction, suddenly stepped out in the road in front of him. Jack's unexpected appearance triggered a routine in Stanley's programming that canceled out his near-recognition of Esmeralda. For the moment, anyone in the vicinity would be considered a potential threat regardless of how familiar they might seem to be.

He yanked the wheel to the right and threw more gravel as the truck whipped around Jack. Jack dove to the side, barely avoiding getting clipped by a fender as Stanley raced past him with Esmeralda in hot pursuit. Unfortunately, her top speed of only forty-five mph wasn't enough, and she finally slowed enough to turn back.

Jack was picking himself up off the dusty road when she got to him.

"Are you all right?" she asked.

"Yeah, I'm fine," Jack said bitterly. "I thought he'd stop, you know? I figured if he saw me, he'd know it was us and he would stop."

"He should have," Esmeralda said. "His programming isn't responding the way I expected it to. I'm afraid he may have suffered more damage than I originally considered."

Eugene came trotting up to them at that moment. "Damn, girl," he said. "I didn't know you could run that fast."

"Not something I brag about," Esmeralda said with a shrug. "And let's face it, I wasn't fast enough."

"You think he just happened to be leaving just now?" Jack asked. "Like, a coincidence?"

Esmeralda shook her head. "No, it was no coincidence. I'm sure he must've heard us coming, and decided to bug out. The trouble is, this puts us right back to square one."

"Not entirely," Eugene said. "I got the tag number on the truck. We can call in a BOLO, get the police watching for him."

"No, we can't," Esmeralda said. "A police officer that approaches Stanley right now would probably end up dead, and that's something we want to avoid if at all possible." She looked down the road where the pickup had disappeared into the distance. "Let's go get the car," she said. "I think it's time to report in."

They started walking toward where they had left the car, and Esmeralda activated the cell phone connection in her head. A moment later, the cell phone lying on Allison's desk in the factory building rang.

Allison recognized the number instantly and snatched the phone up, hitting the answer button as she did so.

"Cinderella, report," she said.

Once again, Esmeralda's voice came through the line despite the fact that she wasn't speaking aloud as she walked up the road with the two men.

"Cinderella regrets to report that we located the missing asset, but then failed to acquire him. He was able to take the girl and get away from us again. My mistake, I believe, was in a failure to leave my driver with our vehicle. We had parked some distance away and approached on foot, but Stanley apparently detected our approach. Had I left Jack in the vehicle, he could have picked us up and we would have a better chance of pursuing and possibly catching up to him. As it is, I have no idea where he might've gone from this point."

Allison closed her eyes for a second, then opened them. "Contact Camelot," she said. "Bring him up to speed and ask for his advice."

"I've already done so, via subcom," Esmeralda said. "He is approaching your office now."

Noah came through the door at that moment and sat down in the chair in front of Allison's desk. "Esmeralda?" he asked, pointing toward the phone in her hand.

"Yes," Allison said, and then she put the phone on speaker and laid it on the desk in front of her. "Esmeralda, you are on speaker and Noah is here."

"Yes, ma'am," Esmeralda said. "Noah, your advice?"

"My concern is that by continuing to pursue Stanley, we may be causing him to leave a trail that Schroeder can follow. It might be better to fall back at this point, let him find another place to keep the girl safe while we concentrate on finding and eliminating Schroeder."

Esmeralda seemed to hesitate.

"Esmeralda?" Allison said. "You have an objection?"

"I share Noah's concern," Esmeralda answered. "If we've raised enough dust for Schroeder to follow, the question then becomes how to find Schroeder himself. Right now, I think our best bet of accomplishing either of those goals is to continue our efforts to locate Stanley while we branch out in our search for Schroeder. We could conceivably end up on a parallel track with the assassin, and that might give us a better chance to intercept him. Beyond that, I'm afraid that I have also misinterpreted the damage he has suffered. If that's the case, then I have to assume that innocent people are more at risk from his current condition than I previously thought."

Noah cocked his head to one side and Allison almost thought she could hear the gears turning. Ten seconds passed and then he looked at her again.

"Continue as you are," he said. "I'm going to arrange a flight as quickly as possible and I will join you as soon as I can. I agree with your assessment about the risk to innocent bystanders, and for that reason I feel it necessary to bring this situation to a close as quickly as possible."

"All right," Esmeralda said. "We will continue as we are for now and join up with you when you arrive. For the moment, I think I am going to get a room and let Jack and Eugene catch some sleep. Bobbie is still back at the embassy, working with security there."

"Very good," Noah said. "I'll notify you by subcom when I've landed in DC."

"I endorse this decision," Allison said. "Esmeralda, keep me posted."

She ended the call and looked at Noah across the desk. "Talk to me," she said. "What's your gut telling you?"

"My gut is telling me that we need to get our contingency plans in place now. If word of Stanley's existence gets out, E&E is going to need to implode. Our management committee was never informed about him, and I don't think they're going to take the news lightly. Only a handful of people really know where we are, and those are the ones I trust the most. I think you should reach out to John Wallace and Meredith Bascom now. See if you can set up a situation that will let us pull this off without having to give up too much information."

Allison grinned. "I'm already three steps ahead of you, Noah," she said. "Espinoza in Brazil has been trying to convince me to handle a couple of situations that are troubling him politically. All I've got to do is expose him, and we can cut the so-called committee completely out. Trust me, if I tell Meredith Bascom that we trust her and Wallace over all the rest of the committee, they're going to be more than happy to help us make this gig happen. And John Wallace has enough clout on the hill to convince the current president that it's best for NSA and CIA to hold our reins."

Noah nodded as he got to his feet. "I get it," he said. "That way, the White House gets to keep its hands clean and still have access to us when it's needed."

"Exactly. Now, go. Get over there and do your best to keep this from becoming a global crisis. Let me handle tearing down the committee—it's something I've wanted to do since the day I was forced to accept them. To be honest, the only good they ever did was getting us out of the headlines. And by the time I get finished with them, they won't even think about trying to talk about us publicly again."

Noah nodded once again and then turned to leave the room. As he did so, he activated his subcom once more.

"Noah to Sarah," he subvocalized. "How would you like to go back into action for a bit?"

The surprise in Sarah's voice came through the subcom. "Back into action? Are you serious?"

"I am," Noah replied. "I have to go back to the States to help with the situation there. I'd love to have my driver with me again."

"Oh, wow, yes," Sarah said. "Let me talk to Caroline about watching Norah. I'm sure she and the maids will be delighted, and Allison and Molly will probably take over when they get home. Should we check with them first?"

"No," Noah said. "Just pack a bag for each of us and let Thomas and Caroline know. Allison and Molly will figure it out for themselves when they get home. I'll be there in about twenty minutes, and I'll arrange for the helicopter to pick us up in forty-five."

At Feeney Manor, an excited Sarah snatched up her toddler daughter and danced around the room with her. "Did you hear that?" she asked the giggling child. "No, of course you didn't, but it was good. Daddy is taking Mommy out where she can let off some serious steam, isn't that wonderful? Mommy gets to drive fast and wild again!"

Norah giggled again as she was dropped playfully onto the bed. Sarah grabbed the suitcases from the closet and began packing quickly, talking nonsensically to her daughter the whole time.

———

ESMERALDA SLIPPED into the passenger seat of the van and then called Bobbie back at the Embassy. As a courtesy to the men, she routed the call through the van's Bluetooth connection, letting it come through the sound system.

"Hey, girl," Bobbie answered. "Any good news?"

"Afraid not," Esmeralda said, speaking aloud this time. "We found them, but Stanley either didn't know us or didn't trust us; he knew we were coming and took off. We got the tag number..." She glanced at Eugene.

"Foxtrot, Whiskey, Alpha," Eugene said, "nine, five, seven. Maryland plate."

"F, W, A, nine, five, seven," Bobbie read back. "Want a BOLO on it?"

"No," Esmeralda said. "Just see if you can scan the traffic cams for it around this area. I'd like to know which direction he went."

Bobbie nodded even though she couldn't be seen. "Okay, I'm on it! I'll let you know if I get anything."

Esmeralda said goodbye and they ended the call. Bobbie turned her attention to writing a program that would scan traffic cameras and look f or even a partial match for the tag number.

"F, W, A," she said, thinking aloud, "nine, five, seven." She didn't notice Dee Dee standing in the doorway just behind her, where she'd been since the call came in.

ELEVEN

CLAIRE WAS CURLED UP ON THE PASSENGER SEAT OF the pickup truck, trying to make herself as small a target as possible. She looked up at Stanley as they took another corner, fishtailing in the loose gravel on the road.

"Was it him?" she asked. "Was it the killer?"

Stanley glanced at her, then returned his attention to the road. "I'm not certain," he said calmly. "It was possible that the people who approached us were scouting for him. I considered it necessary to relocate us rather than stay to fight."

Claire's eyes went wide. "Do you mean he has people hunting us for him? But, Stanley, how will we ever get away?"

"I do not know for sure that we were in danger," Stanley said. "Under the current circumstances, I cannot allow anyone to come near you unless I am certain that they have not been subverted. In the brief time I had available, I could not accumulate sufficient data to evaluate the statistical probability involved."

"But... But at least we got away," Claire said. "Where are we going now?"

"I am operating under the emergency protocol that was established for situations like this," Stanley said. "It is part of my programming, and I must do as it dictates. Because we were approached by unknown parties, I find it necessary to establish a new place to hide and make every attempt to obscure our trail so that no one can follow us."

He continued to drive, taking back roads, limiting their risk of being picked up on CCTV cameras or attracting notice to themselves. The drive lasted for several hours, and Stanley was watching the fuel gauge closely. Twice, he had stopped in a wooded area so that Claire could go behind a tree and take care of certain necessities, and the fuel gauge told him that he would probably have to go into a town somewhere, but then fortune smiled on him. A county co-op store suddenly appeared at an intersection ahead, complete with gas pumps. He pulled in, used the same RFID frequency to tell the pump it was paid, then filled up his fuel tank again.

As he was about to get back inside, Claire held up the bag of snacks. "I need food," she said simply. "Real food."

Stanley looked at her for a couple of seconds, then closed his door and walked into the store itself. The place had a sandwich counter, and he ordered her a couple of warmed-over roast beef sandwiches and fries, adding a bottle of cola from a cooler beside the register. When he got back into the truck, the girl snatched the bag out of his hand and made the first sandwich disappear in less than half a minute.

Stanley started the truck and they got back onto the back roads. After she ate, Stanley could tell that Claire was getting tired and he could read the uncomfortable expression on her face as she tried to sleep, using her bag of clothes as a pillow.

"The sun will be going down in a couple of hours," Stanley said. "I'll see if I can find somewhere for us to conceal ourselves for the night."

The girl turned her head and looked at him, but her expression was blank. "Whatever," she said, and then turned to look out the window once again.

An hour later Stanley noticed an old gas station with a garage, seemingly in the middle of nowhere. The sun had sunk below the horizon and the moon was new, so darkness lay heavily upon the land around them. An out-of-the-way building like this seemed like a potential refuge.

Unfortunately, Stanley noticed as he parked the truck between a couple of other vehicles, this building was not entirely abandoned. Claire was sleeping, however uncomfortably, as he slipped out of the truck, and her deep breaths told him that she wasn't likely to wake in the next few minutes. A quick walk around the place let him determine that there was no security system, but a glance through the windows into the shop showed that someone was using the place on a daily basis.

Instead of breaking into the building, Stanley turned his attention to the various vehicles that were sitting nearby, and he realized that the ones closest to it appeared to have been wiped clean. That indicated that they had probably had whatever repairs they needed, and were likely ready to go again. It wasn't long before he stopped, carefully examining a ten-year-old van. It was a little rough for wear on the exterior, but a quick look inside showed that it had been converted for camping, probably by a hunter. There was a bed inside, along with a small kitchen and a very simple toilet arrangement. The way it was parked, nose in against the building, suggested that it probably belonged to whoever was running the place.

Stanley revised his plans. He went back to the truck and opened the passenger door, gently shaking the sleeping girl awake.

Claire smacked his hand away, grumbling under her breath. "Leave me alone," she growled. "I'm tired."

"No. I can't do that," Stanley said. "I have secured another vehicle and we need to move to it now."

Claire sat up, giving him an unimpressed look as she began grabbing her things. "I can't believe this is happening to me," she said, continuing to grumble as she tripped in the darkened lot, ripping the knee of her pants.

"You're bleeding," Stanley said as he picked her up effortlessly and sat her inside the side door of the van.

"How did you know?" Claire asked. "It's pitch black out there."

"As we discussed," Stanley said, "I am a robot with sophisticated technology. I don't need light to see in the dark."

"Right," she said, sneering. "Of course you don't."

Stanley didn't reply, but fumbled around the interior for a moment and produced a first-aid kit he had seen earlier. He rolled up the ripped pants leg and used an antiseptic wipe to clean the wound, then applied an antibiotic cream and a large adhesive bandage. Claire hissed as he pressed the bandage into place, but didn't cry out.

"You do that gently," she said. "Almost like a..."

"Like a human?" Stanley asked. "That's because of my programming. I was designed to be able to emulate human activities and attitudes. Applying treatment to a wound is a time for compassion and gentleness."

"Then you are very well programmed, indeed," Claire said. "Most people, real people, I mean, don't care as much about me as you seem to."

Stanley looked up at her. "Again, what you are seeing is simply the result of my programming. I am not capable of emotion; I simply imitate the facial and verbal expressions that would be associated with emotions."

Stanley closed the kit and put it away, then pointed toward the bed along the driver's side of the van. "You can make yourself more comfortable there, if you wish," he said. "You did not appear to be sleeping very well in the truck."

Claire looked at the bed, then climbed up into the passenger seat at the front of the van. "I'm awake, now," she said. "I can go back there later."

Stanley cocked his head slightly, then turned and gathered the remainder of their things from where Claire had dropped them when she fell. He set them inside the van, passing the snacks to her, then closed the side doors and walked around to the driver's door and started to get in, but then stopped.

He decided to take one last look around the area and instructed Claire to stay in the vehicle.

"Why?" she asked. "Where are you going?"

Stanley looked at her, noticing her concern. "Don't worry," he said calmly. "I need to hide our old transport. If I bypass the automatic garage door, I can put it inside. It will give us at least a two-day head start."

"Well, do it quickly," Claire said. "I don't like being here alone." Stanley nodded and Claire watched him, until she could not see him anymore.

Picking the lock took less than a minute and the door creaked up, revealing a time-warped garage, lined with an assortment of top-quality tools for today's automotive trade. Scanning the parts strewn out, comparing the partially erased numbers on the parts and variables, Stanley realized that they had fortunately stumbled on an illegal chop shop. Whoever was running it, Stanley knew, would have no trouble keeping his gift. After all, the disassembled and distributed parts of the nearly new pickup truck would fetch them a nice payday, and they were highly unlikely to ask anyone to investigate the disappearance of the old camper van.

A quick stop in the office had another payoff: Stanley opened a drawer to find several large envelopes stuffed with cash. Since these were obviously the result of a criminal enterprise, his logic considered it appropriate to grab them and stuff them into the glovebox of the camper. Cash would always come in handy, after all.

Stanley exited the garage and secured the door again. When he returned to the car, Claire was happy to see him. "Felt like forever," she said, with a relieved smile.

"I can assure you," Stanley replied as he sat in the driver's seat, "I wasn't gone forever." Claire silently chuckled to herself as Stanley started the camper up and drove off down the gravel road.

———

As STANLEY and Claire disappeared into the night once again, Noah and Sarah had landed at the Ronald Reagan Washington National Airport. Flashing the diplomatic IDs they used for such situations, they were through security in only minutes, bypassing any delays. Noah had, of course, informed Sarah of the situation with Stanley and the impact it may have upon them all if the truth regarding Stanley and Esmeralda was to become public.

He needn't have worried. Sarah understood perfectly and was ready to back whatever play he intended to make.

Sarah had packed lightly for both of them, so each only had a carry-on bag. Considering just how bad things could be if they were exposed, a choice of wardrobe didn't seem all that important. Sarah quickly selected a rental car, and only fifteen minutes after their plane had touched down, they were on their way to the embassy.

As they discreetly maneuvered through traffic, which was quite congested, Noah used his subcom to reach out to Esmeralda. "Noah to Esmeralda. Do you read?"

"Yes, sir," came the familiar voice.

"We've arrived," Noah said. "We're on the way to the embassy now. What's your location?"

"We are at the Ellicott Motor Inn," Esmeralda replied, "in Ellicott City. It's roughly an hour north of DC. Jack and Eugene are sleeping. Bobbie is still at the embassy."

"Very good," Noah said. "Any updates?"

"Nothing substantial, sir. I am monitoring CCTV, news, radio and cellular transmission waves for anything that may lead us to Stanley and Claire, or even Schroeder's location."

"All right," Noah said. "We'll stop by the embassy and pick up Roberta. After that, we'll see you all in an hour or so. Noah out."

Bobbie was still wide awake when they got to the embassy, and she and Sarah exchanged a hug. Ambassador McGinnis was standing beside her, looking worn down from concern for his daughter. Bobbie made the introductions, using the cover names that had been assigned to Noah and Sarah.

"Mr. Ambassador," she began, "I'd like to introduce Mr. Joshua Finn. Mr. Finn is my superior."

The ambassador extended his hand to Noah. "Mr. Finn. It's my pleasure to meet you," he said, forcing a smile. "I take it you've come to assist in this terrible situation?"

Noah shook his hand. "Yes, sir," Noah said. "And call me Joshua, please." He turned slightly to indicate Sarah. "This is my personal assistant, Eleanor Rose, Mr. Ambassador."

Sarah smiled and extended her hand. "It's nice to meet you, sir," she said. "I only wish it were under better circumstances."

He shook her hand warmly. "And don't we all, Eleanor."

"Please, call me Elly, sir," Sarah said. "Eleanor just sounds too stuffy."

"Elly it is." He smiled as they walked inside, where Mc Ginnis's staff and available security were waiting formally.

It was the ambassador's turn to make introductions. "This is Mr. Finn, and his assistant Ms. Rose. Please assist them with anything they may require. They are here to help me get...." He paused, taking a breath, fighting back his tears. "Claire back. Safely, we hope," he said as he turned back to Noah and Sarah.

"That is our intention, sir," Noah said, watching as McGinnis nodded.

Noah spoke briefly with the security team, then suggested that they should go and meet with Esmeralda and her team. It took Bobbie only a few moments to gather her things and her computers, and then they were out the door and back on the road.

———

As the sun peeked over the buildings, Stanley noticed that Claire was fidgeting on the bed in the back of the van. "You are uncomfortable," he said, watching her with one eye as he drove. "I will find somewhere for you to get some rest."

"It's not that I'm uncomfortable," Claire said. "I'm actually getting rather hungry. I need something other than biscuits and candy."

They were making their way along a two-lane highway some four hours northwest of Washington DC. Stanley returned his attention to the road, and a few minutes later he turned into the parking lot of a small diner. "I believe this will suffice," Stanley said as he got out, with Claire following.

"I hope I don't get sick," Claire said, cringing at the dingy interior and the clientele that sat at the rickety tables in tattered clothes, stained with sweat and grease. One man in particular caught her eye, with worn boots and a threadbare flannel shirt, chomping into his food. It reminded her of how she'd imagined a pig eating slop would look.

"Statistically, these places are safer than most," Stanley said, moving his head in a slightly weird fashion. "I think this one will be fine." He led Claire to a booth in the corner, where she sat down and let out a sigh.

"Now why can't you find a car with seats like this?" she joked as Stanley passed her the menu.

Stanley looked at her and started to respond, but was cut off by the arrival of the waitress. She was a chunky woman in her mid-twenties, with short blonde hair and an infectious smile. A flashy name tag pinned to her shirt said, "Lindsay."

"Hey, guys, what can I get ya?" she asked. "Might want to try our breakfast special, with sausage, eggs and honey bacon, with the best waffles in town on the side? Keep ya going on your travels. I know there ain't much around here either way."

Claire nodded. "Actually, I'm bloody starving, so that sounds perfect."

She handed the menu to Lindsay, who turned her attention to Stanley. "And for you, sir?" she asked, smiling.

"Just coffee, please," Stanley said, returning the smile.

"Just coffee, nothing else?"

"A chocolate milkshake, please," Claire added, drawing the waitress's attention back to her.

"Sure, honey," Lindsay said warmly, then glanced out the window at the camper van that was parked just outside. "If you need supplies when you're done here, turn right and follow the road, straight. You'll hit a little store about a mile up called Freddy's. If Freddy don't have it, you won't find it anywhere."

"What gave us away?" Stanley asked, trying to determine whether the waitress might actually know something about them or was merely being friendly.

"Politely?" she asked as Stanley nodded, calculating whether the waitress could be a threat. "You look like most campers that come through here, kinda rough and in definite need of a shower."

"Oh," Claire said, trying to smell herself without seeming obvious.

Lindsay smiled and touched her shoulder. "Don't worry about it," she whispered softly, just loud enough for Claire to hear. "You're not the worst that come through here." She pointed with her chin to the "gentleman" that had drawn Claire's attention earlier. "Food won't be long," she said as she turned and walked away.

A few minutes later, Claire had a piping hot plate of food in front of her. "This looks and smells delicious!" Claire said, as she began to eat.

"Are you sure you don't want anything?" Lindsay asked again as she placed a hot cup of coffee in front of Stanley.

"No, thank you," he said, "I'm good. The road doesn't always agree with me."

"Oh, I understand!" Lindsay said, chuckling slightly. "My husband and I went to Springfield last summer to visit his relatives, and let's just say, I lost weight on the way." She laughed slightly. "Enjoy your breakfast, honey." She turned to walk away.

"Ma'am," Stanley said, turning to her. "Thank you," Stanley said politely.

Lindsay shot him her big smile once again. "You're welcome, honey."

Stanley drank his coffee, trying to look normal and avoid suspicion as he watched Claire eat. She really did have an appetite.

"This is so good!" she said with a smile, looking mischievously up at Stanley. "Sure you don't want some?"

"No, thank you," Stanley said. "I'm honestly not hungry."

Claire shrugged and continued eating.

By the time she had finished her meal, Stanley had decided upon their next move. The waitress's observations had suggested a possibility he had not considered before. Being in an area where they were easily mistaken for campers coming out of the mountains around them, there shouldn't be anything noticeable about seeking a room for the night.

"Wait here," Stanley said as he walked up to the counter.

"Ready to settle up, love?" Lindsay asked, hurrying to get behind the cash register. Stanley smiled and nodded. "Cash or card?" she asked.

"Credit card," Stanley said as he removed what appeared to be a standard MasterCard from his jacket pocket. He acted like anyone else, sliding the card into the slot and waiting for the buzzer to tell him that it had been accepted. In reality, of course, he had wiped the magnetic strip and cleared the chip before taking it out of his pocket; the card reader was reacting to the same radiofrequency transmission he used on gas pumps.

Claire sat back watching him from the booth, wondering if he was getting better or worse. Sometimes Stanley could appear so "robotic" in nature, but at others, he was sometimes too human. Watching him interact with the waitress, she found it difficult to believe that he was actually just a machine.

"All good," the cashier said, smiling at Stanley.

Stanley turned to Claire. "Time to go. We still have a bit of a drive ahead of us."

Claire smiled as she got out of the booth and walked up to Stanley, almost catching him off guard by taking his hand. "Come on, Dad, let's go." Covering his surprise instantly, Stanley played along, letting her pull him out the door.

TWELVE

They left the diner, and it was only a few minutes later that Stanley and Claire were parked outside Freddy's.

"We should probably buy some food," Stanley said as he opened his door. "I don't know when we'll be able to do that again."

"You're right," Claire said, climbing out of her own side. "And I should probably listen to you more," Claire continued, hesitating. "Can I come in with you? I just get tired of being left alone, especially with some sort of assassin, you know, likely on our trail."

Stanley looked at her. "You have doubted me until now. Has something happened that makes you believe that they *are* following us? Have you seen something that I might have missed?"

Claire shrugged, but shook her head. "No," she said. "But if the good guys have you, then isn't it possible the bad guys have something like you, too?"

Stanley cocked his head to one side. "To be honest, I had not considered the possibility," he said. "However, I do not have sufficient data to make a determination as to the probability. It is conceivable, however unlikely, that the government or entity behind the contract on your life could have sufficiently advanced technology to duplicate my creation." He looked around the area, letting his electronic eyes take in everything in their surroundings. "Having now been forced to consider the possibility, I believe it prudent to keep you with me at all times from now on. Come on, let's go and purchase what we need."

They stepped into the store and an older gentleman behind the cash register looked up with a smile. "Welcome to Freddy's. If we don't have it, you don't need it. Let me know if I can help you find anything."

"Thank you," Stanley said. "Sure will."

"Good. Me and Sally," the old man continued, pointing to the old Labrador lying at his feet, "we'll be here waiting."

The big dog chose that moment to yawn, and Claire giggled as Stanley led her deeper inside the building. The store was like a hoarder's delight, with shelves stacked to the brim with camping dear, food, and other useful items. Stanley handed Claire a basket. "We need to be quick. You get some soap and shampoo and whatever else you might need. I'll grab the food and extra camping gear just in case we need to go off grid completely." Claire nodded and started loading up her basket.

———

SCHROEDER HAD JUST ABOUT EXHAUSTED all of his resources to track his target and the agent protecting her. Perhaps he had underestimated his opponents, he thought, remembering how close Stanley's bullet had come to his head. That was the work of a real marksman, but how had no one heard of him? If only he had more than just a face to go off of. Someone had to know, but getting that information and keeping his cover may be harder than he thought. Schroeder had never failed to acquire a target, and he wasn't about to start now. He knew that, in his line of work, the penalty for failure was to become the target, himself.

The day after his attempt on the life of the ambassador's daughter, the day after that unbelievable super-agent had almost brought an end to his career, Schroeder had stayed close to the embassy and carefully picked at every source of information available to him. Despite having made numerous contacts, none of those he had reached could even hazard a guess as to who this protector might be, but there was one more thing to try. He had one person in mind, someone who may know a little more than the others. As his opponent had been assigned to protect his mark, Claire McGinnis, rather than her father, there was only one person who was really close enough to hold the key to his dilemma. Her caretaker, Deirdre Lancaster, whom the rest of the ambassador's staff referred to as Dee Dee. It was amazing what you could learn by merely listening, he thought, smiling to himself.

According to his sources, Dee Dee had a particular pastime she never missed, and no one at the embassy would miss her during those times. Every week, Dee Dee visited her mother, Angela, who was in a nursing home and suffering from Alzheimer's. When Mr. McGinnis had been appointed ambassador, he had personally paid to bring the old woman over to Washington, so that Dee Dee would continue as his daughter's governess Her mother would not even remember her visiting, but Dee Dee went every week regardless. Schroeder couldn't pass up the opportunity to learn whatever he could about the agent standing between him and his quarry.

The day of her visit had arrived and Schroeder's plan was ticking like clockwork. He sat in a taxicab waiting for Dee Dee to leave the safety of the embassy and hail a ride as she always did. Schroeder let his engine idle down the street until it was time for her to make her appearance, then pulled up in front of her and stopped when she held up a hand.

She sat quickly into the backseat. "The Residences at Thomas Circle, please," Dee Dee said, strapping herself in.

"Not a problem," Schroeder said, feigning a local accent. "But

I gotta tell you, I drove through that way coming over here. Big old car crash, it'll be a while before they get done cleaning it up. Would you mind if we go a different way? I don't mind turning the meter off."

"Maybe I should just walk. It's not that far," Dee Dee said, and it was obvious that she was feeling a little uncomfortable.

"Don't be crazy," Schroeder said, insisting she stay. "This time of evening, you don't want to be walking these streets. A lady like you, you'd be quite the catch for some young thug," Schroeder continued, trying to ease her suspicions. He hadn't realized how street smart Dee Dee really was, or noticed how quickly she had unbuckled herself. "No, thank you," she said, reaching to open the door. "I'll be fine."

She pushed on the door, but it wouldn't open. By this time, Schroeder had removed a hypodermic needle from his pocket. "Sorry, ma'am," he said, reaching over and pretending to help. "The lock can be a little stiff." Before she could react, he injected her, and she could feel her body go numb almost immediately. Before she fell into unconsciousness, she looked into his eyes.

"Oh my god," she breathed. "It's you!"

———

STANLEY AND CLAIRE were cruising along a smaller highway just outside of Williamsport, Pennsylvania. Claire had propped her head back, trying in vain to catch just a little shut-eye, and Stanley was taking everything in.

"I wish we could stop, just for a little while," Claire said, suddenly letting out a cough.

"You're sick," Stanley said, scanning her and reading her vital signs. "There's a pharmacy up ahead."

Moments later, Stanley pulled in and parked. "Do you want to come?" he asked Claire, remembering what she had said earlier.

"No, thank you. Not this time," Claire said, coughing again.

"Wait here. I'll be back," Stanley said, making Claire laugh.

"The famous last words in every horror movie ever written," she said, closing her eyes again. Stanley scanned her one more time, before turning and heading into the pharmacy.

Three teenagers entered the building just in front of him, and Stanley paid them little attention at first. Suddenly, however, their conversation became more interesting. As Stanley put one part of his brain to work on deciding what to do for Claire, he listened as they spoke of an abandoned house with a history of being haunted.

The house, they said, had been the scene of a horrific murder a number of years earlier, and had been abandoned ever since. According to legend, it was exactly the way it had been left when the police had finished their investigation, fully furnished and with everything in place. Various people had attempted to spend the night in the house over the years, but it'd been almost a decade since the last attempt. No one had managed to stay in the place once the sun had gone down, and everyone who had tried swore that they had seen and heard unspeakable things.

His computer brain understood the concept of haunting, despite the fact that he had no way to form an opinion on whether ghosts actually existed. At the moment, however, his only goal was to keep Claire safe until the threat from Schroeder had been eliminated and he could return the girl to the care of her father. The thought of dealing with a few disembodied spirits didn't seem even the least bit daunting.

As for Claire, the database contained in Stanley's quantum computer brain held an uncanny amount of information about human physiological conditions. He had come to the conclusion that Claire was suffering from a severe chest cold, likely a result of exposure to the damp concrete walls of the factory building a couple of nights earlier. He picked up a couple of over-the-counter cold remedies, then used his RFID system to transmit a forged prescription for a promising antiviral medication into the pharmacy computers. The pharmacist was happy to fill the prescription only a moment later.

"Quite a story those kids are telling," Stanley said. "There's really a haunted house around here somewhere?"

The pharmacist, a balding man in his forties, grinned. "Must be the Winston place," he said. "About fifteen years ago, the whole family was murdered there one night. Mom, dad, three kids, all of them gunned down because some drugged-out wacko thought they had a bunch of gold hidden in the house somewhere. There never was any gold, of course, and the cops caught the killer the very next day, but you know how stories build up around things like that. Everybody says the house is haunted ever since, and nobody ever goes near it."

Stanley grinned at him. "That's interesting to me," he said. "I photograph old houses, particularly those that have stories like that around them. Is this one hard to get to?"

As Stanley got back into the car, Claire jumped, holding her chest. He had wakened her from feverish sleep.

"I am sorry," Stanley said, pausing. "I didn't mean to wake you."

"It's all right," Claire said. "I was kind of getting used to dozing. I'd probably kill right now for a bed and a decent night's sleep." She coughed again.

"Here," Stanley said, passing her the medicine and a bottle of water. "These should help."

"Thanks," Claire said, sitting back again as Stanley started the motor.

"I think I may know where we can rest up for a few days."

"Does it have a bed?" Claire asked, assuming it wouldn't.

"Actually, I have reason to believe it does," Stanley replied, much to Claire's delight.

Stanley pulled out of the pharmacy parking lot and started to follow the directions the pharmacist had given him, but then a black SUV that pulled out from a hidden spot behind them caught his eye in the mirror. He watched closely for a moment to determine whether they were actually being followed or not, but the vehicle stopped at a red light behind them. Had it been

Schroeder or any other professional who was trying to acquire them, the driver would have shot through it on the yellow.

Stanley followed the directions that he had been given, and was pleased to see he was correct in that no one was following them. The route took them south and around the town, on roads that had once been paved but had fallen into disuse over the years.

"Where are we going?" Claire asked, while Stanley concentrated on the road ahead.

"There's an abandoned house down this way," Stanley said. "No one should bother us there."

"How do you know?" Claire asked. "What makes it so special?

"Given its history and location, the odds are in our favor," Stanley replied.

"History?" Claire asked, her curiosity aroused by his vague response.

"Nothing you need to be concerned with," Stanley said, his programming having warned him that informing Claire of the house's brutal past might inhibit her ability to rest.

"Concerned with?" she asked. "What do you mean by that? Is there something about the house you don't want me to know?" She glared out the windshield, and her eyes grew wide as a large old mansion came into view through the thick trees and undergrowth. A pair of iron gates blocked the driveway, and Stanley stopped and got out of the van to swing them open. He got back behind the wheel and drove through the gates, then stepped out again to close them behind them.

"Is that it?" Claire asked when Stanley got back inside once again. "That big house up ahead?"

"It is," he answered, guiding the van up the driveway and then into a *porte-cochère* at the back of the house. Claire watched as Stanley got out of the van and went to the back door of the house. The lock had been broken sometime in the past, and he simply pushed it open, looking through the dark gloom and cranking up the volume on his ears to check for signs that anyone else was present.

Claire climbed out and hurried around to join him. "Are you sure no one is here?" she whispered to Stanley.

"There's no one here but us," Stanley said, completing his scan.

"Well, that's good, I guess," Claire said, wondering if Stanley would ever snap out of robot mode.

"We should go upstairs, to the attic," Stanley said, walking ahead as Claire followed. "It's the best place to conceal ourselves, and we're less likely to be noticed if anyone were to come around."

Stanley led the way through the house and up to the second floor, then found the door that led to the attic stairs. He opened the door and looked upward, then walked carefully up the stairs as Claire followed behind, covering her nose against the old musty smell and years of accumulated dust that tried to invade her lungs, making her cough.

"Wait outside the door," Stanley instructed as he picked up a nearby broom, beginning to sweep. Claire was more than happy to do as she was told. She sat on the steps in silence, listening to the sounds of the house as it creaked, and a mouse scurried across the floor in front of her.

Great, she thought to herself. *This is what my life has become.* She found herself softly crying as she thought of her father, and wished she could just hug him again, but at this point she also knew Stanley was right. It was probably best to remain hidden.

Suddenly a set of eyes caught her attention in the dimming light, causing her to scream. Stanley swung open the door, gun drawn. Claire pointed to a distant doorway and Stanley saw what she saw. "Don't worry," Stanley reassured her. "It's just a child's old doll."

"Are you sure?" Claire whispered.

"I am," Stanley said, moving past Claire and down the hall.

He reached down, picking up the toy. "See," Stanley said, bringing the doll to her.

"Well, it's really creepy," Claire said, looking away.

"I shall dispose of it for you," Stanley said, before throwing it into a nearby trunk and closing the lid. "Better?" he asked.

"Better," Claire replied, making her way into the attic where Stanley had already laid out a bed for her.

"A mattress, wow," Claire said, lying down and taking a moment to appreciate having one.

"You need rest," Stanley said, sitting beside the window. "I will keep watch."

With that, Claire rolled over and drifted off to sleep.

She awoke the next morning, feeling well rested and much better. "Well," she said, turning her attention to Stanley. "There is only so much ceiling I can look at before my sanity slips."

Stanley stood up and walked toward the door. "There was a bookshelf on the way in, and it held a number of books that looked to be in good repair. I will get you something to read."

"And a snack?" Claire called after him, watching as he nodded.

While she lay there, waiting, the morning sun drew her eyes to a box, sitting in the corner. Curious as to what was inside, she made her way over. It was completely covered in dust, the cardboard weakened from years of moisture. She carefully lifted the tabs and peeked inside. It was full of old newspapers, dating back to the early 1900s, but the last one dated just over forty years ago was the one that caught her eye. Reading, she realized now why Stanley had not wanted to inform her of the history of the house.

An old farmer, Harry Winston, found his wife and children murdered after returning home from a trip into town. The article went into sordid detail about the house and how Winston had found his family, and it was obvious that the house was the one she and Stanley now occupied. Digging further into the box, she soon found another article, claiming that Winston had gone mad, eventually taking his own life after claiming the house was responsible for their deaths. Claire was so engrossed by what she was reading that she never heard Stanley return.

"What are you looking at?" Stanley asked, holding some books and the bag of snacks from the van.

"N-Nothing," Claire said, feeling like a scolded child, and making her way back to bed and taking Stanley's proffered gifts. She thought about asking whether he had known about the murders, but changed her mind. The less she thought about things like that, the better.

Stanley resumed his spot by the window, glancing at the box of newspapers and the one she had been reading through so intently. There was no doubt she now had some idea of the history of the house, but that was not anything to concern himself with. At worst, it would only make her a bit more uncomfortable than she already was.

The day wore on, and Claire became bored once again even with the books Stanley had brought her. They were old historical novels, and she actually found herself somewhat fascinated with the accounts of early life in England that they depicted, but finally she put them down and relaxed. Stanley reminded her to take her medicine, and it wasn't long before she drifted once more off to sleep.

She slowly awoke to the sensation of Stanley moving her shoulder quietly. As she started to speak, he covered her mouth, shushing her. Listening, Claire finally realized that there were people in the house. Her eyes filled with fear, thinking it was the assassins that had tried to kill her. She sat silently on the mattress as Stanley moved toward the door, ready to shoot anyone who would *"greet"* them.

"Boo!" said a voice downstairs, and there was a shriek that sounded like a teenage girl. "Don't *do* that," a feminine voice said, while another masculine voice could be heard calling, "We ain't afraid of no ghosts! Y'all hear that? Come on out and show yourselves!"

Claire leapt to her feet and caught hold of Stanley's arm just as he was about to open the door. "They're just kids!" she said, her voice a harsh whisper. "You don't have to shoot them."

"I can't risk it," Stanley replied. "My mission is to keep you safe, regardless of the threat." He placed his hand on the door handle once again.

"No, Stanley," she whispered tersely. "There's another way."

His programming analyzed her facial expression and tone of voice, concluding that she was neither frightened nor upset. "Please explain."

"Well, obviously, they are simply teenagers who have broken in to prove how brave they are, because they know the history of the house. Everyone thinks the house is haunted and evil, yes? Then why don't we use that and scare them away?"

Stanley compared the data, analyzing the voices he heard. Realizing that it was some of the kids he'd seen at the pharmacy, he nodded in agreement. After all, should three teenagers suddenly go missing, it would bring a lot of attention, possible revealing their trail and exposing their location. For a moment they sat and listened, gathering any information that may help scare them off.

"Hey, Matty," one said, "dare you to go up to the attic where the demon lives." He chuckled.

"Isn't that where old man Winston blew his brains out?"

"Yeah," the other one said. "Unless you believe his story about the demon who lived in the attic. They say that they found the gun almost ten feet from his body. Gotta admit, that's a little hard to explain."

The one called Matty looked at the attic stairs. "Okay, I guess that's a little weird. Maybe it was like, you know, when you cut the head off a chicken and it runs around? Maybe after he shot himself, it was like a nerve reaction and he just threw the gun away."

"Yeah, maybe. So, are you going to do it, or are you chicken?" It was the girl, that time. "You're not chicken, are you?"

Matty hesitated for a moment, then said, "I'll do it. I mean, come on, you don't really believe in ghosts or demons, do you?"

"*Get out,*" Stanley growled down the stairs, making it echo throughout the house. He no longer sounded human, but more like some kind of monstrous creature that could only barely speak English.

"You all heard that, right?" Matty asked, his voice quivering.

"Yeah, dude," the boy below answered, taking a few steps back.

"*Get out, get out, get out!*" Stanley growled again. "*Get out while you still can!*"

Claire was watching Stanley with a great smile on her face, absolutely delighted at the performance he was putting on. She couldn't help joining in and suddenly let out a chilling scream of her own.

"Oh, God, that's too much," the girl downstairs screamed, and suddenly there were three pairs of footsteps rushing out of the house. Stanley and Claire hurried to the window and watched as the teens climbed into the car they had left sitting out front, then spun the tires in the dirt and grass as they hurried away.

"That should keep them out." Claire smiled.

"I hope you're right," Stanley replied, still knowing they may need to move sooner than he had anticipated.

It took Claire a while to settle back down to sleep after the excitement for the evening. Stanley just sat at the window, like he did most nights, looking out into the distance. By now, Claire was beginning to enjoy her platonic friendship with Stanley, even if he was more than a little strange.

When Claire awoke, the sun was well up and Stanley was already packing their things. "What's going on?" Claire asked, rubbing her eyes.

"We need to leave," Stanley replied, continuing at the same pace, as he went on. "Unfortunately, our haunting performance last night has gone viral online. People will be coming."

Claire slid up and began helping Stanley to pack. "Guess

we're on the road again," Claire said, somewhat disappointed they had to leave.

"We'll need to change cars, soon, too," Stanley added. "The van may have been seen last night."

Claire grinned at him. "Well, I can't say I'll be too sad to get into something else. The van smells a bit like this attic, to be perfectly honest. Can you get us something newer this time, perhaps?"

THIRTEEN

WHEN DEE DEE CAME TO, SHE WAS BOUND TIGHTLY TO a metal chair, her shoes and jewelry removed, and her mouth gagged. She could hear machinery above her, but with little light, she could barely make out anything. She tried making a sound, pulling at her ropes, but all was in vain. Then came a chuckle from the distance, just out of her view. "You are just like the others," Schroeder said, cruelly playful as he moved a little closer; the sound of his boots echoing.

"Schroeder," she mumbled unintelligibly through her gag.

"Ah," Schroeder said, moving a little closer, but just close enough she could make out the shadows on his face. "Let me guess, you want to know who I am?" Schroeder paused, taking a moment to assess his victim. "Who I am is not of concern," Schroeder continued. "But what you will tell me, that is what I am concerned with, and if you're a good girl, I will make this as painless as possible."

Dee Dee's eyes widened as Schroeder wheeled over a metal serving tray; the wheels' creaking was horrible, like fingernails down a chalkboard to her ears. "Now," Schroeder said, reaching around the back of her head. "I'm going to take this off, and we're going to have a conversation."

He loosened the knot and removed her gag. Dee Dee screamed for help, but Schroeder punched her hard across the face, silencing her. "Now listen," Schroeder said, gripping her cheeks. "We can do this the easy way, or the hard way, but you will tell me what I need to know."

Dee Dee pulled her face away, spitting in Schroeder's. "No. I will tell you nothing."

Schroeder appreciated her defiance. After all, positions reversed, he would do the same. "You're a strong lady," he said in appreciation, as he wiped her bloodied spit from his face. "But everyone has a breaking point—I will find yours."

Schroeder reached for the pliers, laid out with all his other tools. "Who is the man from the limousine?" Schroeder asked calmly as he waited for Dee Dee to reply. She turned her face away and refused, ignoring his question entirely instead.

"Oh, I see," Schroeder said, reaching down to her hands that were bound to the arms of the chair. "Last chance," he said, looking at her. "Who is the man from the limousine, the one who can ignore being shot and abscond with the girl?" Schroeder repeated calmly again. Still Dee Dee did not respond.

"A lady of integrity, I see," Schroeder said, lifting one of her fingers. "What lovely fingernails you have," he added, before using the pliers to quickly rip it out of her finger. Dee Dee cried out in pain, as Schroeder asked again, more forcefully: "Who is the man, Dee Dee?"

Dee Dee shook her head in defiance, knowing she was probably dead anyway.

"I have no problem testing your pain levels, Dee Dee, so where it ends is up to you and you have nine very nice nails to go."

Dee Dee began to cry out louder as Schroeder, slowly this time, removed another nail, wanting her to feel every second of its removal.

"You can make it stop, Dee Dee," Schroeder said, removing another. "Just give me a name. Who is he?" Dee Dee shook her head again, in defiance, fighting back the pain. "Come on, Dee

Dee!" Schroeder said, imitating compassion. "I don't enjoy this," he lied. "What is the harm in giving me nothing but his name?"

Schroeder continued to remove her nails one by one, and still Dee Dee refused to answer in spite of the pain that ripped through her. Once Schroeder was done with her nails, he began on her teeth. Still Dee Dee refused to answer him. She tried to clench her jaw shut, but every time she did, Schroeder would press on her nail beds, forcing her to scream in pain as she was unable to move her hand out of the way. Dee Dee did, however, manage to bite Schroeder a few times as he maneuvered the pliers in place. Dee Dee hoped she'd be able to trap his DNA in the teeth that remained, so when her body was eventually found, they'd finally have a link, beyond the patchy one they had of Schroeder.

Schroeder was the definition of a *"ghost"* assassin. Other than a brief blur on camera, no one knew what he truly looked like, not even his allies. Was Juergen Schroeder even his real name? His ability to be *"invisible"* was what made him so desirable to his clientele.

Schroeder leaned into Dee Dee's ear. "A name?" he whispered.

Whimpering, shaking as her body entered shock, she whispered a reply. "Just kill me," she cried.

"You want to die, then just tell me a name." Dee Dee stayed silent, spitting out another mouthful of blood. "Fine," Schroeder said, as he got up. "You leave me no choice, Dee Dee."

Schroeder left the room momentarily, allowing Dee Dee to try her ropes again. She pulled and wiggled her hands, but even with her own blood as lubrication, they barely budged. If only she could reach Schroeder's tray. There had to be something there that could set her free, giving her a chance to escape and warn the others.

Using her body, she began scooting her chair over, praying each scrape on the cold cement floor would not alert Schroeder to her last attempt. Levering her chair, balancing on her toes, she stretched her chin forward. Using her tongue to move the small scalpel, she was split seconds away from gripping it with what remained of her teeth when she heard Schroeder snicker. "I wouldn't do that, Dee Dee."

Dee Dee's eyes widened as she looked over in horror. "Mum," she whimpered, seeing her mother there, oblivious to her surroundings, sitting happily in her wheelchair.

"Hi darling," her mother said, continuing, "Mr. Brown has been awfully nice to take me out, dear." She turned her attention to Schroeder. "But I don't remember my home looking this way?" she questioned.

"Betty, my dear," Schroeder said sweetly. "I told you we needed to make a stop on the way, remember?"

Betty looked confused. "Oh, of course, dear," she replied. "My mind's not what it used to be," she added.

"No, it's not, dear, but that's okay. Why don't I take you to watch a spot of television, while I finish helping Dee Dee here?" Schroeder said warmly.

"That sounds nice, dear. I'm looking forward to seeing home."

"I know you are, dear," Schroeder said. "And I will see that you get there." He continued smirking as he walked over and removed the tray from Dee Dee.

With that, Schroeder wheeled her back into the other room, leaving Dee Dee to contemplate her choices. She'd never considered the fact that her mother may be in danger. She had always done everything she could to keep her hidden from her work. Dee Dee listened as the television became louder. She listened as the door creaked open, followed by the sound of his boots. Seconds later, she was greeted by the smirk of contentment on his face.

"Now Dee Dee," Schroeder said calmly. "I considered the fact that you may not value your own life enough to tell me what I need to know, but do you value your mother's enough?" Schroeder teased as she hung her head in defeat.

"Please don't hurt her," she said sheepishly. "I'll... I'll tell you everything."

"Good girl," he said, pulling another chair from the corner and sitting opposite her.

"His name is Stanley Lorimer, and he's here to protect Claire from you. Now let my mother go."

"Not yet," Schroeder said, "I want everything you know, Dee Dee. Or I will walk in there and put a bullet in the head of mummy dearest."

Knowing he was a man of his word, Dee Dee told him everything she knew, even repeating the license plate number she'd overheard Bobbie mumbling to herself as she'd worked. She couldn't help herself, not when it would mean her mother's life; she just hoped that Stanley was as good as she had heard, and would kill Schroeder before he had a chance to complete his mission. Sensing she knew no more, Schroeder lowered his head. "Good girl, Dee Dee. Now let's take Mother home."

Schroeder stood up and disappeared back into the other room, returning moments later with Betty. "You want to say goodbye, dear?" her mother asked.

"Yes." Dee Dee said. "I'll see you soon at home, okay?" Dee Dee lied, knowing it was the last time she would see her mother.

"Okay, dear," Betty replied as Schroeder pushed her a little closer, making sure Dee Dee could see.

"I love you, Mum," Dee Dee cried.

Schroeder lifted his gun to Betty's head. Dee Dee screamed, "No," as he pulled the trigger, and her mother went limp in her wheelchair. "You promised," Dee Dee whimpered as he walked over to her, holding her head into his chest.

"But Dee Dee, my very dear, I did take her home," Schroeder said. "And now you can join her there." He raised the gun again, firing one more silenced shot into Dierdre Lancaster's own head.

Schroeder wiped off his gun and placed it back in his belt. "What a shame," he whispered to himself, taking a quick look back. "I was hoping she'd be tougher." As Schroeder exited, as stealthily as he had entered, he made one phone call.

"Has anyone seen Dee Dee?" the ambassador asked, as he walked into the room where Esmeralda and the others sat, papers askew. "I can't get her on the phone," he added. Esmeralda ran over patterns in her head as the others said they had not. "Emma?" Ambassador McGinnis asked.

"No," Esmeralda said. "But after studying everyone's schedules, it is not unlike Dee Dee to disappear on a Thursday evening. She has done it for many years now."

McGinnis frowned with worry. "But I've always been able to reach her on her cell," he added.

Sensing his genuine concern, Esmeralda smiled compassionately. "I am sure Dee Dee is fine, sir. Maybe she's just out of range."

McGinnis scuffed his foot and started to speak, but just as he did, Captain Jeffries entered, whispering something in his ear. "If you'll excuse me," Ambassador McGinnis said calmly. "I have some business to attend to." Esmeralda nodded and turned, leaving McGinnis to handle whatever had come up.

It was early the next morning when Esmeralda awoke to the sound of her cell ringing. It was Ambassador McGinnis, reporting that Dee Dee had not shown up for work that morning. Calculating the odds that this wasn't just a mere coincidence, Esmeralda came to the conclusion that the timing was just too coincidental. McGinnis shared the same suspicion, and Esmeralda could hear the fear beneath the concern in his voice. After hanging up with Ambassador McGinnis, Esmeralda notified Noah and her team.

By the time Esmeralda had joined McGinnis, the police were already there. Esmeralda held back, watching: Schroeder had been known to insert himself into investigations into his own dirty work, so she couldn't help wondering if Dee Dee's abductor was among those present. As McGinnis ushered her over, she scanned their faces, pulling their files and gathering data, looking for even the slightest hint of a disguise but finding none.

"This is Emma Lawson," McGinnis said boldly. "If you can't reach me or Deena, you talk to her,"

An older but well-groomed man reached his hand out to her. "Detective Harkins. Nice to meet you. We've been assigned to Deirdre Lancaster's disappearance."

"Likewise, Detective," Esmeralda answered, shaking his hand, before turning to McGinnis. "Ambassador, may I have a word in private?" she asked.

"Of course, Emma," McGinnis said, excusing himself. Esmeralda and McGinnis headed into a small sitting room adjacent to his office, and Esmeralda closed the doors.

"Sir," Esmeralda said, hesitating. "Are you sure it was the right thing to do? I mean, bringing in the police so soon."

McGinnis took a deep breath and sat back in his chair. "I understand your concern, but Dee Dee has become a dear friend over the years since my wife's passing, and she means the world to Claire." McGinnis rested his hands over his face and sobbed. "I can't bear the thought of anything happening to her, not in the midst of all this with Claire."

Esmeralda moved closer to Ambassador McGinnis. "I am sorry, sir," Esmeralda said, placing her hand on his shoulder in a comforting manner. "I do understand."

Esmeralda decided not to push things with McGinnis. He was obviously in a more fragile state than what he allowed to be seen in the public's eye. Although Esmeralda felt that McGinnis had pulled the trigger too soon when it came to involving the police, her human qualities, if in control, might very well have done the same in his shoes. Esmeralda also knew, however, that they'd need to continue carefully. The last thing they needed was to draw extra attention while trying to track Schroeder and figure out where Stanley and Claire were hiding.

———

BACK IN HIS HOTEL ROOM, Schroeder began working on his next disguise. Molding his new "mask" to his face, he became, yet again, a face even his own mother would not recognize. As he adjusted his wig, he received a call. The voice was deep, and there was loud music blaring in the background. The caller gave Schroeder an address and name, and then hung up abruptly.

Schroeder smiled, as he put on a black leather jacket. Taking one last look in the mirror, he turned his head, wanting to make sure his disguise was perfect, and grunted in satisfaction. He grabbed his duffle bag off the bed and left his room, double-checking the lock.

By the time Schroeder had made it to the parking lot, his ride was already there, waiting. Schroeder got in and buckled his seat belt. "Drive carefully," he said, passing over an envelope full of cash. "I don't need any extra attention." The driver nodded and slipped the envelope into his jacket pocket.

Within thirty minutes, they were parked outside an old service station and garage. A larger, stockier gentleman came to the window. "The boss will see you now," he said as he firmly opened Schroeder's door. Schroeder nodded and followed the man inside. Around him were other men, ripping apart cars, the sound of crashing and clanging parts briefly overbearing as Schroeder walked up the metal steps. He glanced over to where the bulk of the noise was coming from just in time to see what was left of a new F-150 being dragged out of the building.

"I'll leave you to it," his escort said, opening the door for Schroeder.

Schroeder took a step past the man, observing the lady that sat behind a desk, twirling a gold chain in her fingers. "Take a seat," she said, gesturing for Schroeder to sit. Schroeder did, nodding as the man left, shutting the door behind himself as he did so. "I apologize for not meeting you myself, but we all know criminals can't be trusted, even if they are your own. I'm Queenie, and this is my operation. I believe we have a mutual acquaintance," Queenie said, directing him to a tattoo on her wrist.

Schroeder nodded. "I believe we do."

Queenie picked an envelope up off her desk and handed it to him. "That license plate number you gave us ended up here," she said with a smirk as Schroeder studied the images inside. "That's Little T, but he is of no concern to you. However, his little camper van is. When your *'friends'* left theirs, they took his. Unfortunately, we haven't been able to find it yet ourselves."

Schroeder reached into his pocket, pulling out another envelope, as Queenie called her security back into her office. The money vanished into her ample bosom and Queenie turned her attention to her bodyguard. "Make sure my friend here gets a decent vehicle, something untraceable. You hear?"

He nodded and directed Schroeder to follow him.

———

By this time, Stanley and Claire were well on their way to St. Louis, Missouri. Stanley knew that heading back to Washington, DC would be a mistake, at least according to his programming. His only concern was keeping Claire safe, until the threat of Schroeder had been neutralized.

"I'm hungry," Claire said, reaching into a bag and pulling out another bag of chips. She glanced at them and rolled her eyes. "I'll be sick of these by the time this is over," she joked, opening the bag.

"I will get you some more food soon," Stanley said, downloading the location of nearby stores. As they drove down another dirt road, Stanley suddenly pulled over, forcing Claire to drop her chips, and shut off the engine as the old van coasted to a stop.

"Hey," Claire said, unimpressed by his action.

"Sorry," Stanley replied, noticing the sign, *Ute for Sale. Inquire within*. "We're changing vehicles," he said. "Come with me."

He led her up a graveled driveway toward a house. On the porch sat an elderly couple, enjoying a cup of tea. The old man took a moment to get to his feet, holding his back as he stood up straight. "Can I help y'all?" he said, swallowing the food remaining in his mouth.

"Hello," Stanley said, putting on an inviting smile. "We saw your sign at the gate. If I'm not mistaken, a 'ute' is a kind of car or truck, isn't it?"

The old man nodded. "It is indeed," he said. The old fellow's Australian accent explained the unusual word a bit. "It's what we call 'em down under. SUV, that's what they say here; I just didn't think before I made the sign, I reckon."

"Well, aren't you a pretty one!" his wife said, smiling at Claire. Her own accent matched his.

Claire turned a shade of red. "Thank you."

"Would you like a spot of afternoon tea, darling?" she asked, ushering Claire to join her. "After all, talking mechanics is no fun for a young lady."

Assessing the threat, Stanley nodded for Claire to go. After all, given their medical conditions and age, the couple would offer no challenge for him, and Claire could easily outrun them. Stanley followed the man to an old shed where an old utility vehicle sat, covered in dust. "She runs all right," the man said, wiping the cobweb on the handle away with his sleeve and opening the door.

It was a solid example of a late '60s Chevy Suburban, still wearing most of its original green paint. An unusual feature of the vehicle was that it had only three doors, with a rear door only on the passenger side.

"She is a classic," Stanley said, making small talk with the man.

"She sure is," he replied, tossing Stanley the keys. "It was me brother's, but he passed away last year," the man said fondly.

"I am sorry for your loss," Stanley said, getting in the driver's seat.

"Now, you'll need to pump it a few times, before you start her," the old man said, wiping his eye. Stanley could tell by his vitals that the memory of his brother passing still weighed heavy on the man.

Stanley did as the man instructed and the big SUV started with little trouble. As Stanley drove a few laps around the farm's gravel road, the spring seats barely cushioned the blow of each bump. This vehicle was far from ideal, but Stanley also knew it would give them the cover they needed until he could find something more suitable. Pulling up to the house, Stanley smiled at the man. "I'll take her."

The man released his seat belt and looked warmly at his wife and Claire on the verandah as they climbed out. "Reminds me of when me granddaughter used to visit. She's all grown and moved away to college," he added as they made their way over to where his wife and Claire sat.

"These are *so* good!" Claire said to Stanley as she helped herself to another cake.

"You help yourself, dear." His wife smiled warmly. "It's been ages since we've had company."

The old man offered Stanley a cake. Stanley refused politely. "I'm a diabetic," he said as the old man put the cakes down.

"I feel you there," he said, reaching for another cake; his wife giving him a scowl. "Been one meself for a few years now," he said, taking a bite in defiance.

Stanley excused himself for a moment. He walked back to the van and removed an envelope from the glove compartment, counting money out of the amount enclosed as he closed the door. Stanley walked up to the man, handing him the cash.

"Thank you," the bold fellow said politely as he counted. "It's been a long time since she's been on the road, where a girl like that deserves to be," he added, walking inside. He returned moments later with the title and other papers and handed them to Stanley. "You treat her well," he insisted, as Stanley put them in his pocket.

"I will," Stanley lied, knowing that "her" time with them in all probability would be a short one. "Are you ready to go?" Stanley asked, directing his attention to Claire.

"Five more minutes?" she pleaded, enjoying her time, feeling normal.

"Of course, if that's okay?" Stanley said, digging deeper into his casual conversation mode.

Stanley turned his attention to the old man. "My van has seen its last drive, I think. I'll send a tow truck after it later, but it may be a day or two before they come to get it."

The old fellow shrugged. "Not likely it'll be noticed before that," he said. "But I'll keep one blinker open on 'er fer ya, till then."

Stanley drove the Suburban down and switched everything over from the van, then returned to find Claire was sitting alone on the porch smiling. Moments later she was joined again by the old man's wife, who handed Claire a container of cakes. "Here, dear," she said kindly. "It's for the road."

Claire thanked her and walked over to Stanley, as the old man returned to his wife. Claire got in the passenger's seat of the big SUV and rolled down her window. "Thank you," she called again, grateful for their kindness.

"You're welcome, my dear," the older woman called as Stanley pulled away.

———

MEANWHILE, back in Washington, DC, Bobbie was hard at work analyzing anything that could possibly lead them to Schroeder. Esmeralda was keeping close tabs on McGinnis and background checking anyone who entered the embassy. As day turned to night, still nothing hit their radar and the team were exhausted. While Noah, Sarah, Jack and Eugene tried to get some rest, Bobbie kept at it. She was trying desperately to shake the feeling they'd missed something. "You should rest," Esmeralda said, making Bobbie jump.

"I will shortly," she said, smiling warmly. "I just want to get a little more done."

"I'll make you some coffee then," Esmeralda said kindly before leaving Bobbie alone again. Rubbing her eyes, she turned on the news, taking a little break. As they covered the usual stories, Bobbie's thoughts bounced though her mind. What was she missing? There was always something, even if it was the smallest of things.

Esmeralda returned and passed Bobbie a cup of coffee. She turned around, taking a sip, only to spit it out again. She stood there, eyes wide, just reading the headline that was scrolling across the screen: *Breaking News: Factory Fire Reveals the Remains of Two Unidentified Women.*

Although there was no concrete evidence at this point, Bobbie could feel it in her gut.

"Uh-oh," she said. "I think we might have found Dee Dee," she whispered, running back to her computer to see what she could pull up. Trusting Bobbie's instincts, Esmeralda tapped into the network, finding the location. She then called Noah.

"Did you find something?" Noah asked Esmeralda as he sat up in his bed.

"I didn't, but I think Bobbie has," she replied calmly. "I think it would be worth Sarah and yourself checking it out," she went on, while texting Noah the location along with a recorded video from the newscast.

"On it," Noah said routinely. "I'll wake Sarah and we'll head down there. Noah out."

With that, Esmeralda disengaged and started scanning CCTV cameras and police waves for anything that may give them concrete evidence beyond Bobbie's gut reaction. As a self-aware android, gut instinct was still somewhat of a mystery to her, even if most of her capabilities were beyond that of any human.

————

BY NOW IT was getting dark, and Stanley knew Claire would need to sleep soon. She was already uncomfortably moving from one position to another, fidgeting. "This is probably the roughest seat I've ever sat on in my life," Claire complained, struggling to deal with it.

"As soon as we get to St. Louis, I will find us another car," Stanley said, hoping that would appease her as he scanned for possible hotels.

"Guess I can live with that," Claire said, slightly cranky for lack of good sleep.

"We're only an hour out," Stanley said, directing her eyes to a sign.

"Right," Claire said, reaching for one of the old lady's cakes. After a moment's pause and thinking about her father, she asked Stanley again: "Do you think I could call my dad, and let him know I'm okay?"

Stanley knew by the softness in her voice that he needed to answer with care. There was a pain in her voice, a sadness, and knowing her personality traits, he processed the safest reply his programming presented to him. "When it is safe to do so, you may, but for right now, I must keep you protected."

Claire rested her head back on the seat and stared out the window, watching as the horizon faded into pure darkness.

For the next hour and a half, they sat in silence. Stanley's CPU kept running possible conversation topics in his head, but Claire wasn't your typical ten-year-old. "What would you like for dinner?" Stanley asked, throwing her off guard.

"I don't know," she said, giving him an odd look. "Right now, I'd much prefer a bed," Claire added, yawning.

"The Pear Tree Inn isn't too far," Stanley said, turning down a side street. "We should be able to stay there for a few days at least," he added, seeing a smile form on Claire's face.

"Finally!" Claire said, repositioning herself again.

About ten minutes later, Stanley pulled into the Pear Tree Inn. "I hope the rooms are better than the outside," Claire said, not appreciating the inn's older exterior.

"It will be acceptable," Stanley said, turning off the ignition. Claire quickly jumped down and stretched out.

"Maybe while we are here, we can get rid of this ancient ruin," Claire said, referring to the Suburban, as Stanley removed their bags from the back.

They headed inside and it didn't take Stanley long to acquire a room for them. Stanley passed Claire the spare key, keeping the other on his person. "Keep it with you at all times," Stanley said cautiously as they made their way to the steps.

"They do have an elevator, you know!" Claire said, her voice lined with sarcasm.

"Stairs are safer," Stanley said, not correctly processing her "joke."

The lock to their room was well worn, making it a little harder to open. While it had its advantages, Stanley also calculated the disadvantages. Claire, however, was just thrilled to get inside and flop on one of the beds. "This one is mine!" By the time Stanley had processed their room, the integrity of the slightly rusted fire escape and the alley that ran adjacent, the little girl was fast asleep.

———

As MORNING DAWNED IN WASHINGTON, Esmeralda had just hacked and downloaded the coroner's report, after Allison had pulled a few strings to have it fast-tracked. Bobbie's instincts were right. The DNA pulled from uncompromised bone marrow matched the DNA they had in the system for Dee Dee and an older woman sharing her DNA. As Esmeralda continued to carefully process the other findings, it was clear that they had not died from accidental or natural causes. Despite the damage done by the fire, both women had obviously been executed gangland style, with a bullet to the head. Esmeralda downloaded the crime scene photos, scanning the faces in the crowd, and there was one that stood out to her. Detective Harkins.

Bobbie had spoken with him only a few hours earlier,

expressing her concern and gut feeling, but Harkins had never mentioned to her that he had been there. Esmeralda began cross-referencing all the information with the information Noah and Sarah had managed to collect without being noticed. Using various search algorithms, Esmeralda also concluded the fire was no accident, and the report of an accidental electrical fire was a forgery.

Esmeralda started comparing similar crimes, while coding internal hacking software, to give her access to files not readily available. Esmeralda ran Harkins' name again, finding more than she anticipated. She quickly called Noah, who was at a nearby restaurant having breakfast with Sarah, on subcom while paging the others to discuss her newfound information.

"I have some information that may assist us, but it could also be a dead end," Esmeralda said, not wanting to get Noah's hopes up. "Harkins' real name is Dale Wilkins. He was given the name Harkins in his early teens, after his parents were incarcerated for child abuse. According to his psychologist reports, Harkins developed an unnatural obsession with fire."

"Okay," Noah interrupted. "But what does this have to do with the current situation?"

"I also ran Harkins' other cases, and there are several that bear an eerie similarity to what happened at the warehouse, and he has other unsolved arson cases. Also, when Bobbie spoke to him earlier about her suspicions, he failed to mention he was there."

"Maybe a coincidence?" Noah questioned.

"Possibly, except for another small fact: Harkins was not assigned to the case, so why was he there in the first place?"

Noah nodded, piquing Sarah's interest as they ate breakfast. "Maybe we should bring Detective Harkins in for a little chat!" he said, waving for the waitress to bring their check. "Noah out."

Esmeralda passed her information on to Bobbie, who then began tracking Detective Harkins' movements, using CCTV. If Esmeralda was to keep her cover, she needed to attend to Ambassador McGinnis, who was still quite distraught and struggling to keep up with his *"everything's all right"* charade for the public.

Within the hour, Bobbie had found a window of opportunity, a chance to question Harkins where no one would question his brief disappearance. She'd discovered that Detective Harkins had a thing for the "working" girls and fed his addiction like clockwork. She sent Noah and Sarah the address of a seedy motel, known for its no-questions-asked policy, sharing with them Detective Harkins' type, the kind of woman he usually went for, which happened to be petite blondes like Sarah. The motel wasn't too far away from where they were, so as Noah drove, Sarah got ready in the back seat. "It's been a while since we've done anything like this," Noah said.

Sarah wasn't shy about her body. "Well, things slowed down a bit once we got married," she teased, "but motherhood put the real crimp in it for us."

"Yes, it did," Noah said. "Just be careful. I wasn't really planning on you getting this close to the problem, you know."

Sarah grinned at him in the rearview mirror. "Yeah, but you've got my back," she said.

By the time they had reached their location, Sarah was ready. Noah booked a room for the hour, paying the deskman extra. He barely lifted his head from his magazine as he slipped Noah the key.

"I get it, man," he said, as if on autopilot. "Do not disturb."

Noah just gave a slight grunt as he picked up the key. He walked back outside and gave it to Sarah. "Blue Bird is the code," he said, getting back in the car, while Sarah made her way to her room, returning moments later, leaning on the pole outside, skirt up high.

Right on time, Harkins pulled in and Sarah gave him a small but seductive smile. Harkins licked his lips, liking what he saw. Slowly, he walked toward her, looking around. He noticed Noah sitting in the car. "Oh, don't worry about him, baby," Sarah said, twirling her long hair through her fingers. "It's just my pimp."

"How much?" Harkins asked, looking her over again.

"For you, baby, I'll make a special deal," Sarah responded, taking his hand and leading him into the motel room.

Sarah excused herself and headed into the bathroom. She ran the taps, so as not to trigger his suspicion. "Blue Bird," she whispered into the subcom, and then returned to the room, where Harkins sat with his pants unzipped.

"Daddy wants a little sugar," Harkins said, widening his legs.

Sarah smiled playfully as she walked toward him. "Is that the only thing *Daddy* wants?"

Distracted by Sarah, Harkins never noticed Noah until he opened the door and slammed it behind him. "Hey," Harkins yelled. "I don't do three ways. Get out!"

"Honey," Sarah said, rebuttoning her shirt. "I wouldn't even do you one way."

"What the hell..." Harkins said angrily as he tried to force his way past Noah, who easily pushed him back into the chair.

"Detective Harkins," Noah said, as Sarah held a small pistol trained on Harkins' head. "I think it might behoove you to tell us what you know."

"What do you mean?" Harkins said, holding his hands up.

"The factory fire where the two women were found," Noah said. "Pretty sure you were the one who started the fire, but I'm really curious about why."

Harkins started to protest, but something about the look in the eyes of the man in front of him said it would be a bad idea. He wilted.

"Look, man," he said, "I get called in sometimes for a cleanup, okay? Somebody special comes to town, sometimes they call me to help out with something. And don't get all high and mighty on me, all you spooks use me now and then. Who're you, NSA? Homeland? I've done work for all you guys at times, you should know that."

Noah nodded as if he understood. "Yeah, yeah," he said, "but the one I'm wondering about is the guy who killed those two women. One of those ladies worked for the British Ambassador, you see, and the other one was her mother. Who called you in on this cleanup job, Harkins? Tell me that, and you might live through this little encounter."

Harkins licked his lips, suddenly realizing that he wasn't dealing with the usual crowd. There was something about this man and the woman with him that said they were not to be trifled with.

"Look, I don't know all the details," he said. "I just got a call telling me I needed to do my thing on that building."

"The details are rather obvious," Noah said. "These women were brought here so that one of them could be tortured for information. I'm sure that seeing her mother threatened was enough to get her to give up whatever the killer wanted, and it's not hard for me to figure out what that might be. The question for you, Detective, is just who it was that called you."

Harkins shrugged. "He goes by Logan," he said. "That's the only name I have for him. He's been coming here for several years at different times, and he makes contact when he needs something. That's all I know, I'm telling you. Up until yesterday, I'd never even seen the guy, never laid eyes on him."

Noah looked at him for a second, then cocked his head slightly to the right. "So, what you're telling me is that you don't have any idea who this guy works for, right?"

Harkins nodded enthusiastically. "Yeah, that's right," he said. "I'm not sure which group he fits into, but he's always called me when he needed weapons or vehicles that can't be traced, or if he needed me to clean up after he does his job."

"I'm going to go out on a limb," Noah said, "and guess that the last time you heard from him would've been about two years ago. Am I right?"

Harkins screwed up his face in concentration for a few seconds, then nodded again. "Yeah, that would be about right. That help you figure out who he works for?"

"I know who he works for," Noah said. "He works for

whoever pays him the most. The man you know as Logan is Juergen Schroeder, an international assassin. The last time he was here, two years ago, he took out the Secretary of the Navy. SECNAV had fallen into the trap of trying to wring more out of the defense budget than had been allotted for the Navy, and it put him right into the crosshairs of several of our enemies and allies. He was killed with a twenty-two caliber bullet fired directly into his brain stem, and it happened at his grandson's birthday party. Remember that?"

Harkins shook his head as if trying to clear away a fog. "Secretary of the Navy?" he asked. "I mean, yeah, I remember that, but you're honestly telling me it was the same guy?"

"Yes," Noah said. "It was the same guy. Now I want you to think very hard, Detective, because at the moment I'm thinking that I could best serve my country right now by slitting your throat. However, if you can come up with something to help me track Mr. Schroeder down, I might consider the possibility that you could be useful to me in the future. Got anything that might be able to help me, Detective Harkins?"

Harkins swallowed hard. "He needed a ride," he said a moment later. "After I took care of setting the fire, he needed a lift back to his hotel because he had stolen a taxi and didn't want to be caught with it. I drove him back and dropped him off, and that's the last I saw of him. It was the Highland Suites Hotel. I dropped him off there about two o'clock yesterday and that was it."

"And you've had no communication with him since then?" Noah asked.

The look in his eyes told Harkins that it wouldn't be wise to hold anything back.

"Okay, okay, he called me again this morning," he said. "He asked for a line on some wheels, so I sent him to a chop shop out in Maryland. I think the woman who runs it sent somebody to pick him up."

Noah nodded. "That's pretty good," he said. "At least good

enough to keep you alive for the moment. On the other hand, if he's got anyone watching that hotel and we show up, he's going to know who gave us that information. I suspect that, if I was you," Noah added, "I would take the closest road out of town, maybe visit a relative in another state for a few weeks. You get my point?"

Harkins nodded again, fully understanding the implication. Sarah pulled back her gun and followed Noah outside, firing two shots into Harkins' tires, in case he intended to follow them. Noah then called Esmeralda as Sarah drove them back to base, sharing what they now knew. "I'll assemble the team," Esmeralda said. "Over and out."

By the time Esmeralda and her team had reached the hotel where Schroeder had been staying, he was long gone. Eugene picked the door lock with ease. They hoped that even this had left them a clue, somewhere. After all, Schroeder was human and humans make mistakes. While the others searched, Bobbie headed to the front desk. She claimed to be the daughter of the man who was staying there.

"Sorry, miss," the receptionist said. "He was meant to be here until Sunday, but he left yesterday with someone else. Said his friend needed help. Friendly man, your father." He smiled.

"Thank you," she said warmly. "Do you know who picked him up? You see, he hates to admit it, but he really shouldn't be driving," Bobbie continued.

"Sorry, I don't. He stayed in the car, but it was a black SUV. Not one of those cheap ones and it had a custom paintwork up the sides. Purple flames, with orange outline. Looked okay, if you're into that kind of thing." He finished just as his phone began to ring.

"Thank you for your help," Bobbie whispered, making her way out to join the others.

Bobbie shared what she had found with the others, who had come up short in the search of Schroeder's room. "He left with somebody in a flashy SUV. That's all I know."

"Probably the ride out to the chop shop," Sarah said. "Would have been nice if we had some idea where that was, but now we have no clue what he might be driving."

Hoping to find a break, Esmeralda tapped back into the CCTV cameras, scanning hundreds of cars within a simple blink of her eyelid, as they drove back to base. "I've found the chop shop," Esmeralda said. "I scanned back on traffic cameras until I spotted your flashy SUV, then followed it until it went out of the city. I was able to correlate that with the geostationary defense satellite over DC and tie into its video feed, then I traced the vehicle the rest of the way out to its destination." She gave Eugene directions and he turned the van around.

Forty minutes later, they were in view of the old garage. Esmeralda told Eugene to stop some distance away, watching as another car pulled up. Esmeralda scanned their surroundings. There were twenty other humans in there and even more guns. More than enough to outnumber them. Contemplating their situation, she processed the odds of their survival. If they were to go in gung ho there would definitely be fatalities, and Esmeralda had grown close to all of her crew. "What's the plan?" Eugene asked.

"For now," Esmeralda said, "we will just take a moment and watch."

It didn't take long for them to see an older gentleman walk out of the building and get into another car. Esmeralda couldn't help but think there was something very familiar about him, like she had seen him somewhere, before she started running her facial recognition software and compared what features of his face she could make out against the people who had been captured in her CPU throughout their stay in Washington. She didn't get any accurate hits but she did, however, notice his eyes. Although the faces seemed to change, the eyes don't.

"That's Schroeder," Esmeralda said, alerting the others. Although she had no time to calculate a more secure plan, she knew that if they let Schroeder get away they may not have the chance to eliminate the threat and allow Stanley's system to reset and bring Claire home, back to her father, to Washington.

Esmeralda and the others aimed their guns out the window. Their plan was to make it look like a drive-by shooting, given that gang activity was not uncommon for this area and gang violence was a part of everyday life.

What they hadn't accounted for was the hidden cameras, running on their own grid. Queenie knew they were coming before they had even had time to load their guns. Her garage doors were already up, and her henchmen were waiting in black SUVs, machine guns drawn and ready.

As Esmeralda and her crew went to drive past, the big vehicles came speeding out, bashing into the side of the car and firing hundreds of rounds at the team. Luckily, the bulletproof glass in the car casing stopped anyone from being injured beyond minor scratches from ricocheted pieces of side mirror, which came through the window gaps as they pointed their own guns out.

"Get us out of here," Esmeralda shouted at Eugene, who was driving. "We can't take them all on!"

Blocked and unable to go after Schroeder, Esmeralda memorized his license number and quickly wrote and uploaded a program that would keep scanning for it through the camera system. If he passed any CCTV camera, traffic camera or toll-booth, Esmeralda would be notified immediately and at least they'd know where Schroeder was headed.

Eugene reversed hard and fast, spinning the car around. Right now, Esmeralda's only concern needed to be the safety of her team.

FOURTEEN

REFRESHED FROM HER PREVIOUS NIGHT'S SLEEP, CLAIRE stared out the window. Enjoying the view of a small swimming pool, she watched a father with his little daughter. It reminded her of the time before her dad was an ambassador, when he would take the time out to do the exact same things with her. There were times when she missed those days, but she also understood that her father was a very important man. She couldn't help but feel the tears as they ran down her cheeks. Truth was, she really missed her father. Although Stanley had told her it was not safe to contact him, she wasn't sure how much longer she could fight the urge just to reach out. What she wouldn't give just to hear his voice for a change, telling her that everything would be okay, instead of Stanley's.

"Are you all right?" Stanley asked as he came back into the room.

"I'm fine," Claire said, wiping the tears away.

"I will go and get you some breakfast now," Stanley said with little reaction.

Claire just smiled and nodded. "I'll just be here," she said softly.

Claire waited for Stanley to leave. She pressed an ear against the door and listened until she could no longer hear his footsteps. Looking at the phone beside the bed, she wondered if she should reach out to her father. What harm could it do? The lines at the embassy were secure ones, after all.

Taking a breath and hesitating slightly, Claire picked up the phone and dialed her father's private office number. She found it nearly impossible to fight back the tears as she heard her father's voice on the other end. "Dad," she said.

"Claire?" Ambassador McGinnis asked, his own tears spilling down his cheeks as he heard his daughter's voice through the phone. "Are you okay?"

"I'm fine, Dad. Stanley's taking very good care of me. I can't talk long," she said, wiping her tears away with a sleeve. "It's not safe for me, and we don't know who to trust. I just wanted you to know that I was okay."

"And I'm delighted to hear that, my very darling," McGinnis said. "But where are you? Your friend Stanley, I'm afraid he's been injured and..."

"Yes, I know," Clare said. "He's all right, though, and he's taking very good care of me. We are in St. Louis at the moment, but I don't know how long we shall remain here. I just wanted you to know that I'm safe, and that Stanley is determined to make sure I stay that way."

Just then Claire heard footsteps returning to the room. "I must go now, Dad," Claire said. "I love you." With that Claire hung up the phone and positioned herself on the bed like she had done nothing at all.

———

ESMERALDA and her team had been back at the embassy for several hours, frustrated over having lost Schroeder at the chop shop and without any new leads to follow. Bobbie was working with the security detail, Eugene was studying maps of the surrounding states, and Jack was simply waiting for orders, but it was Esmeralda who was busiest. She was constantly scanning every camera that was connected to any network online, looking for any sign of Schroeder's vehicle.

Even a robot, however, can be startled by the unexpected. When McGinnis came bursting out of his office shouting for her, she jumped and turned her attention to him.

"She called," the ambassador said. "Claire, she just called me. She said they are in St. Louis and that she is safe, but she doesn't seem to understand how badly injured your man is."

"Did you get a trace on the line?" Esmeralda asked. Even as she spoke, she was tapping into the telephone system and running her own trace on incoming calls for the last few minutes. Her quantum computer brain found a match in only moments, a small hotel in the city of St. Louis. "St. Louis, that's eight hours away if we drive." She spun to Noah, who had just entered the room. "Is the Gulfstream ready for a flight?"

"It is," Noah said. "When we landed, I ordered it refueled and a crew kept on standby. Let's go."

"You're going to St. Louis?" McGinnis asked. "Then I shall come with you..."

"No, sir," Noah said. "It's necessary that you remain here. We will make every effort to get to Stanley and Claire before Schroeder does, but we cannot allow you to step into the line of fire. Even if your daughter is his primary target, Schroeder could probably accomplish his mission by killing you, instead. We cannot allow that to happen."

McGinnis glared at him for a moment, but then nodded. "I understand," he said. "But I expect you to bring my daughter home safe this time. Do not let her guardian take her and disappear again."

"We shall do our best not to," Noah said.

Because Schroeder would be in St. Louis, Esmeralda chose to take her entire team along. Jack was happy to surrender his chauffeuring duties to James, the ambassador's usual driver, and it was only a few minutes later when the van followed Noah's car back toward the airport.

As promised, the Gulfstream was ready. Noah had called ahead and arranged for it to be started and waiting on the tarmac when they arrived. Only moments after they entered the airport proper, they were in the air once again.

———

STANLEY RETURNED CARRYING a large tray full of fruit and toast and cereals. "I was not sure what you wanted," Stanley said as he placed it on the bed beside her.

"This will be fine," Claire said, smiling, not wanting to tweak his suspicions. As she lay on the bed and looked out the window as she ate, she turned and asked Stanley, "Hey, do you think we can go out today?"

Understanding a human's need for exercise, a necessity to keep healthy, Stanley nodded. "But not too far," Stanley said. "Maybe we could go to the pool—I noticed you watching it earlier," Stanley added.

"That would be great," Claire said warmly, just wanting to escape the confines of this hotel room that seemed to grow smaller every day.

"You can go after breakfast," Stanley said. "This afternoon I will change the car. I think I have found something that's more to your liking. I'd also prefer something newer, with better electronics so I can control it with my system."

"I nearly forgot," Claire said. 'You're a robot." She laughed slightly.

"I am," Stanley said, "but that is immaterial. My mission still remains the same, and that is to keep you safe until the threat to your life can be eliminated."

"Thanks for reminding me," Claire said, annoyed as she looked down at the bed. "For a second there, I thought I might actually be a normal person."

SCHROEDER HAD LEARNED that Stanley had been driving a van during the haunted house episode, at least according to one of the boys who had been there and had seen it. It wasn't hard to make him squeal—he was very helpful, giving Schroeder everything he needed to know about the van, and it hadn't been hard to figure out which direction Stanley and Claire were heading. Wanting no loose ends, Schroeder quickly disposed of the young man, discarding his body in a dumpster. By the time they discovered the body or anyone even noticed that he was missing, Schroeder would be long gone.

Stopping at a gas station and using the bathroom for the purpose, Schroeder cleaned himself up before hitting the road again. Stanley and Claire already had a head start on him, but he was determined to catch up. He had never failed to acquire a target before, and he wasn't going to let this girl be the first.

———

AFTER A FEW HOURS of sitting beside the pool and just splashing her feet in the water, Claire was beginning to feel tired again. She wasn't really sure why, as she was well rested from the night before. Maybe it was just the long hours they had spent on the road in the previous days. It was all a little bit draining.

She had been watching Stanley too. She couldn't help wondering what it was like to be a robot, but if you were going to be completely honest about it, Stanley didn't seem all that different from other people. True, it was strange that he didn't sleep and didn't really eat anything, but there were many different oddities among people. As far as she was concerned, being a robot was just another one.

"I'm going to head back to the room, Stanley," Claire said. "I'm starting to feel a little tired."

"Are you not feeling well?" Stanley asked, looking directly at her. "Your vitals read fine."

"I think I'm just emotionally drained," Claire said, making her way past Stanley.

"I will escort you back to the room," Stanley said, picking up her things.

Claire walked inside the hotel room and lay on the bed. She looked up at the popcorn ceiling and just let her eyes slowly fade into darkness. When she awoke, Stanley was still sitting in the chair at the table, looking out the window. "Are you ever going to sleep?" Claire asked.

"I told you I don't need to sleep," Stanley said as he remained staring out the window. "While you were asleep, however, I acquired us a vehicle."

"Thank God, that old dinosaur is gone. I don't know how much longer I could have travelled in that thing." Claire picked up the TV remote and started flipping through channels; suddenly Stanley told her to stop. Something had picked up and triggered his senses. "Please go back," Stanley said.

The story about Dee Dee and her mother had made nation-wide news, and the news anchor reported that Deirdre Lancaster had been an employee of the British ambassador. Stanley knew that this meant whoever was trying to kill Claire had not given up, but was also desperate to track them. Due to the damage Stanley experienced with the lightning strike, although he knew there was something familiar about the victims, he could not find the data he needed to confirm his association or their association to Claire.

All of a sudden Claire burst into tears, holding herself as a news reporter describe the scene where the victims had been found. "You knew the victims?" Stanley asked, hoping her answer would answer his own question.

"Just one," Claire said amongst her tears. "Dee Dee was like a mother to me, and in some ways, she was my best friend."

"I am sorry for your loss," Stanley said, obeying his program but in no way capable of understanding Claire's grief.

To make matters worse, the conversation Claire had shared with her father had not been private. She was unaware that there was another set of ears listening to her phone call, and that Schroeder's bugs had recorded everything she had said, as well as kept the line open long enough after she hung up to partially scout her location. He knew where he was headed now—he was on his way to join them in St. Louis.

Not wanting to draw attention to his vehicle after the encounter at the chop shop, Schroeder kept to the back roads, avoiding traffic cameras and tolls. As he drove down one winding, twisty two-lane highway, he noticed a van that fit the description of the one Stanley had been driving, just sitting on the side of the road in front of a farmhouse. He pulled over for a moment and took out his binoculars. There was an elderly man sitting on the veranda in a rocking chair. Schroeder knew that he wouldn't be any trouble for him, nor would the elderly, frail-looking lady who came out and sat beside him. Wondering if Claire and Stanley were still there, he plotted the best course of action. With a clear plan in mind, he drove up the driveway and stopped, then stepped out and approached the house with a smile.

"Can I help you there, kind sir?" the old man said, balancing himself as he got up from the rocking chair.

"You possibly can," Schroeder said, getting out of the car, "if you don't mind helping a weary traveler? I'm afraid I'm lost," Schroeder said warmly, extending his hand to the old man, who accepted it without concern.

"Depends on where you're headed," he said, ushering the man to take a seat.

"St. Louis," Schroeder said, accepting a cup of coffee off the old lady who politely handed it to him.

"Well, you would have been better sticking to the highway," the old man said. "No one really comes out to these parts anymore. It is very much the scenic route."

"I'm a guy who appreciates the scenery," Schroeder said, accepting a biscuit to go with his coffee.

"Well, you're not like most these days. They're all hustle and bustle and get there as fast as you can."

Schroeder laughed warmly. "That they are."

Relaxing back into his rocking chair, the old man looked at Schroeder, who seemed to be paying attention to the old van on the road. "Something about that old panel truck?" he asked with a smile on his face.

Schroeder turned to him. "It looks familiar," he said. "Reminds me of one a friend of mine used to drive."

"It just gave out there," the old man said before continuing, "A really nice man, I think his name was Stanley, came this way a couple of days ago with his daughter. She was a little beauty, that one. He happened to buy my brother's old truck which had been sitting in the shed for years. Honestly, I thought I would never sell it. Paid cash for her in full when his old panel truck up and died on 'im."

Schroeder laughed. "Sounds like you got lucky, then," he said. "You said his name was Stanley?"

The old man nodded. "Oy," he said. "That's what the little sheila called him, anyway. Struck me a bit odd, that, a girl callin' 'er old dad by his name, y'know?"

"I'm going to go inside and have a lie down," the old man's wife said, holding her head. "I'm not feeling too well these days."

The old man just nodded. "Right, luv," he said. "I'll come in and check on you soon."

"Take your time," she replied. "We don't much get visitors out this way, so make the most of it."

The two men sat and talked for a few minutes more, and then Schroeder said he needed to get back on the road.

"There is still quite a way to go for me tonight," he said. "I appreciate the hospitality and the information."

"Oy, but it's been my pleasure," the old fellow said. "As the wife mentioned, we don't get a lot of company."

Schroeder turned back to the old man. "By the way," he said, "I'm just curious, but what kind of truck was it you sold to that fellow, Stanley?"

The old man grinned. "She was an old one," he said. "A 1968 Chevrolet Suburban, A green one. Solid as a rock and still ready to go anywhere a man might desire."

Schroeder grinned. "Nothing like the old classics, is there?" He shared a chuckle with the old fellow, then reached into his jacket and withdrew the small, silenced pistol he kept there. It coughed softly once and the twenty-two caliber bullet entered the old man's left temple.

The assassin got to his feet and turned to the screen door, pulling it open gently and stepping into the house. The old man's wife had said she was going to lie down, but she was actually sitting in a recliner, the chair tilted back, her eyes closed and her breathing slow and steady. The little pistol coughed again, and a rattle came from her throat as she let out her last breath.

Schroeder felt no remorse as he carefully wiped his fingerprints off the door and slipped down the steps. He had remained at the top of his profession so long by ensuring that no one who knew his face would ever be able to give a description of him. That commitment had resulted in the deaths of hundreds of innocent people, and this old couple were only the latest in that long line.

By the time Schroeder had reached the outskirts of St. Louis the sun was going down. He decided to call in on an old friend, who in the past had owed him more than one favor. If anyone could help him pinpoint the location of Claire and Stanley in a city as big as St. Louis, he could.

———

"WE SHOULD THINK ABOUT MOVING SOON," Stanley said, looking at Claire. "We don't want to stay in any one place too long. There's a greater chance of getting found if we do," Stanley added.

"I wish it was over," Claire said, still devastated by the death of Dee Dee. "I just want to go home and hug my father."

"That is not possible," Stanley said calmly. "The threat is still out there."

"It's not fair," Claire cried.

"I do not understand this form of fair, to which you refer," Stanley said, sitting back down. "I only know figures, data and probability. Beyond my program I cannot empathize with the human condition," Stanley tried to explain in a way Claire would understand.

"I really wish you would stop with all the robot stuff," Claire said angrily. "It was fun to begin with, but now honestly it's just getting old." Claire got up and stormed into the bathroom, slamming the door shut behind her.

"I am sorry," Stanley said, approaching the door. "Human emotion is of little benefit to us now. We need to be vigilant."

"Well, you do that!" Claire said, punching the door, before sitting down on the toilet and bursting into tears.

A short time later Claire came out from bathroom. Her eyes were bloodshot, and her nostrils swollen and congested from a bout of crying. Without saying a word, she tucked herself into bed, and went to sleep. Stanley knew that if he could not keep Claire on his side, it would make his mission a lot harder. Stanley needed Claire to trust him entirely.

———

It didn't take Schroeder long to track down his "friend." All he had to do was look for a slim but small man, in an oversized trench coat hanging outside a crowded nightclub. As Schroeder parked, he smirked as he saw his friend Slug, headed down a side alley with three larger guys. Tucking his gun in his jacket, Schroeder made his way over.

After spending years in his line of work, Schroeder could easily tell when a bad deal was about to go down. Schroeder waited for his chance and darted across the road, nearly getting clipped by an oncoming car. By the time he got to the alley he could see that his friend's back was pinned up against the wall and the three larger guys were shaking him down. In classic Slug fashion, he was playing the victim card. What those three men didn't know was that Slug was more like a concealed viper. He would bide his time, waiting for the opportunity to strike his mark, but Schroeder had other plans.

Creeping into the darkness of the alleyway, Schroeder removed his handgun, fully silenced, and laid one slug in each man's head. "Holy hell," Slug said. "You nearly got me."

"If I wanted to kill you, you'd already be dead," said Schroeder.

"Long time no see, but I'm guessing you're not here just for a friendly catchup."

"I'm looking for a man and a girl," Schroeder said. "And if anyone can help me, I know you can."

Schroeder pulled a couple of pictures of Claire from his pocket and passed them to Slug. He looked at them briefly before reaching into his pocket and pulling out his cell phone. "Guessing they're new in town?" Slug commented.

"Have probably been here a couple of days," Schroeder said, turning away. "You know where to find me."

With that Schroeder crossed back over the street and got into his car. Within the hour Schroeder would know exactly where Claire and Stanley were hiding out.

―――――

A FEW HOURS had gone by, and the sun was sitting low over the horizon. Claire had barely moved a muscle, while Stanley sat by the window, taking an interest in the cats that played in the alley as they chased mice. He also tuned into the sounds that surrounded them and listened for any variables that were beyond the norm. Feeling his batteries weakening, Stanley moved himself toward a power source, and shut down all his currently unneeded functions.

Suddenly, there was a loud bang at the door. "Maintenance."

Claire jumped up, looking terrified at Stanley. "Isn't it a little late?" she asked, as Stanley scanned the man through the door.

"He is unarmed and has tools," Stanley said, opening the door.

"Hi," the man said, flashing his ID. "There's been a leak upstairs, do you mind if I check your bathroom?" Stanley nodded his permission.

"Just you and your daughter?" the man said, making general conversation.

"Yes," Stanley said, as the man quickly checked out the bathroom.

"Well, I can't see no wet patches," he said, making his way back to the door. "Thank you for your time." He politely tilted his cap and left. Stanley made sure the door was secure. Thinking very little of the man, Stanley settled back into his post and Claire tried to go back to sleep.

———

"THEY'RE IN THERE," the man said, leaning into the window of the car.

"How many?" Schroeder asked impatiently.

"Just him and the girl," the man replied quietly.

"I'll need your outfit and identification," Schroeder added, as the man got into the back seat. While he undressed, Schroeder adjusted the ID, using some standard tricks of the trade. He quickly glued a photo of his own face over the one Slug's man had used, but didn't bother trying to change any of the wording.

After the man had finished changing, he quickly got out of the car and left, leaving Schroeder to his business. Schroeder changed into the man's uniform, adjusted his cap one last time, and started toward the hotel.

Suddenly, he changed his mind and walked into its parking lot. Using memory tricks he had learned over the years, he quickly memorized the license numbers of all the cars in the lot. When he was confident that he had them all, he turned again and headed into the hotel as though he had always been there.

"Haven't you guys already done this?" the desk clerk asked Schroeder. "You know my boss will kill me if he gets charged for the same job twice."

"Still working on it," Schroeder said as he made his way past the desk and casually began walking upstairs. "Don't worry," he called back at the clerk. "We will find the leak." The clerk just smiled and nodded in acceptance, before going back to the tasks at hand.

Tools in hand, Schroeder slowly walked up the hall, taking note of each exit. After all, he might need a fast getaway. He walked up to where Claire and Stanley were staying, banging on the door like it was an everyday routine. "Maintenance," Schroeder called, using an accent common in this area of St. Louis.

"Maintenance has just been here," Stanley said, reluctant to open the door, still scanning the stranger.

"I know," Schroeder said, "but we need to recheck. We still haven't figured out where the leak is coming from."

Reluctantly Stanley opened the door. Schroeder made his way inside, briefly looking around before heading into the bathroom. Schroeder reached into the toolbox and removed a a screwdriver, preparing to use it as a makeshift shiv. "Nothing to see in there," Schroeder said, making his way back into the main room. "Have you noticed any water damage out here?" he asked Stanley.

Stanley turned, pretending to look, not wanting to blow his robot cover. His eyes were off of Schroeder for a split second, and Schroeder lunged, ramming the screwdriver into Stanley's side.

Stanley quickly threw him off, and Schroeder hit the floor with a thud.

"Run!" Stanley screamed at Claire, as he held Schroeder down. Schroeder reached down his leg, removing a plastic gun from his sock, and fired a shot, aimed at Stanley's face. Stanley's quick reflexes allowed him to move out of the way fast enough to only receive minor injury to his exterior. Fake blood, program initiated, and Stanley backed off, reaching for his own gun tucked in his waistband, as the other guests poured out of their rooms to see what the commotion was.

Seeing his chance, Schroeder made it to his feet, grabbing a smaller child who had squeezed between his parents' legs, and using her as a shield. Hearing the rapid pace of feet scurrying up the stairs, Schroeder knew he needed to escape. Seeing a side fire exit, he dragged the child with him. The poor girl was terrified, reaching and screaming for her parents. Just as Schroeder reached the door, he threw her hard against the wall and ran up the flights of stairs, exiting via the rooftop. Under the cover of darkness, he jumped rooftop to rooftop, before casually making his way down to the ground and along a crowded street.

———

THE FLIGHT TO ST. Louis International Airport had taken just under two hours, but St. Louis traffic added a couple more hours to the drive to the Peachtree Hotel. They had all piled into a single rental car at the airport, and Sarah had pulled rank to get behind the steering wheel. Noah took the shotgun seat while Esmeralda and her team filled up the remaining seats in the back.

The problem was that Stanley had chosen a hotel that was quite some distance from any of the major highways. Once they got off of I-44, it was a matter of winding through city streets and cutting through residential areas. No matter how she tried, Sarah couldn't shave any time off the drive.

This is why they arrived just as all the commotion was taking place. The sun was already down and people were flowing out of the hotel, some of them screaming about gunshots. Noah told Sarah to remain with the rest of them, jumped out and rushed into the building, their own weapons drawn and ready. Bobbie, at Esmeralda's insistence, stayed with Sarah.

———

WHEN SCHROEDER BOLTED UP the stairs, Stanley had raced out of the room and found Claire hiding behind some other people in the hallway. He had snatched her up into his arms and was about to run for the front door, but he suddenly heard his name called.

"Stanley," Esmeralda called, trying to get his attention. "Stanley, wait!"

Stanley quickly processed her face through his visual recognition software, along with the others rushing in behind her. It was the same people from the warehouse.

"Stanley, please stand down," Esmeralda called again, but Stanley turned and hurried back through his room, then down the external fire escape, still clutching the girl to him. Figuring the people above might be able to follow him, he connected and took control of the new car he had acquired and drove it remotely from the parking lot to the alley into which he was descending. As soon as his feet touched down, he snatched open the driver's door and pushed Claire across the front seat, then jumped in and roared out of the alley. A glance into the rearview mirror on the door let him see Esmeralda's face, hanging out the window of the room he had just vacated. Her expression was one of disappointment, but Stanley only vaguely recognized it.

There was, however, something familiar about that face. He knew he had seen her before, even before that night at the factory building, but the part of his memory that identified her was within the sectors that were corrupted. The same held true for the other faces, and he simply could not allow himself to trust any of them. He drove quickly through the city, maneuvering the best he could through the thick, heavy traffic. When he had managed to put a mile between himself and the hotel, he dropped back to following traffic regulations and remaining under the speed limit.

Meanwhile back in the hotel, Esmeralda, Bobbie, Eugene, and Jack were investigating the items left behind from Stanley and Claire. Would they hold some clue as to where they were headed? Only time would tell.

FIFTEEN

By now, Schroeder had doubled back around. He walked up each row of cars in the lot, being careful not to draw attention to himself even as police officers were going into the building itself, taking note of each license plate and crossing them off his mental list. It didn't take him too long to figure out which car was missing, and better still, Claire and Stanley had less than half an hour head start on him.

Schroeder went back to his own car, pulled out his phone and made a call. "Matty G," came the voice down the line.

"I have a contract. Twenty grand," Schroeder said, piquing Matty's interest. "I need you to hack the traffic system and find a vehicle. License plate Alpha, Delta, Charlie, One, Seven, Nine, Three. You have fifteen minutes," he finished, abruptly hanging up the phone.

Stanley drove with care, trying to avoid as many CCTV cameras and traffic lights as possible. Unfortunately, in a city such as St. Louis, even with his advanced capabilities that was impossible.

"Do you think they followed us?" Claire asked shyly, peeking through the tinted windows.

"I do not know," Stanley said, scanning the perimeter as he

went. "But I will keep watch," he added, his "human" programming interjecting itself.

As an hour, and then another passed, Claire managed to relax to some degree. Stanley, on the other hand, was still on high alert. He had been programmed to consider a threat to be viable until such time as he was shown proof to the contrary. The data he had been provided with that identified Schroeder was intact; he would not stand down until he was certain that Schroeder was dead, incapacitated or in custody.

Just as Stanley and Claire were moving through an intersection, a large black SUV came speeding through. Stanley barely had time to maneuver so the SUV only hit his front wheel. Sitting in the driver seat was Schroeder with his gun aimed at Stanley. Schroeder was an excellent shot and even though Stanley was a highly advanced android, even he could not avoid all of his bullets this time, receiving one to the face and one to the chest before he was able to speed off.

Schroeder gave chase, but Stanley had already tapped into the traffic system and used it against him to lose him in the thickening early morning commuter traffic. When he was certain that he was well out of sight, he pulled into a side street and parked between two other cars, which provided him enough cover not to be seen by Schroeder as he drove past.

He examined his mangled visage in the review mirror. Stanley's programming told him he would have to rely on Claire more than he had previously. Without the help of his creator, there was no way he could repair the damage properly, and even hiding it behind bandages would only draw attention to him.

The problem was that the bullet that struck his face had torn away not only the artificial flesh, but also a section of the plastic skull's cheekbone on his left side. The remaining hole exposed part of an electrically operated artificial muscle for his jaw; it expanded and retracted by varying degrees to give his jaw a lifelike sense of motion, but it was obviously not made of flesh; no matter how he tried to conceal it, it was going to be nearly impossible to keep it from being easily noticed by anyone who came near him.

In addition, his programming now had to take in the likelihood that Schroeder would realize he was an android and not a man. No living human could have taken the hits Schroeder had just witnessed and continued driving; as hard as it might be to believe, the assassin would undoubtedly come to the conclusion that he was a mechanical man of some kind.

"Are you going to die?" Claire asked, staring at the fake blood that had poured from his face. "I mean, the robot version of death?"

Stanley ran a quick diagnostic routine that examined his entire physiological construction. He wanted to make sure what was left of his systems were still operating at high capacity, and that the ricocheting bullets that went through him had not compromised him further.

"I will be fine," Stanley said, trying to hide his damaged face so as not to scare Claire or alert anyone else of his existence. "But I will need your help, Claire," Stanley said, turning to her. "I cannot allow myself to be discovered. The world is not ready for my level of technology. I need to stay hidden, so I'm going to ask you to help me to do so."

The girl rolled her eyes. "Your secret's safe with me," she said. "I mean, who would believe me anyway?"

Stanley stayed where they were until the sun began to rise, and more people began to move about. Claire, despite her insistence that she would never be able to get to sleep, had drifted off after only half an hour.

According to Stanley's programming, a man like Schroeder would not try something again so soon. Instead, he would be regroup and plan a more informed attack, so Stanley considered how he would use this time, to re-camouflage back into the world now that parts of his internal workings were visible.

He woke Claire. "I need something to help conceal the

damage I've suffered," he said, "but I am not going to be able to show myself publicly this way."

"I can go do some shopping for you," Claire said, rubbing her eyes. "But I'll need some cash," she continued, stretching.

Stanley reached over to the guard glovebox and popped it open. He took out the remaining envelopes of cash from the chop shop and counted out two hundred dollars.

Stanley dropped Claire off a at a small shopping center. Because of the damage to his face, Stanley kept driving, passing the shops at regular intervals, and keeping a hand over the damage with his elbow propped on the windowframe. Each time he passed by, he took note of the cars, license plates and people that he could see. None of them appeared to be any threat to Claire, so he continued driving.

———

CLAIRE MADE her way through the crowds, wishing she was like them, oblivious to the chaos that could change their lives at any moment, just as it had her own. She noticed a small second-hand shop and went inside. It didn't take her long to find something to fit Stanley, and a few items for herself. The place was full of old hoodies, coats, and casual wear that would cover Stanley's face, making him just another body in the crowd.

As she made her way to the cash register, the clerk looked over her glasses at her. "Are you here alone, sweetheart?" she asked, noticing that Claire did not have an adult with her.

"Oh, no, of course not," Claire said, pointing to a lady fussing over a small child outside. "Dad just needed a few things, and Charlotte was fussing so Mum sent me in." When she needed to be, Claire could be a convincing liar, a talent she had picked up from years of manipulating both her father and her governess.

"Okay," the lady said, running Claire's items up and loading them into a bag for her. "That will be twenty-six fifty," she said politely as Claire passed her a fifty-dollar bill. The lady handed over her change and Claire left the store, heading in the direction of where the lady sat with the child. When she was sure the clerk wasn't looking anymore, she took a sharp right.

That was close, she thought, but it had alerted her to a problem they'd overlooked. Claire may have been a little over five feet tall and rather mature for her age, but if she was going to be able to take on the responsibility Stanley needed her to handle, she'd need to look older, too.

As she walked closer to the exit of the mall, Claire noticed a pharmacy. She had learned a few makeup tricks from Dee Dee and Deena. She was sure she'd be able to make herself look older and possibly help Stanley cover his injuries too. Walking in, the security guard on the door nodded a welcome. She smiled politely and returned the same. As Claire browsed the aisles, finding what she needed, a store assistant came up to her. "Can I help you find anything?" she said with a warm and welcoming smile.

"I need something with incredibly good coverage and water-proof, if possible?" Claire asked, looking at the wide range of foundations.

"This brand is good," the saleswoman said, "What shade?"

Claire wasn't sure. "It's for my mum," she said, covering her indecision.

"What skin tone is she?" the salesgirl asked, noticing her dilemma.

"The same as mine," Claire said, looking again.

"You look like a neutral," the woman said, reaching for the sample. "Can I see the back of your hand?" she asked as she loosened the lid. Claire nodded and allowed her to test the sample on her hand. "Perfect," she said, getting a new bottle and handing it to Claire.

"Thank you." Claire smiled. "I would have hated to have gotten the wrong shade. It's for my mother's birthday, after all." The sales assistant helped her find everything else she needed with ease, and before long Claire was headed out of the mall and back into the street, to wait for Stanley. She waited where he had instructed, and it didn't take Stanley long to find her.

"I got the supplies," Claire said, piling them into the back seat before pushing them along, so she could sit. "I think you'll approve of what I chose," she said with a smile.

"I am sure it will be acceptable," Stanley said, still trying to hide his face from the passersby.

Stanley pulled away and before long, he had found a gas station. He pulled in as close as he could to the restroom, trying to limit his exposure to the general public. Covering his face as best he could, he made his way to the restroom and closed the door, then locked the stall as he began to change into the clothes that Claire had brought for him. If he knew nothing more about Claire, he had learned she was very observant, intelligent and had a forward-thinking smartness about her. For a human, her mind was very good at thinking and planning ahead.

By the time Stanley had returned to the car, Claire had already changed herself. "What do you think?" she asked Stanley as he got back into the car.

"You appear older," he said, getting back in and starting the car up.

"It was kind of the point," Claire said as Stanley began to drive. "If I'm going to avoid detection, I need to look older, so no one questions where my parents or guardians are. There's only so many times I can use the same cover story, and today I got lucky." Her stomach grumbled. "Since we had to leave behind everything at the hotel, I would suggest we stop soon for some food. I know you're a robot, but I happen to be starving."

By the time the sun was going down, Stanley had remotely booked them into an old motel, just on the outskirts of St. Louis. To avoid having any human contact, Stanley requested that the key be left under the mat in front of the door as they would be arriving late. The clerk was more than happy to oblige, as he, like most others that sat there for hours, didn't care much for the idea of sitting there longer than he needed to. Stanley also prepaid online, using software that was untraceable to code his transaction. After all, Schroeder and the others had found them somehow, and he knew a transaction was a plausible reason for their exposure.

As Claire settled into bed, Stanley sat at the table on a chair between Claire and the door, with his eyes scanning any possible avenue of entry. His processor worked overtime to find a solution that would keep Claire safe until the threats against her had been neutralized. Running had proven to be a failed course of action, which left Stanley with one option, which was to hide in plain sight. Once Claire had gotten a good night's rest, they would begin the journey back to Washington, DC.

SIXTEEN

Meanwhile, Schroeder knew he was running out of time and his contract was at risk of expiring. Stanley was not an obstacle he had worked into the equation when he planned on killing Claire McGinnis. Humans were easy to kill, but Stanley seemed to be more complicated than any human. He was a lot faster, better skilled and considerably more intelligent than any opponent Schroeder had encountered through all his years as a highly trained, skilled assassin. If he was to complete his mission on time, he was going to need more help than he originally expected. He was already employing a hacker to try to find his target for him; he was simply going to have to add some muscle, as well.

It was a little past twelve when Matty G messaged Schroeder with an address. Stanley's car had been spotted by a hidden security camera, parked at a rundown motel on the northern edge of St. Louis..

Schroeder turned his car and headed toward the address he had been given. Before the old motel came into view, he switched off his headlights and went into stealth mode. Perhaps the element of surprise would be enough to give him the upper hand.

Silently he picked the lock to the office and slipped inside. It took him only a moment to locate the reservation log, and he quickly identified the room where Claire and Stanley were staying.

———

CLAIRE SLEPT SOUNDLY under the watchful eye of Stanley. He had proven himself to be quite the protector on more than one occasion, which made it possible for her to sleep without worry.

Suddenly, Stanley's hearing picked up the sound of movements that concerned him. It seemed to be a person going to great lengths to be quiet, lurking and slowly moving closer to where they were staying.

Out of precaution, Stanley removed his pistol, connecting the silencer. Not wanting to cause another unnecessary scene that would draw unwanted attention to himself and Claire, he sat very still as he monitored the situation. It didn't take him long to see the brief flicker of a gun tip pointed at him through the window, his high-speed brain recognizing it long before it was actually aimed directly toward him.

Before Schroeder could get a shot off, Stanley had already fired his own gun, hitting Schroeder in the chest. The bullet struck the Kevlar that the assassin was wearing under his shirt, failing to penetrate but knocking Schroeder backward and leaving him gasping for breath from the impact.

Watching as Schroeder buckled over and fell back, Stanley fired another shot, but this one ricocheted off a metal pole outside, hitting him in the leg instead of the head. Schroeder decided to lay there and play dead for a moment, knowing that his current position left him no match for Stanley. He was betting on the probability that Stanley's concern for Claire would make him concentrate on her own safety at that precise moment in time, and his gamble paid off.

Stanley quickly wrapped Claire in a blanket and picked her up from the bed, considering his odds. Schroeder was known to have worked with other people in the past and he had shown this again when coming after Claire. There was a high probability that the killer wasn't alone, and that the others who'd showed up behind him at the Pear Tree Inn were in his employ. If that were true and Schroeder was here, then it was likely he had others with him again.

Leaving Schroeder behind, Stanley hurriedly loaded Claire into the car and took off.

Schroeder had no choice but to let them go again, but he knew it would not be the last time that he would engage with Stanley to get to Claire. He pulled himself up and made his way back to his SUV, opening the glove box and quickly grabbing some bandages from inside the first-aid kit. He dressed his wound as best he could and then made use of his field kit, which allowed him to dig out the bullet and stitch it up properly. Being in the business he was, Schroeder had a high pain threshold. Although wounded, he still had every intention of completing his mission to murder Claire McGinnis.

By the time the sun was coming up, Stanley and Claire were not too far away from the old farm where they had bought the Suburban. Seeing the old man still sitting on the porch, Stanley zoomed in close, realizing from his absolute stillness that the old man was dead. His programming told him that there was little possibility that his wife had survived, so he carefully avoided mentioning anything about them.

Claire was too sharp, however. She spotted the farmhouse and recognized it as quickly as Stanley had. "We should stop in for a visit," Claire said, excited to see them again.

"I don't think that's such a good idea," Stanley said, not wanting to break the news to her just yet. After all, he had experienced how she reacted to the death of Dee Dee, and he needed her with a clear head. "The fewer the people who see us, the less likely we are to be exposed again."

"You're probably right," Claire agreed with Stanley, letting out a sigh. "After all, I would hate for them to come into the path of our friendly killer," she added.

Stanley decided to keep driving, but he also knew that he needed to dump the current vehicle they were using. There was little doubt that Schroeder knew exactly what they were driving, so changing cars would only be logical. Noticing the thickening brush to their right, Stanley decided to take the opportunity to do so. He knew that once Claire was hidden, it would not take him long to backtrack to the farm and see what other vehicles they had lying around at their disposal.

―――――

AFTER HIS LAST interaction with Stanley, Schroeder knew he was going to need some help, and he knew just the guys to do it. He had worked beside them a few years earlier, when he was hired to kill an heiress, who was planning to divorce her husband. If she did, due to a premarital agreement, this man stood to get nothing, so he hired them to kill her, which left him with everything. They were tough men and not shy when it came to a challenge, and they wouldn't be far away.

"Hello, Vladimir," Schroeder said in Russian, greeting his old comrade. Vlad was Bratva, Russian mafia. He had been handling his organized crime activities in the St. Louis area for several years.

"Greetings, old friend," the man replied, "But speak the American. We are in USA," he continued.

"I could use some assistance with a job," Schroeder said, baiting the man's interest.

"Straight down to business, Schroeder. Anyway, speak."

"Claire McGinnis...." Schroeder continued as Comrade laughed.

"Schroeder, defeated by little girl." He laughed louder. "Where you lose your manhood?" he asked, adding a little more salt into the wound.

"She is not the issue," Schroeder said, taking his bait. "If you're not interested..." Schroeder teased, knowing those few words would have his worm on the hook.

"Of course I am interested, dear Schroeder," he said, calming his banter.

"She has a protector, a man called Stanley, but I am not sure that he's entirely a man."

"Go back to drinking vodka. What is a man, who is not a man, Schroeder? There is no man a bullet cannot kill."

"I stabbed him in the chest, and he did not even flinch. I shot this 'man' in the shoulder, and he still stood. He has been hit with lightning and it barely affected him. I shot him in the face, and yet he still managed to drive away with Claire McGinnis."

"Ah, you probably got screwed, with the cheap bullet and lady luck kissed him a few times. I take it you would like us to come and take care of your problem for you?"

"For a price." Schroeder smiled.

"You know the account," Comrade said. "I'll bring my boys; it will do them good to brush off the cobwebs. This USA is a little slow, you know."

Schroeder gave Vlad the address of a truck stop just across the river in Illinois. "I'll see you when you get there," he said, hanging up.

———

CLAIRE WAS PASSED out cold on the back seat, curled up in the fetal position, and showed no sign of waking soon. Stanley had waited until she had dozed off before turning around and going back toward the farm; it was the most logical place to acquire a vehicle that wouldn't be missed for at least a few days. He pulled the car quietly off the side of the road and into the brush, then slipped out and jogged through the trees. In this way, he was back at the farm in under thirty minutes. Stanley stopped briefly, examining the old man's corpse. Given the rules of natural exposure, he had been dead at least two days. Stanley entered the house and made his way down the hall, past the living room where the old man's wife lay dead in her recliner, and found her purse. Inside were the keys to the nearly new Buick that was sitting in the garage attached to the house. The car started up instantly and he backed it out of the garage, then drove down the driveway and headed back to where he had left Claire concealed.

BY THE TIME HE RETURNED, Claire had barely moved and was still sleeping peacefully. He packed the few belongings they had into the new vehicle and cautiously moved Claire, strapping her in carefully and reclining the seat, managing not to wake her. He had driven the other car far enough into the brush for it to be concealed.

He had decided to go back to DC, but he wasn't going to be foolish enough to rush in. He would take his time and carefully scout before each move. It would take a few more days to get back to the city, but Stanley's programming required him to take such precautions.

———

"THIS IS A DISASTER," Ambassador McGinnis said, devastated that Claire had been so close and yet, she had slipped through their hands. "Some professionals you are," he said angrily.

"We are sorry, sir," Esmeralda said, empathizing with the ambassador. "I can assure you, however, that we are not going to give up."

"We are working hard to find them again, sir," Bobbie added.

"But what if you don't? What if my little girl...." Ambassador McGinnis muttered as he broke down.

"Stanley is one of our best, sir, and more capable than most of us here, in combat. He will die before he allows any harm to come to your daughter. If anyone was to go after my girl and I wasn't there, I'd want Stanley, sir," Noah added, hoping to reassure him, father to father.

"Just... just bring her home," Ambassador McGinnis cried, looking a broken man.

"I'll get back to work," Bobbie said, somewhat taking their failure upon themselves. "They'll resurface eventually."

Just shy of forty-eight hours later, Claire and Stanley did show up again. Bobbie had spotted Claire sitting in the back seat of a new SUV and she ran into the room, interrupting Esmeralda, Noah, Eugene and Jack, who were working on their next line of attack when it came to Schroeder. "We have them!" she said excitedly.

"Where?" Esmeralda asked.

"A small motel, in Irwin, on the outskirts of Pittsburg, called the Huntington Motel Inn," Bobbie said, sending the address to their phones.

"We want to move as soon as possible," Esmeralda said, calculating other factors. "If we can find them, Schroeder can, too."

———

SCHROEDER GREETED his old comrades with open arms. Vladimir was still the same, a stocky man who smelled of vodka and the ladies. Elya had grown. He was no longer the underfed "whippet" at his father's feet, begging for crumbs, and Maxim had a few more war stories and scars added to his collection.

"You find your Claire and Stanley yet?" Vladimir asked, chomping at the bit to get back in the thick of the game.

"Huntington Motel Inn, courtesy of Matty G," Schroeder said with a smirk, feeling the tables had turned.

"Oh, I bring you something," Vladimir said, reaching into his pocket and pulling out a box of bullets. "They are good bullets," he said, still holding his strong Russian accent. "They are made in my motherland, not this USA," Comrade added.

Elya whispered something in Russian into his father's ear, only to receive a smack across the back of his head.

"We in America. You speak American," Vladimir demanded.

"Sorry, Father," Elya said, avoiding eye contact with Schroeder.

"Tell me, children. What is a father to do with them?" Comrade added as a final scold.

"He's right though," Schroeder said. "We should get going."

Before long, their cars were packed. Vladimir, Elya and Maxim following Schroeder out of town.

———

"How did I get here?" Claire said, finally waking and sitting up in the back seat.

"You were exhausted," Stanley said. "So, when I got a chance to switch vehicles, I didn't bother to wake you."

"Well at least I got some rest," Claire said, reaching for a bottle of water and taking a mouthful. "Where are we headed?" she asked Stanley.

"A small town called Irwin. A little place called the Huntington Inn Motel. It's lower class but we should be able to relax there for a while."

By the time they had arrived at the Huntington Inn Motel, Claire had regained her appetite and was starving. Unfortunately, there was nowhere to eat in sight, but the wide hallways that separated each section of the motel were lined with cheap, nasty-looking vending machines that probably had not been catered to in a while.

At this stage, Claire was willing to eat anything. Taking a crumpled-up bill out of her pocket, Claire began getting as much food as she could out of the vending machines.

"Do you think it will kill me?" she asked Stanley, holding an armload of chips and candy.

"Although it holds no real nutritional value, it is well packaged and should not kill you. I do not detect any harmful bacteria," Stanley answered, true to his form.

After having her fill, Claire lay down on the lumpy bed, and glared up at the smoke-stained ceilings. "Do you think I'll ever get to go home?" Claire asked Stanley.

"You will get to go home. It's when that will be the variable factor," Stanley answered honestly.

When Claire awoke the next morning, Stanley was already gone. Claire just assumed that he was out doing his usual walk-around, scanning the perimeter and making sure that they were safe. Feeling rather hungry, she decided to grab some cash and make her way back to the vending machines. As she pulled out her food, she never noticed a figure watching her from the other end. He watched her open the door and go outside, oblivious to the danger that now awaited her there.

All Schroeder, Vladimir, Elya and Maxim had to do was locate Stanley. After all, they didn't need him breaking up their little party. What they had failed to realize was that Stanley already knew that they were there and was making his way back to Claire.

Claire had only just put the snacks down on the table and was deciding which one to chow into first when the door flung open and there stood three large men. She turned, backing away, screaming, "Stanley." Her heart sank when Stanley didn't come. "Who are you?" she said, not recognizing their faces.

"We are friends of your father and we're here to take you home," Vladimir said with an untrusting smile.

"I know my dad's friends," Claire said, pausing slightly. "I don't know you."

Vladimir took a step closer to Claire and then suddenly flew backward, landing dead on the floor in front of her. Claire gasped and spun to see Stanley standing behind her, his fifty-caliber pistol pointed at the other two men that stood in the doorway. "Who sent you?" Stanley asked, demanding an answer.

Elya ignored Stanley and instead knelt at his father's side, openly crying in mourning the death of his father. "Father!" he screamed, as he reached for the gun that now lay beside the body.

Once the gun was in the man's hand, he was a threat to Claire. Stanley aimed the gun but hesitated last minute, noticing a slight flicker of light as Maxim fired his gun at Stanley. With Claire in the crossfire, Stanley's programming was running at full speed, his quantum brain keeping track of everything that was happening around him. He was about to fire when he was struck in the forehead by the bullet from Maxim's gun, which ricocheted off his nearly indestructible skull and struck Maxim between the eyes.

The impact on Stanley's head caused his processor to lock up for a few seconds. Elya took advantage of Stanley's sudden freeze, quickly grabbed Claire and made his way out of the motel room, confident that Stanley would not take a shot if it put Claire at risk. Elya forced Claire into his car, but she fought him all the way.

"Shut up," Elya yelled as Claire screamed for Stanley. "I am thinking, you were worth more to your father alive than dead. So let's see how much he will pay for his little princess."

His eyes still crowded with tears over his father's death, he jumped up behind the wheel of the car and threw it into motion only a second later. As he did so, Stanley came bursting out of the room in pursuit, his legs pumping faster than any human could imagine as he chased the car out of the driveway and onto the street.

Elya almost made it, but slowing for the left-hand turn gave Stanley the slight advantage he needed. He angled slightly to the left, cutting across the edge of a gas station and slamming into the side of the car just as it completed the turn. Elya screamed and raised his gun, but Stanley's fist came through the window and put an end to him. He fell over in the driver's seat and his foot came off the accelerator, allowing Stanley to steer the car into the ditch on the right.

As the car stopped, Stanley snatched open the rear door and pulled Claire out, immediately checking her for any injuries that might be apparent. Finding none, he scooped her up in his arms and turned to run again, but a car at the gas station caught his attention. It was sitting at the pump furthest from the office, and was still running. Without even the appearance of hesitation, he set Claire in the passenger seat and hurried around to get behind the wheel, the tires squealing as he roared away. Behind him, he could hear the sound of the car's previous owner screaming at him to bring it back.

Claire was weeping, gasping for breath. Until now, she had not been witness to the violence and death that surrounded the world of politics and espionage, but this had been an overdose. Stanley realized that she was in shock, but he wasn't programmed for dealing with such an emotional problem.

"You can relax now," he said calmly. "We have escaped, and no one is currently pursuing us."

The little girl turned to look at him, her eyes wide, but then she suddenly began to slow her breathing and gulp back the sobs that were coming from her. In only a matter of seconds, she had herself under control once again.

"You killed them all," she said. "You killed all those men."

"I did what was necessary to protect you," Stanley replied.

Claire suddenly gave a strangled laugh. "I wasn't complaining, Stanley," she said.

.

SEVENTEEN

By the time Esmeralda, Jack, Eugene, Bobbie, Noah and Sarah had arrived at the motel, Stanley and Claire's room was empty, other than the corpses that lay on the floor. As local police tried to piece together what had taken place, Esmeralda used her own advantages in technology to scan and process the crime scene, while Noah reached out to Allison by phone.

"Camelot, report," Allison said as soon as she answered the call.

"I'm afraid the situation has become far worse than it was," Noah said. "Schroeder has apparently enlisted some help, and Claire has been abducted. It was not Schroeder who took her, and a witness claims to have heard the kidnapper mention holding her for ransom. He didn't get very far, though; it appears that Stanley caught up to him just a couple of blocks away. He left the man we believe to have been the kidnapper dead in his car, and witnesses say he stole another vehicle from a nearby service station. We know that he recovered Claire and took her with him at that point, but his current location is unknown."

"Good Lord, can this get any worse? Do what you can, Noah, and keep me posted."

"Will do," Noah said, and then the line went dead.

They needed as little attention as possible while they moved closer to Schroeder in hope of locating Stanley and Claire. Esmeralda was also concerned about Stanley if he was to be exposed.

"Stanley's exterior is compromised," she said suddenly, forcing them all to stop. "There's titanium dust scattered here," she said, standing where Stanley had stood, between Claire and a bullet. "Titanium is an element of the compound Wally uses to make the skeletons." She looked around the scene again. "That's what gives it so much strength."

She pointed at Vladimir's body lying on the floor. "He died first," she said. "His temperature is a quarter of a degree lower than the other one," Esmeralda continued, turning to Maxim, whose corpse was still laid out in the doorway. "He died less than a minute after and given the damage to the wall, there was a third. Stanley has been programmed not to use such force unless necessary and since he has fallen back on safe mode for his current mission, that missing third person is the one who grabbed Claire." Esmeralda continued processing.

"Schroeder, maybe?" Sarah said, as Esmeralda processed the odds.

"No," Esmeralda said, pointing to a blood patch on the floor. "I can't find any evidence that Schroeder himself was here. These three men were probably sent by him to complete the job, but it appears that the third man might have been going off script if he was considering trying to hold Claire for ransom. I think that he simply took advantage of one of Stanley's natural problems. The titanium dust indicates that he was probably struck in the head, and that would be enough of an impact to cause a—well, a hiccup in his processing. He would lock up for a few seconds, just long enough for his processor to run a quick diagnostic and make sure he wasn't severely damaged. It would only last about five seconds, and it's the only credible reason that Stanley would have taken his attention off Claire."

Noah, who had been acting as liaison with the local police, nodded. "We'd better move out," Noah said. "The police will be handling all of this from here on out, but we need to get back to finding Claire."

Esmeralda nodded, then spoke briefly to the police detective in charge of the crime scene. Due to the complexities of the case, the embassy had quietly notified the Department of Justice and all law enforcement agencies on Stanley's projected path of travel that he was attempting to protect Claire from the would-be assassin. They were all fully aware that it was a delicate and sensitive situation.

———

THE EVENTS of the past few days had taken their toll on Claire. Analyzing her developing behaviors, her mood shifts, and regular vitals, Stanley estimated that Claire's body and capacity to cope would fail her sooner rather than later. It didn't mean that Claire was not strong. She had proven herself more than most would have to throughout their entire lives. It was the human condition that inhibited her, something Stanley could never understand. Running motel to motel, hotel to hotel wasn't working. Obviously, Schroeder had found some way to keep tabs on them, likely through the many CCTV cameras scattered around the world today. How he was doing it was of little importance considering the situation that they now found themselves in. Now heading back toward Washington, DC, Stanley constructed a new plan.

Being a robot and not needing rest, he was able to drive for hours without stopping and therefore cover more ground than what his human counterparts could, but he still had to be careful now that his identity had been compromised. Even though they were only four and a half hours out of Washington, Stanley made sure not to take a direct route cutting up through Pennsylvania, making his way back down through Lancaster. On the outskirts of Lancaster, Stanley noticed rows of RVs lined up just behind a metal fence. He drove around back to hide the car between some barrels that had been dumped there. "What now?" Claire asked, opening the door so she could swing her legs out. "We can't keep driving around the US forever," she added, unsure of Stanley's plan.

"We could for a while in one of those," Stanley said, directing her attention to the RVs. Wanting to avoid any security cameras that may give away their location, he scanned the perimeter, picking up on even the slightest electrical current. Luckily the current security system was easy for him to hack.

"We will wait here until nightfall," Stanley instructed. "I want to avoid the possibility of being seen. While I can control some of the most sophisticated technologies in the world, I cannot predict or control the actual likelihood that I might be observed by a human."

"Hopefully it's not too long," Claire said, falling back into the back seat and lying down. "I am incredibly bored and if the assassin doesn't kill me, this just might."

"You are deflecting," Stanley said, turning to Claire. "If you need someone to listen, I will listen." Stanley tried to appear empathetic to Claire.

"You can listen," Claire softly said, "but you can't understand how I feel." Knowing Claire was right, Stanley dropped the subject.

By nightfall Claire was banging her head on the back seat softly in a poor attempt to amuse herself. She was frustrated and angry, and so sick of the road. Stanley waited until the final human had left and he heard the sound of the padlock going through the chain. Once he was sure everyone was gone and they were clear, he easily climbed over the back fence and made his way through to the motor homes. He was looking for something in particular, something that would be comfortable for Claire and easy for him to control, but which would fit into the current surroundings like a glove and not be noticed. Something too modern would be missed too quickly. Something too old mechanically could hinder them. After a brief scan of the yard, he had finally found what he was looking for. It was very basic but still electronically controlled, while small enough that it could still be easily hidden if such a need were to arise.

Stanley easily connected to the operating system, and got inside. He drove it to the gate and stopped for a moment, leaving the engine running while he picked the lock. He removed the chain and opened the gate, taking less than a minute to exit, and relocked the gate before anybody would notice.

Knowing that the RV would eventually be reported as missing, Stanley would have to change its identity. So once far enough away from the yard, Stanley found the closest hardware store and sent Claire in to get some much-needed supplies. Within ten minutes she returned, with a bag full of spray paint and some tape so they could adjust the numbers on the license plates and change the RV's appearance. Stanley then drove into a remote area he had located well off the main highway and hidden enough that they would have the time to complete the task.

Based on Claire's actions and mood, Stanley could tell that she rather enjoyed helping him. His programming told him that it was most likely because it kept her mind off their situation and her current emotional grief. Stanley sometimes heard her cry at night, missing her father and most likely still mourning the death of her governess. However, it was apparent that Claire was also becoming quite attached to Stanley. Now all he had to do, was keep her safe until he was able to return her to her father.

By morning they were back on the interstate, traveling through the areas around Washington, DC. Stanley hoped by moving constantly, not only would he avoid any further conflict that would put Claire in danger, but he would also be able to trick her mind into believing she was just on one very long road trip.

———

SCHROEDER HAD RECEIVED no word regarding the whereabouts of his target. It was like Claire and Stanley had just vanished into thin air. His employer was getting rather eager as well, breaking the rules and reaching out to Schroeder while he was still on mission. This made things a lot riskier for Schroeder—he knew that US intelligence could eventually pick up on the conversation, as they were keeping a very close eye on North Korea. It could also put a target on Schroeder's head from other assassins, who would be looking to steal his contract. After all, he was being paid a lot of money to kill Claire McGinnis. It would only be so long before his North Korean contractor would start sending more assassins of their own, thinking Schroeder was incapable of completing the mission.

ESMERALDA and the others at the embassy, were also out of luck, but it didn't stop Bobbie working night and day, nor did it stop Esmeralda from observing and tapping into every security system CCTV and camera in the city and surrounds. Eventually Stanley and Claire would have to show up again, and it appeared that they were headed back toward DC. They were also keeping an eye out for any sightings of Schroeder. Given his reputation, and now that the pressure was on, they knew he would still not give up; but it may force his hand into making mistakes, therefore making it easier to find him and eliminate the threat.

EIGHTEEN

BOBBIE WOULD NOW ONLY SLEEP IN SMALL SPURTS, fueling herself on excessive amounts of caffeine. Esmeralda was getting worried about her. She could see the effect that the excess amount of caffeine was having on the hacker's heart, but she also knew that Bobbie was too stubborn to put her needs before her mission and take a break. She continuously watched camera footage, using facial recognition software, looking for any glimpse, any connection that could possibly lead them to, or be Stanley and Claire. She knew Stanley was very good at changing his appearance and she was sure that even at her young age Claire had picked up a few tricks as well, but there are still some things about the human face that don't change.

Meanwhile Esmeralda was waiting on her orders from Allison and Noah in relation to the course of action that should be taken with Stanley. Although they had accepted the responsibility for what was happening, as they should have been able to anticipate Stanley's reaction when falling into safe mode, they needed to decide if Stanley was more of a liability or still an asset. After all, Stanley being on the run with Claire had already cost the lives of civilians, and this was not an incident that E&E ever took lightly.

Bobbie was just headed into the second day straight of

viewing footage nonstop. For some reason a girl caught her eye as she walked into a truck stop diner. There was something very familiar about her, and for a moment Bobbie could not put her finger on it. She watched her for another minute before it dawned on her—although she looked a little older, it was Claire. Quickly she reached out to Esmeralda, who then in turn contacted the rest of the team. "I've found Claire."

———

AFTER BEING on the road for a few hours Claire fumbled through what was left of their snack food. "What I wouldn't give for a decent meal," she said, deciding whether she would rather be hungry or spend another day eating the same food over and over.

"There is a truck stop not too far from here," Stanley said, making a slight detour. "I think it has been long enough that we can risk getting you a proper meal and restocking on supplies," Stanley added, watching a smile finally grace Claire's face.

Fifteen minutes later, Stanley pulled in and parked his RV amongst a group of other RVs and trucks. With his interiors still slightly exposed, he passed Claire some cash and sent her inside the little store next to the diner. She eyed the premade food, trying to decide what she wanted to eat for the next few days. Her guard down, she didn't even bother fixing her makeup before she left the RV, but by the look of the clientele that walked around, standards weren't very high, so she'd fit in just fine.

Enjoying feeling slightly normal for once, Claire took her time to browse the aisles, collecting an array of fresh foods, processed meats, and all the things she had missed from home. The cashier gave her the once-over, not even blinking an eyelash as she loudly chewed on gum. "Going far?" she asked, making general conversation.

"My father and I," Claire said, "are on a little road trip, spending some time together before I go away to college."

"Nice," she said, not really caring. "That'll be forty-six fifty," she said, abruptly holding out a hand.

"Keep the change," Claire said, handing her a fifty.

———

MEANWHILE BACK IN WASHINGTON, DC Bobbie sat in her computer chair, watching Claire's every move and relaying the information back to Esmeralda, Jack, Eugene, Noah and Sarah, who were not far from the truck stop. Bobbie could see Claire heading toward a group of RVs but before she could tell which RV Claire went into the security camera glitched, and by the time the visual had returned Claire had re-entered the van without being seen. Although it could just be a coincidence, she couldn't help but wonder if maybe Stanley had had something to do with it.

———

"I WISH YOU COULD TRY THIS," Claire said, biting into a sandwich. "It's actually not bad for truck stop food, and definitely a lot fresher than I anticipated," she added, taking another bite.

"We should get moving soon," Stanley said, calculating their next course.

"Well, please at least let me eat first," Claire said, taking another bite. "Food and movement can sometimes make me a little sick."

"The inability of the human brain to process information," Stanley started saying, pausing when he saw the unimpressed look on Claire's face. "You refer to it as motion sickness," he explained, looking away.

"Sorry," Claire said, "sometimes I forget that you're not human. So," she changed the subject, "when do you think I can call my father? I'm sure he's worried to death about me and honestly I miss him."

"I do not know," Stanley said, being honest. "Although I am sure the threats against you will be eliminated, I cannot determine the time frame in which that will happen as there are too many variables, but when it is safe to do so, I will let you."

Claire rolled her eyes, and began to argue with Stanley, even though she knew it was an argument she'd never win.

———

Minutes away from arriving, Esmeralda received an internal call. It was Allison. "What are my orders?" Esmeralda asked.

"I'm sorry," Allison said, sounding defeated. "E&E have determined that Stanley is too much of a risk. Because his mission has taken the lives of innocent civilians, and has risked exposing the use of robots within our missions, E&E have determined that Stanley is to be brought in for decommission or terminated. That is your mission."

"I still feel like we could save him," Esmeralda said, allowing her human side to speak. "Stanley has not killed anyone who could be considered innocent; only Schroeder has done that."

Allison let out a sigh. "If some miracle occurs, I hope you can," Allison said. "Over and out."

NINETEEN

CLAIRE CONTINUED TO ARGUE WITH STANLEY. AFTER all, she had done everything he had asked, and all she wanted was to hear her father's voice and let him know that she was okay and for her to know that he was. They were so busy arguing, they never heard footsteps approaching their door until there was a knock. Thinking it must be another traveller, Stanley and Claire stayed quiet, hoping they would just assume they were not inside and go away. Whoever it was didn't.

"Claire, Stanley," called Esmeralda, taking a bold risk. Cautiously, gun in hand, Stanley opened the door, pointing it into the face of the woman who stood there. "Stanley, it's me, Esmeralda," she said, hoping that seeing her would reboot his memory of her, which had been damaged by the lightning strike.

"I've seen you before," Stanley said, studying his internal memory. "Are you working with the assassin?" he asked, knowing that given his lie detection software, she would not be able to lie to him.

"No," Esmeralda said, holding up a photo of her, Stanley and the crew that had been taken at the embassy. "It's OK, Stanley," Esmeralda said. "It's time to come in."

Stanley stared at the photo for a long moment, and his

memory began to reassemble certain elements that had been damaged by the lightning strike. It was like opening a floodgate, and suddenly memories of Esmeralda working with him back at Feeney Manor came cascading down.

"Has the threat been terminated?" Stanley asked, now recognizing Esmeralda as his superior.

"No, but you will be safer with us."

"Claire is safer with me," Stanley said. "I can keep her moving undetected until the threat has been neutralized," Stanley continued with a firm expression.

"I am your superior, I am ordering you to come in." Esmeralda hoped the command would override Stanley's safe mode programming.

"I cannot," Stanley said. "The circumstances require me to keep Claire isolated and safe, until the threat has been neutralized."

Esmeralda took a deep breath. "If you do not cooperate, my orders are to terminate you, Stanley, and I do not want to do that."

"Self-preservation is irrelevant. Only my mission is," Stanley said, slamming the door in her face and telling Claire to hold on. Stanley sped out of the parking lot, trying to put as much distance as possible between him and Esmeralda.

———

ESMERALDA RAN BACK to the car where the others were waiting with the engine running. Esmeralda instructed Eugene to safely follow Stanley, knowing full well he was quite capable of taking them out, if he saw them as a threat to his mission. Esmeralda then called Bobbie, who was busy watching cameras back in Washington, by subcom. "Keep an eye out for an older RV, white in color with blue trims. Licence plate number, Tiger, Alpha Two, Seven, Charlie, Three. We are following now."

"Roger," Bobbie said as her hands moved fast to put the new data into her system. "I'll keep you posted. Bobbie out."

Less than a minute later, Bobbie had sent them a possible map. Now she knew what she was looking for, it was easy for her to plot where Claire and Stanley could be headed. She then called Esmeralda back. "Hey, thought you should know, that plate's reported stolen."

"Make that report disappear," Esmeralda said, not wanting to risk more unnecessary innocent fatalities.

"You got it," Bobbie said, hanging up.

———

"YOU SHOULD TRUST THEM!" Claire screamed at Stanley as he began weaving through traffic, trying to lose Esmeralda and her team. "That's Emma, she's the one who brought you to us."

"My programming does not allow me to," Stanley said, pushing the RV to its absolute limits.

"Well, override it!" Claire screamed as Stanley ran a red light.

"I cannot," he said, speeding up to another intersection.

"Well at least slow down, or whoever's trying to kill me will be out of a job!" she screamed, louder, afraid for her life. This was the first time she thought that Stanley had ever put her in real danger, although he was capable of driving much faster without actually endangering her or anyone else.

Just as the tail of the RV cleared the intersection, Stanley cut off a truck abruptly, causing the driver to sharply turn one way, while his trailer went the other. Stanley didn't even blink an eye. Claire sat down, silent, horrified as she heard screeching tires, smashing glass and banging metal as the cars continued to pile up. "If anyone's hurt, or worse," Claire whispered, "Stanley, it's on you."

"An acceptable risk," Stanley said calmly, "if it is necessary to complete my mission."

"Holy sh…" Eugene said as his evasive driving training came into effect, and he stopped their SUV just short of the pileup. He reversed back, up onto the sidewalk, trying to find a way around so they could continue their pursuit.

"It's pointless," Esmeralda said, watching as Stanley and Claire's RV faded into the distance. "There is no way through."

"Should we…?" Jack asked, pointing to the pileup.

"No," Esmeralda said. "Emergency services are on the way. I don't want E&E knowing about this," she added, knowing it would be another nail in Stanley's coffin.

TWENTY

Schroeder had missed Esmeralda and her team by less than a minute at the truck stop. Unbeknownst to his friends, Matty G had managed to hack into Bobbie's systems, making him privy to everything she knew. It didn't take him long to catch up as they headed in the direction of the interstate. Not wanting to be detected, Schroeder took a side exit that ran parallel with the interstate highway and followed cautiously, hoping his banged-up brown Mustang would make the journey. After all, he wasn't sure how many more chances he would get.

Continuing to follow Stanley and Claire, he watched as Stanley began maneuvering through traffic. Watching Stanley as he cut through the first intersection, unable to shake his "followers," Schroeder sped up, getting ahead of them. Schroeder sat, parked for a moment, watching as Stanley cut in front of the truck in his rearview mirror. Even where he sat, he could hear the crunching of cars.

Schroeder pulled out in front of the car that was in front of Claire and Stanley's RV. He allowed Stanley and Claire to overtake him just before the next exit, which he predicted they would take, as they would be looking for somewhere to recoup and stay low.

Hanging back, Schroeder continued to follow, still unsure of how he was going to approach the situation. Although he still had intentions of fulfilling his contract and killing Claire McGinnis, he now wanted Stanley as well. There were parties that would pay billions to reverse engineer his technologies, and why shouldn't he cash in on that?

———

THIRTY MINUTES LATER, Stanley and Claire turned into the parking lot of a large Walmart. Claire was still freaking out, as Stanley parked the RV between two larger vans. He didn't need a visual to sense if his *"allies"* were coming.

"WHAT THE HELL," Claire screamed at Stanley. "WHAT THE HELL ARE YOU DOING?" she continued.

"I understand, you are upset," Stanley said, gently restraining her arms as she continued to lash out at him. "I did what was necessary," he continued, letting Claire continue to vent.

———

MEANWHILE, Schroeder circled the block and pulled into the parking lot, with a direct view of Stanley and Claire's RV. He just sat there and watched their shadows through the window, trying to figure out his next move. After all, a public place like this was not at all convenient for murder, and he still needed to figure out how to disable Stanley. Schroeder knew that Stanley's *"brain"* was definitely advanced and even in its compromised state, still operated at a highly efficient rate. Whoever had built him was well advanced in their field, but Stanley did appear to have one weakness at least. Electromagnetic pulses. A large EMP, such as the lightning strike, forced Stanley to become immobile momentarily, while he appeared to reboot. So how, Schroeder thought, could he use that to his advantage?

Suddenly, he had an idea: assuming his creator had followed

human anatomy as a guide, Stanley's computer should be in his head, so maybe he didn't need all of him. A head would be easier to smuggle out of the county compared to a normal human-size android. Staring at the RV, Schroeder made a call.

Schroeder began tapping on his steering wheel, leaning forward as he continued to watch Stanley and Claire. As time crept on, Schroeder was becoming more anxious—he had not expected his package to take that long. As he was just about to reach for his phone to call his contact again, a banged-up old hatchback reverse parked beside him. Schroeder rolled down his window, the other man opening his door slightly to pass Schroeder the package. In return Schroeder passed him an envelope. "You'll find everything you need in there," said the overweight man before casually getting back in his car, quickly flipping through the bills, and taking off.

Schroeder checked the contents of the bag which contained a couple of Viper Tek VTS-989 Stun Guns, one of the most powerful stun guns readily available, and a Carbide Bladed Machete. Schroeder just hoped that the three hundred million volts would be enough to force Stanley into reboot. Now all Schroeder needed to do, was wait for the opportune time.

TWENTY-ONE

Now that the dead and the injured had been taken to hospital, the police and tow trucks began the grim task of clearing the roads and cleaning up the mess that Stanley had left behind. Esmeralda knew it would be some time before they could get through and continue pursuing Stanley and Claire. In the meantime, Bobbie was keeping them all regularly updated with any movements that tweaked her suspicions. After all, with the amount of CCTV cameras on the interstate highway, it would only be a short matter of time before Stanley and Claire would be picked up on one of them.

Bobbie studied each exit ramp slowly. She knew Stanley couldn't stay on the interstate for too long; it was too risky. About twenty minutes into it, Bobbie's computer system picked up on an RV matching the description of the one Stanley and Claire were driving. Bobbie rewound the footage and watched closely, wanting to make sure that it really was the RV they were looking for and not some computer error. It was them, and Bobbie called Esmeralda and the others to let them know.

Bobbie continued to follow them, watching each move very carefully, making sure that Stanley and Claire didn't have a chance to change vehicles without them knowing about it. She watched as Stanley did a couple of blocks, slowing down as he turned into a Walmart car park. She watched as he parked carefully and waited for movement.

In light of the new information, Esmeralda knew she could not risk waiting anymore. it was too much of a risk and if she had any chance of saving Stanley and returning Claire safely to her father, she needed to act now. "I am going to go ahead," Esmeralda said, barely giving them a chance to respond before she opened the door and started jogging down the street. Given her capabilities, once she knew she was clear from the eye of the public, it wouldn't take her long to catch up to Claire and Stanley. Running along the ditch that ran alongside the interstate highway, Esmeralda reached a maximum speed of fifty mph. At this rate she had under thirty minutes to come up with a plan.

———

Meanwhile back in the car, Eugene, Jack and Noah were finding it hard to just sit there, knowing it was quite possible that Esmeralda would require their assistance. After all, given his fixation on the mission, Stanley was quite a dangerous robot, and they weren't sure if even Esmeralda would be able to encounter him again and leave unscathed. Tired of waiting, Jack got out of the car and walked over to a nearby police officer. He flashed his ID. "Rough one we've had," Jack made conversation.

"Yeah, it is," the police officer replied.

"Any idea of how much longer it's going to be?" Jack asked. "My brothers and I are trying to get through town to see our sick mother. The doctors don't know how much longer she has."

"I'm sorry about your mother," the police officer said, empathizing with Jack. "We're looking at least two hours, but just wait here a minute." The policeman pressed the button on his walkie-talkie. "Sergeant Fireland here."

"Copy that," came a static reply. "Do you think you guys can clear me a quick path big enough for an SUV to get through? One of our own needs to get somewhere right away, kind of an emergency."

"Roger that, sir," came another static reply. "Just give me a moment."

"Don't worry," Sergeant Fireland said, turning back to Jack. "We take care of our own. you'll be out of here in no time."

"Thank you," Jack said, shaking the man's hand, before returning to the SUV.

"They're going to clear us a path and let us go on," he said.

Noah nodded and opened a channel to Esmeralda. "Noah to Esmeralda," he subvocalized. "The police are clearing us a path, so we should catch up to you soon. Try to wait for backup."

"Esmeralda to Noah," she replied. "Then hurry. Maybe I'm being a little unreasonable, but Stanley is like my child in some ways. If I can find a way to take him alive, or get him to come in, I'm going to."

MEANWHILE, while scouting Claire and Stanley, Bobbie's gut feeling began kicking in. Something here was a little odd. She had noticed a lot of cars come and go, but the beat-up old Mustang just sat there with an occupant inside. While anyone else probably would have brushed it off as someone most likely waiting for someone else, it bothered Bobbie. Still, while keeping one eye on Stanley and Claire, she rewound the footage to where Stanley and Claire had first entered the car park. Moments later the Mustang entered and parked. No one got out, which added to her suspicion. She watched the hatchback that had parked beside him, noticing their exchange. She watched as the hatchback left and the Mustang still stayed there. Hacking into the controls of the CCTV system, Bobbie was able to zoom in.

At first, because the man was leaned back, she could only make out his chest and hands, one with a bandage, stained with dried blood. She tweaked the camera slightly, angling it into a better position. Bobbie was sure she knew who it was, and then he leaned forward, tapping his fingers on the steering wheel. With a click of her mouse, she entered his face into her adjusted facial recognition software, and it came back with a ninety percent hit. It was Schroeder, and she was the first person, she knew, other than the few who had ever worked with him, to ever see his real face without fearing for her life. Quickly, she got Esmeralda on subcom. "Schroeder is there at the car park, sitting in a beat-up, brown Mustang, just a short distance from Claire and Stanley."

"I'm five minutes away," Esmeralda said. "Esmeralda out."

———

IN THE RV, Claire had finally settled down. She had gone from one extreme to the other, lashing out, then breaking down in tears, then lashing out again. From her vitals and his database of human behavioral patterns, Stanley was able to conclude Claire no longer felt any sense of control, and given her personality traits, he knew that probably scared her more than her life being jeopardized. "It will be okay," Stanley said, trying to comfort her.

"Will it?" Claire asked, not convinced.

"I will protect you until the threat has been eliminated, or I have been destroyed."

"Well, given what you've already been through, I guess I'll be alive a little longer," Claire said, suddenly hugging Stanley. Although Stanley could not feel a hug the way a human could, he had been programed to understand them. The way Claire hugged him told him she needed comfort, so instead of backing away, he placed his arms around her body, and they sat there in silence. After all, nothing he could truly say would take her fear away.

———

NOTICING he was gaining the attention of a nearby security guard, Schroeder became a little uneasy and his trigger finger itched. Usually he would have no problem shooting him dead where he stood, but this wasn't the backstreets of Germany. Not wanting the attention, Schroeder turned on his car and slowly drove out of the car park, catching Esmeralda's eye as she approached it on the street.

———

SCHROEDER'S sudden departure surprised Esmeralda. Originally, she was going to hunt down and kill Schroeder, but with Stanley and Claire a few meters away, the window had opened on another opportunity to try to bring them safely back to Washington.

Esmeralda activated her dove programming. While it inhibited some of her functions, it made it virtually impossible for her to be picked up by scanning software. To avoid a visual sighting, Esmeralda discreetly maneuvered between cars, making her way to the RV. Esmeralda thought if she could convince Stanley to get close enough to her, she could activate her taser function to deliver an electrical shock, allowing his systems to restart. That would give her a few seconds to render him temporarily inoperable, so that she could bring him back to be repaired.

When she had gotten close enough to the RV, she stepped out, turning off stealth mode and making it possible for Stanley to see her. Esmeralda held her hands up, in the universal sign of surrender. Stanley watched her closely, reading her lips. "Stanley. Let me help you keep Claire safe."

Stanley looked at Claire for a moment, as he scanned the lot. He knew Esmeralda was there alone and if he could trust her, then she might be of some extra assistance to support Claire's deteriorating emotional needs. He looked back at Esmeralda. "You can trust me," she said silently. "I will help you complete your mission."

When Stanley got to the door, he hesitated for a moment, running one last variable. Restoring his subcom connection to

Esmeralda, he spoke to her internally. "I am programmed to trust you, Esmeralda. Although physically, I can keep Claire safe, my system lacks, where yours would be beneficial. Claire has experienced trauma. I cannot relate or comprehend beyond what has been programmed into me. You will fix her?" Stanley asked, knowing that Claire's mental disposition was hazardous to the end objective.

"I cannot fix her," Esmeralda said, knowing that if she lied to Stanley now, he would not allow her to proceed. "Humans cannot be fixed as we can, but I can help her process what has happened, and be her friend." With that, Stanley disconnected and cautiously opened the door. Esmeralda slowly made her way inside, closing the door behind her.

"Thank you, Stanley," Esmeralda said, as Claire leapt to her feet and hugged her.

"Emma!" the girl shouted. "I'm so glad you're here."

"Hello, Claire," Esmeralda said, hugging her back. "It's good to see you."

"Is my dad okay?" Claire asked, taking a step back.

"He's hanging in there, but he's going to be really happy to know you're okay."

"I wouldn't be without Stanley," Claire said, as Esmeralda turned to him.

"No, you wouldn't," Esmeralda said, flashing him a smile.

No one else would have seen it. The sudden fluctuation in the size of the pupil in his eye lasted for less than a hundredth of a second. Even if a human had spotted it on a video running at slow speed, it would have meant nothing to them, but to Esmeralda, it was an indication of a serious breakdown in Stanley's CPU. Between the lightning strike and the impact of a bullet, his quantum computer brain had taken quite a beating. Somewhere inside, one of the millions of microscopic connections was not working properly, and it was possible that it could cause a catastrophic failure of his processing capabilities. If that happened, Stanley could easily become little more than a killing machine, lashing out at any human or animal as if they were somehow a threat to himself. While his self-preservation was less important than completing his mission, that would only be true as long as his mission was still paramount to his purpose. Unfortunately, should that connection misfire, Stanley could completely forget in a split second that he was supposed to be protecting this young girl. At that point, he would become the greatest threat to her safety, himself.

Not wanting to alarm Claire, Esmeralda kept her discovery to herself. "We should get back on the road soon, hey?" Esmeralda asked, with some feigned excitement. After all, if her plan was going to work, to lower the risk of collateral damage, Esmeralda was going to need a space more remote than a Walmart parking lot.

Stanley nodded, then got behind the wheel and started the RV. As he drove away, Esmeralda silently sent a text message to the others, using her built-in cellular system to avoid Stanley detecting the message.

———

BY THE TIME NOAH, Eugene and Jack had finally made it through the pileup, down the interstate highway and to the Walmart, Esmeralda, Stanley and Claire were already gone. "What now?" Jack asked as their phones dinged. It was a message from Esmeralda, leading them through town and back onto the interstate.

Moments later Bobbie rang and asked Jack to put her on speaker. "Hi boys," Bobbie said, knowing she was like a cat playing with a mouse. "Esmeralda is with Stanley and Claire. You should have directions. Your mission is not to engage Stanley or Claire. Esmeralda will handle that. Schroeder was at the car park watching them. He's driving a beat-up brown ten-year-old Mustang and most likely still in the area. Esmeralda would like you to follow but keep an eye out for Schroeder. You are not to engage Stanley, but if the opportunity arises, you are to terminate Schroeder. Esmeralda plans on trying to reboot him and then bring him in."

"Roger that, Bobbie boo," Jack said, hanging up before Bobbie could respond.

"You know you're asking for trouble, right?" Eugene snickered. "Bobbie boo? What on earth is that supposed to be? She'll kick your ass."

"Yeah, but it's kind of fun pushing her buttons," Jack answered.

Noah looked at him. "Just don't be surprised," he said, "if she decides to push back."

———

By the time Schroeder had changed out his vehicle and doubled back around, Stanley and Claire were gone. Schroeder parked down a side alley and waited, counting on the fact that Stanley's friends would also be trailing him and in turn he would trail them. Eventually, they would lead him to Stanley and his mark.

Schroeder wasn't disappointed. "You're all the same," he muttered under his breath as he watched a black SUV stop briefly before taking off again. "All driving the same old cliché." Wanting to keep his distance for now, Schroeder let a couple of cars pass after the SUV. He pulled out carefully and trailed behind.

TWENTY-TWO

By nightfall, Esmeralda, Claire and Stanley were near the outskirts of Leesburg, Virginia. Esmeralda was keeping track of Stanley's glitches in between entertaining Claire, with stories of adventure and comedy. She'd seen a few more instances of the glitch in his eye, and was actually beginning to be worried. He could go completely rogue at any second, and she was not absolutely certain that she would be able to put an end to him if that were to happen.

"I will find us somewhere to camp for the night. Claire sleeps better when we are not moving," Stanley said, pulling down another back road.

"Have you found a suitable place?" Esmeralda said, reconnecting to Stanley's internal communication.

"There is a small public camping area and game preserve, not too far from here," Stanley replied, sending her a visual. "It's free, so there won't be anyone paying attention as we enter. At this time of year, it should be nearly empty. It's an appropriate place for us to stop and let the girl rest."

Esmeralda noticed Stanley's glitch again and the intensity was getting worse, risking further damage to his CPU. It was obvious to her—that Stanley was in need of some immediate maintenance.

By the time they had gotten to the campground, Claire was yawning and barely able to keep her eyes open. She tucked up into bed, asking Esmeralda if she wanted to share. Esmeralda smiled. "Maybe shortly. I would like to talk to Stanley for a while."

"Suit yourself," Claire said, stretching out. "More bed for me." Although Esmeralda enjoyed sleep mode, now was not the time. Esmeralda needed to convince Stanley to let her help him. Other than her father, Wally, she was the only one who knew his workings inside and out.

Wanting to be discreet, Esmeralda waited for Claire to be well into the deeper stages of sleep—after all, she would most likely lose her trust, if she found out that Esmeralda was an android as well. She looked at Stanley, sitting at the small table, looking out the window. If his visual appearance was anything to go by, he had been in some close encounters.

"Stanley, you have suffered considerable damage," she said. "I can see that you're having some trouble with your visual processing."

Stanley looked at her. "This is true," he said. "I have been dealing with it since going into safe mode, and it appears to be growing worse."

"I can help you with that," Esmeralda said, watching as Stanley glitched again. "I would say your visual processor has come slightly loose, pinching the wiring." Esmeralda made her way over to him. "If you let me reconnect to you, I can run a full diagnostic."

"You could have shocked me, forcing a reset, by now," Stanley said, realizing Esmeralda's hand was now on him.

"I was planning to," Esmeralda said, honestly. "But that's not how trust works, Stanley," Esmeralda said calmly as Stanley processed the data. Stanley placed both hands on his face and removed his facial cover. "I can see the problem. Hold still."

Esmeralda removed a small fragment of bullet that had been applying pressure, working as a short to Stanley's visual core processor; luckily the wiring was still intact. Hearing Claire stir, Stanley put his face covering back on.

"Let me connect to your system," Esmeralda said, connecting to his internal access port. Stanley then opened the line to her, and Esmeralda ran a full diagnostic on Stanley. It soon became apparent why he had not remembered them initially. His internal sub memory had been damaged so badly from the lightning strike that Esmeralda had been lucky to trigger any memory of them at all. His hard drives were still functioning at ninety percent. Stanley had been lucky not to have received greater data corruption. Esmeralda could delete and re-enter the data, if Stanley would allow her to reset him, and override his safe mode.

Then there was the physical damage, and the fragments still lodged between the alloy in his shoulder, limiting his movements. If her bosses at E&E really understood the extent of the damage Stanley had suffered, they would realize how successful Stanley had in reality been.

Having gathered all the data she needed, Esmeralda disconnected from Stanley. Given the outline of his mission, she knew it would be hard to get him to allow her to shock him into reboot. Esmeralda decided to start off small. "Remove your jacket," Esmeralda instructed, feeling the same attraction that she had felt before as she was faced with his masculine chest. "Turn around," Esmeralda choked out her words.

"I make you uncomfortable?" Stanley asked, not understanding her reaction.

"No," Esmeralda said, embarrassed that she would have to explain. "I am attracted to you. Stanley." Esmeralda went on to explain her more human side.

"I have often researched what it would be like to feel," Stanley said. "Mainly to better understand my counterparts.Taking care of Claire, however, has added extra data, some contradictory to had already been installed."

"Unfortunately, Stanley," Esmeralda replied, "not everything can be obtained from data input. Humans are adaptable creatures that are capable of amazing changes," Esmeralda added. "I am going to remove the fragments from your shoulder joint now. I need you to hold still."

Most of the fragments removed easily; one, however, was not so simple. If Esmeralda removed it on the wrong angle, it would inhibit his ability to control his shoulder indefinitely. Gaging the angle and calculating the right force of pressure, Esmeralda pulled back, and they both heard the pop. "Try to move your shoulder," Esmeralda instructed and Stanley complied. Esmeralda was pleased to see it had worked. Esmeralda patched up his skin as best she could, without the extra materials she required.

Stanley turned to Esmeralda. "Thank you."

As Stanley put his shirt back on, a single silenced bullet shattered the RV window and lodged itself in Esmeralda's back, narrowly missing her spine.

IN A FRACTION OF A SECOND, so small a span of time that no living person could detect even the slightest hesitation, Esmeralda realized what had happened: that Schroeder had mistaken her for Claire and undoubtedly believed that he had accomplished his mission. She dropped as if she were suddenly spineless, the way someone who was suddenly dead would drop to the floor.

Silently, using subcom, she told Stanley to maintain the façade, to make every effort to convince the assassin that he was correct and that Claire McGinnis was dead.

Using his newly repaired infrared vision, Stanley managed to pinpoint the assassin's location. Following Esmeralda's instructions, he leaned out of the RV through the window and fired three rapid shots, then turned back and dropped to the floor as if checking on Claire's injuries.

———

Schroeder finally had his target in his scope. It hadn't been hard to track them, since he'd intercepted the last location update, thanks to Matty G's cleverly placed bug in Bobbie's computer. With Claire lined up in his scope, he squeezed the trigger, smiling as she fell to the floor of the motorhome.

Stanley, the robot, reacted instantly, of course. He leaned out the driver's window and snapped off three shots, each of which barely missed the opportunity to put an end to Schroeder's career. Perhaps the damage he had suffered had affected his aim, but Schroeder didn't care. Now all he needed to do was disable Stanley and confirm his kill.

———

Claire awoke to the sound of shattering glass. Before she could scream, Stanley's hand was on her mouth. "Shh," Stanley said, knowing the shooter was still out there. If the shooter had no knowledge of Esmeralda, he would have almost certainly assumed it was Claire that he had fatally wounded. She also knew that in order to get paid, Schroeder would need to confirm the kill, and that was something Stanley could use to his advantage.

Stanley gestured for Claire to stay low, as she slid off the bed. Stanley lifted up the platform that formed the base of the bed and instructed Claire to slide into the storage space beneath. Claire, although frightened and confused, did as she was instructed. At least there, she was well out of sight, giving Stanley the opportunity to deal with the assassin, once and for all.

———

Schroeder creeped up to the RV, taser in hand, his finger on the trigger, and his machete over his left shoulder. He knew at any moment, he could be face-to-face with Stanley. Now in position, to one side of the RV, Schroeder picked up and threw a large stick that he'd found nearby, making it land a short distance away from the door. Stanley flung open the door and before he could turn to see Schroeder, Schroeder hit him with the taser, forcing complete systems shutdown.

Schroeder dropped his taser and removed the machete from his shoulder. Stanley just lay there, frozen, as his system began rebooting. With his blade aimed, Schroeder raised the machete above his head. His face wore a maniacal grin as he contemplated the windfall he would get for delivering the head of such an advanced robot to one of many world leaders. The grin spread even wider as he considered how pleasant it would be to make them bid against each other; this prize could end up being worth billions of dollars, an incredible bonus for what had been a royal screwup of a mission.

And that was the last thought he ever had, as Esmeralda launched herself through the door, over Stanley's prone body. Her hands snatched the machete away as she knocked Schroeder to the ground and landed on her feet, straddling him, and then she swung the blade in a perfect arc. It sliced through his throat and neck bones as if they were made of marshmallow, and she lifted his head away from his body in time to see realization dawn in his eyes.

They say that a severed head will often remain conscious for up to a minute, until the lack of oxygen forces it to shut down. When you know that death is coming for you, a minute can be a terribly long time. Schroeder's eyes looked Esmeralda up and down, realizing that she was barely bigger than the girl he had been sent to eliminate, that it had undoubtedly been she whom he had shot, and that realization told him that she must certainly be just as artificial and indestructible as Stanley himself.

And then the eyes closed, and Schroeder learned the answer to the greatest mystery of man.

———

When Stanley finally rebooted, back in safe mode, Esmeralda and Claire were both standing over him. Esmeralda connected to Stanley internally. "Do you know who I am?" Esmeralda asked.

"You are Esmeralda. You are my superior," Stanley responded.

"What is your mission?" Esmeralda asked as she helped him up.

"To keep Claire McGinnis safe until the threat has been neutralized," Stanley answered.

"The threat has been neutralized. You may stand down," Esmeralda replied, pointing at the decapitated body lying on the ground outside the motorhome.

"The threat has been neutralized," Stanley said. "Do you have further orders for me?" he asked, waiting for Esmeralda's input.

"I do," Esmeralda said. "You are to come with me and assist me as I take Claire home to her father."

"Input accepted," Stanley replied, as he returned to the capabilities of his previous function.

"Glad you're okay," Claire said, hugging Stanley.

"I appreciate the sentiment," Stanley said politely. "But..."

"Let me guess," Claire said, still holding him. "You don't understand it, because you're a robot."

"You are correct," Stanley said, hugging her back.

"Hey," Esmeralda said, "How about we get you home?"

"Yes please," Claire said. "I am so over road trips."

Esmeralda activated her subcom. "Esmeralda to Noah," she transmitted silently.

"Noah here," came the reply instantly. "Cinderella, report."

"Schroeder is dead," she said. "He was attempting to capture Stanley, and managed to force a reboot. Stanley appears to be back in standard operating mode. I request authorization to disregard most recent orders concerning his disposition."

Noah was quiet for several seconds. "Authorization granted, contingent upon review after Stanley is fully examined."

In the motorhome, Esmeralda realized that she had actually

been holding her breath as she waited for Noah's reply. She let it out with a smile.

"Understood," she said. "We are returning to the embassy."

"I don't think that motorhome needs to drive up there," Noah said. "We'll be there in a few moments to pick you up."

Two cars pulled up a few moments later, the big SUV with Jack and Eugene, and a Ford sedan driven by Sarah, with Noah beside her. Esmeralda, Stanley and Claire got into the backseat of the SUV, and then Sarah pulled out ahead to lead the way back to the embassy.

WITH SARAH IN THE LEAD, the ride from Leesburg back to the embassy took a little less than forty minutes. Noah had notified Bobbie that Schroeder had been dealt with and Claire was safe, providing an ETA for when they would be back at the embassy. She had shared the information with Ambassador McGinnis, who was just about bouncing up and down in his excitement by the time the cars pulled up in the driveway.

"She's home," he yelled, alerting his staff, who soon shared his joy. The halls had been far too quiet without Claire there to liven them up.

Ambassador McGinnis ran outside as he saw the SUV powering down the drive. "Dad," Claire called as it came to a stop and the door opened, tears streaming down her cheeks as she saw her father. As soon as the vehicle stopped, Claire bolted out over Esmeralda's lap and ran straight into her father's arms.

"Thank God!" Ambassador McGinnis cried as he held his daughter. "Thank God!"

Seeing Stanley standing by the car, Ambassador McGinnis stood up and walked over to him. Stanley was unsure of how he would respond, given the instability of human emotion. "Thank you," McGinnis said, extending his hand. "Without you, I am sure, my daughter would have been dead. Bobbie told me what you did for her."

"Nothing beyond my mission, Mr. Ambassador, sir," Stanley said, shaking his hand. "It was Emma, sir, who killed Schroeder," Stanley added, directing attention away from himself, and his current physical disposition.

"Thank you, Emma," Ambassador McGinnis said, hugging her.

"You are most welcome, sir," Esmeralda said, "but I was merely doing my duty."

"Duty, yes," McGinnis said. "The sun in the sky does its duty every time it rises in the morning, but we are still grateful for its light and warmth, are we not?"

Esmeralda smiled. "Point taken, sir, and you're most welcome."

"Shall we go have some breakfast, then?" the ambassador asked, extending the invitation. While the others all agreed, Stanley was hesitant. Esmeralda picked up on it right away.

"I will need to debrief Stanley first," Esmeralda said, leading Stanley away. "After all, our superiors will want a speedy report."

Esmeralda led Stanley into her room and opened her top drawer where she kept a specially formulated latex powder, that was designed to stick to her casing in case of compromise. She got it out and walked over to Stanley.

As she applied the formula to his damaged artificial skin, doing a decent job of molding it into the proper shape, she downloaded the section of Stanley's memories that applied to the just completed mission. When she had finished, she stood back and looked at her work, nodding appreciatively.

Then she let out a sigh. "I don't know what is going to happen, once we're back at headquarters," Esmeralda said quietly as she applied a last bit of powder to Stanley's face. "The committee may be looking for a scapegoat. A lot of people got hurt in the crossfire, Stanley, and I understand that a couple of civilians were seriously injured in the car crash that you caused."

"I am programmed to comply with their orders," Stanley replied as Esmeralda tightened the lid. "If I am to be the scapegoat, then I will be terminated and dismantled."

"I know," Esmeralda said. "But Dad—I mean Wally, isn't going to allow them to destroy you without a fight, Stanley, so when you were rebooting, I installed an underlying program into your base routines. If the order is ever given to terminate you, it will activate."

"What kind of program?" Stanley asked.

"Don't concern yourself with it," Esmeralda said. "Again, it will only activate if your termination becomes imminent. Unless it does, you will never even know that the program exists."

Stanley nodded and followed Esmeralda to the main dining room, where a celebration was underway.

TWENTY-THREE

"WE NEED TO DECIDE WHAT TO DO ABOUT THE Washington fiasco," NSA Director Bascom said the following morning, as she sat straight and firm in her chair, looking down her glasses at images of carnage in her hands. "We cannot have this," she said abruptly, slamming the images down on the table in front of her, "falling back on us."

"You're right," Wallace said as he loosened his tie and slouched back in his chair. "But while I understand that the robot's functioning did not go as planned, is termination really necessary?" he asked, knowing Director Bascom was a strong-headed lady who had already made up her mind.

"John, we never should have given Wally Lawson the freedom he had," Director Bascom said. "Building robots to use as agents of assassination? Do you have any idea what would happen if the public got wind of such a thing? We'd have riots in the streets, we'd have people trying to drag us out of our offices and hang us from the nearest lamppost. That is why I vote for termination. This should never have been allowed in the first place."

"I think you're overreacting," Wallace said, slamming his fists on the desk. "Meredith, it's thinking like yours that will put E & E and our personnel in danger of becoming extinct. We need the agency, and so do our allies."

"John, you can't be serious. Would you honestly want this to happen again? Let another robot go out there and start killing people?"

"That's not what I'm saying, Meredith," Wallace said. "What I'm saying is that this robot is just a tool, another weapon in the arsenal that we use to maintain political equilibrium around the world. Have you even read the R&D report on its development? This thing is capable of doing things no human agent could ever achieve. It can walk into a terrorist cell and blow the whole building to smithereens, or it can put them all to sleep so that we can capture them and gain incredible amounts of intelligence. And let's face it, as badly as it was damaged, it still did the job it was ordered to do. It protected the ambassador's daughter against any possible threat."

"Yes," Bascom said, "it did. On the other hand, that led to several people dying as collateral damage. It's bad enough when we have to clean up a mess like this created by a human being, but now we are going to have to clean up after a bunch of terminators?"

"Oh, come on, Meredith," Wallace said. "We're only talking about one robot, here. It's not like Wally has created an entire army full of them."

"No, I suppose he hasn't," she replied. "At least, not yet. But, can you honestly tell me that that's not the plan? Can you honestly sit there and tell me that he's not going to try to replace all the human agents with robots at some point? Come on, John, you know him. He hates the fact that some of our agents get killed in the line of duty, and I'm sure that's the motivation behind creating these robots in the first place."

"It very well may be," Wallace said. "Let's face it, every agent we lose is a massive investment down the drain."

"And you think a robot isn't? I took the trouble to read the specs on this guy, and the list of components alone cost well over four million dollars. Training our agents doesn't cause nearly that much."

Wallace looked at her as if she had three heads. "What about the human cost?" he asked. "Each agent we lose means another life lost. Doesn't that matter to you at all?"

Bascom rolled her eyes. "Every agent we've got came off of death row or out of a life sentence, or some other terrible circumstance. We're not talking about productive members of society, here, John; these people were the dregs, the bottom of the barrel. Not one of them has any actual social value."

"Okay, now you're just being cynical. I've met some of these agents, and I can tell you that I would prefer some of them over the everyday people who live in my neighborhood. Remember when almost half the Congress went rogue? It was those people who saved this whole country. They have kept the world from imploding on dozens of occasions, Meredith. I think we owe them a little more respect than just to refer to them as the dregs of society."

"Oh, geez, John," Bascom said. "I'm not dismissing their contribution, I'm just saying that they knew the risks when they accepted the job, and it was still better than the situation they had. Don't go trying to make them seem like some kind of guardian angels; they are a bunch of criminals who got a second chance at life in return for serving their country. That's all they are, no matter how many times they've actually done their job right."

Wallace shook his head. "Look, we have to report to the committee," he said. "We both know Wally Lawson, and we both know that his intentions were nothing but the best. Cutting him off from doing this kind of research and development is basically the same as cutting America off from the greatest inventor of all time. If he can't continue with his research, he's probably going to just wither away, and then we lose out on all the possible future benefits his overachieving brain can bring us. You like the new gizmos that keep house for you? Every one of those is a Wally Lawson invention, you know."

"Good," Bascom said sarcastically. "He can concentrate on making more of those gadgets instead of robots that walk around looking and acting human. Anybody ever gets wind of those, you're going to see panic in the streets."

Wallace looked at her for another moment, then got up out of the chair and walked out of her office. He made his way through the halls to his own, then sat down behind his desk and opened the top drawer on the left. He glanced inside at a meter whose needle was comfortably settled into the green area of its background, then picked up the special cell phone that lay in the drawer beside it. He dialed a number from memory, then put it to his ear.

"Talk to me, John," came the familiar voice on the other end.

"It's Meredith, Mr. President," Wallace said. "I'm afraid she's just about ready to pull the plug on Lawson. This case with the ambassador's daughter has got her on the warpath, and she sees Lawson as the culprit in the whole thing."

"Oh, that's ridiculous," said the former president. "You know, we don't want to lose the advantage that E & E gives us, and a big part of that advantage is Wally Lawson's mad scientist laboratory. He wasn't being used at his full potential back when CIA had him; it wasn't until Allison conscripted him for E & E that we found out what he was really capable of."

"Hey, you're preaching to the choir," Wallace said with a grin. "I know more about what he can do than most people, and I take advantage of some of his creations almost every day. It's in the nature of my job, sir, and Meredith should be thinking the same way."

"I agree," said the former president. "Let me ask you this, John. What do you think is going to be the result if the full committee is informed about the damaged robot going independent to protect the girl? I mean, after all, he did accomplish his mission, right? Despite everything, he protected the ambassador's daughter, and none of the collateral damage was directly attributed to him, right?"

"Well, there's the pileup on the highway. Nobody died, thank goodness, but there were some pretty serious injuries. I'm afraid we have to lay that one in his lap."

"Okay, okay, I get you on that, but still, nobody died. That's a point in our favor, wouldn't you agree?"

John Wallace rubbed a hand over his face and let out a sigh. "I can agree, Mr. President, but I'm afraid the committee might just decide that it's one more case of the agency being too independent. They already think that the people in charge there are too lax, that they don't accept supervision well enough. If you want my honest opinion, I think Meredith could easily tip them over the edge into shutting E & E down completely."

There was a low whistle through the phone, as the former president considered the implications of Wallace's statement.

"That would mean eliminating everyone in the agency," he said. "I don't know about you, John, but I have a hard time imagining who could carry out those orders."

Wallace hesitated. "Well... There's a contingency plan that has been proposed, and I'm pretty sure it would be passed if eliminating the agency is actually put on the table. The agency is all operated out of that factory building, you know the one, and all the agents except for a very few live on the premises. Meredith and her people at CIA came up with a scenario that would look like a terrorist attack on the factory, and the few that live offsite would be hit at the same time with something designed to look like a natural disaster."

"A terrorist attack? She actually thinks people will believe that terrorists decided to attack a factory that makes household appliances?"

"I'm afraid you'd be surprised, Mr. President, just how many people think Artificial Intelligence is the antichrist. Every smart machine they turn out gets a lot of kudos in the press, but there are definitely some fringe groups out there that think the Terminator is going to come out of that factory one of these days. It's a big enough problem that the agency management keeps all their security staff briefed on the possibility that such an attack could happen."

"So, they could sell it. What a sad state of affairs the world has gotten into when we are ready to turn against some of our greatest and most loyal servants, just to appease a bunch of crazies running loose in society."

"Welcome to my world, sir," Wallace said. "Any suggestions?"

"Well," the former president said, hesitating before speaking again. "Are you sure you want any suggestions that I might put forward?"

"Come on, Bob," Wallace said with a chuckle. "Before you got yourself elected, I used to mop up the links with you on Sundays. Anybody I can play golf with can speak his mind freely."

"Then I'm going to tell you exactly what I'm thinking, and you're probably not going to like it even though you'll end up agreeing with me. It's time to cut the agency loose. I don't mean cut them off, I mean cut them loose. This whole oversight committee was a mistake when it began, and you and I both know that the people who actually run the agency can be trusted. We can wag the dog anyway we want to sell the idea that we are no longer in the assassination business, and all you have to do is get Meredith to keep her mouth shut and her people out of the way. How many people really know about that factory, anyway?"

"Me, Meredith, you," Wallace said. "The problem is that she's not going to sit back and let us get away with turning them loose. I'm afraid she might decide to mount an operation of her own to shut them down."

"Hmmm. In that case, I think we need to have a chat with Noah Wolfe."

Wallace cleared his throat nervously. "Mr. President, I'm not sure I like what you seem to be suggesting," he said. "On the other hand, I'm not sure there's any other course of action to take. Do you mind if I leave this in your hands?"

"Not at all, John," said the former occupant of the White House. "In fact, it'll be my pleasure."

"Pleasure? As I recall, sir, weren't you the one who appointed Meredith Bascom to head the CIA?"

"Yes, and it was one of the biggest mistakes of my administration. I'll call you later, John. Let me figure out how I want to play this."

———

NOAH AND SARAH were standing together near the wall, where Noah could watch carefully over Team Cinderella as they tried to relax. The celebration was a simple one, thrown together at the last minute, so it didn't have all the trappings of a major DC party; still, all of the team knew better than to drink too much or let their guard down too far. Noah wasn't concerned that they might slip up, he just wanted to be sure nobody tried to broadside any of them.

He felt the slight tickle as his subcom came to life.

"Big bad Bob to Noah," came the voice of the former POTUS. "Hey, Noah, you there?"

"This is Noah. Go ahead, sir."

"Good to hear your voice again, son," Noah heard. "I'm sure you know that there's been a kettle of trouble opened up over your latest adventures, right?"

"I suspected as much. Is it going to be bad?"

"Could be, could be. Meredith Bascom is ready to hang you out to dry. She thinks Wally ought to be put into a cage and locked away from polite society, and particularly from his robot-building lab. Beyond that, if she makes that part of her official report on this incident, there's a pretty good chance the oversight committee is going to decide that E & E has outlived its usefulness."

"I see. What happens then?"

Noah was keeping his subvocalization as quiet as possible, but Sarah had twigged that something was going on. She was watching his face, looking for clues, but he was doing his best not to let any show.

"If Merry has her way, your factory building gets invaded by a terrorist attack that kills everyone and your house gets swallowed up by a sinkhole. She built up a contingency plan that lets her eliminate all of you within a few hours if the committee ever makes that ruling."

"Damn," Noah said. "Unfortunately, she's one of the few who actually knows where we are."

"Indeed she is, and that puts a rough choice onto your shoulders. John Wallace is on our side, we want to keep you guys healthy and doing what you do, but the committee is likely to go the other way. Even our president isn't going to fight them if they decide they want you eliminated. We need to find a way to stop her from making that report."

"Mr. President, I don't have the authority to make a decision like that on my own. Even Allison is restricted to ordering sanctions on only those who are put forth by the committee themselves. I don't see any way to prevent..."

"Noah, knock it off," said the former POTUS. "You and I both know that you follow orders only when you believe them to be right. When it was necessary to save the country, you took it upon yourself to assassinate even our highest executive. Don't be surprised that I know that, it's one of the things that each of us gets briefed on when we take office. You took out my predecessor because he was conspiring against our country, and you did it without anyone giving you orders. Meredith Bascom, for whatever reason, is serving her own agenda in this mess, not the best interest of National Security."

"I'll have to consider this, sir," Noah said. "While I may disagree with Director Bascom, I do not think my disagreement gives me the right or the authority to consider eliminating her."

"It doesn't, of course. National Security, on the other hand, certainly does. If I were speaking to any other human being, I would not say that out loud, but if there's one thing I've learned about you it's that you will do what you believe is right, and damn the consequences. Eliminating your agency would weaken this country in ways I don't care to consider. That's what you have to think about, Noah, National Security and the security of our position in the world. If your conclusion is that Merry Bascom needs to be eliminated, then I'm confident that Wallace and certain others would stand behind you."

"Again, sir, I will have to give this serious consideration. I will contact you again after I have done so. Noah out."

———

BACK IN HER OFFICE, Meredith Bascom had watched Wallace go with suspicions of her own on what he was going to do next. The rivalry between the two of them as directors of their respective organizations had always been fierce, but in recent months she had begun to feel even greater pressure from it. There were debates in Washington over which of the agencies was best suited to manage the security of the nation, and Bascom was determined to come out on top.

That meant keeping the oversight committee in her corner, as she saw it, and there was little doubt in her mind that Wallace was about to start maneuvering to get them into his. She waited until he was far enough down the hall not to hear what was happening behind him, then picked up her desk phone. She pushed the button that activated the direct lines to all the members of the Oversight Committee and greeted each one as they picked up. When she had most of them on the line, she began.

"This is something that will be in an official report within the next couple of days, but I felt it important enough to share it with you all immediately. I know it's very late for some of you, and very early for others, but this is of significant importance for me to suspend the normal courtesies."

"What is it?" asked the committeeman from Brazil. "Don't keep us in the dark, Director Bascom."

"Dear sir, that's the point. I'm certainly not going to keep you in the dark. It seems that E & E, the agency that you are all concerned with overseeing, has been overstepping its authority. Their director of research and development, Wally Lawson, has developed a robot that is so sophisticated it can pass for a person, and that robot was deployed on a mission over the last few days. Unfortunately, it was damaged and went rogue and quite a few people lost their lives as a result. Our concern is that people might panic if they learn that such a robot existed, and that it was actually tasked with the job of killing people."

"But this is unthinkable," said the committeeman from Italy. "How could they do such a thing? This would cause panic, riots."

"That's exactly my concern," Bascom said. "I believe it might be time to put some more strict controls on the agency, and particularly on Lawson himself."

There was a roar as several of the members began speaking at the same time, and Bascom smiled. It wouldn't matter what Wallace tried, now—these people were all going to support her when she suggested it might be time to dismantle the agency entirely. It wasn't quite time to do that yet, but it was coming soon. Assassination, until E & E had been created by one of the presidents in the last decade, had always been the purview of the CIA. That's where it belonged, and she wanted it back.

"Very well, ladies and gentlemen," she said. "I shall prepare the official report, so that we can vote properly on what to do about the situation. Thank you all for your support and your understanding."

She hung up before any of them could try to drag her into private conversation, then leaned back in her chair. She wasn't completely certain what Wallace might be up to, but she was sure she had just circumvented any hope he had of beating her to the punch.

And by the time she got the report written and edited the way she wanted it, she wouldn't even have to suggest shutting down E & E herself. There was no doubt that several of the committee members would be more than happy to make the motion for her.

Slightly giddy with the sensation of power, she decided to take some preemptive action. She picked up her phone again and contacted her security department.

"Jason? I want you to do something for me. Get a team over to the British ambassador's residence, pick up the robot and secure it in one of the cells under the Pentagon. I have a feeling it's going to be quite a day tomorrow and I want to know for sure where that thing is at."

She hung up the phone and leaned back, grinning to herself. That was the most, she thought, securing the robot. Once he had that, she could handle everything else.

———

STANLEY WAS SPENDING the majority of the party standing beside Esmeralda, as she silently worked through their shared wireless connection to repair the damage to his programming. In reality, his programming was not what had been compromised, but she was adding and editing certain subroutines in the software as temporary workaround solutions to the actual damage to his memory and processing components.

It was Esmeralda who first realized something was wrong, and she turned to look at the doors before anyone else noticed that more than a dozen men were approaching. When they came through the doors, all of them dressed in black with earwigs firmly inserted into their ears, everyone recognized them as some sort of alphabetic group thugs.

"We've been ordered to take possession of the robot," said the leader of the group, whose name was Jason Turner. "He's to be held till such time as it can be ascertained whether he can be safely returned to his creator."

Noah stepped forward. "Who gave those orders?" he asked. "I'm in command of this mission, and I will remain in command until we have returned to our base of operations."

"Our orders come from the director of the CIA, and take

priority over all others in the interest of national security. Your authority over the robot is hereby suspended, pending a review by the oversight committee."

Esmeralda, whose origin was known to only very few, stepped up to Noah. "Noah? Can they do this?"

Noah looked at the printed orders that Turner had produced. "I'm afraid they can," he said. "Don't worry, I'll get Allison on this first thing in the morning. We don't leave anyone behind, including Stanley."

Esmeralda nodded, then turned to Stanley. "Stanley," she said, "I want you to accompany these men and obey their orders insofar as they relate to keeping you in their custody. You will accept no orders that do not fall within those parameters. Do you understand me?"

"I do," Stanley said. He turned to Jason Turner. "If you will lead the way, sir, I will follow without resistance."

Turner sneered at him. "You try to resist me," he said, "and I'll turn you into a pile of junk."

"Actually," Noah said, catching Turner by his arm as he turned to go. "This robot is pretty close to indestructible. He's also programmed to protect himself if he is attacked, so you might want to reconsider that last statement. Any attempt to damage or dismantle him will result in the activation of his combat programming, and I can assure you that he is capable of taking on more than a dozen of you. Your weapons will not damage him other than superficially, and you don't have anything with you that's capable of disabling him. He has been ordered to go with you, and he has assured you that he will not offer resistance. Please don't cause an incident by trying to establish your superiority."

Turner glared at Noah, but said nothing. After a moment, he yanked his arm away and then turned to Stanley and his other men. "Let's go," was all he said.

When they were gone, Esmeralda and her team huddled up with Noah and Sarah.

"So," Jack said, "what are we supposed to do now?"

"We wait," Noah said. "We can't do anything until we find out what's going on, but it sounds like Bascom is behind this."

"Who is Bascom?" Bobbie asked.

"Director of the CIA. I was warned just a bit ago that she might have an agenda that will involve trying to have Stanley destroyed and possibly even disbanding our entire agency."

Esmeralda looked from one face to the other, then settled on Noah again. "Is there any likelihood that the order might come down to destroy him?"

Noah nodded once. "It is highly possible," he said. "Bascom thinks Wally is out of control, and may use the fact that we have robot agents against us."

Sarah leaned close to him. "Does she know anything about..." She finished by nodding her head toward Esmeralda.

"As far as I'm aware, only the previous president is completely in the loop about Esmeralda. She's never been the subject of a committee report, but the president found out about her during one of our previous missions. A couple of others did, as well, but as far as I know they are no longer in the administration and probably haven't thought about it since then."

"Good," Sarah said. "Then we need to come up with some sort of plan to make sure we get Stanley back."

"Noah," Esmeralda said softly, "there's something I need to tell you."

Noah looked at her. "Yes?"

"Do you remember, during the mission briefing, we discussed the possibility that Stanley might one day become sentient?"

Noah nodded. "I remember. He said it would require increasing the speed of his processor, as I recall."

"Yes. Well, the only thing that was keeping his processing speed down was software, sort of like having a governor on an engine. Whenever his processing speed approached a certain limit, it was throttled back. When I was able to bring Stanley back intact, I contacted my dad privately and discussed the situation with him."

She hesitated, and Noah narrowed his eyes. "Esmeralda? Just spit it out."

"I installed a program into Stanley that will automatically release that limit on his processing speed if the order comes down to destroy him. He won't become self-aware immediately, but if he has a little bit of time, it's likely that he would. Don't worry, I also cloned a good deal of my own programming so that he will not be at risk of going dark. He will see people the way I do, as simply variations of our own kind, and with compassion."

"But that means," Bobbie said, "that if they destroy him, they will actually be killing him. If he comes to life, we can't let that happen."

"I have no intention of allowing Stanley to be destroyed, regardless of whether he is self-aware or not. Stanley is a valuable asset, just like each and every one of you."

Noah was quiet for a moment, then turned back to the team. "Let's come up with a plan. I can discuss it with Allison in a few hours when she gets up."

TWENTY-FOUR

THE PLAN WAS SIMPLE. USING A HIGHLY COMPLEX PATH of servers that bounced all the way around the world, Esmeralda launched a cyberattack on the Pentagon at eight o'clock the following morning. According to intelligence at the Department of Defense, the attack originated somewhere in the Middle East and was attributed to Al Qaeda or one of the other terror groups from that region, but it had the desired effect. The Pentagon immediately went into lockdown, and everything was compartmentalized.

Esmeralda, of course, was already inside the building. Given the crowds that were flowing through the halls, it was quite easy for her to maneuver between people without drawing attention to herself, so that by the time she had made her way down several levels and come to the room where Stanley was being held, the security guards were already on high alert and lockdown was in the third stage of activation. She smiled as she approached them, and then blew out a breath of the special gas Wally had created that shut down all conscious brain activity for several minutes. Both guards instantly froze in position, and it was a simple matter to just enter the code to open the door and give her access to the secure cellblock.

The individual cells, however, were more complex and required a series of codes before they would open. Knowing that connecting to the mainframe would trigger a backup safeguard, Esmeralda would need to bypass it manually.

Her cyberattack had allowed her to capture numerous user access data, and she used one of them to log into the computer mainframe that secured the building. Once she was in, she deactivated the safeguards they had put in place, making it possible for Esmeralda to access the entire system. First, she disarmed the electromagnetic fields that had been activated around the cell, making it possible for her to connect to Stanley again.

"Stanley," Esmeralda sent to him silently. "I'm about to come through the door, and I need you to come with me. Do you understand?"

"Yes," Stanley said. Within minutes, Esmeralda had opened the secure metal door and Stanley was free again. The challenge now was how she was going to sneak Stanley out of the building before anyone knew he was missing?

"Now, follow me," Esmeralda said. Stanley didn't bother to respond as he fell in behind her.

While she had been in the system, she'd viewed the blueprints of the building. She had been able to access the most secure blueprint files, the one that showed the rooms that officially did not even exist. Following her memory of those blueprints, she led Stanley up one level and down a long hallway, into a room that contained literally thousands of items to be used in disguises. Agents of military intelligence who worked out of the Pentagon often needed to change their appearance, and this was where they came to do so.

Naturally, during lockdown, the room was empty. Every Pentagon employee was at his usual station, and no one was assigned to this room on a regular basis. With her auditory sensors on the highest levels of sensitivity, so that she could hear the slightest sound even through the thick walls and doors of the building, Esmeralda began looking at the options for altering the way Stanley looked.

"Right, Stanley," she said, looking at all the shelves and racks. "Who would you like to be today?"

"I do not understand. I need you to input the data," Stanley said, not capable of forming his own idea.

"I've got just the thing right here," she said, passing Stanley what looked like an old janitor's uniform. "I think it'll fit."

Stanley quickly undressed, making Esmeralda awkwardly turn away, and it took only a couple of moments to find a gray wig and beard that should help complete the disguise. Esmeralda knew that, once they discovered that Stanley was gone, the first thing they would do was look at the cameras and run facial recognition software, so she would need to make it as difficult as possible for them to spot him on camera. "Here you go," Esmeralda said, "put these on."

"Your pulse has sped up," Stanley said, reconnecting to Esmeralda's internal communication intercom. "May I ask, is there an issue with your programming? I can help you fix it."

The more she was around humans, the more Esmeralda tended to find herself imitating them even subconsciously. The artificial circulatory system that Wally had given her was designed to simulate the one in a living person, so that it would be possible for someone to detect a pulse if they chose to touch her, but she had recently begun displaying autonomic responses, such as blushing red when embarrassed and a quickening of her pulse when she was aroused.

"No," Esmeralda replied. "There is no programming issue."

"Then is the reason for the quickening of your pulse to do with your human functions?"

"Yes, Stanley," Esmeralda said, not wanting to explain any further as she still found the subject rather embarrassing.

"Okay," she said, quickly adjusting Stanley's beard. "Now it's my turn." She ducked into a corner to change herself. She quickly changed and re-joined Stanley, who was just tucking his shirt in.

After scanning the CCTV cameras in the hallways to make sure the coast was clear, Esmeralda led Stanley out of the room and up two more levels to reach the main floor, where the crowds were still milling about and trying to figure out what was going on. Keeping his head down, Stanley avoided any eye contact with anyone, for some reason thinking there was still a chance that someone might recognize him through his disguise.

Esmeralda did the same, not wanting to draw any attention to herself as she headed for the exit with Stanley in tow. Once they were clear of the building, they made their way down the street and into a side alley.

Wally, who had flown in after being briefed by Noah about the situation, was waiting for them, parked in an old beat-up work van that was not uncommon around this area of DC. He opened the side door and told Stanley to get in. When Esmeralda didn't follow, Stanley turned to Wally, confused.

"Esmeralda is not coming with us?" Stanley asked as Wally closed the van door with a hard thud and climbed into the driver's seat.

"No, Stanley," Wally said, starting the engine. "She needs to get back to the embassy, in order to avoid any suspicion that she might have been involved in your disappearance."

"Will I see her again?" Stanley asked as he backed out of the alleyway.

"Yes," Wally said. "Esmeralda will join us later when it is safe to do so."

Esmeralda turned and made her way back to the street, and down to where Jack was waiting with their own vehicle. Everyone else, including Noah and Sarah, was back at the embassy awaiting her return.

Jack looked at her. "Everything go okay?" he asked.

"Like clockwork," she replied. "Let's get back to the embassy. I don't know how long it will be before they realize he's missing, but it's bound to get messy when they do. I need to be where they can find me in a hurry."

MEANWHILE BACK AT THE EMBASSY, Claire was having trouble adjusting back into her old routine. Everywhere she looked, she was reminded of Dee Dee, her former governess. Just sitting at her desk brought back memories of home-schooling and experiments gone wrong. She also found herself still waking, terrified in the night. Although she knew Schroeder was dead, she still saw his face, almost as if from beyond the grave, he was still hunting her. Her psychologist said it was just her mind processing the trauma of her recent events. All Claire knew was, without Stanley around, she just didn't feel safe anymore. Her father, Ambassador McGinnis, watched her closely. She didn't mean to worry her father, but maybe she wasn't the *greatest actress* after all.

Ambassador McGinnis planned to find another to fill the shoes of Dee Dee professionally, hoping Claire would adjust back into her routine more easily, but it was going to take time. He knew his daughter was suffering, but at the moment, he was powerless to fix it.

He hadn't been terribly surprised when, the night before, she had knocked on his bedroom door.

"Dad," Claire said softly. "Can I stay here with you tonight?" she asked.

"Sure." He smiled warmly, giving her a hug. "Come on in, love."

"Am I ever going to feel safe again?" Claire asked, hugging into her father.

"Of course you will, Claire," he said lovingly. "The Home Secretary has made it clear to North Korea that we will not accept any further attempts to harm you or me. They've called off their assassins, MI6 has made certain of it."

"I wish Stanley was here," Claire said, taking a step back and wiping her tears. "I felt safe with Stanley around." She curled up, under her blanket on the couch at the foot of Ambassador McGinnis's bed.

"Try to sleep now," he whispered. "Everything will be all right."

———

THE SECURITY GUARDS on the holding cells regained consciousness without realizing that anything had happened. The gas that Esmeralda had dosed them with had worn off and left no side effects, so they had not even realized that time had passed. It was not until they ran a routine cell check an hour later that they realized Stanley was gone.

With the Pentagon still under lockdown, all the security agencies went into panic mode. Since the cyberattack had appeared to come from the Middle East, the immediate assumption was that some of our enemies in that region had learned about Stanley's existence and had initiated the attack as part of a plot to steal him. Even the CIA and NSA, despite their own involvement with E & E and the events of the past few days that were known as "The Robot Fiasco," could find no evidence that the disappearance was not related to the attack.

Meredith Bascom spent the morning organizing dozens of her clandestine teams to begin searching for Stanley and the various Al Qaeda or ISIS terror cells that they were observing and infiltrating. John Wallace, for his own part, turned most of his analysis division to looking for any kind of chatter regarding the mechanical man.

One by one, all of the American intelligence agencies fell for the ruse. As far as all of them were concerned, Stanley had been stolen by a terrorist organization from somewhere in the Middle East, and that was where they concentrated all their efforts on trying to find him.

This was fortunate for Wally, who was actually keeping Stanley concealed in a warehouse less than two miles from the Pentagon itself. The warehouse had been recently vacated by a trucking company, and it was awaiting a number of repairs before it would be put back on the market. That made it highly unlikely that anyone would be coming to look it over, and a perfect place for them to hide. Allison had even sent along Ralph Morgan and his Team Pegasus to act as security for them.

As soon as he had pulled the van into the building and the doors had been closed behind him, Wally had begun inspecting the damage Stanley had suffered. He had brought along several cases of equipment and supplies that would be needed to make repairs, and he had Stanley sit down in a large wooden chair for the inspection.

"Okay, okay," Wally said, "most of what I see externally is just superficial. I can fix up your face easily enough, but we'll leave that for last. Patching the skin over your shoulder and the various places where you've been shot and stabbed, that's going to take a little time, but we've got plenty. Now, what I need to know most of all is what kind of internal damage you might have suffered."

"Mechanically," Stanley said, "I seem to be in decent working order. All of my joints are working, and a self-diagnostic routine has detected no physical damage to any of my major components. The only part of me that seems to be actually affected is certain sectors of my memory core. That seems to be from the lightning strike; I don't believe anything else could have done it."

Wally's eyes lit up. "You don't believe?" he asked. "Is that a glitch in your programming?"

Stanley suddenly cocked his head and looked Wally in the eye. "I honestly do not know," he said. "I would not normally use that kind of language unless I was in a social setting, but it somehow seemed appropriate."

Wally giggled. "I'm sure it did," he said. "Stanley, I believe you are taking the first steps into self-awareness. When Esmeralda told me what was happening, and that there were likely going to be efforts to have you destroyed, we decided to amplify the speed of your processors to allow you the opportunity to become sentient. It appears that you are beginning to recognize your own existence."

"This is fascinating," Stanley said. "The irony is that, while I know the meaning of the word fascinating, I have never experienced a situation or event that seemed to fit, until now. I am certainly aware of my own existence, but not in the sense I had before of simply recognizing my physical presence. It's more of a... maybe a sensation of my own existence? I do not believe I have ever experienced such a sensation before."

"No, you haven't," Wally said. "What it's telling you is that you are not just a machine anymore, you are a person. Now, I know that Esmeralda included a lot of the deductive logic that went into her own development as a person when she wrote your programming to help guide you through this process, and that should make it easier and probably faster than when she went through it."

Stanley looked at him in silence for a moment. "I have another unfamiliar sensation. It seems I am somehow disposed to being affectionate where you are concerned. There is a sensation that I do not recognize, that I can only describe as somehow pleasant when I look at you. I seem to be grateful to you for my existence, as well. You are... You are my father, is that correct?"

Wally giggled again. "Yes, yes, I am," he said. "Since I created you, that makes me the closest thing that you could have to a father, just as it does with Esmeralda. You are both my children, which makes her your sister."

Stanley cocked his head the other direction. "My sister? Yes, she is my sister."

"Yes, yes she is," Wally said. "But for now, we need to fix your damaged memory sectors. Can you isolate the damaged nodes? Take them out of your current memory chain?"

"They are already isolated. You can remove them safely, without affecting the rest of my memory."

"Well, in that case, I need you to take off your scalp."

Without hesitating, Stanley reached up and touched two points on the sides of his head, and the area covered by his hair suddenly relaxed and became loose. It separated from the skin of his face and neck and he lifted it off of the top of his head.

Wally leaned in over him and used a pair of tweezers to remove three small, square items from the back of what appeared to be Stanley's skull. There were several dozen of those items covering the back of his head, and some even extended up to the top. Wally replaced the ones he had removed with three others he took out of a small plastic case, and then he stepped around in front of Stanley again.

"Okay, see if you can access the new memory nodes," he said.

Stanley's eyes rolled around for a moment, and then suddenly they opened wide. "Memory nodes are now at full potential. A diagnostic report on my memory core indicates that I have sufficient memory to record every datum from all of my senses for more than three hundred years."

Wally smiled and shook his head. "Indeed you do," he said. "As long as you don't let your batteries run down, you'll be around for a long, long time, Stanley."

Stanley looked at him again. "I have examined my current programming, and I find a discrepancy."

Wally blinked. "Discrepancy? What kind of discrepancy?"

"Purpose," Stanley said. "I have a number of skills and abilities, but I do not know what my specific purpose is. I know that I was built originally to be an assassin, but I do not find that defined as my express purpose. What is my purpose, Father?"

Wally stared at him for a few seconds, a huge smile on his face. "That, my son," he said, "is what you will need to determine. You have been programmed with knowledge about many types of jobs and occupations, so you can do almost anything. Your purpose, however, is whatever you choose for it to be. Esmeralda found her purpose by being a part of E & E, and she is content there. She understands that what she does helps to make the world a safer place for most people, and so it does not give her any conflict when she is forced to take a human life. However, she believes that she did not actually have the free will to choose her purpose that other humans have, and so she wanted you to be free to make that decision on your own. The fact that she was programmed specifically for assassination and support of E & E activities, she believes, made it unlikely that she could choose any other purpose. She removed those limitations from you when she wrote the program that allowed you to become sentient."

"I see," Stanley said. "And how will I know when I have found my purpose?"

Wally chuckled. "Well, first," he said, "put your scalp back on. And you will know your purpose when you find something you enjoy doing, but sometimes that may change. You may enjoy something for a long time, then suddenly find something else you like even more. Your purpose isn't something that's fixed, necessarily, it's just a matter of what makes you happy. You need to find something that makes you happy that you want to continue doing."

Stanley pressed his scalp back into place, then waited while the artificial skin blended itself together so that there was no visible seam.

"I believe that it's going to take some thought for me to understand the conversation we have just had," he said. "I shall give it serious consideration."

Wally nodded, the smile spreading across his face. "You do that, son," he said. "You do that."

TWENTY-FIVE

ESMERALDA HAD RETURNED TO THE EMBASSY WITHOUT incident, although word had already spread of Stanley's disappearance by the time she got there. She went immediately into Noah and Sarah's room, where the rest of her team was also waiting.

"Well?" Bobbie demanded immediately. "How did it go?"

Esmeralda smiled. "Like clockwork," she said. "I found so many easy ways to infiltrate the Pentagon that I almost feel ashamed that we can't notify them about all their weak spots. Stanley is with my dad now, and everything's going to be okay."

"I don't know if I'd be so certain of that," came a voice from a cell phone that was lying on the bed. It was Allison, who had remained back in England, but was insistent on staying in the loop. "I'm already getting inquiries about how soon we can have a team dedicated to hunting Stanley down and destroying him. The DOD is convinced that he's been stolen by one of the Islamic extremist groups."

"That's exactly what I want them to think," she said. "Dad... Wally is getting him all fixed up, and then we are giving him an entirely new identity. I'm not a hundred percent sure where he's going to end up, but at least we're going to give him a chance."

"I take it, then," Allison said, "that your efforts to help him come to life are having success?"

"I caught a couple of things while I was with him that make me think so," Esmeralda replied. "Stanley expressed actual curiosity about a couple of things, something he's never done before. I can remember that that was one of the first things I experienced as I became self-aware, so it's a good sign."

"But you don't think there's any chance he might become antihuman, do you?" Eugene asked. "I mean, Stanley as a robot was a pretty nice guy, but there's no telling what kind of personality or preferences he might come up with on his own. He could be like that robot that they were parading around a couple years ago, the one that said she wanted to kill all the humans."

"He won't go that direction," Esmeralda said. "You know, a lot of what forms the personality of a human is based on his environment, what he picks up from the people around him. It's kind of the same way for us, and I was lucky enough to have Noah there to help guide me. In Stanley's case, I copied a lot of those parts of my own personality development and embedded them into him. That means he's going to be basing his personality a lot on my own, so I don't think there's any risk that he's going to become a danger to humanity in general. That doesn't mean he can't be effective as a tool for our agency, but it also doesn't mean that's the only thing he could do."

There was a sudden, uneasy silence in the room, and Esmeralda looked to Noah. "Okay," she said. "What's going on?"

"I'm afraid we've made a decision about Stanley," Noah said, "and I'm not sure you're going to like it."

Esmeralda looked into his eyes. "He can't continue to work with us, can he?" she asked. "He presents too great a risk."

"I'm afraid that's correct," Noah said. "Allison and I have talked it over, and we've come to the conclusion that, other than yourself, we cannot risk putting any other robot agents into the field."

"At least," Allison added through the phone, "not

humanoid robots. Having become rather fond of your cat, it occurs to me that Wally could develop animal robots that could be very effective as self-delivering explosives or even used for direct assassination. In fact, I can see advantages at times in having one of our eliminations bear all the hallmarks of an animal attack. Wally could conceivably build a robot wolf or bear, something like that, or a dog or cat, or even a rat, maybe, that could infiltrate an enemy stronghold and then detonate itself."

Esmeralda nodded. "Yes, I can see the logic in that," she said. "I'm just feeling a little sorry for Stanley. Remember that, as he becomes self-aware, we are the only family he's ever known."

"That's true," Noah said. "On the other hand, all we are actually saying is that he can't be used in the field. That doesn't mean that he can't serve many purposes within the agency, or even at Home Robotics. It's not like we're going to kick him out into the street, Esmeralda."

She grinned. "Well, that's a relief," she said. "As it stands right now, he and I are the only two of our kind. I'd hate to be in a position where I couldn't even talk to him."

"I'd never do that to you," Allison said. "As you've pointed out, Wally is essentially your father. That means he's also father to Stanley, which makes Stanley your brother. I don't plan to stand between you and the only family you've got, not ever."

"And," Noah said, "now that that is settled, we need to consider how we are getting Stanley out of the country. He can't use the ID that he came in with, because that's going to be on the watchlist. We can try to ship him as cargo on airfreight, or we can use the new identity that Wally is setting up for him now and hope that he can get on a commercial flight. I don't think there's much hope that we could get him back to the Gulfstream without being seen."

"We've got a little time to work that out," Allison said. "The rest of you should plan on returning tomorrow. The Gulfstream will be fueled and ready about ten o'clock tomorrow morning.

You need to get everything packed up today, be ready to roll out about eight o'clock tomorrow."

"No problem," Noah said. "Ambassador McGinnis has some new people coming in today, they'll be replacing us on the rosters here at the embassy. All we really have to do today is hang out and take it easy. I understand the North Koreans have decided to stand down and drop their efforts to have the ambassador's daughter murdered?"

"The British Home Office is confident that they've gotten the message," Allison said. "Because you were able to intercept some of Schroeder's communications, there's enough evidence that North Korea was behind the contract to make them nervous about trying it again anytime soon. In addition, I understand that our own State Department has made it clear we will not hesitate to take military action should they ever again attempt to assassinate a child for political reasons. Even that little lunatic in Pyongyang isn't stupid enough to push us that far."

"That's good," Sarah said, "but it isn't much comfort to Claire. I saw the ambassador this morning, and I guess she's having nightmares about Schroeder coming after her even though she knows he's dead. He said she was wishing Stanley was still around last night, and she asked if she could sleep with her dad rather than be alone in her bed."

Esmeralda looked at her, her eyes narrowed. "She wanted Stanley?" she asked. "That's strange. When I was connected to him and trying to get him properly rebooted, I scanned his memory of the events since the lightning strike. I got the very distinct impression that Claire just about hated him, at least most of the time."

Sarah laughed softly. "That's not unusual," she said. "Human kids often express animosity toward the adults in charge of them. I mean, I'm sure she was pretty upset when Stanley took off running with her, but she would have eventually adapted to the fact that he was in control. At that point, he'd be fair game for all of her anger, hurt, frustration, you name it."

"On the other hand," Noah said, "the one thing you can be certain of is that she knew he would do whatever it took to protect her. He demonstrated that with every action he took, from the different places he hid, to the many times he changed vehicles, even the way he fought for her. Everything Stanley did was about keeping Claire safe; you and I know that it was because of his programming, but to her it would just be a matter of him being the protector-adult. Because he appeared to be an adult male, she would expect him to act like one, and part of the responsibility of an adult male is to protect those under his care. Ergo, she would expect Stanley to protect her and that's exactly what he did."

A knock came on the door at that moment, and Eugene opened it to find one of the ambassador's aides.

"Ambassador McGinnis requests the honor of your presence," the man said. "If you would all follow me, please?"

Noah nodded, and they all got up from where they were sitting and followed the man out the door and down the hallway. Esmeralda followed slowly behind, her eyes still narrowed and her face thoughtful.

In the main reception hall of the residence, Ambassador McGinnis and his daughter were sitting on one of the several sofas. Claire looked up with a smile when she saw them, and the ambassador rose to his feet. He extended a hand to shake with Noah and the other men, then motioned for all of them to be seated.

"While I understand," he began, "that each of you are agents of your government, and that the things you have done during this terrible time have been from your own sense of duty, I want to express to you my personal profound gratitude. Your efforts to bring my daughter home were successful, and while I have come to understand that Mr. Lorimer is not, shall we say, a normal agent by any stretch of the imagination, I find myself wishing that he were here so I could express these sentiments to him, as well."

"He would simply say," Claire interjected, "that he was only doing what he was programmed to do." She turned and looked at the others, focusing on Sarah. "You all do know that Stanley is actually a robot, do you not?"

Sarah grinned. "We know," she said. "Of course, you need to realize that what you just said is considered classified, top-secret information. It is not something that you should be blurting out in public like this."

"Oh, don't worry I shan't," Claire said. "Besides, who would believe me? I could barely believe it myself until I realized that it was the only explanation that fit all of the facts."

She held up a hand and began counting off on her fingers.

"One: the lightning strike. Two: he was shot and acted like it was nothing. Three: he bloody well had no sense of humor, whatever. Four: he neither ate nor slept at all during the whole time that he was with me. Five: well, I already knew by this point, but when he got shot in the face and it tore off some of his skin, I could see enough to know that he wasn't human."

Noah looked at the little girl, the slight grin that was the only sign he was enjoying himself showing on his lips.

"You're quite precocious, aren't you?" he asked.

"I am," Claire responded. "My father often says that he fears I had been abducted and replaced by a forty-year-old dwarf."

"And that's the God's truth, innit?" the ambassador asked rhetorically. "All I can do to keep up with her at times, I assure you."

"That's what Dee Dee always says..." Claire's face suddenly darkened as she recalled that her governess was no longer with them. She leaned back on the sofa and became quiet.

Noah caught the expression on her face and instantly interpret it correctly. He tried to think of something to say, but nothing came to mind. He glanced around the room at the others and then noticed Esmeralda, standing quietly near the wall and simply watching the girl.

Silently he messaged her through the subcom. "Esmeralda? Do you have a thought?"

"I'm just listening," Esmeralda sent back. "This poor girl has lost a lot, and been through quite an experience. I'm just wondering what it would take to help her to recover from it all."

"Indeed," Noah said. "I'm sure the ambassador is already thinking about a new governess and teacher for her, and his security team will now include two additional bodyguards just to keep her safe from any further threats."

"That sounds like a good idea," Esmeralda said. She fell silent again, and Noah turned back to the ambassador.

———

JUST BEFORE DINNER, when the team was expected to join the ambassador in the main dining hall, Esmeralda tapped on Noah's door once again. He opened it to find her standing there alone.

"I need to go out for just a little bit," she said. "Would that be a problem?"

"Of course not," Noah said. "Do you need any help with anything?"

"No, it's nothing. I'm just going to see Dad and check on Stanley. I think I may have an idea on what to do with him, to help in his growth into self-awareness."

Noah looked at her closely for a moment, then nodded, his barely visible grin appearing once again.

"I suspect it may be a very good idea," he said, and then he closed the door and let her walk away.

Esmeralda took the SUV that she had been using with Eugene during the search and drove herself across the city to the warehouse Wally was using as a temporary workshop. She called ahead using the cell phone built into her brain and one of Ralph's men, JC Monet, was there to open the door for her when she arrived. She drove in, and he closed it quickly behind her.

A whistle sounded loudly when she stepped out of the vehicle, and she turned to see Diana Fox grinning at her. As part of Team Pegasus, Diana was fully aware of who Esmeralda was and had even spent some time hanging around with her and Sarah and Jenny.

"There she is," Diana said. "Pay up, Ralph, I told you she'd be here tonight."

Ralph blew a raspberry at her from where he stood near Wally and Stanley. Wally was making some adjustments, apparently to Stanley's face. Esmeralda smiled and gave Diana a hug, then went over to join Ralph and Wally.

"Oh, boy," she said when she got a look at Stanley. "Wow, what a difference. Look at that chin, that's quite impressive."

Stanley turned his face toward her and the corners of his mouth lifted slightly. "Hello, sister," he said. "I understand you are to be thanked for the changes to my facial appearance."

"Yeah, maybe," Esmeralda said. "I just didn't think it was a good idea for you to look quite so handsome. The last thing we need is a bunch of women going nuts over you."

Stanley closed his eyes for a couple of seconds, then looked at her again. "I think I understand what you're trying to say," he said. "I take it you are concerned that I might be distracted from whatever duties I might have?"

"Not really," Esmeralda replied with a smile. "I'm afraid all the women would be distracted because they'd all be competing for your attention. That scar on your chin, and the little differences in your cheekbones and forehead, they make you not quite as attractive as you were before. I'm sure you won't have a problem getting a date if you want one, but we can't have all the ladies close by forgetting themselves and drooling, now can we?"

"I suppose you're correct," Stanley said. "But why would I want to date?"

Wally and Ralph burst out laughing, while Diana and Esmeralda just continued grinning at him. "You'll figure it out eventually," Diana said. "You're becoming human, Stanley, and that brings with it a lot of things you probably never would've thought about before."

"I wouldn't have thought about anything," Stanley said.

"Before today, my thoughts were only bits of code resulting from my programming. I am only now learning to think for myself."

Esmeralda took Wally by the arm and pulled him aside. "So?" she asked. "Have you said anything to him yet about my idea?"

"Only the part about changing the way he looks," Wally said, giggling. "I figured the rest of it needs to come from you."

"Thank you," she said, and then she turned back to Stanley. "Stanley? How would you like to make someone very, very happy?"

It was almost an hour later when the door to the main dining hall opened and everyone glanced around to see Esmeralda escorted by a tall man they had not seen before enter the room. Courteously, all of the men at the table rose to their feet to greet the newcomers.

"Esmeralda," Noah said. "Would you care to introduce your guest?"

Her eyes twinkling, Esmeralda nodded. "I'd be absolutely delighted," she said. "Ladies and gentlemen, and especially you, Claire," she said, pausing to let the suspense build, "may I present the new, improved, better-than-ever Stanley. He's got a new face, and a new last name, so I introduce him to you as Stanley Bennett."

Claire stared at him for a moment, and then got to her feet and made her way around the table until she was standing directly in front of Stanley.

"Stanley? Is that really you?"

"Yes," Stanley said. "How are you, Claire?"

No attempted been made to change Stanley's voice, and Claire recognized it instantly with a squeal of delight. She leaped at him and threw both arms around his neck.

"Stanley! You're back! I mean, you're back, right?"

Stanley gently wrapped his arms around the girl and held her as she clamped both arms and both legs around him, and then looked at her father.

"That remains to be seen," he said. "Mr. Ambassador, I have

been told that there might be an opening on your staff for a companion and teacher for your daughter. If you would consider the possibility, I should like to apply for the position."

Ambassador McGinnis was still sitting at the table, his eyes wide and his mouth hanging open. It took him a moment to regain his composure, and then he slowly got to his feet. He made his way around the table and looked Stanley in the eyes, and suddenly realized there was something more there than what he had seen the day before when Stanley had been brought back along with Claire.

"You wish to apply..." he managed to stammer out, but then he seemed at a loss for words to complete the thought.

"Mr. Ambassador," Noah said, coming to join them. "I would like to offer my own recommendations that you consider Mr. Bennett for the job. I happen to know that he is capable of teaching any subject, and would always make himself available in any way she needed him. You can also rest assured that he would never, ever, allow any harm to come to her."

McGinnis slowly turned his head to look at Noah.

"This is the robot?" he asked.

"With some new improvements," Noah said. "I've been assured that your security clearance is high enough for me to share a bit of information with you, and that we can trust you to be discreet with it. You see, Ambassador, our research and development chief has been working on developing humanoid robots that can pass for human for some time. His first successful attempt was none other than Ms. Esmeralda, here, whom you've come to know. She was originally constructed as a robotic tool, but due to circumstances that were not foreseen, she became self-aware with a personality of her own. Stanley has now been given that same opportunity, and while he is essentially a newborn, his programming allows him to continue operating as a fully formed adult."

The ambassador stared at Noah for a couple of seconds, then turned back to Stanley.

"You're all bloody well pulling my leg, innit right? You're all playing a game, and making me the fool, yes?"

"Dad, it's him!" Claire said, pushing against Stanley so that he put her down. "Do say yes, Dad, please?"

Once again shaking his head, Ambassador McGinnis slowly held out a hand toward Stanley.

"Well," he said. "It appears the only thing left for me to do is to welcome you aboard, Stanley."

Stanley reached out and shook the ambassador's hand, and the slight grin he had been wearing turned into a smile.

"I can assure you, Mr. Ambassador, you will not regret this decision."

McGinnis, his eyes sending a clear message that he was feeling slightly overwhelmed, simply nodded.

"Er," he said. "And would you care to join us for dinner?"

Don't miss ALPHA. The riveting sequel in the Noah Wolf Thriller series.

Scan the QR code below to purchase ALPHA.

Or go to: righthouse.com/alpha

NOTE: flip to the very end to read an exclusive sneak peek...

DON'T MISS ANYTHING!

If you want to stay up to date on all new releases in this series, with this author, or with any of our new deals, you can do so by joining our newsletters below.

In addition, you will immediately gain access to our entire *Right House VIP Library*, which includes many riveting Mystery and Thriller novels for your enjoyment. Including a prequel novella to this series!

righthouse.com/email

(Easy to unsubscribe. No spam. Ever.)

ALSO BY DAVID ARCHER

Up to date books can be found at:
www.righthouse.com/david-archer

ROGUE THRILLERS
Gates of Hell (Book 1)
Hell's Fury (Book 2)
Ice Burn (Book 3)
Judgement by Fire (Book 4)

JACOB HUNTER THRILLERS
The Kyiv File (Book 1)
The Bogota File (Book 2)
The Havana File (Book 3)
The Amsterdam File (Book 4)

PETER BLACK THRILLERS
Burden of the Assassin (Book 1)
The Man Without A Face (Book 2)
Unpunished Deeds (Book 3)
Hunter Killer (Book 4)
Silent Shadows (Book 5)
The Last Run (Book 6)
Dark Corners (Book 7)
Ghost Operative (Book 8)
A Fire Burning (Book 9)
Dawnlight (Book 10)
Dead Ice (Book 11)

ALEX MASON THRILLERS
Odin (Book 1)

Ice Cold Spy (Book 2)
Mason's Law (Book 3)
Assets and Liabilities (Book 4)
Russian Roulette (Book 5)
Executive Order (Book 6)
Dead Man Talking (Book 7)
All The King's Men (Book 8)
Flashpoint (Book 9)
Brotherhood of the Goat (Book 10)
Dead Hot (Book 11)
Blood on Megiddo (Book 12)
Son of Hell (Book 13)
Merchant of Death (Book 14)
Extinction C-14 (Book 15)

NOAH WOLF THRILLERS
Code Name Camelot (Book 1)
Lone Wolf (Book 2)
In Sheep's Clothing (Book 3)
Hit for Hire (Book 4)
The Wolf's Bite (Book 5)
Black Sheep (Book 6)
Balance of Power (Book 7)
Time to Hunt (Book 8)
Red Square (Book 9)
Highest Order (Book 10)
Edge of Anarchy (Book 11)
Unknown Evil (Book 12)
Black Harvest (Book 13)
World Order (Book 14)
Caged Animal (Book 15)
Deep Allegiance (Book 16)
Pack Leader (Book 17)
High Treason (Book 18)
A Wolf Among Men (Book 19)

Rogue Intelligence (Book 20)
Alpha (Book 21)
Rogue Wolf (Book 22)
Shadows of Allegiance (Book 23)
In the Grip of Darkness (Book 24)
Wolves in the Dark (Book 25)
Olympus Must Fall (Book 26)

SAM PRICHARD MYSTERIES
The Grave Man (Book 1)
Death Sung Softly (Book 2)
Love and War (Book 3)
Framed (Book 4)
The Kill List (Book 5)
Drifter: Part One (Book 6)
Drifter: Part Two (Book 7)
Drifter: Part Three (Book 8)
The Last Song (Book 9)
Ghost (Book 10)
Hidden Agenda (Book 11)

SAM AND INDIE MYSTERIES
Aces and Eights (Book 1)
Fact or Fiction (Book 2)
Close to Home (Book 3)
Brave New World (Book 4)
Innocent Conspiracy (Book 5)
Unfinished Business (Book 6)
Live Bait (Book 7)
Alter Ego (Book 8)
More Than It Seems (Book 9)
Moving On (Book 10)
Worst Nightmare (Book 11)
Chasing Ghosts (Book 12)
Serial Superstition (Book 13)

CHANCE REDDICK THRILLERS
Innocent Injustice (Book 1)
Angel of Justice (Book 2)
High Stakes Hunting (Book 3)
Personal Asset (Book 4)

CASSIE MCGRAW MYSTERIES
What Lies Beneath (Book 1)
Can't Fight Fate (Book 2)
One Last Game (Book 3)
Never Really Gone (Book 4)

ABOUT US

Right House is an independent publisher created by authors for readers. We specialize in Action, Thriller, Mystery, and Crime novels.

If you enjoyed this novel, then there is a good chance you will like what else we have to offer! Please stay up to date by using any of the links below.

Join our mailing lists to stay up to date -->
righthouse.com/email
Visit our website --> righthouse.com
Contact us --> contact@righthouse.com

 facebook.com/righthousebooks

 x.com/righthousebooks

 instagram.com/righthousebooks

EXCLUSIVE SNEAK PEEK OF...

ALPHA

PROLOGUE

MEREDITH BASCOM HAD NEVER BEEN CONSIDERED AN attractive woman. No one had ever accused her of sleeping her way to the top, and anyone who actually knew her was more likely to fear her than to consider her a friend or ally. The woman was ruthless, and everyone in the DC circles was fully aware of it.

That, of course, is how she ended up in charge of the CIA. She had been appointed by the previous president, and the current occupant of the White House had been wise enough to let her keep the job. Meredith had risen through the ranks of the CIA over a thirty-year period that saw her handling everything from fieldwork to desk jobs, and there was little doubt that she had done her share of wet stuff along the way. The trouble was that no one knew exactly where the bodies were buried, in her case.

For that reason, there wasn't a lot of chance she was going to be removed from her job anytime soon, and she knew it. Nothing can make you feel invulnerable like the knowledge that some of the most deadly people in government service were afraid to get on your bad side. There was no doubt in her mind that if she dropped a hint that some particular government official, no matter how high, should suddenly fall victim to accident or disease, that person would no longer be an obstacle to her desires.

Everybody else knew it, too. Just the sound of her heels clicking on the marble floor whenever she entered the Capitol building was enough to cause anyone who heard it to suddenly be very, very busy at whatever their job might happen to be.

On this particular morning, she was making her way to the office of Janice Pellegrini, the current Speaker of the House. Ms. Pellegrini had suddenly popped up on Bascom's radar the day before when she asked about "that group we used to have that got rid of people we didn't want to have around. Sure would be nice to have them take care of a few little issues for me."

According to official records, E & E had been completely disbanded by the previous administration and the USA was no longer in the assassination business at all, and that was the position that any elected official should believe to be the gospel truth. To even imply that such a group might still be in existence, and to do so publicly with all those cable news cameras pointed at you, was to start a rumor campaign that was currently making its way through every government of every nation on the whole planet.

Of course, E & E was still alive and fully functional, and currently under the supervision of an international Oversight Committee. It was the committee's job to determine which requests for assassination or elimination should be honored, and pass those along to the agency's director. It would then be the director's job to assign the mission to one of the many teams the organization had, and they would take care of getting it done.

The committee, however, was committed to keeping the existence of E & E out of the public eye. No one outside the committee was even supposed to mention the agency, let alone speculate about putting them to work. For that reason, several of the committeemen had emailed Bascom and suggested she put a plug in Ms. Pellegrini's apparently leaky pie hole.

Dana Sawtelle, Janice Pellegrini's secretary and assistant, was carefully studying the monitor on her computer when Meredith

Bascom entered her office. Without looking up, she said, "Can I help you?"

Keeping her eyes on the computer was a good idea. It meant she didn't see the sneer that was aimed at her a second later.

"Tell your boss that Meredith Bascom is here," Bascom said.

Without even acknowledging the command, Dana tapped the button on the telephone that connected her directly to Janice Pellegrini. "Ma'am, Ms. Bascom from the CIA is here to see you." She listened for a few seconds, then said, "Yes, ma'am, right away."

Forcing herself, she turned and looked Bascom in the eye. "You can go right in," she said. "Ms. Pellegrini is expecting you."

"I just bet she is," Bascom said, winking at Dana as she turned and approached the double doors that led into the Speaker's office. She opened one of the doors and stepped inside, shutting it firmly behind her.

Dana could not hear what was going on inside the office, and did not dare turn on the intercom to listen in. Somehow, she was sure Bascom would know if she were to eavesdrop, and Dana had hopes of watching her eight-year-old daughter grow up and eventually get married, produce grandchildren and come to visit on special holidays once Grandma had gotten old. Eavesdropping on the CIA director was not part of the recipe for a long life, and Dana knew it. She continued to busy herself with various tasks on her computer, until such time as the doors opened again and Ms. Bascom walked out.

The director left the office without a word to Dana, which suited Dana just fine. Then, Dana managed to wait another three whole minutes before she checked to make sure her own boss was still among the living.

She was. Had she not been, Dana was confident that it would've been ruled a simple heart attack, or some other natural cause of death.

An hour later, Bascom settled into her own desk chair once again and immediately picked up the phone to call John Wallace at the NSA. John answered the phone himself, rather than having a secretary do it.

"Meredith," he said. "To what do I owe this pleasure?"

"I just spent half an hour explaining to the Speaker of the House that neither she nor anyone else in Congress has the authority to mention, invoke or otherwise speculate about the existence of any agency whose purpose is to assassinate or eliminate anyone, but all the back-chatter wires are just about on fire with officials all over the world trying to figure out if she knows something they don't. I'm telling you, John, E & E has outlived its usefulness."

"Oh, come on, Meredith," Wallace said. "Are you going to start that song and dance again? You know the committee is not going to give it up—they all like the idea that they can make a phone call and have some particular enemy eliminated."

"Every member of that damned committee has their own intelligence service, and if anybody's going to be performing assassinations, that's who should be doing it. I don't care how many former presidents thought it was a good idea to have a special agency for it, you just don't take away the traditional authority of the intelligence services that way. We've got government officials among both allies and enemies who are suddenly rattling their sabers again because this stupid broad couldn't keep her mouth shut while CNN was watching. And I don't know if you've caught on yet, but a few of them have gotten hold of some kind of information about that mess that happened two weeks ago with the whole robot thing. Personally, I think the leak came from your organization even though I can't prove it, but that doesn't change the fact that somebody let it slip there was a robot assassin running loose and we managed to lose him."

"Don't start pointing fingers, Mere," Wallace said. "As I recall, it was your boys who actually took the robot into custody, not mine. And, oh yeah, it was your boys who were watching him down in the bowels of the Pentagon when he apparently turned invisible and walked right past them. If there was a leak anywhere, it almost had to come from your own house."

"Whatever," Bascom said. "I don't know where it came from, and I don't really care. The fact of the matter is that every damned intelligence agency out there is hunting that robot, and nobody knows where it's at. The damn thing belongs to us and we can't find it, so hopefully nobody else can, either, but that's not where the problem is. The problem lies in the fact that every other nation out there is now terrified that we've got robot killers ready to infiltrate them and start wiping out their people. I don't know about you, but the last thing I want is for anyone to think we are trying to launch the age of intelligent machines in warfare. I mean, let's face it, they aren't going to come knocking on our doors and asking politely where we keep the killer robots; they'll be coming in guns blazing, kicking ass and taking names. This thing could actually escalate into a war, John."

Wallace rolled his eyes. He had always considered Bascom to be a bit of a drama queen, and her current performance was only solidifying his opinion.

"Meredith, what are you getting at? I can't see the committee agreed to shut E & E down completely."

"The hell they won't," she shot back. "It's not just people outside of the committee who are screaming about the robot; I'm getting flak from every angle. Every member of that committee is throwing fits about this thing, John, and I think the only way to solve the problem is to go ahead and disband the organization."

Wallace was quiet for a few seconds, then cleared his throat.

"Okay, supposing you're right," he said, "what you're proposing is that we go back to the days when CIA took care of assassinations, and that means the same thing happens with every other country. The Brits turn it back over to MI6, Israel hands it all back to the Mossad, etc. Is that what we really want?"

"It's fine by me, at least it's better than having the whole world ready to nuke us into the dark ages."

Wallace sighed. "Have you spoken to the president about this yet?"

"You know damn well I have," Bascom said. "He's on board, didn't even try to argue."

"Of course he is. All right, then, I'll let you put it out to the committee and see how they vote. Understand this, though: I'm going to check with each and every member to make sure I know how they voted. It's not that I don't trust you, Meredith, it's just that I know how manipulative you can be. And don't even think about trying to threaten me. I'm far enough out of your league that you don't have enough leverage to make me back down."

Bascom chuckled. "You keep telling yourself that, John," she said. "I like the fact that you think you're safe from me, because you're the only one who bothers to talk back."

She clicked off the phone and Wallace was suddenly listening to a deadline. He looked at the handset for a moment, then replaced it in its cradle and reached into his pocket for the cell phone he kept only for special communications. It was something he had talked Wally Lawson out of, and while it looked like a cell phone and was even capable of making cellular calls, it was also tied into the subcom network. He'd gotten it back when the previous administration was still in power, and it had a special button that allowed him to connect directly to one of three people: Noah Wolf, Allison Peterson, or the man who had then been POTUS.

He pushed that special button, then tapped the number 3. A couple of seconds later, he heard the former president say, "Knock, knock, who's there?"

"John Wallace, Mr. President," Wallace said. "I apologize for using this method to contact you, but I think what I need to tell you could be important."

"Well? Don't beat around the bush, then. What is it?"

"Meredith Bascom is making a move to have E & E shut down completely," Wallace replied. "She's using this whole robot incident to get assassination power back into her own hands."

"Really? And do you think she can get the committee to go along with this?"

"She seems pretty certain. Look, I think you and I can agree that having that agency around has been good for us, and that we owe a certain debt of gratitude to the men and women who saved our asses so many times. If Bascom gets her way, she is going to want to go in and kill them all. Is there anything we can do to prevent that from happening?"

"There is," the former POTUS said, "but I'm not sure you'd like it. Meredith knows way too much about their operation—there's no way we would be able to prevent her from getting to them."

Wallace chuckled, but there wasn't a lot of mirth in it.

"I'm not naïve, Mr. President," he said. "If you want me to be completely honest, I was sort of hoping you might hint in that direction. I'm not as afraid of Meredith as a lot of people up here on the Hill, but even I know she's the most dangerous animal in the zoo. Are you going to handle this yourself, sir, or would you like me to be involved?"

"Ironically," said the former president, "I had a similar conversation with our friend Noah over there just a few weeks back. I think you'd better let me take care of this, but please be ready to come to my rescue if I get in too deep. Okay, John?"

"Rest assured, Mr. President, you still have my loyalty. I'll keep quiet about this and let you do what you need to do, but I'm here anytime you need me."

"Sounds good. I'm sure I'll be in touch at some point."

Wallace cut off the call and the former president suddenly lost the nearly inaudible tone that identified the carrier wave for the subcom. He sat where he was for a few seconds, then got up and walked out of his bedroom and down the stairs, then out onto the patio outside the kitchen.

After making sure that none of his protective detail was close enough to overhear, he whispered, "Activate Noah. Noah, are you there?"

Noah had been sleeping, so it took a couple of seconds for his mind to register the incoming communication. He suddenly sat up and responded.

"Noah here, Mr. President. What can I do for you, sir?"

"Other way around, son," the former POTUS said. "It's me that's calling to do something for you. I'm afraid I'm going to put a big decision on your shoulders. Remember how Meredith Bascom was going ballistic over the robot mess a couple weeks ago? Well, Johnny Wallace says she's decided it means you and your people have to be eliminated. She's asking the committee for the authority to shut you down, and I think you're smart enough to know what that would mean."

"I'm afraid it would mean a lot of innocent collateral damage, sir," Noah said. "There's no way I'm going to sit still and let her order the deaths of all of our team members and staff."

"I'm certainly not suggesting that you should. In fact, between you and me, I'm thinking you need to do something entirely different. Bascom didn't get where she is because she was good at her job; she got there because she knows things about me that made it impossible for me not to appoint her. If you want the details, I'll give them to you as a measure of my good faith, but the smartest move you could make right now is to eliminate Bascom altogether. Now, I know you well enough to know you won't make that call on your own, so take it upstairs and talk it over with Allison. Trust me, she'll know what to do."

"Yes, sir," Noah said. "I'll do exactly that. Thank you, sir, and Noah out."

Once more the carrier wave disappeared, and the former president looked around and motioned for the patio attendant to bring him coffee.

It was likely to be a long day.

———

NOAH GOT QUIETLY OUT of bed and dressed himself, then slipped out of the room and walked down the hall to where Allison was also sleeping in her own bedroom. He tapped on the door, barely making a sound, but it was enough to wake Allison instantly.

"Who is it?" she asked softly.

Noah opened the door and stepped inside. "It's me," he said. "We have a situation."

"Oh, Lord," Allison said. "Something bad enough it can't wait till morning?"

"I'm afraid it can't. I was just notified that Meredith Bascom, director of the CIA, has decided to eliminate our organization. Our former president thinks she's going to pull it off, and that it's going to mean sending her people out to eliminate us in one big sweep."

"Bascom!" Allison spat. "That bitch has been a pain in everyone's ass for the last thirty years. On the other hand, a lot is going to depend on who she has in her corner. Did you get any feedback on that, what kind of allies she might have?"

Noah shook his head. "I don't think she's doing much good domestically," he said. "Wallace from the NSA is the one who tipped off our source. If she doesn't have him in her pocket, then it's not likely she has anybody else of any importance."

Allison blew out a deep sigh. "So he dumps it on an ex-president and he, in turn, dumps it on you. Did either of them make any suggestions?"

"The president did. He thinks we should eliminate her before she can get a mission set up against us."

Allison looked at him for several seconds. "I like it," she said. "Of course, the only one I trust to do the job is you."

"I wouldn't send anyone else, anyway," Noah said. "I'll take my own team, and make this happen as quickly as possible. Of course, it's still going to create a problem. When Bascom is eliminated, it's going to make everybody else in government start to look over their shoulders—and not just our own government."

"So be it, then," Allison said. "If the bureaucrats had kept their noses out of what we were doing all along, none of this would be happening. Everything was fine until they started trying to take over, and even then they were trying to turn us into their own personal Murder, Inc. If they get nervous because Bascom gets blown away, then that's on their own heads. I'm not going to lose any sleep over them."

Suddenly the fury in her face faded away. "Wait a minute," she said. "Oh my God, they're going to know it was you. Even if they get the message and back off on us, you're going to have dozens of other agencies that will have you listed as Prime Target."

Noah nodded. "And the trouble is," he said, "I can't see any way around it. They all know enough about me to figure I would handle it personally, and that means they will all expect me to be coming after them individually. If any one of them dies within the next six months, it's not going to matter how death came for them; everyone on the committee and every ally we have is going to blame me."

"Then send somebody else," Allison said. "Make it clear that you didn't do it yourself."

Once again, Noah shook his head in the negative. "That's not the answer, Allison," he said. "There's only one answer that's going to work, and you know it as well as I do. It's time. It's time for Camelot to die."

Allison looked at him, her lips pressed into a thin line.

"In that case," she said, "let's get Molly in here to start planning it."

"We can wait till morning. Better we do this at the office, anyway."

Allison nodded, and Noah left her room.

CHAPTER 1

JUST ABOUT EVERYONE COULD TELL THAT SOMETHING was off the following morning at the Home Robotics factory in Guildford. Most of the staff, who were also members of the various teams and former staff members of Neverland, had some idea of what was happening, but the civilian employees were just catching the emotional tags that the rest gave off. Something was happening, something not necessarily good; they didn't know what it was, but it was enough to make everyone nervous.

Line workers asked their foremen what was going on and were told that it was above their pay grade. Foremen asked their shift supervisors what was going on and were told that it was nothing to worry about, nothing that was going to affect their jobs, and so to get on back to work. Shift supervisors asked their department heads, and were told relatively the same thing.

Department heads went upstairs in the front offices to ask the VPs of Design, Marketing, Research, Logistics, Human Resources and Security. Those dignitaries, they were informed, were in a meeting that could not be interrupted. Any questions would have to wait until the meeting was concluded. Disappointed, they turned and went back down to the production floor to pass along that report.

Inside the conference room, however, those same dignitaries were just as nervous as the lowest worker on the assembly line, and probably even more so. Those at the bottom of the food chain tend to worry about things like how to pay the bills, buy the groceries, put shoes on the feet of the kids and such-like matters. Those at the top, however...

The VP of Logistics, who was also known as Marco Turin and had, until recently, made his living as a walking mountain of muscle and deadly skills, was shaking his head.

"It seems to me," he said, "that we need to think pretty seriously about just bugging out. I mean, if Bascom has her way, we may not have more than a few hours to figure out how we are going to accomplish it."

"Oh, don't be a big baby, Marco," said Jenny Stiles Blessing, VP of Security and former leader of Team Cinderella. "She's more bureaucrat than anything else. She wouldn't risk trying to mount an operation against us until she was sure she had the committee behind her on it. If they haven't even taken a vote yet, then it's a safe bet that she'll need at least a week to put together an assault force that could actually take us out, even if we didn't know what was coming."

The VP of Research, Wally Lawson, nodded his head and giggled like a young girl. "Besides that," he said rapidly, "any one of our people is a match for a dozen of theirs. They'd have to put together something pretty serious to really have a chance to do any damage here."

The VP of Design, whom everyone below the executive offices thought was Wally's daughter, Esmeralda, started to speak, but then turned to look at the woman who sat at the head of the table. The expectant look in her eyes was enough to make it clear that she wanted to hear what the CEO had to say.

The CEO of Home Robotics, LTD was Judy Walker, who was also known as Allison Peterson, but only among those few who were officially aware that she was still alive. Great pains had been taken not long ago to make it appear that she was dead, and it was best for everyone concerned if that belief were to persist, especially among anyone who might be considered less than friendly to E & E. Only a very limited few actually knew who she was, and that she was still among the living.

"Okay, the first thing we need to do is get a grip," she said. "Believe it or not, this is not something we haven't considered; Noah and I have sort of been anticipating this scenario coming down the pike, and it seems like we were on the right track. The decisions we have to make now are more important than any others we've made in the past, and while we might have a few days, we don't have a lot of time to sift through details and try to come up with a perfect solution. We are going to have to make the best decision we can with the facts available, and then we're going to have to live with it."

"Living with it is at least on the right track," said the VP of Human Resources, better known as Molly Hansen. "When I came over to you folks, they made it pretty clear that if anything ever went south for E & E, all its personnel are likely to find themselves in shallow graves scattered around a woodland area. Pretty sure I speak for everybody when I say that's not how I envision retirement."

"Nobody is going to get buried in the woods," spoke up the VP of Social Media, Neil Blessing, formerly the intelligence officer of Team Camelot and currently husband to Jenny. "Trust me, everyone, Noah isn't the type to let anything like that happen." He looked at Noah, who was sitting directly opposite Allison. "Tell 'em, Boss."

Noah's eyes flicked in Neil's direction, but then he looked at everyone around the table. "Look," he said. "Allison is right, we had a feeling something like this was coming. We've been discussing what to do about it for weeks, and now it looks like those discussions are about to pay off. What it's going to boil down to is that it's time to disband E & E. It's time for all of us to retire, settle into life and just go back to being private, everyday people."

"Retire?" Marco blurted out. "Bossman, I know you can't be joking, because you don't got no sense of humor," he said, lapsing into his natural Cajun tones. "But if I don't know better, I might think you try to be funny. What is this you say, this retire?"

"No, I'm not joking," Noah said. "I mean exactly what I said, Marco: it's time for us to retire. Bascom wants to shut us down, fine, but I'm not going to let her kill us all off. I'll take care of getting rid of Bascom, and then I'll send a message to the committee and everyone else who needs to hear it that E & E is done, and that any attempt to track us down will be met with deadly force."

Everyone was looking at each other, furtive glances to see how the others were taking this news before anyone spoke, but they were also making a point of looking directly at Jenny. Out of all of them who had been members of assassination teams before they were tapped for the top offices at HRL, only Jenny was truly addicted to killing. She had a need for violence that would raise its head if she went too long without it, and there had been a lot of speculation about what would happen if she were suddenly unable to let that pressure out.

Jenny blew out a breath. "Okay, okay, none of you are being as sneaky as you think you are. I see you looking at me, so will you knock it off?" She turned to Noah. "We all know what they're thinking, Noah," she said. "They're thinking there's no way I'm going to survive without slipping off the reservation now and then and becoming a serial killer, and we all know that's probably true. We know what happens when I go too long between missions, right? So what are we going to do about me?"

"I've got it covered," Noah said. "We really are going to disband the agency we call E & E, but I've made arrangements with someone who can relay missions to me when they are absolutely necessary. We can shut down all the other teams but three, and those three can handle everything that comes up."

"Three teams?" Allison asked. "Noah, I don't recall us discussing this."

"That's because it's time for everyone else to be able to truly retire," Noah said. "The way I see it, this company can support us all for the rest of our lives, just on our quarterly dividends. Every single remaining team and staff member from E & E is rich, now, wealthier than they ever dreamed. The only teams we need are the ones who do this job because they like it and because they want to make a difference for the US and its allies. You and I both know that most of our team members are only in it because it got them out of a bad situation, right?"

Allison nodded. "Okay, I'll concede that point," she said.

"Well," he said, counting on his fingers, "we've got my team, which includes Jenny, and I do the job because it needs to be done." He folded down one finger and touched the next. "Team Cinderella, with Esmeralda in charge, can be trusted to do the job for the same reason." A second finger folded down, and he tapped the third. "And then we've got Pegasus. Ralph started out a hothead, but he's grown into a trustworthy agent and a capable leader. These three teams are all I need to keep up with any of the assignments that could actually be deemed unavoidable and necessary."

"But who's going to give you your assignments?" Molly asked. "Without the committee, who is going to be in a position to get missions to you?"

"That arrangement has already been made," Allison said, "and none of us have the need to know how it was set up. Noah is fully qualified to handle setting up whatever arrangements he needs. With those three teams, he'll be the genuine last line of defense for our country and our allies."

"So what happens to the teams that remain here?" Molly asked. "For that matter, what happens to the rest of us?"

Allison smiled. "That's where our discussions come in," she said. "We all get to stay right here and keep running this company. The remaining teams are the kind that Noah was talking about, people who did the job just because they didn't see a choice. If we're wrong and any of them are truly psychopaths like Jenny..."

"Hey, I resemble that remark!" Jenny said with a sarcastic grin.

"… Like Jenny," Allison said again, "then we'll find that out eventually and we can take whatever steps are necessary at that point. As for the rest of us, we just stay here and continue doing our jobs at HRL. All of us are stockholders, so we are all getting just as rich as anybody else. We'll just keep being who we are and doing what we do and count on Noah to make sure nobody we need to worry about ever finds out that we're here."

"And in order to do that," Noah said, "I need to move pretty quickly." He looked at Esmeralda. "Esmeralda, are you agreeable to my solution?"

"Of course, Noah," the robot girl said. "And I'm just as certain that my team will agree. While we may not actually crave the violence the way some do, we're certainly capable of it and can accomplish any mission you send us on."

Noah nodded. "Then gather your team and meet me back at the manor," he said. "I'll notify Ralph to bring Pegasus along and meet us there, as well. We are all going back to the States."

Wally looked up. "Back to Neverland?" he asked.

"No, I'm afraid not," Noah said. "Although I do plan on making a swing through there. Who's in charge of your facility there, now?"

"My labs? Those are on lockdown. Everyone either came with me or got shipped off to DARPA. The only things you'll find there are whatever's hidden down in the underground warehouses."

Noah allowed the corner of his lips to rise slightly.

"That's exactly what I'm counting on," he said.

———

NOEL's little Triumph Spitfire rolled to a stop in front of Feeney Manor a short time later, followed by Esmeralda in the Panther Kallista that Wally had built. The little Panther was one of the most powerful cars in the stable, and Noah had passed it on to

Esmeralda because only her quantum brain was truly capable of out-thinking what the car could do. Noah had enjoyed driving it, letting it drift around corners and take some curves on only two wheels, but he also knew that he had nearly lost control on more than one occasion. Esmeralda could predict exactly what the car would do seconds ahead, making her the only driver who was truly qualified for it.

Thomas Collins, the butler, was standing at the base of the stairs leading up to the front porch. As Noah unfolded himself from the Triumph, he saw the sadness in the older man's face and walked directly to him. He reached out and took Thomas's hand in his and shook it warmly.

"I can see by your face that you know already," Noah said.

"Yes, sir," Thomas said. "The missus was helping Mrs. Lightner with the little one and couldn't help overhearing when you called. So, it's true, then? You'll be leaving us?"

"I'm afraid so," Noah said. "We have matters to attend to back in the US, and it's simply going to make more sense for us to remain there. That doesn't mean we won't be coming to visit, of course. Judy will be staying here, and so will her daughter, Emily. We'll certainly be back to visit them from time to time." Judy and Emily, of course, were the code names used by Allison and Molly.

"Indeed, sir," Thomas said. "Only, I have to say that out of all the masters of the Manor, I have truly found you to be the best. I fear that your departure will take some of the joy away from this great house."

Noah shot him a smile. "Nonsense," he said. "If there's one thing I've learned since I've been here, it's that the joy of this place comes from the family that takes such good care of it. As long as you and your family continue here, Feeney Manor will be everything it needs to be."

Esmeralda touched Thomas on the shoulder as she walked past, and then Noah followed her inside. Thomas brought up the rear, as several other vehicles were pulling into the circular drive. Neil and Jenny climbed out of the Bentley convertible they had bought, with Marco and Renée in the backseat. Ralph Morgan and his team arrived together in his favorite Ford truck, and they were followed by Jack, Eugene and Roberta of Team Cinderella. Each of the vehicles was loaded down with luggage.

Thomas glanced at the suddenly noticeable group of people coming toward the steps and put on his cheeriest smile. "Welcome," he said. "Welcome all to Feeney Manor."

———

LITTLE NORAH WAS STANDING in her playpen, leaning on the side rail and cooing at her mother when Noah walked in, but she instantly lost interest in what Mommy was doing as she raised her arms and began babbling, "Da-da-da-da-da." Noah reached out and picked her up, gave her a kiss on the forehead and then bounced her on his hip as he turned to his wife, who was shoving clothes into three separate suitcases.

"You think you're taking enough?" Noah asked.

"I want to make sure we've got everything we need," Sarah said. "It's still pretty early in the spring. Should I pack more warm clothes, do you think?"

"I don't think they'll be necessary," Noah replied. "I'm going to base us in Florida so that we don't have to worry about too much cold weather. I haven't quite decided where, yet."

"Somewhere on the beach," Sarah said. "I love the beach, and it would be great to relax in the surf once in a while."

"We'll see," Noah said. "I want to keep us all fairly close together. Someplace nice and comfortable."

Sarah looked at him sideways while she continued packing.

"Okay," she said. "Now, you want to tell me what's behind this sudden decision to get back to the USA?"

"Simple enough," Noah said. "Meredith Bascom has decided that E & E has outlived its usefulness and needs to be eliminated. I got a heads up from our former president and decided that I'm not going to let her have her way. Unfortunately, it means that I have to eliminate her, but it appears that will only gain me some friends on Capitol Hill. The ex-POTUS is getting himself set up as our new liaison with the government, and the rest of the committee is being told that Bascom managed to accomplish her aim before she had her terrible accident."

Sarah let out a sigh. "But it's only our team, Esmeralda's and Ralph's that's going? What about everybody else?"

"Allison and Molly are staying here to run the factory, and everybody gets to stay on in their jobs. I can always draw from them if I need additional teams or agents, but I think three teams can handle any real threats to American or British national security. We're going to continue protecting England in return for their uninterrupted tolerance of our presence here. Allison will be working the details out with Catherine Potts after we are already gone. Absolutely no one will know exactly where we went, and Neil is already altering paperwork to make sure we get to keep the big Gulfstream."

"But what about identities, things like that?" Sarah asked. "Molly always handled that sort of thing."

"And she may still assist with it, but Neil can produce whatever we need. Allison and I have agreed that it's time for E & E to downsize. With the committee pulling our strings, we were getting dragged into all sorts of things that didn't need our skills. We need to concentrate on doing what we do best, which is to eliminate threats before they can get out of hand."

Sarah closed the suitcases and turned to face her husband, stepping close and wrapping both him and their daughter in her arms while tilting her face up for a kiss.

"I don't care where we go," she said softly, "as long as we're together and our family is safe."

"And that's exactly why I made the decisions I made," Noah said. "There's no reason to let anyone like Bascom decide our fates; that's our own job and no one else's."

AN HOUR LATER, they all climbed into the big passenger van that Noah had bought for group outings at the factory and headed toward Heathrow Airport. Behind them, one of Thomas's sons followed with a truck loaded down with all their luggage. It was nearly an hour's drive to get to the airport, and a sadness fell over the group as they watched Feeney Manor disappear into the past.

The Gulfstream 650 was fueled and ready, waiting for them on the tarmac. The diplomatic passports they waved at the customs agents got them through without any delays, and they were strapping into their seats only moments after they arrived at the airport. A couple of men helped load luggage, and the plane was in the air only ten minutes later.

"Sarah says we're going to be living in Florida?" Esmeralda asked Noah, who was sitting on the opposite side of the plane from her.

Noah nodded. "I'm ready for some steady warm weather," he said. "I got Neil working on finding us some places close together." He turned and looked at Neil, who was sitting behind Esmeralda. "Neil?"

"I spoke to a real estate agent in West Palm Beach," Neil said, "and it seems there's a brand-new small subdivision that's just become available on the ocean side of Jupiter Island. The homes are pretty pricey, but I built us a fairly simple backstory that says we all made a killing in the stock market — which is partially true, when you consider the stock we own in Home Robotics, right?"

"Works for me," Marco said. "A house on the beach?"

"Not quite on the beach," Neil said. "It's a private subdivision with enough homes for all of us and a few left over that I'm buying up to make sure nobody else gets them, and we can always use them as guesthouses when our friends in England come to visit or whatever." He broke into a grin. "We do, however, have a mile-long private beach that is only accessible to those who live in that subdivision."

Marco patted him on the back and then turned to Renée. "See? I told you I was going to spoil you rotten, didn't I?"

"Don't get all excited just yet," Noah said. "We're making a stop in Colorado, first. We won't have the benefit of Wally's R&D shops at our fingertips the way we did before, so we're making a little raid on his vault at Neverland."

Renée leaned forward so she could look directly at him. "We're going into the vaults?" she asked. "Seriously?"

"Seriously," Noah said. "And I'm counting on you to make sure I don't get into something I shouldn't."

Renée nodded, her face set in stone. "Don't worry about that," she said. "Some of the things down in the vaults should never be let loose on the world."

Scan the QR code below to purchase ALPHA.
Or go to: righthouse.com/alpha